The Redemption of Philip Thane

The barouche's window was shoved up and a dark-haired man stuck his head out. His brown eyes met hers and then he smiled, a bold, appreciative, devil-may-care smile that transformed his features into something beyond ordinary good looks.

It was pure, powerful, unadulterated *charm* that illuminated his face and made him strikingly attractive.

So attractive, in fact, that Margaret felt a delicious tingle running through her.

It had been so long since she had felt anything like this. She was just about to smile back when his emboldened gaze raked over her from head to foot in a frankly piratical manner, and the warm exciting tingle was quenched in a heartbeat.

She didn't mind the appreciative smile, but she certainly didn't enjoy being ogled like that, in a way that made her glad she had on several layers of clothing impenetrable to the human eye.

His smile widened, and in a smooth, deep, cultured voice (which nearly sent *another* tingle shimmering through her before she managed to suppress it) he said:

"Why, hullo there. Aren't you a sight for sore eyes."

Also by Lisa Berne

THE WORST DUKE IN THE WORLD
ENGAGED TO THE EARL
THE BRIDE TAKES A GROOM
THE LAIRD TAKES A BRIDE
YOU MAY KISS THE BRIDE

LISA BERNE

THE REDEMPTION OF PHILIP THANE

THE PENHALLOW DYNASTY

AVONBOOKS

An Imprint of HarperCollins*Publishers*

Untitled excerpt copyright © 2021 by Lisa Berne.

THE REDEMPTION OF PHILIP THANE. Copyright © 2021 by Lisa Berne. All rights reserved. Printed in the United States of America. No part of this book may be used or reproduced in any manner whatsoever without written permission except in the case of brief quotations embodied in critical articles and reviews. For information, address HarperCollins Publishers, 195 Broadway, New York, NY 10007.

First Avon Books mass market printing: December 2021

Print Edition ISBN: 978-0-06-285240-3
Digital Edition ISBN: 978-0-06-285241-0

Cover design by Amy Halperin
Cover illustration by Anna Kmet

Avon, Avon & logo, and Avon Books & logo are registered trademarks of HarperCollins Publishers in the United States of America and other countries.

HarperCollins is a registered trademark of HarperCollins Publishers in the United States of America and other countries.

FIRST EDITION

Printed in Lithuania

21 22 23 24 25 SB 10 9 8 7 6 5 4 3 2 1

For the wonderful, extraordinary, phenomenal, marvelous, delightful, amazing, and stellar Cheryl Pientka

Acknowledgments

With immense, vast, enormous, epic, massive,
fathomless, and infinite gratitude to:
Lucia Macro
Sophie Jordan
Julia Quinn
Leslie Ruder
Frauke Spanuth
Gillian Green
And to you, dear reader.
Thank you! ♥

Do you need a prod?
Do you need a little darkness to get you going?

—*from "The Fourth Sign of the Zodiac"*
by Mary Oliver

Chapter 1

Surmont Hall
Somerset County, England
January 1819

Philip Thane wasn't handsome, precisely, but people seldom realized it when caught by his raffish charm, as women in particular often were. He was a tall, broad-shouldered man in his late twenties, with long muscled limbs and glossy brown hair and arresting brown-green eyes, and he sat in an elegant armchair in the equally elegant drawing-room with a kind of negligent grace that suggested nothing but confidence in his time-honored powers of persuasion.

Unfortunately for Philip, Mrs. Henrietta Penhallow, who sat opposite him, indomitably upright despite her advancing years, was well-acquainted with his history and exploits and so was not disposed to admire or applaud, and instead looked at him rather fixedly with her still-sharp blue eyes.

"How kind of you to drop by, Philip," she said dryly. "I daresay you were in the neighborhood."

Undeterred by this less than subtle jab—as Surmont Hall, the Penhallows' vast ancestral estate, lay in the Somerset countryside and far from Philip's usual cosmopolitan haunts—he merely smiled a smile more than once described as devastating, and breezily replied:

"No, I came here expressly to see you, Aunt Henrietta. It's been far too long since I've had the pleasure of your company."

The old lady's silvery eyebrows went up at this form of address. She was not Philip Thane's aunt, and in fact the lines of familial connection between them were tangled and hardly substantial. However, she let it pass.

"I trust," she said, "that you have recovered from your wound, which I believe you sustained while in Vienna? I was informed it was nearly fatal."

"Oh, it was nothing, really," responded Philip, in the tone of one who had stubbed a toe, perhaps, or narrowly avoided a collision with a lamp-post, and anyone unaware of the actual circumstances of his injury would have no idea that he had been shot point-blank in the chest by a jealous husband who had rather vehemently objected to Philip's dalliance with his wife.

A satirical smile curved old Mrs. Penhallow's mouth. "I'm glad to hear it."

Philip nodded, and crossed one long leg over the other, entirely at his ease. He wore a beautifully tailored burgundy jacket, elegant buckskins, and tall gleaming top-boots, all in the latest mode and crafted of the finest materials and obviously very expensive. His many-caped greatcoat, tall hat, gloves, and natty portmanteau he had left in the Great Hall under the gimlet eye of the butler Crenshaw who had received them with an unflappable politeness which somehow also managed to convey quite a bit of disapproval.

I regret to inform you that no bedchamber has yet been assigned or prepared, sir, as I was unaware of your imminent arrival, Crenshaw had frigidly said, to which Philip had carelessly answered:

Nobody was. Is your mistress about? The old one, I mean.

And so he had been ushered into this luxurious drawing-room where Henrietta Penhallow had received him with a surprise tempered by shrewd appraisal, then invited him to take a seat although she had not, so far, called for refreshments.

Chattily Philip said, "I hope all the family here is well, ma'am?"

"Thank you, yes."

"That's excellent news."

"Indeed it is."

"This is a charming room."

"How kind of you to say." The same satirical smile remained on the old lady's face.

"The proportions are superb."

"I agree."

"Nice to have a fire, for it's devilish cold out today," he remarked.

"Very."

"Everyone said it would snow, but I knew it wouldn't."

"Oh?"

"Yes, I have an uncanny knack for predicting the weather, you see."

"Indeed."

"Yes, it just comes to me somehow. Speaking of the uncanny, I was accosted by quite a character in your quaint little village—Riverton, isn't it?—earlier today. I'd just gotten out of the coach from Bristol and was standing there on the high street wondering how I could get myself ferried over to Surmont Hall, when an old woman, whom I've never seen before in my life, marched up to me and said, rather in the manner of an ancient Greek oracle, 'You're right on time.' As if she'd been waiting for me. Your obligatory village madwoman, I daresay."

"That was Mrs. Roger, no doubt," said Henrietta Penhallow. "A goodwife in full possession of her wits who's widely believed hereabouts to be possessed of mystical powers. Last year, for example, she predicted that a cow belonging to one of our local farmers, a Mr. Moore, would be delivered of an albino calf, and she was correct. And apparently she was able to locate her neighbor's long-lost watch by the deployment of a divining-rod which, she says, has been in her family for generations."

"Oh, I don't believe in such things, Auntie, do you? A lot of silly superstitions and primitive claptrap, that's all."

Those silvery brows went up again at a yet more cozy form of address, but Henrietta only went on, musingly:

"There was a time, several years ago, when Gabriel swore it was Mrs. Roger who helped him find Livia when she had gone missing."

At this reference to Henrietta's grandson and his wife, Philip nodded without much interest. "Well, at any rate, Mrs. Roger hustled me over to where her husband happened to be standing with his gig—quite the convenient stroke of luck for me!—and told him to drive me to Surmont Hall. Odd—I wonder how she knew I was bound here? I must have mentioned it, I suppose. Good God, only picture it—me in a *gig* sitting side-by-side with one of your worthy yokels. I don't know how I held onto my countenance. You're quite in the middle of nowhere, aren't you, ma'am?

Don't you find yourselves awfully dull with nothing to do?"

"As Gabriel and Livia manage the estate, and together they not only look after the welfare of our tenant-families but also are raising a family of their own, it could hardly be said that there's nothing to do. As for me, I provide whatever help is needed in estate management, I spend many happy hours in my greenhouse, and additionally am active in supporting various charities, both local and distant."

Philip laughed and waved a dismissive hand in the air. "I meant jollification, ma'am—assemblies, dinners, balls, that sort of thing. Not *work*."

"You say the word as if it leaves a bad taste in your mouth," observed Henrietta Penhallow dryly. "But rest assured that the neighborhood is a lively one, and that we all enjoy a great deal of visiting among family and friends, especially upon celebratory occasions. As you may have heard, last year my great-granddaughter Jane married our neighbor the Duke of Radcliffe, which was a most delightful event. And his sister is shortly to marry our vicar Mr. Pressley."

Philip gave an amused smile, imparting a strong impression of one heroically refraining from rolling one's eyes, then continued to chat in his easy, self-assured way on subjects of more sophistication and scope, lightly touching on the latest London *on-dits*, the blackballing of Lady Caroline Lamb from the hallowed halls of Almack's as well as from the *haut ton* in general, the further expansion of the Prince Regent's girth which no longer made riding feasible (not least for any horse selected for the dubious honor of having the Regent's enormous derriere lowered onto its back), the sad demise of Queen Charlotte back in November, and the publication of several notable works of literature including Miss Austen's *Persuasion* and John Keats' *Endymion.*

Mrs. Penhallow listened equably for some time, her hands folded in her lap, but when Philip began to comment upon the celebrated actor Edmund Kean's deliberate sabotage of his role in *The Fatal Accusation to Drury Lane,* she interrupted him without ceremony.

"What is it that you want, Philip?"

His dark brows went up. "Want, Aunt Henrietta? Whatever do you mean?"

"I mean that it would save us both a considerable amount of time if you would simply divulge the actual reason for your sudden arrival upon my doorstep."

If Mrs. Penhallow anticipated that that these forthright words, uttered with a slight but distinct tinge of acid, would discompose Philip Thane, she was destined to be disappointed, for he merely smiled his charming smile and remarked affably:

"You always were one of my favorite relations, ma'am."

"Flattery will get you nowhere. I repeat: why are you here? Do you need money?"

"Now that you mention it, I *am* just a trifle under the hatches," he acknowledged unblushingly.

"When are you not? I suppose your step-grandparents, your mother, your half-sister *and* your half-brother—not to mention all your acquaintance among Polite Society and the other, rackety circles you frequent—have turned you down in your requests for pecuniary assistance."

"Your discernment, dear ma'am, never fails to astonish."

"Rather, let us say that old habits die hard, and that I am more familiar than I would like to be regarding your way of life. It takes no amazing leap of intelligence to surmise that your pockets are once again to let."

"A gentleman," answered Philip, in a voice of the utmost reasonableness, "must be seen to live as one."

"And handsome is as handsome does, if we are to sit here bandying aphorisms."

"Surely, Auntie, you wouldn't care to see a member of your own family languishing in debtors' prison. Or worse. Only think of the embarrassment."

"As you have caused the family a great deal of embarrassment for well over a decade, Philip, a little additional mortification would hardly be noticed."

This blunt statement generated within Philip Thane a tiny, minute frisson of concern. He leaned forward and said in an earnest voice:

"A small loan, ma'am, would have me right as a trivet."

Mrs. Penhallow chuckled sardonically. "You must know your reputation as someone who has never once repaid a loan, not even during your schoolboy days at Eton."

"That's ancient history. I've changed, Auntie, I assure you."

"Have you?"

"Yes. Absolutely."

"You will pardon my skepticism. I have, by now, little confidence in your ability to change."

Philip leaned forward a bit more. "The thing of it is, ma'am, I've come all to pieces. If you send me away with nothing, I'll be at my wit's end. And look at it this way—send me away with *something*, and I'll spare you the further burden of my presence."

His voice was earnest, his expression appealing. Somehow he managed to evoke the pitiful sensibility of a forlorn, needy, yet adorable puppy without in the least detracting from his graceful masculine vigor.

Henrietta eyed him thoughtfully.

A lesser woman might feel a pang of grandmotherly concern; she might feel her heart softening, her resistance to his wiles waning.

Such a woman might reach into her reticule and dispense wads of bank-notes, as might a doting grandparent give a naughty child a toy, if only to bring a smile back to his face.

She, however, was made of sterner stuff.

After several minutes of silent contemplation, which to Philip Thane began to feel like hours, then years, and possibly even decades, Henrietta brought her elbows to the padded arms of her chair, laced her fingers together, and made a little meditative temple of her two forefingers. Over it she slowly said:

"You might, perhaps, execute a small commission for me."

A look of relief spread across Philip's face. "By all means, dear ma'am. What is it?"

"You will recall my mentioning that I am engaged in various philanthropic endeavors. Late last year our bailiff brought to my attention the efforts of an agricultural cooperative in Whittlesey—where his brother lives—to remain viable after an especially bad harvest."

"Whittlesey?" repeated Philip vaguely.

"A town in Peterborough County, some forty miles north of Cambridge and approximately two hundred miles from Surmont Hall."

"Ah."

"Being deeply interested in agrarian matters—farmers being, of course, this country's backbone for time immemorial—I made a sizable donation to the Straw Bear cooperative. Its president wrote back with a nicely worded letter of thanks, and invited me to say a few words to the townsfolk during their annual Plough Day festivities, which denote the community's hopes for a prosperous growing season."

Farmers? Growing season? *Plough Day?* Oh, good God. Philip felt his eyes begin to glaze over with boredom, but, as his position was precarious, and might even be said to be hanging by a thread, he made a determined attempt to keep his expression one of alert interest.

"While appreciative of the president's invitation," Henrietta continued, "I felt it better to assign someone else to go in my stead, and suggested to one of our local agriculturalists, Sir Gregory Stoke, that he travel to the festival, so that he could deliver some remarks at the opening ceremony, which is next week. He agreed. However, this morning I learned that Sir Gregory has fallen ill with an acute and incapacitating attack of gout. I was just about to send an express to the cooperative's president, detailing the unfortunate change in plans, but now, it may be, I don't have to."

Gazing at Philip over the little temple of her forefingers with cynical shrewdness, Henrietta went on:

"It is said that when a door shuts, a window flies open. Therefore I shall designate you to serve as the representative of the Penhallow family and to make a short but appropriate speech at the ceremony and otherwise help suitably mark the occasion. You shall leave within the hour, traveling in one of the Penhallow barouches and staying at the various inns where I have reserved rooms on Sir Gregory's behalf. On the assumption—and let us be clear, my dear Philip, this is merely conjecture on my part—that you behave creditably throughout, I will be glad to provide you with remuneration for your services." Henrietta suddenly chuckled, and added:

"A novelty, is it not? You'll be paid for working. Ha! Let no one assert that *I* am lacking in family feeling."

Philip leaned back in his seat, his mind racing. He

did not want to travel to some godforsaken hole of a town somewhere to the northeast, he did not want to issue pithy remarks upon the occasion of an agrarian festival, and he did not want to waste his precious time mingling with a bunch of dull provincials.

On the other hand—since he and Henrietta Penhallow *were* bandying aphorisms during this increasingly unpleasant and uncomfortable exchange—beggars couldn't be choosers, and he was unnervingly close to being an actual beggar.

He had no choice. He'd have to make the best of it.

He would allow himself to be dragged to Whittlesey, but the moment his obligations were discharged he'd flee the place with such dispatch the bumpkins' heads would spin like tops.

And his life would be his own again. Things would go on as they had before.

The tension in his shoulders melted away. He said, lying through his teeth:

"I look forward to this marvelous opportunity, Auntie."

"Do you? Splendid. One last thing, my dear Philip. While I would hardly claim to be omniscient, or that I have eyes and ears everywhere, I must admit—without false modesty—that I have a reputation for being well informed when it comes to matters that concern me. So I trust you will behave yourself accordingly."

Into Philip's mind rose a hideous vision of Henrietta Penhallow and Mrs. Roger, the Riverton oracle, as Shakespearean witches huddled around a black smoking cauldron and cackling in a sinister way over entirely accurate visions of himself in faraway Whittlesey, mystically projected among the wisps of smoke.

A chill danced up his spine, and he told himself

not to be a damned fool. Solvency beckoned. Debtors' prison receded. *All would be well.*

"I do hope," said Henrietta blandly, "the weather will be propitious for your journey."

"Oh, it won't snow. I can feel it." He smiled at her, with the newly restored poise of one who enjoyed complete mastery of the world around him.

"Splendid," repeated Henrietta Penhallow, dismantling the little temple of her fingers, and if her answering smile was both dubious *and* sardonic, Philip Thane chose to ignore it.

Four days later . . .
The Hare and Hounds Inn
Brampton, England

Well, *damn.*

Standing in the dilapidated courtyard of the equally dilapidated inn, her gloved hands akimbo at her waist, Margaret Allen stared grumpily at the stagecoach which lay all askew on the frozen hard-packed dirt, the iron shaft which connected the two front wheels having snapped a mile or two back, causing the body of the coach to crash onto the ground, the wheels to break, and the horses to rear in alarm.

Luckily neither horses nor passengers had been injured, but everyone had had to trudge in the bright sunshine of a bitterly cold morning to the little village of Brampton where, it seemed, the repair of the shaft would take a day or two, or maybe more, and nobody seemed to have any idea when replacement wheels could be secured. Furthermore, no other public conveyance was expected for several days.

Which meant, Margaret thought with annoyance, they were trapped here.

And she wasn't looking forward to spending any time in the bedchamber assigned to her as she had seen for herself that the sheets were damp, dirty, and crawling with fleas; and that every surface was covered in a thick layer of dust. There was somewhere else she very much wanted to be, only a half-day's journey from here.

Tantalizingly close, yet out of reach.

And time was of the essence.

Double damn.

Abruptly, to her ears came the sounds of horses' hooves and jingling harness, and with eager strides she hurried out to the road.

A large black barouche, pulled by a team of four big horses and its body glinting in the sun like an oversized jewel, was approaching—and heading in the right direction.

Now *this* was more like it.

Margaret waited until the barouche was within a stone's throw, then she waved to the coachman who brought the horses to a halt and looked inquiringly down at her from his high perch on the box.

"May I be of assistance, ma'am?" he said, but before Margaret could answer the window was shoved up and a dark-haired man stuck his head out. His brown eyes met hers and then he smiled, a bold, appreciative, devil-may-care smile that transformed his features into something beyond ordinary good looks.

It was—the realization winged through her mind— pure, powerful, unadulterated *charm* that illuminated his face and made him strikingly attractive.

So attractive, in fact, that she felt a delicious tingle running through her.

It had been so long, so dreadfully long, since she had felt anything like this. Inside herself Margaret swept aside a pang of old grief and renewed loss, and was just about to smile back when his emboldened gaze raked over her from head to foot in a frankly piratical manner, and the warm exciting tingle was quenched in a heartbeat.

She didn't mind the appreciative smile, but she certainly didn't enjoy being ogled like that, in a way that made her glad she had on several layers of clothing impenetrable to the human eye.

Margaret crossed her arms over her chest.

Blast it all, wasn't it just her bad luck that the first vehicle to pass her way contained an irksome libertine.

His smile widened, and in a smooth, deep, cultured voice (which nearly sent *another* tingle shimmering through her before she managed to suppress it) he said:

"Why, hullo there. Aren't you a sight for sore eyes."

If it weren't for the fact that she was rather desperate, Margaret would have enjoyed giving vent to the tart retort hovering on her tongue. Instead she said, with as much civility as possible:

"Good morning, sir. Might I inquire as to where you're heading?"

"To Whittlesey."

Margaret felt her heart bound with sudden hope. "That's where I'm going as well, but I find myself stranded here due to an unfortunate mishap with the stage. I know this is a great and presumptuous favor to ask, sir, but have you any extra room inside?"

"Not only do I have extra room, dear lady, I'm the sole passenger. And the seats are . . . very capacious."

At the silky innuendo in his too-charming voice, Margaret's temper rose still higher and she almost abandoned her resolve to be civil. But then she realized how she might give him back his own, in a way that allowed her to maintain her dignity *and* would soon have her on the road again. Her little plan was devious, admittedly, but after all, turnabout was fair play.

So she smiled and sweetly said, "How kind, sir. Won't you have your coach come into the courtyard while I gather up my things?"

He returned her smile, looking not unlike a cat expecting to be served a delectable bowl of cream. "By all means."

Margaret went back into the courtyard and whisked herself inside the dumpy, dusty inn, returning some five minutes later with her portmanteau and bandbox, Aunt Seraphina, and young Mr. Lawrence, a fellow passenger who had joined them in Watford and was also on his way to Whittlesey, and who kindly insisted on carrying Aunt Seraphina's luggage along with his own.

Together they bade farewell to the disappointed proprietor whose eyes had brightened at the prospect of some paying guests, then emerged into the courtyard where the coach stood waiting with the door wide open and the steps let down. The dark-haired man, who was clad in a dashing many-caped greatcoat, Margaret could now see, and a tall stylish hat along with a pair of beautifully polished boots, was leaning against the gleaming black side-panel of the barouche with his legs crossed at the ankle in a very debonair manner.

She watched as his anticipatory smile faded and onto his face came a look of surprise and dismay.

Ha *ha*, she thought triumphantly, doing her best to keep her expression as bland as a baby's, and as she and her companions came close, she said in a sweet, demure tone:

"Thank you *so* much, sir, for your generosity in allowing us to accompany you to Whittlesey. May I introduce you to my aunt, Miss Allen, and to Mr. Lawrence, a new acquaintance of ours?" She added, even more sweetly:

"And I am Miss Margaret Allen."

So of course he had no choice but to reply, "I'm Philip Thane, at your service," although his voice did lack a certain graciousness; after which he handed Aunt Seraphina and herself up into the barouche, while Mr. Lawrence helped the coachman secure their luggage behind and then climbed in, and finally Mr. Thane did also.

Margaret was pleased that Mr. Thane also had no choice but to sit opposite Aunt Seraphina, and she repressed a laugh as she watched the two of them sizing each other up, Aunt Seraphina with her brows beetled and Mr. Thane looking increasingly disgruntled.

The carriage began to roll and Margaret leaned back against the plush velvet squabs.

"My," she remarked, in a satisfied, cheerful tone, "what comfortable seats. How wonderfully capacious they are."

Mr. Thane shot her a look of annoyance and folded his arms across his chest.

"Thane," said Aunt Seraphina, as if the word was foreign to her, and managing to sound both doubtful and haughty at the same time. "I don't believe I know the name."

Mr. Thane shot *her* a look of annoyance. "I'm a relation of the Penhallow family, and my step-grandparents are the Duke and Duchess of Egremont." He paused, as if waiting for gasps of amazement or a burst of applause, and when none were forthcoming, he added, sounding just as haughty as Aunt Seraphina:

"You *have* heard of the Penhallows, I assume."

"Who hasn't?" interjected Mr. Lawrence. "Pretty much the first family of England, aren't they? Came along with the Conqueror, chummy with royalty, plump in the pocket, immense seat in Somerset, and so on and so forth."

"Draping yourself in a cloak of reflected glory, aren't you?" said Aunt Seraphina to Mr. Thane. "Is this really your barouche?"

The temperature inside the coach seemed to drop about twenty degrees and so Margaret thought it prudent to reenter the conversation, such as it was. She said:

"What takes you to Whittlesey, sir? Is that where you live?"

He actually shuddered. "Good Lord, no. It will be my first and—I assure you—my only time there. I'm going to give a little speech at the Plough Day ceremony." There was a complete and utter lack of enthusiasm in his voice.

"I say, sir, that's splendid," exclaimed Mr. Lawrence. "I'm a journalist for the Watford *Bugle,* and I'm writing an article about tomorrow's events. Care to offer up any early tidbits?" He looked as if he were about to dive into his rucksack and produce a pencil and paper on the spot.

"No," Mr. Thane responded, sarcasm creeping into his tone, "I prefer to leave you in suspense about my scintillating remarks, which will doubtless render my entire audience of rustics, provincials, hobnails, yokels, chawbacons, hicks, bumpkins, and loobies spellbound."

"Good as a thesaurus, aren't you?" said Aunt

Seraphina, not very pleasantly. "You might want to include 'hawbucks,' 'joskins,' and 'lumpkins' while you're busy denigrating the good citizens of Whittlesey."

"If it comes to that, you're quite the thesaurus yourself, ma'am," returned Mr. Thane, also not very pleasantly.

"I ought to be, as I'm a lexicographer who's published three of them, and am at present working on my fourth."

"Indeed. How charming, marvelous, wonderful, captivating, glorious, delightful, and sublime."

Aunt Seraphina, unmoved by Mr. Thane's gibe, pulled some white lace tatting from her enormous reticule and began wielding her mother-of-pearl shuttle with ferocious speed and dexterity.

"If that's truly your attitude, Mr. Thane," said Margaret, "I can't imagine your speech will go over particularly well."

He shrugged. "For any normal human being, it's difficult to get excited about an event called Plough Day."

"Oh, I don't know about that. I'm quite excited to witness it myself."

"Why, for God's sake?"

"Because I'm interested in folk-lore and old cultural traditions."

He stared, then drawled, "Oh, like your esteemed aunt, you're *blue*."

"If by 'blue,' you mean we actually have brains, despite the ghastly misfortune of being women, then you're correct. Plough Day is a custom dating back several centuries, possibly linked to the Nordic invasions of the eighth century, and I for one can hardly wait to see the Straw Bear."

"I know there's a Straw Bear cooperative, but please, please, don't tell me there's an actual bear draped in straw."

"No, not an animal, but apparently somebody gets all covered over in sheaves of straw, and—"

"Surely not voluntarily."

"It's said to be a great honor," Margaret went on, repressing a real urge to swing out her foot and kick him in the shin, "and the Straw Bear is meant to personify the winter season. His appearance on Plough Day symbolically represents the banishment of winter, so that crops can grow again and the people will flourish."

"How childishly sweet."

"Just because a custom springs from ancient beliefs very different from our own contemporary ones doesn't mean they're worthy of your scorn. Besides, even if it's only a fable, it's still a lovely one. It makes people feel hopeful and engaged in their community—a very meaningful sentiment in my opinion."

"Rubbish. Fables are for children, not for adults. The people of Whittlesey need to grow up."

"Your outlook on life," said Margaret, "is inspiring."

"Thank you."

"I was being sarcastic."

"No, really?"

At this Margaret pressed her lips together, hard, in order to prevent herself from tumbling deeper down the rabbit-hole of a conversation which was clearly going nowhere, then realized that Mr. Thane was looking at her with a fresh gleam of interest in his brown eyes which, she now saw, had within them hints of deep forest green. He went on:

"How the devil did a beautiful woman like yourself end up delving into such dull stuff? Why aren't you married?"

"Brazen," interpolated Aunt Seraphina in a color-less tone, without looking up from her tatting. "Brash, impertinent, impudent, brassy, shameless."

"First of all," Margaret said rather snappishly to Mr. Thane, her resolve already weakening, "it's not dull to me. As for the 'how,' it probably has something to do with the fact that I come from a family of aca-demics in Oxford."

"I'm sorry to hear that," he said in a voice of spuri-ous sympathy, and Margaret was so irritated that her strength of will reasserted itself and she didn't even bother telling him that it was none of his business as to why she was unmarried at the supposedly advanced age of twenty-five, and that she didn't appreciate his comments about her appearance, and also that she was pretty confident his speech tomorrow wasn't going to be received with much fanfare; and instead she reached into her reticule and pulled out a book, with which she silently and determinedly beguiled the time—some four or five hours—until they reached Whittlesey.

Dusk had begun to fall, blanketing the town in soft shades of dark blue, violet, and murky gray. They passed houses, shops, offices, inns, a little theatre, some restaurants, taverns, a central square with a festive-looking platform liberally strewn with bunting, and sidewalks filled with people going to and fro, huddled close against the cold in their coats, pelisses, shawls, and hats.

"Where can I drop you?" said Mr. Thane. "Unless you're also staying at the Apple Street Inn." He looked with transparent and annoying significance at Mar-garet, who replied without regret:

"We're staying at the Woodhull Inn."

"As am I," chimed in young Mr. Lawrence.

Mr. Thane banged on the roof and the barouche
came to a stop. He pushed open the window, stuck
his head out, and told the coachman to find the
Woodhull Inn, after which he quickly closed the
window, shutting out the chilly air. They could hear
the coachman asking a passerby for directions, and
soon the barouche started rolling again. It was just a
few minutes later that it came to a stop once more, in
the courtyard of a modest but well-kept hostelry all
lit up with lights inside which rendered it very cozy-
looking in the deepening twilight.

Margaret was so happy to find herself in Whittlesey, when only a few hours ago it had seemed a real
impossibility, that she felt a sudden rush of gratitude
toward Mr. Thane and impulsively she said to him:

"Won't you join my aunt and me for dinner, Mr.
Thane? By way of a small but heartfelt thank-you.
You as well, Mr. Lawrence."

Mr. Lawrence gave a boyish grin. "I say, that sounds
awfully jolly. Thanks ever so much."

But Mr. Thane shook his head and fixed his eyes
soulfully upon her. "No, my dear Miss Allen, two's
company and four's a crowd. I prefer to loom large
in your imagination instead. Envision me as a desperate man, in lonely contemplation of a beautiful face
and an even more beautiful figure, consoling myself
as men have done for time immemorial."

"Lewd," remarked Aunt Seraphina, putting away
her tatting. "Lecherous, lubricous, satiric, dissolute,
dissipated."

"Irritable," said Mr. Thane in a thoughtful voice.
"Cantankerous, crabbed, curmudgeonly, waspish,
prickly."

"Offensive, disrespectful, repulsive, rude, objection-
able, displeasing."

"Belligerent, combative, bellicose, aggressive, martial, hostile."

The coachman pulled open the door and swung down the steps. "Well," said Margaret, glad to thus put an end to the escalating hostilities between her aunt and their unlikely benefactor, "thank you again for the ride, Mr. Thane. We'll see you tomorrow morning, bright and early."

"Just how bright and early do you mean?"

"Why, the ceremony begins just after sunrise."

"Of course it does," he replied in a very bitter way, and Margaret, suppressing a strong desire to snicker, accepted the coachman's hand and stepped down into the courtyard, deftly avoiding a slushy puddle, and also looking forward to a big dinner, a nice long bath, a book, and so to bed.

Chapter 2

Someone was knocking on a door.

"Wake up, sir," said a voice, apparently from outside the room, "it's Plough Day."

Knock knock knock.

"Mr. Thane," said the voice, "you asked to be awakened in time for the ceremony. It's Plough Day, sir."

Groggily Philip opened his eyes, and realized he was lying on his back in a singularly uncomfortable bed, but where?

He stared without comprehension at the unfamiliar ceiling above him.

Then it came to him: he was in his dowdy, quaintly decorated room at the Apple Street Inn, in Whittlesey.

Knock knock knock.

"I'm awake, damn it," he said loudly.

"Very well, sir."

Philip shoved aside the bedcovers and got up, goose-bumps rising on his flesh in the chill of the room despite his fine cambric nightshirt, and went to the window, pulling aside the curtain to look out into the street.

It was a clear, bright day, and the sky was a soft

cloudless blue. On the ground lay scattered splotches of gray slush. He could see hordes of people all walking in the same direction—toward the center of the town. Eager, no doubt, to partake of the Plough Day fun.

He groaned under his breath, and for a few peppery moments thought about packing it all in, jumping into the barouche, and getting out of this repugnant place as fast as possible.

But then he thought about the very small quantity of bank-notes he had in his possession, along with a very small number of coins, together comprising all the money he had left in the world until he fulfilled his commission for Henrietta Penhallow, and he changed his mind.

So he got dressed and went out into the corridor, down the stairs, and into the common-room, hoping in his bad mood and with all his heart to avoid speaking to anybody, but before he got to the door leading to the street, the proprietor Mr. Lancross came sailing over, neatly cutting him off, and although Philip could have shoved him aside with a flick of his arm, it was just too damned early for violence.

"Good morning, Mr. Thane."

"Is it?"

"I—uh—well, I—" His brow furrowed, Mr. Lancross glanced to the windows, as if seeking verification for the goodness or the badness of the day. "It's not snowing, at any rate, which will make for a fine Plough Day, sir."

"Nothing will make for a fine Plough Day."

"Nothing? Oh, sir, surely not—"

"Well, it's been lovely chatting with you, but if you'll excuse me, I've got a speech to make."

"A speech, sir? Why, that's very impressive."

"Yes, I know. No doubt the town will erect a statue in my honor. Good day." Pointedly Philip waited for Mr. Lancross to move from out of his path, but he only brought his hands together into a nervous sort of tangle and said:

"I was just—I was just wondering, sir—your room was reserved for the one night only. Do you happen to know when—when you'll be vacating it?"

"As soon as possible, my dear fellow. I said *good day*."

Mr. Lancross bowed. "Very good, sir." He stepped aside, and Philip toyed with the idea of challenging *this* inane assertion also—whatever Mr. Lancross was referring to, it was clearly not, in fact, good at all—but gave it up and left the inn. God *damn* it, it was cold. How he loathed winter! But here he was regardless, in the very worst season, in the very worst place and among the very worst people. He might as well give the very worst speech while he was at it. Just get it done and get out, and get his money.

His jaw set in morose resentment, Philip made his way toward the town square. He turned onto a sidewalk fronting a variety of stores and shops and almost stumbled into a rickety table, covered with a neatly ironed cloth, behind which sat two middle-aged people, a man and a woman, dressed in the dowdiest clothes imaginable and yet who looked so cheerful and friendly that he actually leaned away from them, as one might attempt to avoid a bad smell.

The woman picked up a basket and held it out to him. "A donation for the convalescent home, sir? For our brave war veterans."

"Sorry, I'm in a hurry," Philip answered, with an indifference he didn't bother to conceal, and walked on without in the least picking up his pace in an attempt to demonstrate speed. They should be donating to *him*, for deigning to grace Plough Day with his presence. He passed a few more shops and then a high sweet voice said:

"Why, goodness me, if it isn't Philip Thane!"

He came to an abrupt halt. A little old lady, bundled up to her eyeteeth and looking positively cylindrical in her various shawls and wraps, stood on the sidewalk beaming up at him. He said, "Do I know you?"

"Surely you haven't forgotten me, Master Philip! *Matron!* From your dormitory at Eton. Such a wee, scrawny lad you were, too! I'll always remember the time I found you a-crying in the laundry, as if your poor little heart were broke in two. I just about burst into tears myself. But look at you now!" she went on approvingly. "So tall and handsome, and dressed so fine. Life's treated you well, hasn't it? Just fancy meeting you here, after all these years, Master Philip! Why, it's quite the Plough Day miracle!"

He stood staring down at her. How could this be happening? What kind of ghastly, miserable, unfortunate coincidence was *this*? A miracle? No—a damned catastrophe! The cruel opening of a book he'd slammed shut a long time ago . . . until now.

Ghosts rose up. Eton, long ago. Him, crying, hugging a sack of dirty clothes as if it would bring back the person he had lost forever. His poor stupid heart *had* been broken. How many times had he hidden in the laundry, weeping like a baby? A rising dam of memories threatened to burst within him, and to forestall it Philip curtly said:

"Yes, quite the miracle, Matron. Goodbye."

He strode on without waiting for a reply, wrenching himself back into the present, then walked into a lamp-post and nearly clocked himself. He stood dazed for a moment, half-blinded, then pulled him-self together. He was Philip Thane, dammit, sort of an Egremont, practically a Penhallow, lord of all he surveyed, smarter than most, blue-blooded and stout-hearted, and a man whose charms no lady could resist.

And so he straightened up again, tall and proud. Then he continued toward the town square, where he came upon a crowd of people gathered in happy anticipation, talking and laughing, congregating in convivial groups small and large, their breaths puffing into little white clouds in the chilly air. Somebody was playing a pipe, somebody was banging a drum, and it all sounded so lively and jolly that Philip longed with every fiber of his being to grab the pipe and drum and crush them under his boot.

But he didn't.

He kept walking.

The only thing keeping him going was the thought of Henrietta Penhallow's money, and an intense determination—bolstered by a supreme confidence that had never let him down—to cajole her into giving him more than she'd intended.

Because he *deserved* it, by God.

Warm and snug in her thick wool pelisse and cozy hat, Margaret looked around with pleasure from her place near the festive bunting-bedecked platform in the town square. What a delightful scene lay all about: how much fun everyone was having! She sent a smiling glance to Mr. Lawrence next to her, he being busy jotting down his impressions in his notebook. Suddenly she spotted a tall broad-shouldered figure coming toward the platform, and in her good mood feeling very willing to let bygones be bygones she called out:

"Mr. Thane! Good morning!"

He came near and she saw at once that he was looking quite saturnine, just as he had yesterday when he'd dropped them off at the Woodhull Inn: annoyingly suave and sardonic and full of himself. But today, for some strange reason, his stylish hat was set askew on his dark locks, as if he'd bumped into something and didn't realize it.

"Good morning," she repeated, smiling at him. "May I?" She reached out a gloved hand toward the brim of his hat, but he caught at it with his own and pressed it to his greatcoat, somewhere in the region where his heart—assuming he *had* one—would be.

"My dear Miss Allen, I didn't know you cared."

Margaret snatched her hand away. "I *did* care, briefly, that your hat's on all wrong, and I'm starting to regret that I did."

Mr. Lawrence unsuccessfully stifled a laugh. "I say, Mr. Thane, you won't want to give your speech looking like *that*. As if you've been in a brawl and lost."

In a very huffy way Mr. Thane straightened his hat, and said to her, "Where's your doughty aunt? Compiling additional pejorative adjectives to deploy against me?"

His tone was sarcastic, and Margaret struggled to remind herself that it was thanks to him that she was here at all. With as much civility as she could muster she replied, "My aunt is at our inn, working on her book."

"And missing out on Plough Day? How I pity her."

"Rest assured, I'll fill her in on everything she missed."

He gave a loud sigh of mock-relief. "*Now* I can give my speech with true peace of mind."

Margaret said, between slightly clenched teeth, "I can hardly wait."

"You and everyone else here."

No sooner had Mr. Thane uttered this than the merry sounds of the pipe and drum fell away, and the crowd fell silent too, turning as one toward the platform in joyful expectancy.

"Well," Margaret said to him, "I believe that's your cue."

"Oh, goody." Mr. Thane went up the wooden steps of the platform, introducing himself to the various town dignitaries clustering there, one of whom, Margaret saw, gestured him toward the front. Mr. Thane walked to the railing, swept his gaze over the crowd, and began speaking in an obsequiously earnest voice.

"Good people: we are gathered here today to celebrate farmers, farming, agriculture, growing seasons, winter, the end of winter, crops, future crops, and also tradition, Whittlesey, springtime, straw, bears, *and* straw bears. Plus, ploughs. Which is spelled P-L-O-U-G-H-S, by the way, not P-L-O-W-S. You're welcome."

He paused in a very theatrical way, and there was a faint, obedient smattering of applause from the crowd.

Margaret could see the tiniest of smirks on Mr. Thane's face, and she glanced next to her at Mr. Lawrence, who was looking nonplussed as he scribbled in his notebook.

Up on the platform Mr. Thane nodded with patently false modesty. "Thank you very much. You're a wonderful audience. And now, the moment you've all been waiting for. The true star of the show, the cynosure of all eyes, the harbinger of seasons past, present, and future. Ladies and gentlemen, I give you . . . the Straw Bear!"

Mr. Thane gestured with an exaggerated sweep of his arm, and, looking to the far edge of the crowd, Margaret saw people eagerly yielding to a great round figure all covered in sheaves of clean shining hay, from its head down to its ankles. The figure lumbered forward and everyone began applauding, those closest to the Straw Bear reaching out to pat at the sheaves—a gesture which signified hope for an early spring. The pipe and drum resumed their merry, lilting beat and some people began to move and sway in happy little dances, both singly and together.

Margaret watched, fascinated, tapping one of her feet in time to the music.

A deep voice said in her ear:

"The bear's quite light on its feet, isn't it?"

It was Mr. Thane, and Margaret glanced up into his attractive but sardonic face. "I suppose," she said, without warmth, "you think you can do better?"

"I flatter myself that yes, I *can* dance better than a bear."

Margaret wrinkled her nose at him. "He's not a bear, and you know it."

"Are you *sure*?"

"What I'm sure of is that your speech wasn't exactly the most inspiring thing I've ever heard. Just as I suspected."

He shrugged. "The important thing is that I did it, and it's done. Huzzah and all that. I'm leaving just as soon as the horses can be hitched to my barouche."

At this Mr. Lawrence lifted his head from his notebook. "They say there's a snowstorm coming in."

"There's not."

"Oh, really? Well, if that's the case then, sir, any

chance I could tag along till Northampton? If it's on your way?"

For a moment Mr. Thane looked as if he wanted nothing more than to say no, but he answered, with obvious reluctance, "Unfortunately it *is* on my way." Then he turned his dark eyes to her. "I suppose you and your aunt would like to tag along also? That is, *if* you've partaken sufficiently of the glorious festivities?"

Insulted by his tone as well as his choice of words, Margaret was just about to spurn his lackadaisical offer of a ride . . . with a few choice words of her own. But she checked herself. She had had the opportunity— yesterday evening and also this morning—to talk with several local folk about Plough Day and the Straw Bear, and had taken copious notes. She had also made inquiries about available transport and had discovered to her dismay that there were no stage seats to be had for several days.

As little as she would look forward to more time spent in the cynical Mr. Thane's company, still less would she look forward to cooling her heels here in Whittlesey for an extended period of time as there was a colloquium in Oxford on the subject of fairy folk, the ballad of Tam Lin, and superstition at which she was slated to speak. So she suppressed her annoyance at his sarcastic manner, and responded with what truly was genuine gratitude (and amazing forbearance):

"Thank you, yes. If going to Oxford doesn't take you too far off your route, sir?"

"No, it's no inconvenience to me at all."

Well, as long as it doesn't inconvenience *you*, Margaret thought tartly, but managed to refrain from saying it out loud.

Within the hour they were on the road, hot bricks beneath their respective pairs of feet and the four horses carrying them swiftly along. Mr. Thane had adroitly managed, this time, to seat himself opposite Margaret, and from time to time their knees bumped. He apologized, but with so little sincerity that she ignored him, keeping her eyes firmly on her book—gratitude having faded away into prickly irritation and her forbearance in danger of fading away also. What an obnoxious, *un*attractive man! She really would be glad to see the last of him.

Some thirty minutes after leaving Whittlesey, they had just passed through the tiny market town of Oundle when Aunt Seraphina, looking up from her tatting and out the window, said:

"It's snowing."

"Not much," said Mr. Thane, but five minutes later it was obvious that they were driving right into a storm. It was as if the dense gray sky above was purposefully dumping large, heavy snowflakes on them, like pouring sand out of a box; they could barely see ten feet ahead.

"What the *hell*," he said, ignoring the disapproving glance Aunt Seraphina gave him. "It wasn't supposed to snow."

"You said that already," Margaret pointed out. "And yet there it is."

"Thank you for that trenchant observation, Miss Allen." There was a distinct snarl in Mr. Thane's voice.

The barouche came to a stop and the coachman climbed down to knock at Mr. Thane's window. He shoved it up and a blast of cold air came inside along with a rushing swirl of snowflakes. "What is it?" he demanded.

"A big tree fell and is blocking the way, sir," said the coachman.

"Can't you move the damned thing out of the way?"

"Doubtful, sir. Even with your help and the other gentleman's."

"Besides," put in Margaret, "you wouldn't want to make the horses travel in such a heavy snowstorm, Mr. Thane, would you? And of course it would be dreadfully uncomfortable for your coachman."

"We've got to go back to Whittlesey, sir," said Mr. Lawrence. "No other choice."

"I agree. Tell the coachman to turn around," Aunt Seraphina said, adding sharply, "And close that window before we all get frostbite."

"Mighty peremptory of you, ma'am," replied Mr. Thane, still with that snarl in his voice. "May I remind you that this is *my* carriage, not yours?"

"Hoity-toity! If you want to go on, young man, you can walk. *We're* going back."

He stared at Aunt Seraphina with dark brows drawn together, looking so flummoxed that Margaret had to suppress an unholy feeling of glee.

"Well, sir?" snapped Aunt Seraphina. "Which is it to be? Go with us or freeze to death on the road?"

"Do hurry and make up your mind," Margaret interpolated. "Your coachman's lips are turning blue."

Mr. Thane turned his glowering gaze to the window, muttered "*Damn* it," then went on in an unpleasant tone to the coachman:

"We're going back to Whittlesey."

He slammed the window shut.

The coachman climbed onto his box again, maneuvered the barouche around, and soon had them rolling briskly on their way. Nobody said anything. Margaret had opened up her book again, Aunt Seraphina was serenely tatting, Mr. Lawrence had leaned back against the squabs with his eyes closed, and Mr. Thane was staring out the window looking very morose, as if still in disbelief at how the weather had personally, atrociously, and viciously betrayed him.

Unlike yesterday when he had dropped off the two Misses Allen and Mr. Lawrence at their inn, today there was no sudden invitation from the younger Miss Allen to join them for dinner.

Not that *he* cared, thought Philip, pacing around his same dowdy room at the Apple Street Inn which, incidentally, had started to become far too familiar. He supposed he should have been grateful that it was still even available—and it *was* the nicest room in the place, thanks to Henrietta Penhallow's generosity on behalf of her neighbor the gouty agriculturist Sir Something-or-Other—but all he could summon up was a grumpy feeling of ill-temper.

He should have been well on his way back to Surmont Hall by now.

Instead, he'd had to cool his heels for a hideously long boring afternoon and evening while he waited for tomorrow to come when he could bolt out of here. He'd had luncheon and dinner sent up, additional expenses for which Henrietta Penhallow, of course, would pay. It occurred to him that he ought to be keeping a running tally so that he could be reimbursed in full.

So he went to the table where a couple of pencils were set in a tray and some sheets of paper were stacked beside it, and he totted up some numbers.

Every penny counted when one was, well, temporarily improvident.

Philip did another lap or two around the room, then went to the window and pulled the curtain aside. At least the snowstorm back near Oundle hadn't arrived. With luck, by the time they got there tomorrow the road would be nice and clear again.

Gloomily he stared out into the darkness.

After a while he found himself thinking again of the younger Miss Allen.

What a shame that such a lovely face and figure was inhabited by a peevish, impertinent personality. Why, aside from that first promising moment yesterday when their eyes had met, she standing in the road and he inside his barouche, she had actually behaved as if she didn't find him in the least bit attractive. What the devil was wrong with her?

Then Philip turned around, and his gaze fell upon the empty bed.

Inspiration struck.

Happy, familiar inspiration.

Why not go out and find some agreeable company, rather than sulking here all alone, pacing about like a caged animal?

Half an hour later he strolled into the crowded taproom of the Publick House and stood with his back to the bar, looking around. It was filled with cheery Plough Day revelers, bustling in and out of the taproom and the big adjacent dining-room, and Philip would not have been surprised if the Straw Bear happened to lumber in and request a pail of honey.

He was pleased to identify several possible candidates who would no doubt be thrilled to be noticed by him. One comely young lady, in fact, had already responded to his gaze upon her and was toying with a strand of her light brown hair, winding it round and round her finger and looking self-conscious. A good sign.

Miss Margaret Allen had light brown hair, he suddenly recalled. It was shot through with bright threads of gold, as if dappled by the sun. And it looked very silky—just the sort of hair that would slide through one's fingers in a delicious sensual way. Also it would be marvelous to bury one's face in it, breathing in that faint haunting scent of hers. Roses, wasn't it? The kind of scent that made one think of summer, and warmth, and vast blue skies, and gardens in bloom and a world filled with infinite potential . . .

All at once Philip realized that the comely woman halfway across the room had hunched her shoulder, dropping her gaze down and away, and he also realized that he had been staring like a man just about to start drooling over a steak.

Now *that* wasn't his usual style at all.

He was urbane, polished, self-assured, in control at all times.

Foolish wayward thoughts of Miss Allen had thrown him off his stride.

Annoyed, he gave himself a mental shake, dismissing Miss Allen and her hair and her scent and also her deep blue eyes all fringed with tawny-brown lashes and her gorgeous mouth and her ripe delectable figure from his mind.

Then he strolled over to the table where the comely woman sat.

"Why, hullo there," he said, making his voice friendly, but not eager. Warm, but not needy. Soft, but not uncertain. In short, pitch perfect. "Aren't you a sight for sore eyes." And he was rewarded when she looked up at him and smiled. He had regained the ground he had lost by staring; in her eyes shone a message he needed no words to comprehend.

Maybe it wasn't so bad after all, being stuck in Whittlesey for just one more night.

The Plough Day banquet was over, and Margaret stood in the spacious, brightly lit foyer of the Publick House, waiting as Mr. Lawrence went to retrieve her pelisse and hat. It had been a long, interesting day, and she had accomplished everything she'd hoped to by coming to Whittlesey. The Straw Bear really had been quite remarkable. She began to mull over her notes, mentally adding some further observations, but was jerked out of her abstraction by a high-pitched trilling laugh.

"Oh, Mr. Thane, aren't you *naughty*," came a voice, lilting with flirtatious approval, and Margaret looked to the doorway to the taproom, through which the tall broad-shouldered form of Mr. Thane emerged, a pretty young woman (with hair, Margaret couldn't help but notice, almost the same shade as her own) clinging to his arm. Together they strolled near and Mr. Thane's eyes came to meet her own with audacious coolness and even, Margaret thought, with the smugness of a cat who'd gotten his bowl of cream.

He nodded, once, and she did the same. There was nothing that needed to be said: earlier today he had, in a grudging manner, repeated his offer of a ride, and they had all agreed to be ready to leave first thing in the morning tomorrow.

Then Mr. Thane and his companion had passed her, going out into the night together, and Margaret found herself idly thinking how well put together Mr. Thane was. He walked with the easy grace of an athlete, and there was no denying that he wore his beautifully tailored clothes with understated elegance.

What a shame that such a fine-looking face and figure was accompanied by an annoying, impertinent personality. Aside from that first intriguing moment yesterday when their eyes had met, she standing in the road and he inside his barouche, he had done nothing but aggravate and provoke her. Why was he like that?

And why was she wasting her time even thinking about him?

Annoyed, Margaret gave herself a mental shake, dismissing Mr. Thane and his fascinating face and broad shoulders and deep charming voice from her mind, and went to meet Mr. Lawrence. She put on her things and together they walked back to the Wood-hull Inn, parting when Mr. Lawrence nipped into the common-room to have a drink, and she proceeded into the private parlor set aside for the exclusive use of herself and Aunt Seraphina.

She found her aunt sitting by the fire with her stockinged feet cozily propped up on a stool, a glass of claret near her on a side-table, and deep into her book.

Margaret shut the door behind her and went to sit in an armchair opposite Aunt Seraphina, who closed her book and said:

"You look rather sober, my dear. Was the Plough Day banquet unpleasant? I do hope that scoundrel Mr. Thane wasn't bothering you."

"Oh, he wasn't at the banquet," answered Margaret, putting out her chilled hands to warm them in the fire's heat. "Although I did see him for a moment in the foyer."

"Is that why you're looking so pensive? He accosted you there?"

"Oh no, he didn't accost me at all. He was with someone else."

"Let me guess. A lady-friend."

Margaret nodded, and her aunt sniffed and said:

"I'm not surprised. I knew him for a rapscallion the moment I met him."

"Yes, but Aunt, what does it matter? It's none of our business what he does. And after he drops us off in Oxford, we'll never see him again."

"Goodbye and good riddance, *I* say. Now, do tell me about the banquet."

So Margaret leaned back in her chair and folded her hands, now all warm and toasty, in her lap, and told her aunt about the people she had met and the interesting conversations she had had.

"I'm pleased you had a good time, my dear. And where was our nice Mr. Lawrence throughout all this?"

"Well, he was flirting quite a lot with some of the young ladies there," replied Margaret, "though I must say he didn't seem to be having much luck."

"Unlike Mr. Thane," remarked Aunt Seraphina in a caustic tone. "What a disagreeable, licentious young man he is. And how unfortunate that we met him."

"Oh, he *is* rather awful, but he couldn't be all bad," Margaret said, trying hard to summon up a spirit of fairness. "He must have some good qualities, don't you think? Perhaps we just haven't seen them. He's clearly intelligent, and he can be well-spoken. And he does have nice eyes, when he isn't leering at one like a rake in a badly written novel."

"You truly do see the best in people, my dear."

"I try, though I don't always succeed." Margaret smiled wryly at her aunt, then turned her gaze to the leaping flames of the fire, wondering what Philip

Thane was doing right now (having, in fact, a very good guess), and also trying to imagine his face when he was smiling without sarcasm or concupiscence but instead with real warmth, and decided that he would be exceedingly attractive like that.

Then she wondered all over again at herself for thinking of Philip Thane at all.

Chapter 3

He was walking through a dense, impenetrable fog that seemed to chill him to his very bones.

He was almost blind in the fog, but still he moved with as much speed as he could.

He had to get somewhere. Get *away*. A sense of urgency clawed at him, quickening his every movement. Hurry, hurry—

All at once he slammed into something hard, nearly clocking himself, and he fell back.

Slowly now, with greater caution, his hands outstretched, he moved forward again, until his fingers touched something hard and icy cold.

Metal.

He felt at it.

It seemed he'd stumbled against some cold, hard, metal bars, set so narrowly together that he could only thrust his hand between them, and for sure not his head or his body.

Was he . . . in a cage?

There were more bars to his left, just as narrowly set together.

He kept moving. More and more bars.

It was hard to tell with all the fog obscuring his

vision, but after a while—he couldn't have said how long—as he went round and round, he became convinced that he was indeed enclosed in a cage.

That he was *trapped* in a cage.

There didn't seem to be a door anywhere, much less one that he could swing open.

How the devil could this have happened?

He had somewhere to go! Somewhere to be!

Didn't they (whoever *they* were) know who he was?

He was an important man.

He *had* to get out of here.

Roughly he grabbed at the bars and tried to rattle them.

They didn't move in the least.

He tried again, with all his strength this time, grunting and groaning.

No movement at all.

He *was* trapped. A chill of horror skittered up and down his spine.

Help! he shouted. *Help! Someone help me!*

His voice seemed to fade away with alarming quickness, and he stood there with his hands hanging useless at his side, blinded, shivering in the cold.

All at once the fog beyond the bars parted, like a curtain in a theatre.

Three old ladies seemed to materialize out of nowhere.

He squinted at them, his heart pounding in his chest. Who were they?

It seemed to take a long time before he could identify them.

One was Henrietta Penhallow, elegant and indomitably straight, smiling at him in that satirical way she had.

Next to her stood Matron. From his dormitory at

Eton. She was shaking her head, looking mournful, and crooning under her breath, *I'll always remember the time I found you a-crying in the laundry.*

He shouted back, *Shut up!*

But she didn't, only kept on shaking her head and crooning out loud those embarrassing, soul-shriveling words.

He tore his gaze away from her, to the third and final old lady, who was staring at him with hard, contemptuous little eyes, as if she had thoroughly assessed him and found him wanting.

It was Mrs. Roger, the so-called village oracle who had met him upon his arrival in Riverton, then hustled him over to the gig which had carried him to Surmont Hall. She'd said something, hadn't she? Something portentous?

Frantic, he tried to remember what it was, but his stupid brain wouldn't cooperate. Besides, he was so cold he was shaking like a leaf. It was difficult to think at all.

Now he watched as old Mrs. Roger raised a gnarled hand, pointing a knobby forefinger as if accusing him of something dreadful.

Why?

He'd done nothing wrong, he was unjustly accused, why was he trapped in this prison?

He opened his mouth to scream, but nothing came out, and horror engulfed him so profoundly that he sank to his knees under the weight of it and let his chin drop to his chest, desperate to avoid the gazes of the three terrible old ladies—

With a sudden sharp intake of breath Philip snapped awake.

He lay there in the chilly dimness, realizing that he was in a bed, not in a cage, and felt a wave of deep, welcome relief wash over him.

But . . . which bed? Where?

It came to him then as he stared at the unfamiliar ceiling above him.

He was in his dowdy, quaintly decorated room at the Apple Street Inn, in Whittlesey.

And last night he had brought someone back here. He'd forgotten her name, but he turned in the bed and groped for her.

Unfortunately the rest of the bed was empty.

Damn.

She must have slipped out in the night.

That was too bad.

He'd have enjoyed another go-round with her right now.

Philip lay back against his pillows. Already his dream—his nightmare—was receding, and for that he was glad. He would have liked to have fallen asleep again, but glancing at the curtained window he could see just the faintest intimations of dawn glimmering around the edges.

He gave a loud yawn, and stretched. Soon it would be day, and soon he'd be on the road and gone from here. It couldn't happen fast enough, as far as he was concerned.

Someone knocked on the door.

"Wake up, sir," said a voice from outside the room, "it's Plough Day."

Knock knock knock.

"Mr. Thane," said the voice, "you asked to be awakened in time for the ceremony. It's Plough Day, sir."

Philip jerked his head toward the door.

Did the voice really say that it was Plough Day?

Plough Day was *yesterday.*

Was the person in the corridor stupid and confused, or playing a strange little game?

Knock knock knock.

"I'm awake," Philip said loudly.

"Very well, sir."

Philip shoved aside the bedcovers, got up, and went to the window, pulling aside the curtain to look out into the street.

It was a clear, bright day, and the sky was a soft cloudless blue. On the ground lay scattered splotches of gray slush, and hordes of people were all walking in the same direction—toward the center of the town.

It looked like yesterday's view.

The same weather, the same slush, and what looked a lot like the same number of people.

How strange.

And the voice had said that it was Plough Day.

Again?

"What the devil," Philip muttered out loud, staring.

He turned about and looked uneasily around his room, as if somehow the bed, the armoire, the table, the fireplace, or the sofa would be able to pipe up and tell him what was going on.

But of course they didn't.

A fact which he found oddly comforting.

Then he glanced again at the table.

On it were a couple of pencils set in a tray and some sheets of paper stacked beside it.

Puzzled, he went closer. Where was the paper with the tally of his expenses?

He rifled through the papers; they were all blank.

Next he looked under the table.

Nothing.

This was strange also. Was it possible that Miss What's-her-name from last night had absconded with his tally?

It seemed unlikely, but then again, he hardly knew her.

Perhaps she had taken it as a little memento of their enjoyable night of passion.

A bizarre choice for a memento, though.

Had she taken anything else?

Philip searched through his things and found that all his possessions were still there, though they weren't quite in the same configuration as last night.

Reassured, he got dressed, whistling under his breath, and went out into the corridor, down the stairs, and into the common-room, keen to make his way to the stables to tell the coachman to get the barouche ready for departure, but before he got to the door leading to the street, the proprietor Mr. Lancross came sailing over, neatly cutting him off, exactly as he had done yesterday morning.

"Good morning, Mr. Thane."

"Yes, it is." *Because I'll never see you, or this miserable inn, again.*

Mr. Lancross glanced to the windows. "It's not snowing, which will make for a fine Plough Day, sir, won't it?"

"I beg your pardon?"

"I said that it's not snowing, sir, which will make for a—"

"I heard you the first time," Philip interrupted curtly, looking hard into Mr. Lancross' face. Was *he* playing games, too? "What day is it today?"

"Why, it's Plough Day, sir," replied Mr. Lancross, and if he was making a sly joke, he was doing a masterful job of it. His expression was earnest, pleasant, entirely without guile.

What the *hell*, Philip thought. He glanced around the common-room and saw, to his uneasy surprise, that the same people seemed to be in the same spots they were yesterday morning.

Were *they* in on the joke as well?

It seemed unlikely that everyone in the Apple Street Inn had banded together in a sinister conspiracy to torment him, but, feeling more and more befuddled, Philip found himself thinking that it might even be possible. Hadn't he said just the other day to Miss Allen, *The people of Whittlesey need to grow up.*

Was this some fiendish juvenile prank?

A panicky chill ran through him, and he shuddered. He had to get out of here. *Now.*

"Well," he said, "goodbye," and walked around and past Mr. Lancross, who said from behind him:

"I was just—I was just wondering, sir—your room was reserved for the one night only. Do you happen to know when—when you'll be vacating it?"

Yesterday Mr. Lancross had asked him this same question, and he had answered: *As soon as possible, my good man.*

But today he only said, vaguely, "Soon."

He hurried outside. God *damn* it, it was cold. As cold as it had been in his nightmare? he suddenly wondered. Gripped by a horrible deepening anxiety, he paused on the front portico for a few moments, like a man lost in the woods standing at a crossroads leading he knew not where. Then he decided to postpone his plan to go to the stables, just for a little while, and instead he walked with long strides toward the town square.

He had to see for himself what was going on there.

In all likelihood, nothing.

Then he'd give a hearty laugh at the joke, and proceed at once to the stables.

In a few minutes he turned onto the sidewalk fronting a variety of stores and shops and almost stumbled into that same rickety table, covered with a neatly ironed cloth, behind which sat the same two middle-aged people, the man and the woman, dressed again in those dowdy clothes and still looking repulsively cheerful and friendly.

Nothing unusual about that, Philip told himself. Probably they did this a lot.

The woman behind the table picked up a basket and held it out to him. "A donation for the convalescent home, sir? For our brave war veterans."

"Sorry, I'm in a hurry," Philip replied, which was, in fact, the truth. Quickly he passed a few more shops and then a high sweet voice said, sending a fresh purl of horror through him:

"Why, goodness me, if it isn't Philip Thane!"

And there was Matron, bundled up to her eyeteeth as she had been yesterday, looking positively cylindrical in her various shawls and wraps, standing on the sidewalk beaming up at him. *Maybe she's senile,* Philip thought. *Maybe she forgot that she saw me yesterday.* He said, carefully:

"Hullo, Matron."

"You remember me, Master Philip!" she said in delight. "Even after all these years! My, doesn't our time together at Eton seem so long ago? And you such a wee, scrawny lad, too! I'll always remember the time I found you a-crying in the laundry, as if your poor little heart were broke in two. I just about burst into tears myself. But look at you now!" she went on approvingly. "So tall and handsome, and dressed so fine. Life's treated you well, hasn't it? Just fancy meeting you here, Master Philip! Why, it's quite the Plough Day miracle!"

With a massive effort of will Philip tamped down that excruciating memory of himself hugging a sack of dirty clothes, weeping like a baby, along with all the others that threatened to rise within him. "It's Plough Day?" he said, even more carefully.

"Yes indeed!" Matron beamed up at him. "And such fine weather as we're having for it, too!"

"Yes, very fine," he responded, hardly knowing what he was saying. "Goodbye."

Quickly he walked on, right into the exact same lamp-post, and nearly clocked himself. He stood dazed for a moment, half-blinded—*exactly* as he had been in his dream—then with another massive effort of will pulled himself together.

There had to be a perfectly good reason for all of this.

He was looking forward to giving that hearty laugh, demonstrating that he had a very good sense of humor even when the joke was at his expense, and then getting out of here, once and for all.

Philip continued toward the town square, where to his infinite dismay he came upon a crowd of people gathered in happy anticipation, talking and laughing, congregating in convivial groups small and large, their breaths puffing into little white clouds in the frigid air. Somebody was playing a pipe, just as they had yesterday, and somebody was banging a drum, *just as they had yesterday,* and it all sounded so lively and jolly and *familiar* that Philip had to admit, with another chill of horror streaking up and down his spine, that something *was* wrong, especially when he looked to the bunting-bedecked platform and saw the exact same dignitaries standing up there.

Had the world gone mad?

Or . . . had *he* gone mad?

It was a crisp, bracingly cold morning, but Margaret was warm and snug in her thick wool pelisse and cozy hat. Here she was in Whittlesey on Plough Day, and wasn't she just so lucky? And she'd found such a nice place right near the bunting-bedecked platform in the town square, too. A delightful scene lay all about: how much fun everyone was having, herself included. It reminded her of other festivals she had attended over the years—the same jolly, convivial atmosphere. That must be why this one felt a bit similar.

She sent a smiling glance to Mr. Lawrence next to her, he being busy jotting down his impressions in his notebook. Suddenly she spotted a tall broad-shouldered figure coming toward the platform, and in her good mood feeling very willing to let bygones be bygones and not let yesterday's aggravating carriage ride linger in her mind, she called out:

"Mr. Thane! Good morning!"

He came near and she saw at once that he was looking quite different than he had last night when he had dropped Aunt Seraphina, Mr. Lawrence, and herself off at their inn. Then he had been annoyingly suave and sardonic, and openly bitter about having to get up early for Plough Day. Today, however, he was pale and rather haggard, and also, for some strange reason, his stylish hat was set askew on his dark locks, as if he'd bumped into something and didn't realize it.

"Good morning," she repeated, smiling at him. "May I?" She reached out a gloved hand toward the brim of his hat, but he caught at it and gripped it tightly.

"Miss Allen, if I were to ask you a question, would you promise to tell me the truth?"

"Yes," she returned cautiously, "as long as it's not too personal."

"It's not personal at all. What day is it today?"

Startled, she stared up into his pale, tense face. "Have you forgotten? It's Plough Day."

He groaned out loud. *"Et tu, Brute?"* His grip on her hand tightened, almost hurting her, and she tugged it away.

"What's wrong, Mr. Thane?"

"I was hoping your answer would be different."

"But why? Oh, is it because you're nervous about giving your speech? There's nothing to be worried about. Everyone here is looking forward to it."

"I couldn't care less what people here are looking forward to. I'm worried about *me*."

Margaret's surge of concern for him dissipated as quickly as it had arisen. "Of course you are."

"I say, Mr. Thane, why is your hat all topsy-turvy?" put in Mr. Lawrence. "You won't want to give your speech looking like *that*. As if you've been in a brawl and lost."

"I already gave my speech," Mr. Thane retorted. "Why would I want to give it again?"

Now Mr. Lawrence was the one looking startled. "What do you mean, you already gave your speech?"

"I gave it yesterday."

Mr. Thane sounded so firm and insistent that Margaret shared an even more startled look with Mr. Lawrence. She said:

"Do you mean that you *practiced* your speech yesterday?"

"No, I mean that I gave it yesterday. Here. In front of all of you. Don't you understand plain English?"

No sooner had Mr. Thane uttered this than the merry sounds of the pipe and drum fell away, and the crowd fell silent too, turning as one toward the platform in joyful expectancy.

"Well," Margaret said, "I believe that's your cue."

"That's exactly what you said yesterday."

Mr. Thane's voice was filled with such conviction that for a crazy moment Margaret found herself wondering if she *had*. Then she rallied. "Nonsense. Are you going to give your speech or not?"

He was staring at her, looking quite haunted, and then at last he said: "Oh, all right."

"You'll be fine," Margaret said, impulsively reaching out to straighten his hat.

"Maybe." With obvious reluctance he went up the wooden steps of the platform, introducing himself to the various town dignitaries clustering there, one of whom, Margaret saw, gestured him toward the front. Mr. Thane walked to the railing, swept his gaze over the crowd as if in disbelief, and said:

"Good people: we are gathered here today to celebrate Plough Day. Again. Doesn't it seem just like yesterday that we celebrated it? How time flies when one's having fun. Here's to farmers, farming, agriculture, ploughs, and all that."

Mr. Thane paused, and there was a faint, obedient smattering of applause from the crowd. Margaret could see on his face that same expression of stunned disbelief, and when she glanced next to her at Mr. Lawrence, she saw that he was looking nonplussed again as he scribbled in his notebook.

Up on the platform Mr. Thane continued to gaze at his audience as if he had never before in his life seen a group of human beings gathered together; as if he was looking at visitors from another planet. "And now— once again—the Straw Bear."

He gestured in a rather anemic fashion, and, looking to the far edge of the crowd, Margaret saw people eagerly yielding to a cylindrical figure all covered in sheaves of hay, from its head down to its ankles. The figure lumbered forward and everyone began applauding, those closest to the Straw Bear reaching out to pat at the sheaves—a gesture which signified hope for an early spring. The pipe and drum resumed their merry, lilting beat and some people began to move and sway in happy little dances, both singly and together.

Margaret watched, fascinated, tapping one of her feet in time to the music.

A deep voice said in her ear: "I gave my speech. Are you satisfied now?"

It was Mr. Thane, and Margaret glanced up into his haggard face. Just as she had predicted yesterday, it wasn't exactly the most inspiring thing she'd ever heard, but instead of issuing a tart critique, she only said:

"Well, at least you did it."

"Yes, huzzah and all that. I'm leaving just as soon as the horses can be hitched to my barouche."

At this Mr. Lawrence lifted his head from his notebook. "They say there's a snowstorm coming in."

"I don't care."

"Oh, really? If that's the case then, sir, any chance I could tag along till Northampton? If it's on your way?"

For a moment Mr. Thane looked as if he wanted nothing more than to say no, but he replied: "Unfortunately it *is* on my way." Then he turned his dark eyes to her. "I suppose you want to come too."

"And Aunt Seraphina, of course?"

"Why not? She can use the time to compile additional pejorative adjectives to deploy against me."

Margaret bristled at his tone. But then she recalled that she had made inquiries about available transport

and had discovered to her dismay that there were no
stage seats to be had for several days.

As little as she would look forward to more time
spent in the cynical (and, frankly, rather bizarre) company of Mr. Thane, still less would she look forward
to cooling her heels here in Whittlesey for an extended
period of time as there was a colloquium in Oxford on
the subject of fairy folk, the ballad of Tam Lin, and
superstition at which she was slated to speak.

Fortunately she had had the opportunity—yesterday
evening and also this morning—to talk with several
local folk about Plough Day and the Straw Bear, and
had taken copious notes. She could leave town satisfied with her work here. So she responded with what
truly was genuine gratitude (and amazing forbearance):

"Thank you, yes. If going to Oxford doesn't take
you too far off your route, sir?"

"No, it's no inconvenience to me at all."

As long as it doesn't inconvenience *you*, Margaret
thought tartly, but again, managed to hold her tongue.
She merely nodded, and he said to her and Mr. Lawrence in an irritatingly peremptory manner:

"Hurry up then. If you're not standing in the courtyard of your inn with all your baggage in half an hour,
I'm leaving without you."

"**W**ell, here we are again," said the elder Miss Allen,
sliding her tatting and mother-of-pearl shuttle back
into her capacious reticule. "Unfortunately."

Mr. Lawrence woke up from his nap with a glottal
snort and glanced out the window. "At least the snow
didn't follow us here."

"Yes, that was lucky," agreed Miss Margaret Allen.

"And hopefully tomorrow morning we'll be able to try again. If that suits you, Mr. Thane?"

At the sound of his name Philip gave a start. He'd barely been paying attention. In his mind, over and over again, he kept seeing the same storm they'd run into, just outside Oundle. And the same big fallen tree blocking the way. *Just like yesterday.* And here they were, back where they started, in the courtyard of the Woodhull Inn. "What did you say?" he muttered to Miss Allen.

She was, he noticed, looking at him rather fixedly.

"I said," she replied, enunciating her words with special care, "that I hoped we could leave again tomorrow morning. If that's suitable for you also, of course."

"Tomorrow?" he said vaguely, as if it were a word he'd never encountered before.

"Yes, tomorrow."

"Perhaps."

"Going to run off without us, young man?" said the elder Miss Allen, her brows beetled.

"I'm sure Mr. Thane meant that it's all dependent on the weather," put in the younger Miss Allen hastily.

Her aunt gave an audible, skeptical sniff.

There was a knock on the door of the barouche, and the coachman, having put down the steps, opened the door to hand the ladies down. After her aunt had clambered out, Miss Allen turned to him and said:

"Mr. Thane, are you all right?"

"Why wouldn't I be?"

"Well, it's just that you—well, you look—"

"Incredibly handsome? I know."

Her lovely mouth thinned and she took the outstretched hand of the coachman, whisking herself out of the carriage without a second glance. Mr.

Lawrence, looking at him with a kind of nervous doubt, scuttled after her. When their baggage had been removed from behind, the coachman came to him and said:

"Back to your inn now, sir?"

"Yes. And shut the damned door. I'm freezing in here."

The coachman did, and they soon began to roll. Arriving at the Apple Street Inn, Philip found it not the least bit surprising that his room was still available. He dodged Mr. Lancross' attempts at further conversation, trudged up the stairs, flopped on the bed, and lay there for quite some time, staring up at the ceiling.

He supposed that when it got dark, he could make his way over to the Publick House and that there was a very good chance he'd find Miss What's-her-name again.

A few practiced smiles, a few deft compliments, and she'd be hanging on his arm like a limpet all the way back to his room.

A fine interlude they'd shared together last night, too.

Even though her hair hadn't been particularly silky, not as Miss Margaret Allen's looked to be, and she hadn't smelled of summer roses, either.

Still, she had sufficed.

But he felt no anticipatory stirring of his loins.

In fact, he didn't feel much of anything besides a nauseating blend of bewilderment and dread that made his stomach hurt.

So after a while, he crawled under the covers of the bed, still fully dressed, turned onto his side, and pulled the covers over his head, waiting with as much patience as he could muster for this foul, horrible, harrowing, miserable, ghastly, discombobulating, and thoroughly upsetting day to end at last.

Having parted from Mr. Lawrence, who nipped into the common-room to have a drink, Margaret went into the private parlor set aside for the exclusive use of herself and Aunt Seraphina.

She found her aunt sitting by the fire with her stockinged feet cozily propped up on a stool, a glass of claret near her on a side-table, and deep into her book.

Margaret shut the door behind her and went to sit in an armchair opposite Aunt Seraphina, who closed her book and said:

"You look thoughtful, my dear. Was the Plough Day banquet not to your liking? I do hope that scoundrel Mr. Thane wasn't bothering you."

"Oh, he wasn't there," answered Margaret, putting out her chilled hands to warm them in the fire's heat. "Not that I expected him to be, after his condescending remarks about Whittlesey. I daresay he wouldn't wish to lower himself to socialize with the *hoi polloi*."

"Possibly," said Aunt Seraphina in an acid tone, "he was embarrassed to show his face after the speech he gave this morning."

"I see the word got around."

"Yes indeed. Apparently it was the worst Plough Day speech in living memory—even when considering the speech seven years ago by an alderman so drunk that he toppled off the platform, tearing all the bunting as he went, rolled around in it, and rose to his feet looking so much like an Egyptian mummy come to life that several people screamed and at least two women fainted."

"That does sound memorable," agreed Margaret. "I'm sorry to say, however, that I think I would have laughed."

Her aunt smiled. "I believe I would have also. Did you want to laugh when you heard Mr. Thane's speech this morning?"

Margaret thought back. "No. Actually I was puzzled. Mr. Thane looked so pale, and even rather wild-looking."

"Suffering from the aftereffects of drinking, perhaps?"

"I don't know. But he insisted that he'd already given his speech *yesterday*, which was odd."

"I suppose he was joking, although in very poor taste. It seems just the sort of thing a rapscallion like that would do—simply for the fun of confounding you. Dear me! What a disagreeable young man Mr. Thane is. How unfortunate that we met him."

"I'm not at all sure that he was joking, Aunt. He looked serious when he said he'd given his speech yesterday. And at first he didn't even seem to know what day it is."

"You think he's unbalanced, my dear?" Aunt Seraphina looked grave.

Margaret nodded. "It's possible."

"If that's so, then perhaps we ought not to accept a ride in his carriage tomorrow."

"Oh, but Aunt, I *do* want to get out of here and back home! There's that colloquium on fairy folk, the ballad of Tam Lin, and superstition at which I'm speaking, you know. Besides," she added, "I don't think Mr. Thane is dangerous. Just—a trifle off."

Aunt Seraphina still looked grave. "I propose that we withhold our decision until the morning."

"Agreed." Margaret watched as her aunt opened up

her book again, and she turned her gaze to the leaping
flames of the fire, wondering what Philip Thane was
doing right now.

He *was* rather awful, but still she hoped that he
was all right.

Chapter 4

Philip rolled onto his side and, with his eyes still closed, gave a sleepy yawn as slowly he drifted up into consciousness. Something was tugging at him. Something about . . . yesterday. What was it?

It came to him after a few moments.

He had gone to bed very early, without even bothering to take off his clothes. No doubt they were all wrinkled and creased by now. It was lucky that he'd brought along extras of everything. He smiled. How foolishly overwrought he had been as he'd tucked himself in. He should have strolled over to the Publick House, cozied up to Miss What's-her-name, and had themselves a fine time together.

He yawned again and rubbed his face, still drowsy. What *was* it he'd been so upset about?

Ah! He remembered it now, and with the easy detachment of a fading dream.

A stupid prank being played on him, that was it. As if Plough Day had repeated itself. Expertly done, too, with lots of people in on the gag. Even Miss Margaret Allen.

He wouldn't have thought it of her, really.

Although—despite her stunning good looks—she *did* have a rather peevish, impertinent personality.

Maybe she'd been getting back at him for his witty remarks and clever repartee. Some people just couldn't stand being around others of superior intellect and more illustrious bloodlines.

He gave a luxurious stretch, toying with some subtle insults he could lob her way on today's journey out of town. How he'd laugh inside himself watching her stew all the way to Oxford!

Knock knock knock.

"Wake up, sir," said a voice from outside the room, "it's Plough Day."

Philip's eyes opened wide in sudden horror and he actually gasped out loud.

Knock knock knock.

"Mr. Thane," said the voice, "you asked to be awakened in time for the ceremony. It's Plough Day, sir."

Knock knock knock.

"I'm awake," he said, but the words came out in a stifled sort of rasp and so he forced himself to say them again, more loudly. *"I'm awake."*

"Very well, sir."

Underneath the covers he groped frantically at himself and made a ghastly discovery.

He *wasn't* wearing his clothes from yesterday.

Instead he was wearing his fine cambric nightshirt.

And unless he had engaged in a neat act of sleepwalking last night, getting up from the bed, changing out of his clothes, and putting on his nightshirt, all without having the slightest awareness of what he was doing, that meant . . .

"No, no, no, *no*," he said hoarsely into the placid silence of his room. "Not again."

He shoved back the covers, bolted out of bed, and

went to the window, wrenching aside the curtain to look out into the street.

O God: it was a clear, bright day, and the sky was a soft cloudless blue. On the ground lay scattered splotches of gray slush, and hordes of people were all walking in the same direction—toward the town center.

The same weather, the same slush, the same people.

Frozen into immobility, Philip stared, bewildered and horrified, out the window.

The conclusion was inescapable.

It really was Plough Day. *Again*.

How was this happening?

Why was it happening?

And what was he going to do about it?

His mind was a whirling, swirling storm of confusion, but somehow he found something to grasp onto—like an alpine climber gaining just the tiniest bit of a hand-hold, just enough to keep him from falling off a mountainside and meeting a horrid fate at the bottom.

He would go find Miss Allen.

Never mind that she was so alluring and beautiful. Or that she could be peevish and impertinent. What was more important right now was that she was calm, steady, sensible, clever, sure of herself.

If anyone could help him, it would be her.

His heart pounding violently in his chest, his brain gone to panicky mush, Philip scrambled into his clothes and went out into the corridor, down the stairs, and into the common-room, veering wildly when Mr. Lancross came sailing over and nipping out the door before that worthy could say a word.

With long strides Philip made his way toward the town square, barely noticing the cold, and when he turned onto the sidewalk fronting a variety of stores and shops, this time he managed to give plenty of clearance to the rickety table, covered with a neatly ironed cloth, behind which sat those two middle-aged people, the man and the woman, dressed in their dowdy clothes and looking so cheerful and friendly.

He practically ran past them, before the woman could even pick up the basket, but came to a screeching halt when he heard it.

That high sweet voice exclaiming in wonder.

"Why, goodness me, if it isn't Philip Thane!"

And there was Matron, bundled up to her eyeteeth as she had been before, looking positively cylindrical in her various shawls and wraps, standing on the sidewalk beaming up at him.

Dimly Philip was aware that his eyes were bugging out from his head in a very undignified way, but he couldn't seem to stop himself.

Matron said, with jocular reproach:

"Surely you haven't forgotten me, Master Philip! *Matron!* From your dormitory at Eton. Such a wee, scrawny lad you were, too! I'll always remember the time I found you a-crying in the laundry, as if your poor little heart were broke in two. I just about burst into tears myself. But look at you now!" she went on approvingly. "So tall and handsome, and dressed so fine. Life's treated you well, hasn't it? Just fancy meeting you here, after all these years, Master Philip! Why, it's quite the Plough Day miracle!"

Philip opened his mouth, but nothing came out save for an odd, desperate-sounding sort of croak. Like a frog. *Was* he a frog? Anything seemed possible. He scurried away, like a mouse fleeing a cat—no, like a frog fleeing whatever it was that stalked it—snakes? Eagles? He hadn't the slightest idea—and walked right into the lamp-post again, nearly clocking himself. He stood dazed for a moment, half-blinded, then somehow managed to pull himself together, more or less, and moved on, his muddled mind fixed on one thing and one thing only.

Miss Allen.

It was a crisp, bracingly cold morning, but Margaret was warm and snug in her thick wool pelisse and cozy hat. Happily she looked all around from her place near the festive bunting-bedecked platform in the town square.

Yesterday it had seemed all too likely that she'd be stuck in Brampton for goodness knew how long, but here she was in Whittlesey for Plough Day. How lucky she was! If Mr. Thane managed to behave with a modicum of civility this morning—without leering at her, like a rake in a badly written novel—she'd be sure to thank him again for ferrying them here.

Margaret cast another cheerful glance around. What a delightful scene lay all about: how much fun everyone was having! They were so nice and friendly, too—she felt right at home here, almost as if she knew them already.

Smiling, she looked at Mr. Lawrence next to her, he being busy jotting down his impressions in his notebook. She wondered if he felt the same way, too—the same subtle sense of familiarity, even after only one evening in town. But probably not; she was likely having this sensation because she'd been to other, similar festivals, and they'd begun to blend together.

Suddenly Margaret spotted a tall broad-shouldered figure coming toward the platform, and in her good mood feeling very willing to let bygones be bygones she called out:

"Mr. Thane! Good morning!"

He came near and she saw at once that he was looking quite different than he had last night when he had dropped Aunt Seraphina, Mr. Lawrence, and herself off at their inn. Then he had been annoyingly suave and sardonic, and openly bitter about having to get up early for Plough Day. Today, however, he was white as a sheet and alarmingly haggard, and also, for some strange reason, his stylish hat was set askew on his dark locks, as if he'd bumped into something and didn't realize it.

"Good morning," she repeated, rather carefully this time. She wanted to reach out a hand and straighten his hat, but decided to wait on that until she had a better understanding of what was going on with him. Really, he looked quite wild.

"Miss Allen, may I talk with you?"

"If you like," she answered, still carefully. "But it's just about time for the speeches to begin, don't you think?"

"I'm not giving my speech. I already did it twice."

"I beg your pardon?"

"I already gave my speech twice."

She could feel her brow wrinkling in puzzlement. "Do you mean that you *practiced* it twice?"

"No, I mean that I've given my speech two times already. Up on that platform. Two days in a row."

He spoke with what seemed like genuine, painstaking sincerity, and Margaret stared at him. Was he pulling a prank? Or—worse—was he drunk? It would be early in the day to be imbibing, but Mr. Thane struck her as someone who might indulge that way. And over the years she'd seen plenty of hollow-eyed Oxford students staggering about in the morning, reeking of alcohol. Cautiously she sniffed at him, but there was no distinctive aroma of spirits about his person. How baffling.

"If you're done smelling me, can we go someplace where we can talk? Please."

Margaret didn't have time to be embarrassed at being blatantly caught out, for no sooner had Mr. Thane uttered this than the merry sounds of the pipe and drum fell away, and the crowd fell silent too, turning as one toward the platform in joyful expectancy.

"Mr. Thane," Margaret said to him, "I believe that's your cue."

Vehemently he shook his head, and his hat tilted even more precariously to one side, giving him, along with his pale countenance and haggard expression, a pitifully deranged appearance. So Margaret, who could never walk past a person in need, or a dog or a cat or a horse in trouble, without intervening, said:

"Very well, Mr. Thane. I'll come with you. Where would you like to go?"

"Anywhere but here."

"We'd better hurry then, before they come and try to escort you up onto the platform. Mr. Lawrence, could you please let them know that Mr. Thane was called away for an emergency? And could I trouble you to take some notes about the Straw Bear, if you can? I'd be so grateful."

"Of course," replied Mr. Lawrence, and bounded away and up the platform steps.

Margaret slid her arm through Mr. Thane's and hustled him away from the town square. He went willingly and she felt almost as if she was leading a scared dog on a leash. It was impossible to hold onto her earlier resentment and disdain. *What* a different Mr. Thane from yesterday!

Gone was the suave, confident, arrogant man who had leaned against his barouche with casual grace, expecting to share its capacious interior with herself and herself alone.

In his place was a man who looked as if he had seen a ghost.

Strangely, she found him more attractive like this.

He seemed less like a caricature of a smooth-talking libertine and more like an actual person.

They paused together on a sidewalk across from the town square, and Margaret saw that they were standing outside a little restaurant. "Shall we go inside? We can have something to eat, and talk."

He nodded listlessly, and Margaret felt comfortable enough to reach out a gloved hand to the brim of his hat and gently straighten it. He grabbed at her hand and held it tight.

"I knew you could help me," he said hoarsely.

"I'm afraid I haven't helped you at all, Mr. Thane." With that same gentleness she pulled her hand away, then led him into the restaurant, where they found a table in the corner. They sat across from each other and curiously Margaret studied his face. His dark eyes were fixed on her own, and she noticed that within their brown depths were some fascinating forest-green flecks.

She said, "I don't understand, Mr. Thane. Didn't you come to Whittlesey for the specific purpose of giving a speech?"

"I told you, I *did* give my speech. Twice."

Doubt, uneasiness, and suspicion all rose in her again. Was he playing her for a fool? "What do you mean? Explain it to me simply, please, as if I were a child."

"It *is* simple. Plough Day has happened three days in a row. The exact same Plough Day."

"What can I get you?" It was the pot-girl, come to take their orders. They each ordered a coffee, and Margaret asked for a pastry platter, too. Perhaps Mr. Thane would feel better with some food in him. She knew she would, at any rate.

When the pot-girl went away, after casting an inquisitive glance at Mr. Thane, Margaret leaned back in her chair. "You say that you're experiencing Plough Day repeatedly?"

"Yes. As I just said, this is my third one." He still spoke in the earnest tone of one telling the absolute, unvarnished truth.

"But Mr. Thane, that's impossible, you know."

"It may be impossible, but it's still happening."

"*I'm* not experiencing Plough Day repeatedly."

"I can't explain it. I just know that *I* am."

There was a brief silence as they looked at each other.

"I'm not saying I believe you," Margaret said, "because I simply can't. But even if I did, what would you possibly think I could do? I'm not a magician, or—or a sorceress."

"I know that," he said, leaning forward, his expression eager, even desperate. "But you're clever. Bookish. Anyone can see that. Can't you think of *something*?"

Into Margaret's mind popped a quote from the *Bhagavad Gita*, the ancient Sanskrit text. In a thoughtful voice she murmured, "'He is never born, nor does he die at any time, nor having once come to be will he again cease to be. He is unborn, eternal, permanent and primeval.'"

Mr. Thane sat up straight. "See? That's what

I've been trying to tell you! I've become *permanent* somehow."

She shook her head. "I really don't think it applies to *your* situation. Even if it were true."

"But it *is* true. You've got to believe me, Miss Allen."

Their coffees came, along with a large plate filled with freshly baked pastries. Margaret chose a muffin and took a bite. "Don't you want anything? It all looks so good."

"No. What can I do to convince you that I'm telling the truth?"

She had another bite of her muffin and a sip of her coffee. Then she said, "Tell me everything that happened this morning."

The words tumbled out of him. "I woke up and it was Plough Day again. I could tell because I was wearing my nightshirt, not the clothes I'd had on last night, and also it was obvious just by looking out the window. Everything looked exactly the same. So I got dressed again and came rushing over to the town square, and on the way I saw the same people, just like on the other Plough Days, and they all said the same thing, and I ran into the same lamp-post, and—"

"Wait," Margaret interrupted. "You ran into a lamp-post? Is that why your hat was tilted so oddly when I first saw you?"

"Maybe. I don't know."

She peered at him. Wasn't there a faint red patch on his forehead? "How hard did you hit the lamp-post?"

"Pretty hard. So after that, when I got to the town square, I could see that everything was exactly the same, and—"

"Did you lose consciousness when you hit the lamp-post?"

"No, I was only a little dazed. Why does it matter? Why aren't we talking about the fact that I'm living Plough Day over and over again?"

"Mr. Thane, do you truly want my assistance?"

"Yes," he answered, sounding very eager. "Have you figured out how to fix things?"

"What I'd like to do is to take you to the infirmary."

"The infirmary? Why? I'm not ill."

"You did run into a lamp-post," she said gently.

"So?"

"So is it possible that you're suffering from—from delusions after a blow to the head?"

He stared at her and his shoulders visibly slumped. "You think I'm mad."

"I think we should go to the infirmary."

"You said you would help me."

"I'm *trying* to help you, Mr. Thane."

There was a long silence. Then he sighed, a deep, deep sigh that seemed to emanate from the very depths of his being. "All right, let's go."

Quickly Margaret had another sip of her coffee and two bites of her muffin. "I'm ready."

The pot-girl, when asked, told them how to get to the Whittlesey infirmary, and in a few moments Margaret and Mr. Thane were outside again and walking toward Plympton Street. They hadn't gotten far, though, when Mr. Lawrence, pink-cheeked from the cold and with his rucksack hanging from one shoulder, hurried over to meet them.

"I say, here you are! I've been looking for you everywhere. I wrote up some notes for you, Miss Allen. The Straw Bear was *ripping*." He pulled a couple of pieces of paper from his rucksack and gave them to Margaret, who slid them into her reticule with a smile of thanks. Mr. Lawrence went on:

"Mr. Thane, if you don't mind my asking, are you planning to leave today? We—the Misses Allen and I—were hoping we could tag along with you till Northampton. If it's on your way? There aren't any stage seats to be had for several days, you see, which means we're more or less stuck here."

"Join the club."

"Sorry?"

"Never mind."

"The thing of it is, sir, that if you *do* decide to leave, it might be wise to do it sooner rather than later. There's supposed to be a snowstorm coming in."

"Mr. Lawrence, might we postpone this discussion for now?" Margaret interposed. "I'm taking Mr. Thane to the infirmary."

"Oh, are you? Now that Miss Allen mentions it, you do look a little under the weather, sir," Mr. Lawrence said kindly to him. "Can I be of any help?"

"I'm still ambulatory," replied Mr. Thane testily. "Unless you'd like to sling me over your shoulder like your rucksack."

"I say, sir, I don't think I could. You're quite a bit taller and I daresay you outweigh me by several stone."

"Do come along, Mr. Thane," said Margaret, sliding her arm through his. "Thank you *very* much for the notes, Mr. Lawrence."

Tacitly accepting her gentle dismissal, Mr. Lawrence said, "Hope you feel right as rain again soon, sir. I'm off to try and get an interview with the mayor. Wouldn't that be jolly? My editor would be ever so pleased with me."

He rushed off, and Margaret—once again feeling as if she were leading a frightened dog on a leash—accompanied Mr. Thane to the infirmary.

There she made no mention of Mr. Thane's delusions, hallucinations, fantasies, lies, falsehoods, mis-
statements, or whatever they were, and merely told
the doctor that Mr. Thane had hit his head on a
lamp-post.

"Hmmm. Yes, there's a slight red mark on the left
side of the forehead," observed the doctor. "Doesn't
look serious in the least. A hale and hearty specimen,
aren't you, sir? Splendid muscle tone, full head of hair,
perfect teeth, and you look as strong as an ox. How
many fingers am I holding up?"

"Three."

"And now?"

"Two."

"Any ringing in the ears?"

"No."

"Any dizziness, or feeling like you're going to faint?"

"No."

"Headache?"

"No."

"Hmmm. Any other symptoms?"

Margaret and Mr. Thane exchanged a glance, and,
very reluctantly, he said:

"I've been living through the same day over and
over again."

The doctor's eyebrows shot up high in his face. "Eh?
What did you say?"

"I'm living Plough Day over and over again."

"I see," said the doctor, his tone now quiet and
grave. "Did this—ah—realization come to you before
or after you hit your head?"

"Before."

"Are you certain?"

"Yes."

"Hmmm. I'm afraid, sir, this sort of thing is beyond

my scope. You may wish to consult with a practitioner in a larger town, such as Peterborough or Cambridge. Someone who specializes in—ah—matters of the mind."

Mr. Thane's eyes brightened. "Now why didn't I think of that?"

To Margaret he instantly looked much more like the jaunty, devil-may-care Mr. Thane of yesterday. But after the bizarre events of the morning, she didn't know whether to feel glad or sorry, and why was Mr. Thane so pleased at being shunted off elsewhere in search of doctors dealing with mental impairment?

With new energy Mr. Thane jumped to his feet. Breezily he thanked the doctor, and then he was the one hustling *her* out onto the sidewalk.

"Well, I'm off then," he cheerfully announced.

"Off where?"

"I'm going to Cambridge, just as the doctor suggested."

"You're going to find a different doctor?"

"Good Lord, no. They're all quacks. I'm going to Cambridge because it's in a different direction, you see."

"A different direction from where?"

"From Somerset, which was where I was trying to go before," he explained. "Don't you see? Those two other times we got stuck just outside Oundle because of the snow, and that big fallen tree. I'll go south to Cambridge, then I'll divert around to the southwest, avoiding the storm. Why, I'll be back in Somerset in no time." All the lines of worry and despondency had left Mr. Thane's face, and he was positively glowing with good cheer. "Goodbye then."

He strode off, and Margaret stood on the sidewalk staring after his rapidly retreating form, aware that her jaw had dropped with a combination of surprise, uneasiness, and annoyance.

Surprise at Mr. Thane's lightning-fast turnaround in mood.

Uneasiness at his state of mind, and the idea of him careening off to the south all by himself.

Annoyance because he hadn't even offered to take her, Aunt Seraphina, and Mr. Lawrence with him. Like Mr. Lawrence, she too had made inquiries about available transport and had discovered to her dismay that there were no stage seats to be had for several days. So while Mr. Thane could go speeding away, the rest of them were trapped here. Which meant that she was probably going to miss that colloquium back in Oxford on the subject of fairy folk, the ballad of Tam Lin, and superstition at which she was slated to speak.

Well, *damn*.

Margaret stood, fulminating, on the sidewalk for a few more moments, and then she restored her jaw to its usual position. There was nothing she could do about the situation. And besides, why had she let herself embrace, even if only briefly, the notion that Mr. Thane would offer to bring herself and the others along?

She thought about it.

Because he had said, *Those two other times we got stuck just outside Oundle because of the snow.*

He'd said "we."

And somehow she nearly assumed they'd go along with him *again*.

And *she* didn't even have the excuse of hitting her head on a lamp-post.

Margaret, she told herself sternly, *do snap out of it. Mr. Thane is gone, and now you need to get on with your own life.*

So she went back to the little restaurant—the Cup and Saucer—where she ordered another coffee and some more of those delicious pastries, read over Mr. Lawrence's excellent notes, added some of her own, enjoyed a large and satisfying breakfast, and tried very hard within herself to wish Mr. Thane well on his madcap journey out of town.

*K*nock knock knock.

Philip gave a start, jerked from his stunned, miserable abstraction by the sound. Blearily he looked out the window of the barouche. It was the coachman who had rapped on the door. After a few moments Philip pushed it open and the coachman said:

"Here we are again, sir."

"I can see that." It seemed to take all of his strength to lift himself from the seat and to slowly descend from the barouche into the courtyard of the Apple Street Inn.

"Hope they'll still have a room for you, sir."

"Somehow I'm confident they will. Take care of the baggage, will you?"

"Certainly, sir."

It was very cold in the bright light of full afternoon, and Philip stood there shivering.

Yet he couldn't bring himself to go back inside, where he would, in all likelihood, have to face the proprietor Mr. Lancross and his fulsome greetings, and then find himself trudging up the stairs, flopping on the same old bed, and lying there for quite some time.

Maybe forever.

Philip turned on his heel and left the courtyard, walking blindly, without purpose or direction.

A leaf in the wind.

He couldn't have said how long he walked, except that at some point he heard a voice.

A feminine, pleasantly husky, familiar voice saying: "Mr. Thane! You're back!"

Chapter 5

Abruptly Philip stopped in his tracks. He blinked, as if he were just waking up from a deep, dark sleep. There before him on the sidewalk stood Miss Margaret Allen, ravishing in her dark green pelisse and fashionable hat in the exact same shade of green and embellished with a charming spray of pink artificial roses that complemented her golden-brown hair quite beautifully. She was, he saw, looking up at him with an expression of surprise and concern that he found both touching and demoralizing.

"What happened?" she asked. "Why couldn't you get to Cambridge?"

"Because we drove right into a snowstorm, and the road was blocked by a big fallen tree."

Her deep blue eyes went wide. "Just like . . . just like you said happened outside Oundle."

"That right." His voice was flat.

"Oh dear."

"That about sums it up."

"Perhaps tomorrow you could try a different direction, as long as it got you heading toward home."

"I haven't any home."

"I thought you were going to Somerset."

What the hell, he thought, he had literally nothing to lose by telling her the truth. "That's where my relation Henrietta Penhallow lives. It's her barouche, and I'm returning it to her."

"Oh, I see." Miss Allen received this information, which hardly cast him in a good light, without a blink. "But—yesterday you mentioned your stepgrandparents, the Duke and Duchess of Egremont. They must have a country seat somewhere, don't they? Isn't that your home?"

"No, not really. They merely put up with me out of familial obligation." It was only after he blurted this out that Philip realized, to his shamed horror, just how vulnerable and desolate he sounded.

But then he also realized how Miss Allen's expression softened. It was full of sympathy and concern. She reached out to grasp his arm and quietly said:

"Oh, Mr. Thane, I'm sorry."

It was the tender note in her voice that undid him.

He reached out for her and the next thing he knew, she was in his arms, body to body, her soft rounded form pressed hard against his own. For a moment she was stiff and still, as if shocked by the sudden contact between them, and then she hugged him back, evidently not caring a whit that they were standing together, quite visibly, on a public sidewalk.

After a few seconds Philip realized in dazed wonderment that he felt better.

Much, much better.

So much better, in fact, and in very familiar ways, that he began feeling like his old self.

He wasn't chilly anymore, but had begun to warm up in an extremely pleasant way.

All over.

Through and through.

Especially in a certain part of his anatomy that showed signs of springing into eager life.

Into her charming shell-like ear he said, infusing into his voice a soft caress:

"I knew you could help me, Miss Allen."

He felt, rather than saw, the shiver that went through her—not of cold, he well knew, but of reflexive pleasure.

Now was the time to press his advantage. He pulled away, just a little, to look soulfully down into her face. "Come with me."

"What? Where?" she asked, sounding just a tiny bit breathless.

A good sign, that. Also, her cheeks had flushed an enchanting pink color, and her lips had parted. Invitingly?

"Come to the Apple Street Inn," he murmured caressingly. "To my room. We can be alone there."

But Miss Allen stiffened again, then detached herself from his embrace and stepped a pace back. "I beg your pardon, Mr. Thane, but I'm afraid you've misinterpreted my hasty gesture."

"But it felt good, didn't it? And I can make you feel . . . very, very good."

For the briefest moment he saw a responsive flicker in those deep blue eyes of hers, and then they went cold.

"Apparently," she said, in an equally arctic tone, "you think that I'm a weak-kneed ninny, overcome by a simple hug—initiated, I might add, with genuine compassion—and by a seductive little whisper in my ear."

"No," he said, backpedaling as his vision of being deliciously and carnally intertwined with the voluptuous Miss Allen began to recede, "I don't think you're a ninny at all. Weak-kneed or otherwise. I assure you. Truly."

"You were looking at me just like you did yesterday, when you thought you'd have me all to yourself in your barouche."

"Not yesterday, and not *my* barouche," he pointed out, rather feebly, but Miss Allen rolled right over him.

"I daresay this whole entire thing *has* been a prank after all. You've been pretending to be afflicted in order to lure me right into your bed. A very *capacious* bed, I'm sure."

"No," he said, yet more feebly. "Not *that* capacious. Only room for two, really."

"Unlike the seats in your barouche."

He didn't even bother to try and correct her again about the "your." Instead he said, like a man grasping at straws that were basically out of his reach: "Why don't we go get a coffee? And talk?"

"I'm done talking with you, Mr. Thane," said Miss Allen, cold and composed and with a finality that came at him like a bludgeon. "Good day."

"Wait," he said, still grasping. "Where are you going?"

"Back to *my* inn. I'm going to have a nap and a bath and then I'm off to the Plough Day banquet at the Publick House."

"Have fun," he said, but with a palpable sarcasm he couldn't repress. "Maybe you'll get to share a mug of honey with the Straw Bear."

Miss Allen's lips thinned. "I can't believe I spared a moment to feel sorry for you."

"I feel sorry for *you*. You could have come to my room and had the most amazing afternoon of your life."

"Goodbye, Mr. Thane," she coldly said and, turning her back, walked briskly away.

"Ladies and gentlemen," said the mayor in a loud, carrying voice as he wrapped up his rather long and rambling speech, "thank you for your kind attention. Now, please join me in welcoming, as we do every year, our wonderful Straw Bear!"

He gestured with a sweep of his arm, and, looking to the far edge of the crowd from her place near the bunting-bedecked platform in the town square, Margaret saw people eagerly yielding to a great round figure all covered in sheaves of clean shining hay, from its head down to its ankles. The figure lumbered forward and everyone began applauding, those closest to the Straw Bear reaching out to pat at the sheaves—a gesture which signified hope for an early spring. The pipe and drum resumed their merry, lilting beat and some people began to move and sway in happy little dances, both singly and together.

Margaret watched, fascinated, tapping one of her feet in time to the music. How lucky she was to be here in Whittlesey! Yesterday it had seemed all too likely that she'd be stuck in Brampton for goodness knew how long, but thanks to Mr. Thane she'd made it after all. Plus, she had had the opportunity—yesterday evening and also this morning—to talk with several local folk about Plough Day and the Straw Bear, and had taken copious notes.

That was the good news.

The bad news, however, was that she'd made inquiries about available transport and had discovered to her dismay that there were no stage seats to be had for several days.

And as much as she liked Whittlesey, and felt surprisingly at home in it—as if it was somehow a familiar place she'd visited before—she really didn't want to stay on here for an indefinite period of time. For one thing, there was a colloquium in Oxford on the subject of fairy folk, the ballad of Tam Lin, and superstition at which she was slated to speak.

Early this morning, as she'd walked with Mr. Lawrence to the town square, she had made up her mind to ask Mr. Thane about his departure plans, and inquire if it would be at all possible for herself, Aunt Seraphina, and Mr. Lawrence to tag along to some convenient point where they might find other transportation.

She wouldn't particularly look forward to more time spent in the cynical, rakish Mr. Thane's company, but—as the pungent old saying went—*needs must when the devil drives.* Not, of course, that she meant to cast any aspersions on Mr. Thane's coachman, who looked like a perfectly nice fellow and who, based on yesterday's journey here, was a capable driver.

On Mr. Thane, however, Margaret might be more willing to cast aspersions.

He hadn't even shown up to give his speech.

How rude and selfish!

And, very likely, how *typical* of him.

There had been a scramble up on the platform when it was time for the ceremony to begin, and the mayor had had to step in and—it was painfully obvious—revise his speech at the last minute.

A voice said into her ear:

"I say, that Straw Bear's *ripping*, isn't he?"

Margaret turned and smiled at Mr. Lawrence, who had been busily jotting down his impressions in his notebook. "Yes, he is," she agreed.

"Too bad Mr. Thane didn't arrive in time," Mr. Lawrence remarked. "I was rather curious as to what he was going to say, especially after all those less than favorable things he said about Whittlesey on the way here yesterday. Can't say I was surprised he didn't make it, though—got the distinct impression he's one of those chaps who doesn't ordinarily get out of bed before noon. One of those *haut ton* London types, I daresay. I mean—you saw his boots, and that great-coat of his. All those capes." Mr. Lawrence spoke with wistful admiration.

"So what? Anybody can buy a pair of boots. A true gentleman keeps his word."

He nodded. "Are you really going to ask if we can join him on his ride out of town?"

"Yes, even if I have to literally drag him out of bed," answered Margaret, a martial gleam in her eye, envisioning herself with Mr. Thane's ankles in her hands as she wrenched him from a decadently comfortable sleep and onto the floor with a satisfying thump.

"Would you like me to go with you to his inn? Miss Allen?"

Margaret gave a start, realizing that she had allowed herself to get distracted by wondering if Mr. Thane had delightfully hairy legs. They *were* muscular—she'd already seen that for herself. His fashionable breeches didn't disguise this interesting fact. Quickly she pulled herself together. "No, that's all right. I know you're hoping to interview the mayor. Wish me luck with the elusive Mr. Thane."

Mr. Lawrence grinned. "He's the one who's going to need the luck, I suspect."

Margaret smiled at him again, and then went with brisk steps to the Apple Street Inn, where she asked the proprietor if Mr. Philip Thane had rung for his breakfast or, perhaps, descended to the common-room or a private parlor to have it there.

"Mr. Thane's gone, ma'am," replied the proprietor.

"Gone?"

"Yes, that's right, ma'am. Left bright and early, he did. Said he was going to Peterborough to avoid the snowstorm some say is coming in."

Margaret thanked him, then gazed, fulminating, around the large and handsomely furnished common-room though, to be honest, she wasn't really *seeing* it in her aggravated state.

Aggravated, and strangely forlorn.

After a while she gave herself a mental shake, and chided herself:

Why on earth do you so stupidly feel abandoned? Mr. Thane had absolutely no obligation to offer a ride to people he only met yesterday, and whom he had been tricked into accommodating in his barouche, thanks to you. Besides, it's not as if we got on like a house on fire.

Even as she thought this, Margaret was aware of a faint, haunting sensation.

It took her a few moments to identify what it was.

Why, she had actually seemed to imagine that Mr. Thane *had* taken them along on other rides out of town. Futile rides, which had only resulted in bringing them back to Whittlesey.

Margaret, what is *the matter with you? What a ridiculous idea.*

And yet . . .

As she left the Apple Street Inn and made her way back to her own inn, Margaret still couldn't quite shake that niggling sensation of familiarity. It seemed to stubbornly cling to her while she went over her notes, while she enjoyed a pleasant luncheon with

Aunt Seraphina in their private parlor, while she went
again to inquire about any sudden availability on the
stage (speaking of futility), and also while she went for
a long, invigorating walk around the town, peeping
into storefronts, offering a donation to a nice couple
raising money for the local convalescent home, petting
all the dogs she encountered, buying some peppermint
confits at an apothecary shop, chatting with a freckle-
faced little boy in a jaunty red cap who had crouched
down to stroke the butcher's tabby cat, and otherwise
amusing herself.

And that strange sensation abruptly intensified
when she was walking along Plympton Street and
saw, coming her way, none other than the exceedingly
elusive Mr. Thane himself.

As they drew closer together Margaret thought,
startled: *Goodness gracious, what's happened to him?*

Gone was the suave, confident, charming man from
yesterday who had leaned against his barouche with
casual grace, expecting to share its capacious interior
with herself and herself alone.

In his place was a pale, haggard man with haunted
eyes and dark hair that was rather disheveled.

Strangely, she found him more attractive like this.

He seemed less like a caricature of a smooth-talking
rake and more like an actual person.

When they each came to a halt, as if by unspoken
mutual consent, two or three feet apart, she said:
"You're back."

She watched as his brown-green eyes traveled over
her. Not with the same bold, piratical, annoyingly
comprehensive gaze from yesterday, when she had
gone out to the road in Brampton to flag down his
carriage, but with a slow, dazed wonderment, as if
he were just now waking from a deep, dark sleep. She
went on:

"What happened, Mr. Thane? I heard you were going to Peterborough."

"We drove into a snowstorm long before we got there, and also the road was blocked by a big fallen tree. So we had to turn around."

"Oh. That's too bad." Her earlier sense of injury was reanimated by his use of the word "we," and with some tartness she added, "It seems you're stuck in Whittlesey with the rest of us, then."

He only nodded, and, noticing again just how pale and distraught he was, she mustered herself to continue in a more civil manner:

"Mr. Thane, are you all right?"

"No."

"What's going on?"

"Nothing."

"Are you sure?"

He nodded again. She said, doing her best to rise above her lesser feelings and to sound encouraging and also *not* to be secretly issuing a hint:

"Well, you can try again tomorrow."

"I won't. There's no way out."

Startled again by both his words and his tone, heavy with conviction, she stared up into his face. "Whatever do you mean?"

"I mean that I've tried to leave, but that it's no use. I *am* stuck here in Whittlesey."

"But Mr. Thane, you won't be here forever, you know," said Margaret reasonably. "Snowstorms come and go, and people do travel."

"Not me. Not anymore."

"You're not making any sense. You came to Whittlesey to make a speech—which you didn't even give—and now you're saying that you're stuck here?"

"That's right."

"I don't understand you."

"You never did."

"What?"

"I tried to explain it to you, but you wouldn't believe me."

"Tried to explain it to me when, exactly? I haven't seen you since yesterday, when you dropped us off at our inn."

"You couldn't be more wrong."

His voice had taken on an accusing tone, as if she had somehow failed him in some way, and even though she had absolutely no idea what he meant, Margaret felt herself starting to bristle. But she tried again.

"Are you *certain* you're all right, Mr. Thane? You look—well, you look . . ."

"Incredibly handsome? I know."

Her mouth hardened as she tried to suppress a sudden flare of temper. "I was going to say that you look a trifle unwell."

"Quite the personal remark, isn't it, Miss Allen? I, for example, would never dream of saying that you look vacuous and stupid."

The poorly suppressed flare of temper now exploded into a kind of inner fireball which made her feel hot all over. "Why, you rude and arrogant man!" she snapped. "How dare you!"

"How dare I? Why not? A condemned man can say whatever he likes. It doesn't matter."

"It matters to me, you—you *toad*." Margaret spun on her heel and stormed away, back to her inn and up into her bedchamber, where she paced round and round until, at last, her temper finally cooled.

That *loathsome* man.

What a terrible shame that such a fine-looking face and figure was accompanied by an odious, bothersome, awful, contemptible personality. Aside from that first intriguing moment when their eyes had met yesterday, she standing in the road and he inside his barouche, he had done nothing but aggravate and provoke her. Why was he like that?

And why did she even care?

Huffily Margaret tried to take a nap, failed, paced around her room some more, took a bath, got dressed for dinner, and went off to the Plough Day banquet with Mr. Lawrence, determined to put Mr. Thane out of her mind once and for all.

Philip stood on the sidewalk staring after Miss Allen's rapidly retreating form. When finally she had vanished around a corner, as if disappearing from his life forever, he gave a long, long sigh which felt as if it was emanating from the very depths of his being, and then went to the edge of the sidewalk and sat down. His handsome, stylish, expensive boots were in the gutter, but he couldn't summon the energy to care.

In fact, it seemed highly appropriate somehow.

Philip couldn't have said how long he sat there, his brain churning with the speed and savagery of a determined milkmaid in a terrific hurry to make butter.

The good news was that he *wasn't* mad.

He knew this with absolute certainty now.

Somehow, in some bizarre and mysterious and inexplicable way, the world really had rearranged itself to trap him in Whittlesey on Plough Day, over and over and over again.

This was also the bad news.

No matter how hard he tried to escape, every morning he was going to wake up on the exact same day.

Over and over and over again . . .

These ghastly words looped around his brain, repeating themselves, like a bell tolling with soul-crushing finality.

"Oi, mister, what's wrong with you?"

Philip looked up and to his left. Standing near him on the sidewalk was a little boy, perhaps eight years old, slender and fine-boned and with a generously freckled face, dressed neatly in nankeen breeches and a dark blue woolen coat. On his head was a red wool cap set at a jaunty angle.

He said to the little boy: "Just about everything, I'm afraid."

"Are you in trouble?"

"Yes."

The little boy nodded and sat down next to him, planting his feet, in sturdy brogues, into the dirty gutter with sublime nonchalance. "Did you do something naughty?"

Philip thought. Now *this* was a difficult question to answer. It might take him all day to do justice to it, so in the interest of keeping things simple he merely said, "Yes."

"You looked like it. When *I'm* naughty they make me sit in a chair in the corner, with my face to the wall. Didn't they have a chair for you?"

"No, not really."

"How long do you have to sit here?"

"As long as I want to."

The little boy looked hard at him, his brow wrinkling. "Do you mean that you can get up whenever you want?"

"Yes."

"I call *that* unfair! I can only get up when they tell me I can. You're lucky."

Philip gave a short, sharp laugh. "If you say so."

"Well, I do. Must be nice to be a grownup, and do whatever you please."

"It's a bit more complicated than that."

"If you can get up from being punished whenever you like, then *I* say it's better," declared the little boy.

Rather than let himself be drawn into a philosophical argument with an eight-year-old who showed signs of sticking to his guns with infinite pugnacity, Philip didn't at once respond. A cold wind rattled past, sending a few dried winter leaves and other detritus scudding along the gutter at their feet, and the little boy plucked from amongst the flotsam and jetsam a battered-looking crisp and popped it into his mouth.

"Ha! They'd make me sit in that chair for *that*," he said with satisfaction. He poked around with a none too clean forefinger, searching for another crisp, but without success. "Damn," he said, and then he laughed. "That'd be another half an hour in the damn chair. I'm not supposed to use bad words. Like 'damn.'"

Philip was starting to feel a faint, unwilling affection for the boy and his unquenchable spirit. "Speaking of being naughty, why aren't you in school?"

"Because it's Plough Day, mister," said the little boy, condescendingly. "Don't you know *anything*?"

"Apparently not."

The little boy seemed to find this reply quite acceptable, for he only nodded and went on in a confiding tone:

"I was supposed to go home for luncheon, but I thought I'd go and roast some chestnuts instead."

"Won't you be in trouble for not showing up for your luncheon?"

"Probably."

"That's too bad."

The little boy shrugged. "That's life, isn't it, mister? Do what you want, then get punished for it." Abruptly he added, "Ever find a four-leaf clover?"

"Can't say that I have. Why? Have you?"

"Not so far. Want to know what I'd wish for if I did?"

"I really do."

"I'd wish that I could do what I want, and *not* get punished."

Philip thought this over. "In other words, you could do anything without having to face any consequences."

"That's right. I'd never go to school again, for one thing. Or take a bath. I'd go to bed whenever I like, and eat crisps every day. And sweets. Bags and bags of them." A dreamy look had come onto the little boy's face. "I'd have a horse, too, a great big tall one, as high as a house. That way Edmund couldn't get at me."

"Who's Edmund?" asked Philip, but rather absently. His brain had kicked into high gear again, and he felt as if he were on the verge of an important discovery. A great and wonderful discovery . . .

"Edmund Carter. He's a dreadful toad and I hate him. He's awfully mean to me."

"I'm sorry to hear that."

"*Oi* there!" It was a new voice coming from down the street, female, high-pitched, and exasperated. "Thomas Abernathy! You come right here!"

The little boy jumped to his feet. "Damn! It's my mum. She's not bad, you know—just a bit of a fuss-bucket. Well, see you later, mister." He gave Philip an insouciant smile and ran off, laughing merrily, in the opposite direction from the voice. In about thirty seconds Mrs. Abernathy, stout and red-faced and wearing a big purple hat that might have been fashionable ten years ago, came trundling up to Philip and scowled down at him with arms akimbo.

"You're just as bad as *he* is! And you a grown man, sitting in the gutter!"

"To be clear," answered Philip coolly, "it's my *feet* that are in the gutter, madam."

She gave a snort and trundled off again in hot pursuit of her recalcitrant son. Just to spite her, Philip remained sitting where he was for a while longer. Besides, he didn't want this fascinating new idea of his to slip away from him.

He was thinking about his conversation with young Thomas.

"Ever find a four-leaf clover?"

"Can't say that I have. Why? Have you?"

"Not so far. Want to know what I'd wish for if I did?"

"I really do."

"I'd wish that I could do what I want, and not get punished."

"In other words, you could do anything without having to face any consequences."

All at once Philip broke into a grin.

His mood had lightened so much and so quickly that he almost felt giddy.

You could do anything without having to face any consequences.

Well, well, well.

What a *very* intriguing possibility.

Very, very, very, *very* intriguing.

He'd better test it out, though, to be sure.

How, exactly?

Philip got to his feet and looked around. Arrayed before him in a row was an expensive-looking restaurant, a tobacconist's, a toy-shop, a jewelry store, a dentist's offices, and a modiste's.

Yes, that would do.

He strolled into the jewelry store and went to its main display case, which was filled with necklaces, aigrettes, bracelets, brooches, rings, and so on. A clerk came over and said:

"May I be of assistance, sir?"

"Yes, what's your priciest item?"

The clerk removed from the case a pretty diamond and ruby necklace which he held out for Philip to peruse. Rubies weren't his favorites, but it really didn't matter.

"May I?" he said to the clerk, who let Philip take it in his own hand. He held it up to the light, observing how it sparkled.

"There's a matching set of earrings, sir."

"No, this is perfect. Thanks." Philip slid the necklace into a pocket of his greatcoat. "Happy Plough Day." And he turned around and strolled out of the jewelry store, onto the sidewalk again, and sauntered off.

He could hear the flabbergasted clerk calling after him, but he neither stopped nor picked up his pace. Instead he whistled a little under his breath, and smiled.

Chapter 6

The Plough Day banquet was over, and Margaret stood in the spacious, brightly lit foyer of the Publick House, waiting as Mr. Lawrence went to retrieve her pelisse and hat. She'd managed to shake off her bad mood and to have a nice time at the banquet, where she'd chatted with quite a few of her fellow guests. Although she *had* been dogged again by that curious sense of familiarity—a feeling which itself was becoming familiar.

"I say, Miss Allen! *Here's* a bit of news!" Mr. Lawrence had come rushing over, holding her things and his face alight with excitement. "Mr. Thane's been locked up in the constabulary house!"

So much for her valiant attempts to keep Mr. Thane out of her mind, and her life. Goodness, he was like a bad penny—always turning up.

Wait—why had she used the phrase "always turning up"?

She had only met Mr. Thane yesterday.

To Mr. Lawrence she said, with a curiosity she was unable to repress: "What did he do?"

"He robbed the Whittlesey jewelry store."

Margaret's eyes went wide. "What?"

"Yes, it seems he asked a clerk to show him a very expensive necklace, and then he pocketed it and walked away."

"He *walked* away? He didn't *run*?"

"No, they're saying that he walked out of there as cool as you please. Almost as if he *wanted* to be caught."

Margaret's brain was whirling in amazement. She was recalling the odd conversation she'd had earlier today with Mr. Thane, and the strange things he had said to her. Was it possible that there was something seriously wrong with him? That he was—well—unbalanced?

And in the beginning of their conversation, she remembered, he had looked pale and haggard and distraught.

Then he'd crassly insulted her, and she had stalked away in high dudgeon.

Feelings of guilt now tugged at her.

Should she have stayed, and somehow tried to help him in some way? Been more patient and sympathetic and understanding?

So Margaret, who could never walk past a person in need, or a dog or a cat or a horse in trouble, without intervening, said to Mr. Lawrence:

"Let's go see him."

"Yes, let's," replied Mr. Lawrence eagerly, and Margaret could tell that his journalistic instincts were aquiver, especially when he mentioned that he'd already asked for directions.

Together they walked to the constabulary house, where Margaret's air of pleasant self-assurance gained them immediate admittance.

They found Mr. Thane in a cold, drafty cell, sitting on a bare uncomfortable-looking bench, with one long booted leg crossed over the other and appearing quite peaceful. He looked over at them and said with the dangerously charming smile with which he had favored her yesterday, as she'd stood in the road near his barouche:

"Oh, hullo."

In turn Margaret looked hard at him. He didn't seem at all troubled, as he had just a few hours earlier. Now he seemed alert, relaxed, even gleeful. She said, "You've been charged with theft, Mr. Thane, and the jewelry-store clerk has given sworn testimony to the fact. I asked if you could be released on my recognizance—and I offered to pay the surety fee—but they said you're to be held here until tomorrow morning, when the magistrate will speak with you then and adjudicate your sentence."

"It's possible that the magistrate is in for a nasty surprise."

"What kind of surprise?" asked Mr. Lawrence curiously.

"I may not be here in the morning."

"Planning on breaking out? By Jove, how *ripping*. Just the sort of story I like to write about."

"Oh, there's no need for an escape attempt," Mr. Thane answered, with so much peacefulness that Margaret stared at him even harder. "If it happens, it'll happen all by itself. And I'll simply wake up in my bed at the Apple Tree Inn."

"Forgive me, sir, but that makes no sense," said Mr. Lawrence.

For the briefest moment, Margaret had a strange, unnerving feeling that she *did* understand what Mr. Thane meant. She seemed to have a gauzy, insubstantial memory of sitting across from Mr. Thane—in a restaurant?—and him saying:

I woke up and it was Plough Day again. I could tell because I was wearing my nightshirt, not the clothes I'd had on last night, and also it was obvious just by looking out the window. Everything looked exactly the same. So I got dressed again and came rushing over to the town square, and on the way I saw the same people, just like on the other Plough Days, and they all said the same thing, and I ran into the same lamp-post, and—

A little dazedly Margaret put a hand to her forehead, as if *she* had run into a lamp-post and rattled her brain so badly that she was having memories of something that hadn't happened.

Or—maybe she'd had a dream last night after meeting the charismatic, provocative Mr. Thane, and her mind had somehow concocted a wild story about him, and about them having a meal—breakfast?—together, and he was regaling her with his own wild story? A dream within a dream, that sort of thing?

It was all rather confounding.

Then she reminded herself that she'd come here to try and help him, not puzzle over the intricacies of her own mind. Gently she said, "I'll come back in the morning, Mr. Thane, and speak with the magistrate myself. He should know that you're not well, and—"

"Rubbish," he interrupted. "I've never been better."

"Now that you've robbed a jewelry store?" inquired Mr. Lawrence. "And been incarcerated?"

Mr. Thane smiled again. "That's right. Well, it was kind of you both to stop by. I'll probably see you tomorrow at the Plough Day festivities."

"*Today* is Plough Day," Mr. Lawrence reminded him gravely.

"And will probably be again tomorrow." Mr. Thane was unshakably serene.

Margaret said, just as grave as Mr. Lawrence, "Is there anything we can do for you before we go?"

"Yes, how about a kiss for a poor condemned man?"

He was so saucy and brazen, and with that charming devil-may-care air about him again, that for a few moments Margaret once more felt a vertiginous sense of confusion. *Should* she feel sorry for him? Should she be angry at him? Should she . . . kiss him?

He *did* have a very enticing mouth, and he looked as if he knew what to do with it, too.

A delicious tingle of heat spun through her.

It had been quite a while since she'd felt such a jolt of fiery carnal interest.

Too long.

Wouldn't it be wonderful to be held in his arms again? Not quarreling, not to be at loggerheads with each other, but to willingly kiss and be kissed?

She actually took a half-step toward Mr. Thane and his glossy dark hair and his interesting mouth and his broad shoulders and long muscled limbs and his remarkable brown-green eyes, but checked when she saw that knowing smile of his widen.

Good heavens, you poor foolish girl, whatever are you thinking? she scolded herself. And why on earth had she thought about being in Mr. Thane's arms *again*, when of course she had never had that dubious pleasure? Hastily she retreated a step, and out loud she said:

"I'll be back in the morning, Mr. Thane."

"So you say."

They left him sitting calmly on the bench, leaning against the wall and with one leg crossed over the other, looking as if he was anticipating a very full and rewarding day to come instead of the fate which most likely was awaiting him: a visit from a magistrate, a fine, and, quite possibly, a sentence of further incarceration.

Mr. Lawrence murmured, "Poor fellow ought to be in Bedlam."

Margaret only nodded somberly.

Together they walked back to the Woodhull Inn, parting when Mr. Lawrence nipped into the commonroom to have a drink, and she proceeded into the private parlor set aside for the exclusive use of herself and Aunt Seraphina.

She found her aunt sitting by the fire with her stockinged feet cozily propped up on a stool, a glass of claret near her on a side-table, and deep into her book.

Margaret shut the door behind her and went to sit in an armchair opposite Aunt Seraphina, who closed her book and said:

"You look rather serious, my dear. Was the Plough Day banquet unpleasant? I do hope that scoundrel Mr. Thane wasn't bothering you."

"Oh, he wasn't at the banquet," answered Margaret, putting out her chilled hands to warm them in the fire's heat, and told her aunt about visiting the incarcerated Mr. Thane at the constabulary house.

Aunt Seraphina shook her head with a kind of gloomy wonderment. "As you know I wasn't impressed with Mr. Thane based on his demeanor and behavior on the way here, but I never thought he'd sink to these appalling depths. Are you really going to visit him tomorrow morning, my dear?"

"Yes, I am. I don't know why, Aunt, but somehow I feel a kind of—well, a kind of obligation to help him if I can."

Aunt Seraphina looked doubtful, but then she

brightened. "If you succeed in having him freed, then perhaps we can get places in his barouche—*if* he's lucid, that is. I know you're slated to speak at that colloquium on fairy folk, Tam Lin, and superstition, and I'd like to get home myself. It would be the least Mr. Thane could do, to repay your kindness to him. Although I suspect that he'll ogle you all the way to Oxford."

"A small price to pay, to get us home again."

They talked for a while longer, Margaret joining her aunt in having a glass of claret, and after that she went up to her room and so to bed, determined to get up early to make her way back to the constabulary house *and* to stop speculating as to what it might be like to kiss the unfathomable Philip Thane with his dangerously attractive smile.

Someone was knocking on a door.

"Wake up, sir," said a voice from outside the room, "it's Plough Day."

Knock knock knock.

"Mr. Thane," said the voice, "you asked to be awakened in time for the ceremony. It's Plough Day, sir."

Groggily Philip opened his eyes, and realized he was lying on his back in a singularly uncomfortable bed, but where?

He stared without comprehension at the ceiling above him.

Then it came to him: he was in his dowdy, quaintly decorated room at the Apple Street Inn, in Whittlesey.

Wait—did the voice say that it was Plough Day?

Knock knock knock.

"I'm awake," he said loudly.

"Very well, sir."

Philip shoved aside the covers, jumped out of bed, and went with long strides to the window, pulling aside the curtain to look out into the street.

It was a clear, bright day, and the sky was a soft cloudless blue. On the ground lay scattered splotches of gray slush, and hordes of people were all walking in the same direction—toward the town center.

Seeing this, he smiled a great broad smile.

He still had absolutely no idea as to why this was happening or how, but now he knew one thing for sure: he was going to make the most of it.

So he got dressed and went out into the corridor, lightly descending the stairs and into the common-room where he cut short Mr. Lancross the proprietor who had just opened his mouth.

"It's Plough Day, right?"

"Yes indeed, sir."

"Well, that's excellent. Have a nice day. *I* am." He strode out of the inn and made his way toward the town square, indifferent to the cold for once, and when he turned onto the sidewalk fronting a variety of stores and shops, he breezed past the rickety table, covered with a neatly ironed cloth, behind which sat those two middle-aged people, the man and the woman, dressed in their dowdy clothes and looking so cheerful and friendly.

Then came that high sweet voice exclaiming in wonder.

"Why, goodness me, if it isn't Philip Thane!"

And there was Matron, bundled up to her eye-teeth, looking cylindrical in her various shawls and wraps, standing on the sidewalk beaming up at him. He checked his stride and she went on with jocular reproach:

"Surely you haven't forgotten me, Master Philip! *Matron!* From your dormitory at Eton. Such a wee, scrawny lad you were, too! I'll always remember—"

"I do beg your pardon, ma'am," smoothly he interrupted, "but I believe you've mistaken me for someone else. Happy Plough Day."

He breezed on, neatly avoiding the lamp-post with which his forehead had gotten all too familiar in recent days, and continued toward the town square, where he came upon the usual crowd of people gathered in happy anticipation, talking and laughing, congregating in convivial groups small and large, their breaths puffing into little white clouds in the chilly air.

Somebody was playing a pipe, somebody was banging a drum, and it all sounded so lively and jolly that Philip did a little gliding chassé, and when he saw a pretty young woman smiling at him in open invitation, he reached out his hand and took her extended one in his own and gracefully twirled her, just as if they were dancing in a ballroom.

Then he released her hand, gave her a low jaunty bow, and kept walking toward the bunting-bedecked platform, near which Miss Allen stood, ravishing (as always) in her dark green pelisse and fashionable hat in the exact same shade of green and embellished with a charming spray of pink artificial roses that complemented her golden-brown hair quite beautifully.

Next to her stood Mr. Lawrence (as always), scribbling away in his notebook.

"Mr. Thane!" called Miss Allen, smiling. "Good morning!"

"Good morning," he said, smiling back. "Happy Plough Day."

"To you as well. Isn't it a beautiful day?"

"Very."

"I feel so lucky to be here. Thank you again for making it happen. I hope your inn suits you, and that you slept well last night?"

"Like a baby."

"Oh, I'm glad. We're all so excited to hear your speech."

He smiled again. What kind tact on Miss Allen's part. Plus, she'd made no mention of the constabulary house, or of stolen necklaces, surety fees, magistrates, doctors, snowstorms, fallen trees blocking the road, or anybody blurting out *I haven't any home. . . . They merely put up with me out of familial obligation* and betraying oneself in a ghastly mortifying way. He said placidly:

"How sweet. Thank you."

No sooner had he uttered this than the merry sounds of the pipe and drum fell away, and the crowd fell silent too. He could see them turning as one toward the platform in joyful expectancy.

"Well," Miss Allen said to him, "I believe that's your cue."

"I believe it is." Philip went up the wooden steps of the platform, introducing himself to the various town dignitaries clustering there, one of whom, the mayor, gestured him toward the front. Philip walked to the railing, swept his gaze over his rapt audience, and began speaking in his most persuasive, earnest, and appealing voice.

"Good people: we are gathered here today to celebrate farmers, farming, farmers everywhere but especially farmers in the dell, hi-ho the derry-o, the rat takes the cheese, the cheese stands alone, blah blah blah, so on and so forth, et cetera, et cetera, et cetera. Oh, and bears. There's one now."

He gestured in a very theatrical way to the far edge

of the crowd, many of whose members were looking less rapt and more nonplussed, but who, after
the faintest smattering of applause, all joined in with
their fellow revelers and turned to watch as that silly
Straw Bear lumbered forward, all covered in sheaves
of clean shining hay, from its head down to its ankles.
People began to applaud, with more vigor this time,
and the pipe and drum resumed their merry, lilting
beat; some people started to move and sway in happy
little dances, both singly and together.

Philip turned to the mayor. "I do hope that suited,
sir?" he said earnestly, exactly as if he had just delivered the best and most cogent, articulate, meaningful,
inspiring, and profound speech anyone had ever given
in the whole history of the world.

The mayor looked both nonplussed *and* taken
aback. "Well, I—I—that is—well, it certainly was—
er—memorable, Mr. Thane."

"Honored to be of service." Grinning inside himself but keeping his face perfectly straight, he added,
plagiarizing Miss Allen without the slightest remorse:
"I know that Plough Day is a custom dating back
several centuries, possibly linked to the Nordic invasions of the eighth century, and I for one was absolutely thrilled to see the Straw Bear. I know it's a great
honor to get all covered in straw like that, and that
his appearance personifies the winter season—it symbolically represents the banishment of winter, so that
crops can grow again and the people will flourish.
Isn't that marvelous? It makes everyone feel so hopeful and engaged in their community, don't you think?
I know *I'm* feeling hopeful and engaged. Well, thank
you again, sir, for the opportunity to say a few heartfelt words today. I couldn't be more grateful. Happy
Plough Day."

"Happy Plough Day," mumbled the mayor, and with long buoyant strides Philip went down the platform steps and over to where Miss Allen stood watching the Straw Bear lumbering about. He went close and said in her ear:

"I do believe I've discovered my vocation."

She glanced up into his face. "Oh, really?" she said in a distinctly neutral tone. "And what might that be?"

"Giving speeches. Did you see how I held the crowd spellbound?"

"Actually, I didn't see that at all."

"Odd. You must not have been paying attention."

"That must be it," she said, now with a slight edge to her voice.

"I say, Mr. Thane," said Mr. Lawrence, "if you don't mind my asking, have you any idea as to when you're leaving town? We—the Misses Allen and I—were hoping we could tag along with you till Northampton— if it's on your way, that is. There aren't any stage seats to be had for several days, you see, which means we're stuck here."

"There are worse things."

"Yes indeed. It's just that I'd rather not hang about Whittlesey for days and days, you see."

"Oh, I don't know. You might grow to like it here. I am."

"Really?" said Mr. Lawrence, surprised. "The way you talked about Whittlesey on our way here, I'd have thought you'd be champing at the bit to leave."

"I've changed my mind. I'm going to stay on here for a while."

"Oh." Mr. Lawrence looked disappointed.

Philip gave a mental shrug, then turned his eyes

to Miss Allen to see if *she* was looking disappointed, too. He knew, of course, that she wanted to leave also. But he saw that she was gazing up at him with a rather puzzled look on her lovely face. "What's the matter?" he said to her.

Miss Allen didn't respond, and he had to repeat his question.

She gave a start. "It's nothing, really."

"I do hope you're not too upset about not leaving today," he said, unable to resist the temptation to needle her. It was fun watching her get all testy and prickly. Her cheeks always turned a charming shade of pink and those expressive, deep blue eyes of hers sparkled like jewels.

"I daresay it wasn't meant to be," she answered, still with a faintly puzzled air and unfortunately without getting pink and prickly.

"My feeling exactly," he agreed affably. "Are you going to the Plough Day banquet tonight?"

"Very likely."

"I'll probably see you there, then."

"Truly?" She lowered her voice. "You're going to mingle with all the rustics, provincials, hobnails, yokels, chawbacons, hicks, bumpkins, and loobies, as you so eloquently described them yesterday?"

"You have an excellent memory, Miss Allen," he said with even more affability. "And now, if you'll excuse me? I have things to do." He gave her a jaunty little bow, and strolled away.

Margaret watched as Mr. Thane's tall, broad-shouldered form receded amongst the crowd. She actually *did* have a very good memory, but now she found herself struggling with a kind of uneasy doubt.

Why had Mr. Thane's inane speech sounded some-how familiar to her?

Maybe it was because she'd been to festivals similar to this one and heard a lot of speeches—some better than others.

Also, it could sound familiar because she had, after yesterday's annoying conversation in his barouche, been expecting him to deliver a subpar speech, and so it merely confirmed her prediction.

And speaking of Mr. Thane's barouche, it seemed a sure bet that she wouldn't be seeing the inside of it again anytime soon. Which was unfortunate, as she had, like Mr. Lawrence, made inquiries about avail-able transport and had discovered to her dismay that there were no stage seats to be had for several days.

As little as she would look forward to more time spent in the cynical Mr. Thane's company, still less would she look forward to cooling her heels here in Whittlesey for an extended period of time as there was a colloquium in Oxford on the subject of fairy folk, the ballad of Tam Lin, and superstition at which she was slated to speak.

But apparently she too was stuck here.

There was nothing she could do about it, however, and so Margaret resigned herself to the fact. She kept herself busy all day, talking to people about Plough Day and taking notes, sharing a hearty lunch with Aunt Seraphina in their private parlor, and going for a long invigorating walk about the town, peeping into storefronts, offering a donation to a nice couple rais-ing money for the local convalescent home, petting all the dogs she encountered, buying some peppermint confits at an apothecary shop, chatting with a freckle-faced little boy in a jaunty red cap who had crouched down to stroke the butcher's tabby cat, and otherwise amusing herself.

She would rather have died than admit it aloud, but she was really quite curious to see if Mr. Thane, after giving that abysmal speech, would have the nerve to show up at the banquet tonight.

"**H**i-ho the derry-o," said Miss Janney, giggling, nibbling on his ear like a hungry rabbit just given a carrot. "Best Plough Day speech I ever heard. Aside from the time that alderman fell off the platform."

"Thank you," said Philip, polite but distracted, as there seemed to be a lot of breasts everywhere and it was a bit hard to think.

"The rat takes the cheese," added Miss Tellington, giggling also, and slid down his bare chest to take something in her mouth that most definitely wasn't cheese. (Speaking of hard.)

"We're *so* glad you came to Whittlesey," Miss Janney said. "Ain't we, Sally?" she said to Miss Tellington, who only made agreeable affirmative noises as her mouth was full.

"We spotted you right away when you gave your speech this morning," the talkative Miss Janney went on. "I says to Sally, I says, 'Ooh, here's a looker,' didn't I, Sally? And then when you came walking toward us after your speech, I says to Sally, I says, 'Ooh, look at all them *capes* on his coat! And them *boots*! And brown eyes to fall down into, just like a well! Think we can sneak him up to our room? He's such a looker!' And so we asked you, and you said yes right away, and here we are, with none the wiser!" she finished triumphantly, nibbling at the bare skin of his throat.

"Yes," said Philip rather hoarsely, reaching out for a dangling breast. It had to be Miss Janney's. Miss Tellington's were unavailable at the moment. "Here we are."

"Best Plough Day ever," Miss Janney said, giggling. And Philip had to agree.

Chapter 7

Margaret had another bite of her roast beef and suppressed a sigh. She was having a perfectly nice time here at the banquet, and had met lots of very nice people, but there was no denying that it all seemed a trifle flat.

Slightly boring, perhaps.

Even somewhat routine.

It was galling to confess it, but she was just a teeny-tiny bit sorry that Mr. Thane hadn't made an appearance after all. If nothing else, he would have livened things up. Maybe he'd have recited *all* of "The Farmer in the Dell." Or sung it. And everyone could have joined in with the refrain.

Hi-ho the dairy-o, the cheese stands alone.

Margaret, she said sadly to herself, you're a chucklehead.

Both of her neighbors to left and right were chatting with *their* neighbors at the moment, and so Margaret felt herself drifting further into a funk.

The cheese stands alone.

That was what she felt like.

Alone, and lonely.

Even surrounded by all these people.

She brooded darkly, poking with her fork at some herb-encrusted potato wedges on her plate.

What on earth had caused Mr. Thane's sudden turnabout regarding Whittlesey? Yesterday in his barouche she'd gotten the distinct impression that he wouldn't spend a minute more here than he had to.

Her mind stretched backward in time, to that moment when she'd been standing in the road and she'd seen that big black shiny barouche barreling her way, and going in the right direction. Her heart had lifted with hope. Possibly she *would* get to Whittlesey after all.

Then Mr. Thane had shoved up the window of the barouche, stuck out his dark head, and smiled at her—a bold, appreciative, devil-may-care smile that had aroused in her a delicious responsive tingle.

Looking back, Margaret realized that for her, that one singular moment had held a world of tantalizing possibilities.

Like a locked door creaking open . . .

For five years she had allowed—no, *disciplined*— her unruly heart to cool into ice, at least where men were concerned. Her focus had been on her studies and her work, her family and her friends, her charities and her pets.

Hers was a good life, a fortunate life, and never had she lost sight of that, but in one elemental way it had been a lonely one for quite some time.

Yesterday she had looked into Mr. Thane's bright, intelligent, fascinating eyes, had felt the pull of his potent charm, and for a split second had wondered if *here* was a man who could interest her again—talk with her, joke with her, laugh with her, dance with her, and more . . .

So that her icy heart would melt, and she would *feel* again.

Feel all the things a person in love felt.

The giddy anticipation of waiting, with exquisite impatience, to be in the same room as one's beloved.

The joyous thrill of being together again, even if only after a short time apart, and seeing his eyes light up when he saw her.

The intoxicating rush of desire, crackling along one's spine, filling up all the empty spaces inside with a pooling, honeyed warmth, with a ravenous hunger that wouldn't be denied.

The joy of knowing another person so intimately, so deeply, so completely.

Of course, it helped if one's beloved wasn't—as it turned out—a dreadful, cavalier, small-minded ass who five years ago had broken one's heart in two, and in a cruel callous way that sometimes made one afraid that it would never, ever heal.

So when yesterday Mr. Thane had shamelessly raked his eyes over her, like someone who could see through multiple layers of clothing to the bare body beneath (and practically licked his lips at what he saw, too), well, that had ended the magical moment of possibility.

She had no interest in trying to redeem a rake.

What was the point of loving someone conditionally, anyway?

I'll love you, but only if you change.

Or, worse:

I'd love you, but only if you were different.

A poor, weak, miserable sort of love, in her jaundiced opinion.

Margaret sighed, not bothering to try and repress it this time.

"You're woolgathering again," said a familiar, deep, cultured voice, quite near her, and as her heart gave a wild jump Margaret dropped her fork, which

clattered onto her plate, and she looked up to see that
Mr. Thane had come upon her unawares.

Her jaw dropped in astonishment.

He was wearing stylish dark breeches, those tall
dark boots of his, a gorgeous embroidered waistcoat, and a white full-sleeved shirt of rich expensive
cambric.

What he *wasn't* wearing was a neckcloth *or* a
jacket, a shocking omission which revealed thanks
to the open vee of his shirt the interesting fact that
he had a hard-planed chest (with soft, dark hair on
it) and also the even more interesting fact that on his
smooth, sturdy, yet elegant neck he had an enormous
violet-colored love-bite.

To Margaret's unspeakable consternation an actual
and ridiculous flash of jealousy shot through her as she
wondered just who it was who'd administered those
enthusiastic nips. It was only after a severe internal
struggle that she managed to subdue this unfortunate
response. But as she brought her eyes up from Mr.
Thane's neck to his face she could see that he *knew*
what she'd been looking at, and maybe, just maybe,
he also knew how she had reacted.

He smiled, a silky, piratical, discerning, and horribly
charming smile.

Margaret could feel herself flushing wildly, and her
brain scrabbling about like a greedy chicken pecking
for grain. At last it seized on a useful old maxim from
the ancient Chinese military strategist and philosopher
Sun Tzu—*Attack is the secret of defense*—and so she
said, infusing her voice with a cutting tone:

"I see you're dressed for an evening on the town,
Mr. Thane."

Much to her annoyance his smile only widened.
"You noticed. How flattering." To Margaret's left-

hand neighbor, Mr. Smith, he blandly said, "I do hope you don't mind, old chap, but Miss Allen and I are bosom friends and I *must* sit next to her. You've had her to yourself for far too long, you know. A bit selfish of you, really. Do go find somewhere else to plant yourself." When Mr. Smith got up, rather huffily, Mr. Thane thanked him with such exaggerated courtesy that Margaret longed to snatch up her fork and sink it into his muscular thigh.

Mr. Smith went away; Mr. Thane gracefully sank into the vacated seat and waved a casual hand in the air, attracting the attention of a nearby waiter to whom he said:

"Clear everything away, will you? I want something to eat. Two of everything, please."

"Two, sir?" said the waiter, surprised.

"Actually, make it three."

"Right away, sir. A glass of wine also?"

"No, bring a bottle."

"Yes, sir." The waiter whisked up Mr. Smith's plate and utensils, then bustled away, and Margaret said to Mr. Thane:

"*Three* of everything?"

He smiled serenely. "Yes, that's right. I'm hungry as a horse. I've had a lot of exercise today."

All sorts of images threatened to rise in her mind, chiefly being that of a naked Mr. Thane and his glossy dark hair and his delicious mouth and his broad shoulders and long muscled limbs and hard-planed chest and his compelling brown-green eyes as well as other, equally interesting body parts. Margaret clamped down hard on her stupid intemperate brain and merely said, in an even voice, "I'll just bet you did."

"Yes, it was quite vigorous." Mr. Thane placidly nodded, then turned to his neighbor at his left, an

elderly lady clad in stately puce and sporting a monu-
mental befeathered turban in the same eye-catching
shade. Affably he said to her:

"Didn't I see you at the Plough Day celebration this
morning, ma'am? I gave the big speech, you know."

"I do know," answered the old lady in a freezing
tone. "It was a disgrace."

"Really? Perhaps I should have toppled off the platform, like that drunken alderman did several years
ago, and got myself all wound up in bunting."

"It might have been an improvement. 'Hi-ho the
derry-o' indeed." The old lady took the napkin from
her lap and set it next to her plate, then began to
gather up her skirts.

"Wait," Mr. Thane said, his voice so abruptly earnest and mild and winsome that the old lady paused.

"Yes?"

"Lend me a tenner, won't you? I'll pay you back
tomorrow."

The old lady stared, then gave a sound that was
something in between a snort and a puff and which
entirely smacked of outraged disbelief. She got up and
marched away, the feathers in her turban fluttering angrily. Unperturbed, Mr. Thane turned back, nodded
his thanks to the waiter who had returned with a fresh
place setting and a large bottle of wine, and after his
wineglass was filled he lifted it and said to Margaret:

"Shall we toast?"

"To what? Attempting to swindle one's table-
partner?"

"My, you're peppery this evening," he remarked.
"Is your roast beef that bad? Or is it because you
missed me? *I* was going to suggest we toast to Plough
Day."

"Oh? How high-minded of you," returned Margaret, and lifted her glass too, reminding herself that she *had* rather wished that Mr. Thane would show up, and also admitting that he had, for better or for worse, livened things up, and also somehow lured her out of her melancholy funk. Still, she wasn't going to let down her guard. And she was definitely not going to stare at either that tantalizing chest of his or that very, very, very obvious bite-mark. She said in a neutral tone:

"To Plough Day."

"To Plough Day," he echoed, but with much more enthusiasm.

They clinked glasses.

"My favorite day of the year," said Mr. Thane, and drank down all of his wine at once. He grimaced. "By Jove, this stuff is awful." Then he poured himself another glass and drank it all down too. "How much have *you* had?"

"About half a glass."

He lifted up the bottle. "Have some more."

"No, thank you. It *is* awful. How could you drink two glasses of it?"

Mr. Thane poured himself another glass and drank it down. "Three. I'm thirsty."

"From all that exercise."

"Why, yes."

The waiter now returned, balancing three plates on his arm, and slid them all in front of Mr. Thane. "Here you are, sir. Fish croquettes, roast beef, and Cornish hen."

"Splendid. Can you bring me a loaf of bread and another bottle of wine?"

"Of course, sir," answered the waiter, looking surprised again, and went away. Mr. Thane briskly tucked into the croquettes, and Margaret, unable to resist needling him just a little, said:

"I've got some potato wedges and mushrooms in Bechamel sauce if you want some extra."

He reached out with his fork, speared a couple of the wedges, and popped them into his mouth. "Thank you. They're not bad, are they? Could use a bit more thyme, though." He went on with his croquettes, and Margaret watched, bemused, as he proceeded to neatly demolish everything on all three of his plates, along with the bread the waiter soon brought, on which he spread lavish quantities of butter before devouring it—exactly as might a man who hadn't eaten for days and who also had no thought of tomorrow.

"We're so often told that moderation is the key to a happy life," she commented. "But I can see that's an aphorism which carries no weight with you."

"Moderation is overrated." He drank yet another glass of wine. "Are you going to finish your roast beef?"

"Somehow I've lost my appetite."

"A shame." Deftly he switched one of his empty plates with hers and began to eat what was left of her roast beef, potatoes, and mushrooms. "The sauce isn't half bad, either."

"Maybe you could ask for more."

"An excellent idea." He flagged down the waiter. "More of those mushrooms, *garçon*, *tout de suite*. And another loaf of bread while you're at it. Also, dessert. Heaps of it." Then he picked up his wine bottle and with the utmost casualness drank directly and deeply from it, astonishing Margaret all over again.

"I hope you don't explode."

"Unlikely."

"Honestly, I think you might."

He looked soulfully at her with those brown-green eyes of his. "Why, Miss Allen, I didn't know you cared."

"Well, I don't, Mr. Thane, but if you *did* explode it

would make a mess and I'm afraid my gown would be ruined."

"Spitfire," he said appreciatively. "By the way, I like the one you're wearing tonight. It brings out the blue of your eyes."

Margaret fought down a flutter of warmth inside her. It was a new gown, in periwinkle silk, and she loved its delicate spangled trimmings around the short puffed sleeves and the hem and bodice, too. She merely responded, "Speaking of clothing, why didn't you bother wearing all of yours to the banquet?"

He shrugged. "I didn't feel like it."

"Is that your modus operandi in life, then? You don't do things you don't feel like doing?"

He smiled. "It is now. Did you see how that lady in puce couldn't keep her eyes off my chest? That's probably the real reason she fled. Too much proximity to my overpowering masculine virility."

"That, and perhaps she didn't feel like lending you ten pounds."

"No, I think it was my masculine virility. Why does anyone wear puce, incidentally? It looks like dried blood. So what were you thinking about when I came over? Your lovely brow was furrowed and you seemed rather sad."

Margaret felt another one of those fiery little flutters at his use of the word "lovely," and, a trifle disarmed, she gave him a wry half-smile. "Was it that obvious?"

"To me it was. What was on your mind?"

"I was thinking about the past."

"Never do that. It's a complete waste of time."

"I disagree. I believe that looking to the past can help us make better decisions in the future."

"Wrong again. Don't worry about the future. Try living in the present."

She looked at him curiously. "Is that what you do?"

He nodded, and pushed away his last emptied plate. "Now more than ever. Oh, good, here's dessert."

The waiter had arrived, nearly staggering beneath the weight of a tray packed full with half-moon cheese-cakes festooned with ribbons of fresh lemon-peel, pistachio ices in dainty china cups, ratafia cakes, and even a couple of oranges, all of which he disbursed onto the table in front of herself and Mr. Thane, who pitched in with fresh abandon.

Margaret watched with a kind of helpless fascination, then finally said, "You remind me of a *gulon*."

"A what?" he asked thickly, having just taken a large bite of cheesecake.

"In Scandinavian folk-lore, a *gulon* is a creature that gorges itself until it's too swollen to move."

Mr. Thane chuckled. "That's good to know. I'll be sure to commit the term to memory."

"Will you really?"

"Honestly, probably not."

"Averse to a little learning?"

"As I was kicked out of Eton, I suppose I am."

"I'm afraid to ask why."

He took another bite of cheesecake. "Like Saint Augustine, I struggled with concupiscence."

"Loftily expressed, although I can't help but notice the use of the past tense."

"Yes, after a while I stopped struggling with it, and life instantly became much easier. Also, more fun."

"Then your syntactical linking of yourself with Saint Augustine is specious. *He* eventually overcame his lecherous tendencies, you know, and refrained from pursuing every woman he met."

"I must say, this strikes me as a very indelicate

topic. I wouldn't have thought it of you, Miss Allen. You *look* like a lady, at any rate. Orange?" He held one out to her, and Margaret accepted it and began to peel away the tough dimpled skin.

"As yesterday on the coach ride here you accused me of being blue, Mr. Thane, I can't imagine why anything I say would shock you."

"And yet you do. Not that I'm objecting, mind you." He smiled again at her, with the full potent force of his charm, and Margaret could almost *literally* feel her guard wavering, and in a highly unnerving way.

So she put down her half-peeled orange and hid her hands beneath the table, then pinched the sensitive juncture of flesh between her thumb and forefinger, hard, as one might furtively do in order to fight off an overwhelming wave of sleepiness. *Snap out of it, you weak-kneed ninny,* she scolded herself.

"What are you doing with your hands?" he asked, in his voice a shimmer of lazy insinuation that brought another wild flush to her face. "And in public, too. You shock me again, Miss Allen." He helped himself to four more macaroons. "Speaking of the coach ride here, you never answered my question. Why aren't you married? It's hard to believe you weren't snapped up years ago by some dashing young fellow with an eye for the main chance."

Margaret stiffened. She would never accuse Mr. Thane of possessing supernatural abilities, but it felt as if he had, in a very cavalier way, just shot an arrow into her defenses, piercing them and leaving her horribly, painfully exposed. There wasn't any way he could have known she'd been brooding, less than half an hour ago, about the very reason why she remained single, and which threatened to break her poor bruised icy-cold heart all over again.

Philip admired the pretty flush that mantled again in Miss Allen's face. Really, it made ribbing her entirely worthwhile. He picked up her orange and finished peeling it, then pulled it apart and held out a juicy crescent. "Have some orange."

Mutely she shook her head, and brought her hands up onto the tablecloth where she interlaced her fingers in a way which gave her a faintly judicial air.

"Don't you want it?" he inquired, and when she shook her head again he ate the orange himself. By now he was rather uncomfortably full but thought he could manage to finish off the rest of the wine, probably without swelling up like a *gulon* and then exploding, although there *was* a chance they might have to roll him over to his inn, just like a giant ball, and shove him up the stairs, along the corridor, and into his room, where they'd have to heave him into his bed and hope it didn't collapse under the weight of his newly acquired *avoirdupois*.

Idly he wondered how the immensely corpulent Prince Regent, a casual acquaintance of his, managed to eat like this pretty much every night. It took up a great deal of time which might have been better used, say, wenching or gambling, and also it was quite boring listening to him complain about his bouts of indigestion, the bloating, the fetid eructations, the interminable straining at stool, and so on and so forth.

Luckily, *he* didn't have to worry about such things.

Any fleeting discomfort he might feel would be gone—poof!—in the morning, and he would rise from his bed as lean and as trim as ever.

Happy Plough Day!

Suddenly Miss Allen said, levelly, "Why aren't *you* married?"

"Why would I want to do that? I'm far too busy having a good time."

"Did—do—your *amours* feel the same way?"

He shrugged. "How would I know?"

"Did you ask them?"

"I repeat: why would I want to do that? Haven't you heard the old adage about discretion being the better part of valor?"

"I'm not sure valor has anything to do with it."

"I could be mistaken, but I'm getting the distinct impression that you're critical of my way of life."

"Why would I be? We're strangers who met yesterday by chance, and with any luck we'll both go our separate ways as soon as possible, and never have to think of each other ever again."

"Your cunning plan may be thwarted," he said lazily. "They say there's a snowstorm coming in, which will play merry hob with anybody trying to come *or* go. So we may be stuck here together for a long, long time." He watched as her lovely mouth thinned.

She said, rather snappishly: "It's a big enough town. I daresay we can manage to coexist without being forced to spend time in each other's company."

"I'll miss you."

"Ha. You'll probably be busy getting more *exercise*."

Philip watched with deep appreciation as not only did Miss Allen flush all over again with that charming pink color, but her eyes also dropped, as if against her will, to his exposed neck. Then she brought them up to his, a hard jewel-like sparkle in them, slapped her napkin onto the tablecloth, and got up.

"Goodnight, Mr. Thane."

"You're not leaving, are you? The night is still young."

"I'm going back to my inn."

"Would you like me to escort you?"

"No, I wouldn't dream of tearing you away from those remaining ratafia cakes. Goodbye."

"If you insist. See you tomorrow, Miss Allen."

"Not if I can help it," she said in a grim and tight-lipped manner, and then she went away, looking, Philip couldn't help but notice, nearly as ravishing from behind as she looked from the front.

There was no doubt about it, Miss Allen was a fine-looking woman.

He wished she had stayed so that they could needle each other some more. He actually *did* miss her a little. Somehow, though, he didn't think she missed *him* in the slightest.

Well, that was her loss.

Philip took hold of the wine bottle and slouched low in his seat, tipping it onto its two back legs in an enjoyably precarious way. He took a long pull of the wine, then held it out invitingly to the fellow who was sitting to the right of where Miss Allen had been and who was staring in disapproval at him, Philip, with his mouth set in an upside-down U and his large bushy eyebrows drawn together in a manner that gave him the amusing look of having only one eyebrow, rather like a fuzzy caterpillar which had crawled above his nose and decided to stay there. "Have a drink," Philip said pleasantly to Mr. Caterpillar Face. "You look as if you could use one."

"Thank you, no," answered Mr. Caterpillar Face without any cordiality at all.

"Suit yourself." Philip took another long pull of the wine, after which he brought his chair back down and scooted over to Miss Allen's vacant seat. To Mr. Caterpillar Face he said, "Were you at the Plough Day celebration this morning? I would have remembered if you had been. You have a very distinctive eyebrow, you know. Or do I mean *eyebrows*? In case you didn't realize, I gave the big speech. Not to brag, but it was probably the best speech anyone's ever given, with the possible exception of Mark Antony at Caesar's funeral."

Mr. Caterpillar Face looked even more disapproving. "I *was* there—"

"At Caesar's funeral? Come, come, sir, you couldn't be *that* old. You don't look a day over eighty."

"For your information," said Mr. Caterpillar Face, freezingly, "I am forty-seven years old."

"To be sure you are," replied Philip in a soothing tone.

"*And* I was at the Plough Day celebration *this morning,* in the back, where I did have the misfortune of hearing your so-called speech."

Philip nodded, keeping his face exquisitely straight as he continued boastingly: "That's why I didn't notice you, I daresay. There were a lot of people there. Hundreds, maybe thousands. All dying to hear what I had to say." He leaned closer, which, he could tell, put Mr. Caterpillar Face in the tricky position of trying to decide whether to lean away, which he probably wanted to do, or to remain where he was, to show that he wasn't going to be swayed in any way by whatever Philip chose to do. "You look like a fine outstanding chap," he said to Mr. Caterpillar Face in a mild, earnest, affable voice. "Lend me a tenner, will you? I'll pay you back tomorrow."

Mr. Caterpillar Face made exactly the same sound as Puce Lady had—something in between a snort and a puff and which smacked of outraged disbelief. And just like Puce Lady, he got up and marched away, although, unfortunately, he wore no turban and so there were no feathers to flutter angrily atop his head.

Philip laughed, and finished off the wine in a single long swallow.

Altogether he had made not one, not two, but *three* people get up and stalk away from him. So far. He eyed the other people sitting around the table, all of whom were conspicuously and disapprovingly avoiding his glance. Fat chance of any of them loaning him money.

And he *would* like to have some money.

He might, he thought, try a different tack tomorrow.

But what might that be?

He pondered this interesting question.

Then he grinned.

He knew just what he was going to do. Ho *ho*, he could hardly wait for tomorrow. It might even top today in terms of sheer brilliant fun.

Also, he had something else he wanted to do right now.

He'd longed to do it his whole entire life, but had never quite summoned the nerve.

Now, however, he had all the nerve he needed, and more.

So Philip stood up and said to his table-mates:

"Not only am I the world's best speech-giver, but I'm also an amazing magician. Watch *this*."

He took a firm grip with both hands on the edge of the tablecloth. "Hey presto!" he called out and in a very theatrical way yanked hard on the cloth.

There was a tremendous crash as plates, glasses, utensils, dishes large and small, the big crystal centerpiece filled with flowers, and so on, all tumbled in a scattered heap onto the floor.

In the sudden aghast silence which followed, Philip viewed the carnage thoughtfully. "Whoops."

Then he laughed, dropped the tablecloth, said, "Send me the bill," and strolled away, out of the Publick House and into the chilly dark of night, whistling a little under his breath.

Happy, *happy* Plough Day!

Chapter 8

Warm and snug in her thick wool pelisse and cozy hat, Margaret looked around from her place near the festive bunting-bedecked platform in the town square and bit back a sleepy yawn. Here she was, in the very midst of the Plough Day celebration, and wasn't she just so fortunate? A delightful scene lay all about: how much fun everyone was having! She was, too, although she *was* rather tired. She hadn't slept well last night. She'd tossed and turned, and had a lot of disturbing dreams, most of which featured Mr. Philip Thane.

That in itself was disturbing.

She had only met him yesterday, after all.

In one of the dreams, she now recalled, Mr. Thane was swollen up as round as a ball, and had bounced gleefully about the room, causing everyone else to scatter like panicked chickens, which only made him laugh.

In another dream, she had been alone in a vast crowd, weeping about something, and nobody had noticed, which made her feel like the loneliest person in the whole entire world. Then Mr. Thane had walked over to her, parting the crowd in a magisterial way, just like Moses subduing the Red Sea, and said, *Why are you so sad, darling Margaret?*

In yet another dream, Mr. Thane seemed to be telling her not to wear puce, and that he was sorry for everything, and that he loved her. Then he gave her a beautiful fresh orange which, when she began to peel it, had a rotten, dank, smelly interior and she had dropped it with an exclamation of disgust.

And in still another, she had seen three elderly ladies—all strangers to her—huddled around a black smoking cauldron and cackling as if at something agreeable. Wisps of smoke rose from the cauldron and among them appeared a ghostly, ethereal representation of Mr. Thane looking very fine and dashing in his many-caped greatcoat and dark shining boots. Together the three old ladies had chanted: *Double, double toil and trouble, fire burn and caldron bubble. Time doth spin round and round, to each other you are bound. Double, double toil and trouble, fire burn and caldron bubble. Thwart it with your true love's kiss, thus the charm brings sweetest bliss.*

Which was strange, because that wasn't how the Song of the Witches in Act IV of *Macbeth* really went.

Margaret gave her head a bewildered shake, as if trying to clear these odd vague memories from her brain. Her glance fell upon Mr. Lawrence next to her, he being busy jotting down his impressions in his notebook, and then she suddenly spotted a tall broad-shouldered figure coming toward the platform. It was none other than Mr. Thane, and Margaret felt a sudden, secret sense of embarrassment at having dreamed about him last night. Not that he would ever know, of course. But still she felt a real constraint as she called out:

"Mr. Thane! Good morning!"

He came near and she saw at once that he was looking quite different than he had last night when he had
dropped Aunt Seraphina, Mr. Lawrence, and herself
off at their inn. Then he had been annoyingly suave
and sardonic, and openly bitter about having to get up
early for Plough Day. Today, however, he was fresh-
faced and smiling, which was such a big change that
Margaret found herself staring at him in surprise.

"Good morning, Miss Allen. Happy Plough Day,"
he said pleasantly in his deep, cultured voice.

"Happy Plough Day, Mr. Thane," she returned,
but a trifle mechanically.

"What's the matter? You're looking at me as if I
have two heads."

With an effort Margaret gathered up her scattered
wits. "I do beg your pardon. It's just that you're so
different today."

"Am I? How so?"

"Frankly, after what you said yesterday about Plough
Day, I wasn't even sure if you'd show up to give your
speech."

"A gentleman always keeps his word," he said with
affable reproach. "How painful it is to be so miscon-
strued. I dreamt about you last night, by the way."

Margaret gave a giant start and could feel herself blushing wildly. "Oh, really?" she replied, in as
dampening a manner as possible which was meant to
indicate her complete and total disinterest in hearing
all (or any) of the details, even though inside herself
she was, in fact, burningly curious to know. "Nobody
likes to hear other people talking about their dreams,
you know."

"You will, though. I dreamt that you were a mighty
queen on a throne, wearing a spectacular crown of
sapphires and diamonds which brought out the blue

of your eyes in a very fetching way. And I kneeled before you, kissing the hem of your gown."

Margaret had to tamp down a flattered, warm little flutter within her. "It was only a dream," she said in a repressive tone. "And so here you are after all. I'm sure everyone is excited to hear your speech."

He smiled down at her. "Justly so. What did *you* dream about last night? Judging by the dark circles beneath those lovely blue eyes of yours, you had a restless time of it."

"I slept very well, thank you," she lied.

"If you say so. Good morning, Mr. Lawrence."

"How do you do, sir. Splendid day today."

"Yes, it is. I do hope you'll be able to capture for posterity as much of my speech as possible."

"I'll try my best, sir."

"I know you will."

No sooner had Mr. Thane said this than the merry sounds of the pipe and drum fell away, and the crowd fell silent too, turning as one toward the platform in joyful expectancy.

"Well," Margaret said to Mr. Thane, "I believe that's your cue."

"I believe it is." He went up the wooden steps with a light, graceful tread, introducing himself to the various town dignitaries clustering there, one of whom, Margaret saw, gestured him toward the front. Mr. Thane walked to the railing, swept his gaze over the crowd, and began speaking in an earnest, cheerful voice.

"Good people: as we all know, there are holidays, and then there are *holidays*. Who needs Christmas, who needs Boxing Day, who needs Twelfth Night, when there's Plough Day? I for one don't. Here we are, assembled together in glad fellowship and celebrating all things agricultural—and what could be more important, more meaningful? Because *we* know that farmers are this country's backbone, and have been for time immemorial."

He paused, smiling in a way which encompassed the entire crowd, the members of which responded by breaking into applause. He dipped his dark head in acknowledgement and continued:

"On a personal note, I'd like to tell you all about my very own Plough Day miracle. Originally, I wasn't even supposed to be here. No, just a few days ago I was visiting with my dear relation, Mrs. Henrietta Penhallow—"

A ripple of awed amazement went through the crowd.

"Yes," Mr. Thane continued as if unaware, "my dear, close, affectionate relation Mrs. Henrietta Penhallow at her magnificent country estate in Somerset, all fifteen thousand acres of it—"

Another ripple of awe.

"—and as it turned out I just happened to be in the right place at the right time. Her representative to come here and deliver a few words honoring Plough Day had fallen ill. Of course I jumped at the chance to take his place—who wouldn't?—and here I am. To tell you the truth, I feel like the luckiest man in the world. I was supposed to be heading out of town after I'd given my speech this morning, but do you know what?"

He paused in a very expectant way, and several people called back curiously: "What?"

"Here's the thing. I love it here so much that I've decided to stay on for a while. Not just for today, but for a long, long time. For me, every day is Plough Day. And I hope it is for you, too." He smiled again.

"Well, that's enough about me. I couldn't be prouder, or more excited, to usher in the big moment you've all been waiting for. The true star of the show, the cynosure of all eyes, the harbinger of seasons past, present, and future. Ladies and gentlemen, I give you . . . the Straw Bear!"

Mr. Thane gestured grandly with a sweep of his arm, but instead of turning her head right away to see the Straw Bear for herself, Margaret stood gazing up at him with narrowed eyes. She'd been listening to his speech with a skepticism which had rapidly burgeoned into a strong suspicion that Mr. Thane was playing a joke on everyone here.

It would make perfect sense, too, given his comments yesterday about the good people of Whittlesey.

Mr. Lawrence had asked Mr. Thane for some early tidbits of his speech, and he had refused, saying in a sarcastic tone:

I prefer to leave you in suspense about my scintillating remarks, which will doubtless render my entire audience of rustics, provincials, hobnails, yokels, chawbacons, hicks, bumpkins, and loobies spellbound.

Indignation burned inside Margaret, and she watched, fuming, as Mr. Thane jovially shook hands with all the various dignitaries up on the platform, then lingered to talk to each of them in turn. Huffily she turned away, only then realizing that she was missing out on the very reason why she'd come here in the first place: the Straw Bear himself.

And there he was, making his slow way among the crowd, a great round figure all covered in sheaves of clean shining hay, from its head down to its ankles. As he lumbered forward, everyone was applauding, those closest to the Bear reaching out to pat at his sheaves—a gesture which signified hope for an early spring. The pipe and drum had resumed their merry, lilting beat and some people were moving and swaying in happy little dances, both singly and together.

Margaret watched, fascinated, tapping one of her feet in time to the music, although in the back of her mind she was conscious of a sense of disappointment. She'd been hoping that Mr. Thane would be leaving Whittlesey today, and that he'd offer—or agree—to take herself, Aunt Seraphina, and Mr. Lawrence along as well, at least to some convenient point where they might find other transportation. She had made inquiries about the stage and discovered to her dismay that there were no seats to be had for several days.

It seemed, therefore, that she was trapped here, and for who knew how long.

As this realization came to her, Margaret was further aware of an odd, creeping sense of . . . inevitability.

As if she wasn't really *that* surprised there was no way out of Whittlesey.

And why on earth would that be?

In last night's dream, she all at once recalled, Mr. Thane had been telling her something about a snow-storm coming their way. And then she heard again the three elderly ladies chanting:

Double, double toil and trouble, fire burn and caldron bubble. Time doth spin round and round, to each other you are bound. Double, double toil and trouble, fire burn and caldron bubble. Thwart it with your true love's kiss, thus the charm brings sweetest bliss.

A deep, familiar voice said reproachfully in her ear:

"You're looking at the Bear, but I'd bet a tenner you're not *seeing* him. Woolgathering again, aren't you?"

It was Mr. Thane, of course, and Margaret glanced

uneasily up into his handsome face. "What do you mean, I'm woolgathering *again*?"

"Oh, nothing. Can I buy you some breakfast?" He held up his hand and invitingly waggled a wad of what looked like quite a few pound notes. "I'm flush with cash now."

"'Now'?" she echoed. Abruptly she remembered him mingling with—lingering among—the dignitaries on the platform. "After you gave your speech, did you demand *payment* for it?"

"My dear girl," he said, his voice reproachful again as he slid the notes into a pocket of his greatcoat, "you do me a grave injustice. My speech was entirely a charitable act. I merely borrowed the money to finance a few personal needs. Don't worry—I'll pay it back tomorrow."

"How will you get the money to do that?" she responded suspiciously.

He smiled. "Something will turn up. Come have breakfast with me. You look as if you need it. Are you always so prickly and defensive first thing in the morning?"

"No, only when I'm forced to have a conversation with you. Are you really going to stay on here in Whittlesey, or was that all a part of your long running joke—I mean, was that all a part of your *speech*?"

"Spitfire," he said appreciatively, and with the full potent force of his considerable charm.

Margaret had to sternly repress a responsive flare of warmth within her. "Well, are you?"

"Yes, I'm staying on. I like it here."

"Even amongst—" Discreetly she lowered her voice. "—all the rustics, provincials, hobnails, yokels, chawbacons, hicks, bumpkins, and loobies you so casually denigrated on the ride here?"

"You forgot to include hawbucks, joskins, and lumpkins. Your doughty aunt would be disappointed in you."

She stared up at him, baffled, but stuck to her guns. "What happened between yesterday and today, to make you change your mind so profoundly about Whittlesey?"

"Oh, it's a long story. Are you going to have breakfast with me or not? We could go to my room at my inn, and have it sent up. Wouldn't that be awfully cozy?"

To her surprise Margaret had actually been wavering about his invitation, but naturally she had been assuming that he meant having breakfast in a *restaurant*. In a cold voice she said, "I'm afraid that would be a little too cozy for my taste, sir."

"A shame. It would have been the best breakfast you've ever had."

"I loathe innuendoes."

"I was talking about oatmeal."

"Really."

"Last chance, Miss Allen."

"You already know my answer."

"That's too bad. I'll miss you. Good day then." He tipped his hat and sauntered off, and Margaret watched him make a beeline toward two pretty young women who bridled coyly at his approach. Miss *her*? Ha. He'd found consolation right away.

"I say, how does he do it?" said Mr. Lawrence wistfully.

Margaret saw that he had followed her gaze, to where Mr. Thane now stood chatting with the two young women, who were looking up at him as if they were very, very hungry and *he* was going to be their breakfast.

"It must be all those capes on his greatcoat." She was being sarcastic, but regretted it right away when Mr. Lawrence eagerly said:

"Do you really think so?"

Tired of talking about Mr. Thane, tired of *thinking* about him, Margaret replied, "Who knows? I'm going back to my inn to have breakfast. Would you like to come with me?"

"No, I'm hoping to get an interview with the mayor."

"Good luck," she said, and walked into the crowd, being sure to make a wide detour around Mr. Thane and his new friends, who already seemed to be getting on like a house on fire.

"**W**e're *so* glad you came to Whittlesey," Miss Janney said. "Ain't we, Sally?" she said to Miss Tellington, who only made agreeable affirmative noises from down below as her mouth was full.

"We spotted you right away when you gave your speech this morning," the talkative Miss Janney went on. "I didn't understand most of what you said, to be honest, because you used a lot of long words, but I says to Sally, I says, 'Ooh, here's a looker,' didn't I, Sally? And then when you came walking toward us after your speech, I says to Sally, I says, 'Ooh, look at all them *capes* on his coat! And them *boots*! And brown eyes to fall down into, just like a well! He's such a looker!' And then there we were, the three of us talking away like we'd known each other forever, and Harriet came over too, and *she* said you was such a looker too, and then she says, 'Ooh, can't we all sneak up to your room, Sally? We done it before, lots of times,' and so we asked you, and you said yes right away, and here we are, with none the wiser!" she finished triumphantly, nibbling at the bare skin of his throat.

"Yes," said Philip rather hoarsely, reaching out for a dangling breast. It was either Miss Janney's or Miss Bing's. Miss Tellington's were unavailable at the moment. "Here we are."

Miss Janney giggled. "Ooh, Matilda's gonta be so *mad* she didn't come to Plough Day! She said it was gonta be too cold out."

Miss Bing giggled too. "Not cold in here."

Gently Philip pinched whoever's nipple it was. "I feel sorry for Matilda."

"Me too," Miss Janney said, still giggling. "And for Ella, too."

At this Philip lifted up his head, dislodging Miss Bing who had been tracing the tip of her tongue along his ear. "Who's Ella?"

"Our friend. She didn't come either. Poor chuck. She missed out on the best Plough Day ever."

"Maybe we can make it up to her and Matilda somehow," said Philip, even more hoarsely, and decided he'd figure out how just a little bit later. Now wasn't quite the time for any heavy thinking.

After a pleasant breakfast with Aunt Seraphina in their private parlor, Margaret had gone to work on her notes, and by midday felt that she had had a very productive morning *and* she'd managed to shake off that odd, niggling sensation of inevitability.

Mostly, that was.

It did seem to cling to her, just a trifle, while she enjoyed an equally pleasant luncheon with her aunt, while she went again to inquire about any sudden availability on the stage (no luck there, alas), and also while she went for a long, invigorating walk around the town, peeping into storefronts, offering a donation to a nice couple raising money for the local convalescent home, petting all the dogs she encountered, buying some peppermint confits at an apothecary shop, chatting with a freckle-faced little boy in a jaunty red cap who had crouched down to stroke the butcher's tabby cat, and otherwise amusing herself.

However, she *had* succeeded in banishing Mr. Thane from her mind, which gave her a cheerful, proud, even rather smug feeling of mastery.

This happy feeling lasted until the precise moment when she and Mr. Lawrence were heading toward the Publick House for the Plough Day dinner and she saw, rolling along the street with an ostentatious lack of speed, the showiest curricle she had ever seen, with its high, wide seat all padded in shiny crimson leather and enormous wheels painted a gaudy bright yellow, pulled by a pair of flashy and expensive-looking bays and being driven by . . .

Margaret blinked and felt her mouth dropping open in surprise.

King Louis XIV of France?

Who, incidentally, had been dead for over a hundred years.

She stared.

Then blinked again.

For it was—inevitably—Mr. Philip Thane, dressed like the Sun King in one of his most famous portraits, complete with a towering wig of long dark curls, a neck-frill of exquisite white lace, ruffled sleeves, and a massive furred cloak of dark blue velvet embroidered all over in gold fleur-de-lis, along with short, puffy, white silk breeches, from which his long and undeniably muscular legs emerged clad in white stockings.

From his lean hip dangled a shiny golden sword, and on his feet were elegant, historically accurate red-heeled shoes.

Next to her Mr. Lawrence murmured in an awed undertone: "What the devil . . . ? Begging your pardon, Miss Allen."

Margaret didn't tear her eyes away to glance at him or even acknowledge his apology, as she'd just realized that Mr. Thane was surrounded by—she counted them—no less than five women, each of whom looked exactly like an eighteenth-century china shepherdess.

They were all dressed in short green-and-white ruffled gowns which belled out around them in a riot of starched petticoats, revealing their ankles *and* their old-fashioned shoes; on their gowns' broad hems were fastened frothy lace, pale green bows, and bands of looped, embroidered daisies. On their heads they each wore a straw bonnet topped with a giant spray of curling, improbably pink feathers and clutched in their hands was a tall beribboned crook.

Altogether, it was a sight not soon forgotten.

And it wasn't just herself and Mr. Lawrence who were gawking. Dozens of other people stood stock-still, gazing at the remarkable spectacle before them.

The curricle rolled slowly past, and Margaret's eyes met Mr. Thane's.

He nodded at her, once, as would a mighty king deign to acknowledge a humble subject, and, torn between amusement and ire, Margaret reminded herself to close her mouth.

Mr. Lawrence gave a long sigh, one that seemed to emanate from the depths of his being. "*Five* women," he murmured, sounding very melancholy.

All at once Margaret seemed to have a vague memory of Mr. Thane saying placidly to her, *Moderation is overrated.*

Which of course he hadn't.

For a brief moment she felt a vertiginous sense of disorientation, as if she'd somehow slipped out of time and place.

Then she gave herself a shake.

She was standing on a sidewalk in Whittlesey, it was Plough Day, she'd arrived here yesterday after traveling from Brampton in Mr. Thane's carriage, and she was just about to go to the banquet with Mr. Lawrence.

As for Mr. Thane's placid remark, she must have dredged up a memory from her dreams last night.

"Shall we go on?" she said to Mr. Lawrence, who agreed, and together they made their way to the Publick House and found some seats, Mr. Lawrence, with another muttered apology, diving toward a table where sat several lively young people just his age.

So Margaret sat down at a different table and did her best to chat amiably with her fellow table-mates although, truth be told, she was rather preoccupied. And for some strange reason she was feeling lonely, too, despite the presence of the others around her. The dinner seemed to stretch on and on and she really began to wish it were over.

She sighed, almost as deeply as Mr. Lawrence had on their way here, and toyed with her fork at the last of her herb-encrusted potatoes. They were quite good, although they could have used a bit more thyme.

"Good Lord, you're woolgathering *again*. My dear girl, you think too much," said a familiar, deep, cultured voice, and as her heart gave a wild thump Margaret dropped her fork, which clattered onto her plate, and she looked up to see that Mr. Thane had come upon her unawares.

He was dressed in the latest fashion, in stylish dark breeches, a gorgeous embroidered waistcoat, a plum-colored jacket that fit him to perfection, and a spotless white cravat which was expertly tied into a simple but dashing configuration.

"Good evening, Your Majesty," she said wryly.

He smiled and gave a low, elaborate bow. "I might greet you the same way."

"That was just a dream of yours," she reminded him, "and pray don't kiss the hem of my gown."

"It's a very pretty one."

Margaret had to repress a little flutter of pleasure at the compliment, as it was a new gown and this was the first time she'd worn it. She did love its delicate spangled trimmings around the hem and the bodice and the short puffed sleeves, and the soft sheen of its periwinkle silk.

Her neighbor to her left, Mr. Smith, said:

"Splendid speech this morning, sir. I enjoyed every word of it."

"Thank you so much," said Mr. Thane, with an air of complete and total modesty that Margaret knew was completely and totally false. "I enjoyed *giving* every word of it."

"I see that you're acquainted with Miss Allen here," said Mr. Smith, and rose to his feet. "Do take my seat."

"How kind," said Mr. Thane, and gracefully sank into it as Mr. Smith ambled away and found another seat at a nearby table, where he was hailed by everyone there—a cordial response which only intensified Margaret's feelings of loneliness.

"What were you brooding about when I came over?" asked Mr. Thane. "Did you have a horrible day without me?"

"No, I had a pleasant and productive one. And how was *your* day?"

"Also pleasant and productive."

"I'm glad to hear it. I didn't realize there was a costume ball this evening."

"There wasn't." He signaled to a waiter, who bustled over and inquired:

"Some dinner, sir?"

"No, I'm quite satiated. Just a glass of wine."

The waiter nodded and bustled away.

Margaret was tempted, very tempted, to make a sarcastic remark about his use of the word "satiated," then thought better of it, discretion being, of course, the better part of valor. "That was quite a carriage, and those outfits were . . . memorable."

"Thank you," he said placidly.

"A good use of your hard-earned money, no doubt."

"Oh, I agree. Although the term 'hard-earned' doesn't apply, you know."

"I do know. So why Louis the Fourteenth?"

"Because long ago, I auditioned for a role in the school play as Louis and to my immense disappointment wasn't cast. So I'm making up for lost time, you see."

The waiter arrived with a glass of wine which he set before Mr. Thane, who lifted it up and took a sip. He grimaced. "By Jove, this stuff really is awful."

Margaret nodded. "Yes, it is. What was the play?"

"It was written by one of the classics masters and was an extended dialogue between Louis the Fourteenth and England's own James the Second, in which Louis was portrayed as lecherous, lubricous, satiric, dissolute, and dissipated, and James as saintly, upright, virtuous, high-minded, and chaste."

"I'm not so sure that it was an accurate portrayal of James."

"No, but it was intended to be patriotic, you see, and staged on Guy Fawkes Day. And naturally you can understand why I wanted to be Louis—he got to stride about the stage boasting of his innumerable conquests, twirling his mustaches and demanding that everyone admire his shapely legs, and also ordering that all his political enemies be clapped in irons and tossed into the Bastille. James just sat there like a lump, looking down his nose and making tutting noises every ten lines or so."

"Your choice of roles is indeed understandable. And what about the shepherdesses in the play? What did they do?"

"Unfortunately there weren't any in the script."

"Then why were they a part of your—ah—entourage today?"

"Oh, because my friends wanted to join in, and aside from a few dowdy witches' outfits that's all the costumers had to offer."

"Ah. And they didn't care to join you here at the banquet?"

"Honestly, I couldn't persuade them to take off the costumes."

"How disappointing for you."

"So true. Would you like to join us? I'll bet they'll listen to *you*. Especially if you go first."

Margaret stiffened. Curiously enough, she'd been feeling less lonely at Mr. Thane's arrival, and even though their conversation wasn't exactly the most profound one she'd ever had, still it had been rather fun to trade a few barbs. But his audacious invitation quenched all her pleasurable feelings; it was like dumping a bucket of cold water onto a kindled fire.

She actually shivered a little.

Philip watched as Miss Allen's mouth thinned and her eyes went cold, but tore his own eyes away from her when Puce Lady, sitting to his left as she had last night, apparently thought it a good time to insert herself into his *tête-à-tête* with Miss Allen.

"Well! The *indecency*! Sir, you are no gentleman!" she exclaimed severely, glaring at him. "I've never been so shocked in my life!"

"My dear ma'am, what's shocking is your open admission of eavesdropping. A highly unladylike behavior, I might add."

Puce Lady bristled. "Your behavior is *far* worse, and you know it!"

"So you admit to eavesdropping. I rest my case."

Predictably, she gave a sound that was something in between a snort and a puff and which smacked of outraged disbelief. She got up and marched away, the feathers in her turban fluttering angrily, and Philip turned back to Miss Allen, hoping she would be as amused as he was, but instead he saw that she, too, had risen to her feet.

"Don't go. The night is still young."

"Maybe so, but I'm going back to my inn anyway," she answered, in an all too familiar grim and tight-lipped manner.

He stood up also. "I'll escort you."

"No, you won't. Goodbye."

"See you tomorrow," he called after her, and watched as she went away, looking, as usual, nearly as ravishing from behind as she did from the front. Why, he wondered, had he issued that brazen offer to her? If he'd stopped to think for half a second, he'd have known she wouldn't accept, and that she'd get all offended and haughty. And now she was gone. His good mood somewhat evaporated, Philip picked up his wineglass and drank it all down, grimaced again, and when he'd put the glass back onto the table he noticed the cloth, all white and smooth and tempting.

"Hmmm," he murmured aloud. "Second time's the charm, perhaps."

So he took a firm grip with both hands on the edge of the tablecloth, and without bothering to forewarn the remaining people sitting there, he yanked hard and maybe even with more force than was really necessary.

There was a tremendous crash as plates, glasses, utensils, dishes large and small, the big crystal centerpiece filled with flowers, and so on, all tumbled into a scattered heap on the floor.

In the sudden aghast silence which followed, Philip viewed the carnage with faint annoyance. "Damn."

Then he dropped the tablecloth and strode away, out into the chilly dark of night, not to *his* inn but to a boarding-house in a different part of town. He had to sneak in from the back, but all his new friends were waiting for him. They were still dressed in their identical shepherdess costumes, which made it difficult to tell them apart—not that it mattered.

At some point later, when they were all agreeably tangled up again, Philip suddenly found himself thinking about Miss Allen and her beautiful face and lush figure and the way her expressive blue eyes sometimes sparkled just like sapphires and how her lovely mouth thinned in a way which made him wonder what it would be like to slowly and gently tease her lips apart with his own and kiss her until she was smiling and flushed and warm all over.

"Ooh," he vaguely heard someone saying, and "Oh *my*," and then somebody else giggled, and after that a sweep of long dark hair descended onto his chest, tickling him. He swept it aside rather impatiently, thinking of Miss Allen's shining, silky, tawny hair and how he'd like to bury his own face in it and breathe in her delicious scent of summer roses, and more . . .

There were hands and mouths and limbs all over him, and inviting orifices everywhere, and yet here he was, distracted, with Miss Allen looming large in his mind.

Would she be the least bit flattered that he was thinking about her at a time like this?

Probably not.

Somebody attempted to sit on his face, giggling, and he shifted himself away.

He'd had a flash of inspiration.

As much fun as it had been with the shepherdesses, it was time to move on—and straight toward the feisty, intellectual, ravishing, *and* aloof Margaret Allen.

He'd begin his campaign tomorrow.

There was no doubt in his mind that he would succeed.

After all, he had all the time in the world.

And no woman could resist his wiles forever.

Chapter 9

It was a bright, sunny morning, and Margaret should have been glad that here she was in Whittlesey, joining in the lively Plough Day celebration, and with a splendid vantage-point right next to the festive bunting-bedecked platform, too. A delightful scene lay all about: how much fun everyone was having! Why should *she* feel so blasé, as if she'd seen it all before? She wasn't even excited about the Straw Bear's imminent appearance—and after all the trouble she'd gone through to see him at last.

What on earth was wrong with her?

She sent a troubled glance to Mr. Lawrence next to her, he being busy jotting down his impressions in his notebook, but of course he couldn't explain what was bothering her. Suddenly she spotted a tall broad-shouldered figure coming toward the platform: it was Mr. Thane, all stylish and elegant in his greatcoat and fashionable hat and shining dark boots.

As he came near she saw at once that he was looking quite different than he had last night when he had dropped Aunt Seraphina, Mr. Lawrence, and herself off at their inn. Then he had been annoyingly suave and sardonic, and openly bitter about having to get up early for Plough Day. Today, however, he looked pleasant and fresh-faced and mild.

"Good morning, Miss Allen. Happy Plough Day."

"Happy Plough Day," she returned, though a trifle mechanically.

"Are you all right?"

"Why wouldn't I be?"

"You seem a bit downcast."

"I'm fine."

"If you say so."

"I do say so," she said, aware, to her chagrin, that she sounded childish and petty. "Are *you* all right?"

"What do you mean?"

"You look very different today."

"Do I?"

"Yes, you're looking quite cheerful for someone who clearly didn't want to be in Whittlesey making a Plough Day speech. Frankly, I wasn't even sure if you'd show up."

"Indeed? But here I am, bright and early. A gentleman always keeps his word."

No sooner had Mr. Thane uttered this than the merry sounds of the pipe and drum fell away, and the crowd fell silent too, turning as one toward the platform in joyful expectancy.

"Well," Margaret said to him, "I believe that's your cue."

"I believe it is." He went up the wooden steps with a light, graceful step, introducing himself to the various town dignitaries clustering there, one of whom, Margaret saw, gestured him toward the front. Mr. Thane walked to the railing, swept his gaze over the crowd, and began speaking in an earnest, cheerful voice.

It all seemed so strangely familiar—simplistic platitudes about holidays, agricultural things, miracles, his famous relation Mrs. Henrietta Penhallow, and how lucky he was—that Margaret didn't even bother to actually listen. Mostly she was brooding over the fact that there were no stage seats to be had for several days. After only one night in Whittlesey, the town had somehow lost its novelty, and she wanted to leave.

But it seemed she was trapped here, and who knew for how long.

Damn and *double* damn.

Even *triple* damn.

Oh, Margaret, you're acting like a complete chucklehead, she scolded herself. *Do perk up and leave off the pointless self-pity.*

A familiar voice said in her ear:

"You're missing out on the Straw Bear."

Margaret gave a start, and looked up into Mr. Thane's handsome, pleasant face. "What?" she said, rather wildly. "Where?"

He gestured to the edge of the crowd, and obediently Margaret turned her head and saw the Straw Bear himself making his way among the crowd, a great round figure all covered in sheaves of clean shining hay, from its head down to its ankles. As he lumbered forward, everyone was applauding, those closest to the Bear reaching out to pat at his sheaves—a gesture which signified hope for an early spring. The pipe and drum had resumed their merry, lilting beat and some people were moving and swaying in happy little dances, both singly and together.

"Remarkable, isn't he?" said Mr. Thane, without a trace of sarcasm or mockery.

Margaret shot a suspicious glance up at him. But his expression was still pleasant and mild and friendly.

What a very, very different Mr. Thane from yesterday.

"Now that my speech is done, I'm going to be

heading out of town, Miss Allen. Would you and your aunt care to join me? And you too, of course, Mr. Lawrence."

At this Mr. Lawrence lifted his head from his notebook. "They say there's a snowstorm coming in."

"I hadn't heard that. But hopefully we'll get lucky."

"I say, I hope we *will*. I'd love to tag along with you till Northampton, sir. If it's on your way, that is."

"Absolutely," said Mr. Thane graciously, then looked at her. "As is Oxford, Miss Allen."

Margaret felt her spirits lifting and her bad mood melting away. "Oh, Mr. Thane, that would be marvelous! *Thank* you! There aren't any seats on the stage for quite some time. I was worried that we'd be stuck here for ages."

"Is that why you were looking out of sorts?"

She nodded, beaming. "But not anymore! When can we leave?"

He smiled back, and Margaret couldn't help but think how very attractive he was. She wondered why she hadn't noticed it before. Had she completely misjudged him? He replied:

"When would be convenient for *you*? I'm ready anytime."

"Oh, the sooner the better."

Within the hour they were on the road, hot bricks under their respective pairs of feet, and Margaret was so happy that she nearly burst out in song. And it was all thanks to this new, surprising, rather captivating Mr. Thane.

"**W**ell, here we are again," said the elder Miss Allen, sliding her tatting and mother-of-pearl shuttle back into her capacious reticule. "Unfortunately."

Mr. Lawrence woke up from his nap with a glottal

snort and glanced out the window. "At least the snow didn't follow us here."

"That's something, at least," Philip agreed pleasantly. "If we're lucky, it won't pass through Oundle toward us. And hopefully someone will be moving that fallen tree later on today." He sent an inquisitive glance around the barouche's interior. "Shall we try again tomorrow morning? If that suits all of you?"

"By all means, Mr. Thane," said the elder Miss Allen, bestowing upon him an approving smile. "Thank you."

Philip smiled back at her, careful to keep his own smile neither too wide nor too small. Too much would be a grin; too small might seem unenthusiastic. He'd exerted himself to be a paragon of respectful deference all morning and now he had his reward: Margaret's aunt, that doughty old iceberg, had been visibly thawing toward him, even going so far as to permit him, at his request, to rewind a length of thread that had slipped off its spool and gotten tangled up. It had been tedious, displaying all that respectful deference, and of course wasting time going to the predictably futile effort of attempting to get away from Whittlesey, but foundations must be laid.

"I know you're disappointed, Miss Allen," Philip said to Margaret. "But there's always tomorrow, you know."

She had been staring out the window, looking rather pensive, but now she turned her head and gave him a smile. "Yes, very true."

It wasn't a particularly warm or beaming smile, being polite more than anything else, but still a smile was better than a frown, scowl, glare, glower, grimace, and so on.

There was a knock on the door of the barouche, and the coachman, having let down the steps, opened the door to hand the ladies down into the courtyard of their inn. He and Mr. Lawrence followed.

"I suppose we're stuck here for the day," said Mr. Lawrence. "Shall I go get our rooms back, ladies?"

"I took the precaution of asking the proprietor to hold them for you," Philip said. "On the off-chance we'd be returning, I didn't want you subject to any inconvenience."

"How clever of you, Mr. Thane," said the elder Miss Allen warmly. "*And* thoughtful. Thank you again."

"It was nothing, ma'am," he replied in a modest tone.

A bustle commenced in the courtyard as the luggage was unloaded by the coachman and two of the inn's staff, and Philip took advantage of the elder Miss Allen's distraction as she reminded the staff whose bags belonged to whom. He stepped close (but not *too* close) to Margaret and said, in a respectful, modest, earnest, deferential tone leavened by just a touch of humorous playfulness:

"I wonder if I might console you for your disappointment by taking you out for luncheon."

"Thank you, but I should stay and help my aunt with the luggage."

"Nonsense," interjected the elder Miss Allen, handing a bandbox to the coachman. "It'll all be settled in a trice. Do go and enjoy yourself, my dear."

"Yes, but what about you, Aunt? What will you do?"

"I'll have some luncheon myself, and then I'm going to work on my galley-sheets, very likely taking up every inch of the private parlor with my books and papers and having a marvelous time and being of absolutely no use to anyone else. Mr. Lawrence, would you care to join me for a bite to eat? My treat, you know."

"I say, that *would* be jolly. Thanks ever so much, ma'am."

Her concerns plainly allayed, Margaret turned to Philip and said, "Shall we then, Mr. Thane?"

He held out his arm in a courtly gesture. "Let's."

Together they walked to the Cup and Saucer restaurant and found a cozy seat in the corner. He was glad that he'd managed again to borrow money from the town dignitaries this morning and so he had plenty of cash. But he didn't want to start out displaying extravagance; far better to begin, in a modest way, in this hilariously rustic little place. How long would it take before Margaret fell into his arms, he wondered. She smiled at him from across the table, more warmly this time, and he made a mental bet with himself that it would be around suppertime.

They gave their orders to the pot-girl and Philip said, enjoying himself very much:

"That *was* a shame about Oundle."

"Yes, but how could we have known? It was worth a try."

"Nothing ventured, nothing gained." An aphorism which had multiple meanings, he thought, picturing the voluptuous Margaret all naked and rosy and in his eager arms. What a gain indeed!

"If at first you don't succeed, et cetera," she responded. "Hopefully tomorrow, the second time will be the charm."

"I'll drink to that," he said, only marginally registering the fact that he'd deployed that same phrase about charms last night at the Publick House, and in a cheerful gesture he raised his water-glass.

They clinked glasses and he went on:

"Yesterday you mentioned being interested in folk-lore and old cultural traditions. That's what brought you to Whittlesey, I think you said. To experience Plough Day and see the Straw Bear."

"Yes, that's right."

"I'm awfully sorry I was such a dreadful ass. I hadn't slept well the night before, and I'm afraid I let it get to me. My behavior was unpardonable, frankly."

She smiled again. "One never feels quite oneself after a bad night. Consider yourself pardoned, Mr. Thane."

"That's very gracious of you, Miss Allen. How did you come to be interested in folk-lore? If you don't mind telling me, that is."

"Are you sure you want to hear? I've found, over the years, that many people find folk-lore obscure and even rather dull."

"I do want to hear," he replied, naturally refraining from mentioning that he happened to be one of those people and also heroically keeping his eyes from glazing over with boredom as they very much wanted to do. Instead he kept his expression one of alert interest. Ha! He'd thought playing Louis XIV would be his greatest theatrical triumph? *Today* was already shaping up to be the performance of a lifetime.

"Well," Margaret said, "it's simple, really. When I was five years old, my father told me the story of *The Odyssey*. Modified, of course, for my age. He said it was an old, old story that people had been telling each other for a long time. And the parts I liked best had to do with the gods and goddesses, the mystical creatures, the magical elements. They were real and yet not-real, both at the same time. I was fascinated.

"After that we went on to Aesop's *Fables, Odo's Tales*—a fourteenth-century collection of innovative

Welsh stories—and *One Thousand and One Nights,* though I hated the framing-device which has poor Scheherazade telling tales in order to save her life. It made me anxious. And angry at the stupid king. How I longed to do away with him!

"At any rate, growing up in a house with a mother who studies ancient Greek texts and a father who teaches the classics, I developed a deep interest in—and a love for—old stories, specifically the ones ordinary people have told each other over the centuries. And so, in a small way for now, I'm traveling here and there, listening and learning, and writing these stories down in order to preserve them. They're a part of our heritage—and in my opinion a national treasure."

Struggling to bite back the jaw-popping yawn which threatened to betray him, Philip took a hasty drink of water to disguise it, and brightly said, "Hence the Straw Bear and Whittlesey."

"Just so." She smiled and nodded.

To his immense relief the pot-girl returned with their meals and he and Margaret began to eat their pork cutlets and buttered green beans. He repressed a chuckle. Cutlets and green beans! How quaint.

"Oh, this is all so delicious," she said, picking up a roll and proceeding to spread upon it a lavish amount of butter. "I was so hungry. Usually I'm worthless until I've had my breakfast and at least two cups of coffee."

"I hustled us out of town with unseemly speed. My apologies for that, Miss Allen. We'll take time for breakfast tomorrow."

"There's no need to apologize—I was keen to go, and to get back home to Oxford. There's a colloquium on the subject of fairy folk, the ballad of Tam Lin, and superstition, you see, at which I'm slated to speak, and I'm very excited about it."

"Why, that's very impressive," he said, lying through

his teeth and also secretly congratulating himself on the masterful way in which he maintained both his tone and his expression of deep interest. "Won't you tell me more about it?"

"Really?"

He could see, with a thrill of triumph, that she was pleased and flattered by his response. He nodded, and she began to talk again, and while she did, her soft, pleasantly husky voice lively with enthusiasm, he passed the time by nodding every few sentences or so, murmuring, "How interesting," and envisioning her again without any clothes on and with her glorious shining hair unbound, spilling about those delectable plump shoulders of hers. He could hardly wait. The tedium would all be worth it.

She didn't go on for long, actually, being concise and succinct about her topic and her speech, but it did seem rather like years to one with more amorous preoccupations on his mind.

"Very impressive indeed," he told her, as he set aside his knife and fork, and patted his mouth with his napkin. "That *was* delicious. I'm almost as full as a *gulon*."

"You know that term?" Margaret said, her lovely eyes wide with delight.

"Yes, it's Scandinavian, isn't it?"

"That's right. Now *I'm* very impressed."

"Don't be. I must have come across it in a book somewhere." Inside himself Philip was gloating. They were getting on like a house on fire! Maybe they'd end up in his bed *before* suppertime. *Keep flattering her by asking about her interests,* he told himself. It would be deadly dull, and of course it would be much more enjoyable to talk about himself and *his* interests, but it seemed pretty clear he was making good progress. So he said:

"You mentioned that you were writing down the stories you encounter in your travels, Miss Allen. Tell me more about that."

She paused for a moment, then leaned forward. "Well, I know it's ambitious," she answered in a confiding tone, "but when I have enough of these folk-tales, from all over the country, I'd like to publish them in a book."

Philip couldn't help it. He burst out laughing. "Good God, who would want to read *that*?"

She stiffened at once and he could have kicked himself. "I mean—I meant to say, what a fascinating topic," he said, stammering as frantically he backpedaled as best he could, desperate to regain lost ground. "Absolutely fascinating. *And* engrossing. Riveting, really. You must have an enormous brain in order to tackle such a complex subject, and I'm sure you'll find a publisher right away and it will sell a lot of copies—a thousand, probably, perhaps several thousand. Who knows, perhaps more than that. You're really a very impressive person, Miss Allen. Very, *very* impressive."

"I'm not particularly impressive." Her voice was frigid, and in her eyes was now a hard jewel-like glitter. "What I *am* is gullible. I should have known from the start that *yesterday's* Mr. Thane is the *real* Mr. Thane." She took her napkin from her lap and slapped it onto the tabletop, and got up.

"Wait," he croaked, in a horribly frog-like manner. "Don't go. Please."

"Thank for you the luncheon, sir," she said with awful formality. "And pray erase from your mind all thoughts of taking my aunt and me along with you tomorrow. We'll find some other way of getting home."

"It—it could be a long while. The snow might come

in, you know, loads of it," he gabbled. "Mounds, piles, heaps! You have your colloquium, and your speech to give, and I'm sure your aunt wants very much to go home—only think of *her*."

"I'm quite confident that when I tell her all about this charming luncheon, she'll understand my disinterest in ever spending another single minute in your company. Good day."

He watched, crestfallen, as Margaret turned and stalked away and out of the restaurant.

Left alone, he stared at the door through which she had vanished.

Damn it to *hell*.

All his hard work today was for nothing.

It was her fault, really, for being interested in such dull things. Why did she have to have a brain inside that delectable body?

And now he had to entertain himself somehow for the rest of the day, while he waited until tomorrow— when he could start all over again.

Maybe he'd go see what his shepherdess friends were up to.

He was rather tired of them still, but what else was there to do in this godforsaken town?

"**Y**ou mentioned that you were writing down the stories you encounter in your travels, Miss Allen," said Mr. Thane, looking across the table at her with bright, interested eyes which, she noticed dreamily, had within their brown depths some intriguing green flecks. "Tell me more about that."

Margaret paused for a moment, amazed. *What* a different Mr. Thane from yesterday! Gone was the sardonic, cynical, lascivious fellow who had just about made her blood boil, and in his place was . . .

A kind, intelligent, courteous, generous, attentive, and attractive man.

An *extremely* attractive man.

She was vividly aware of his masculine solidity, the long length of his body and its easy, graceful lines; the way his brown hair, with its interesting hint of chestnut, curled ever so slightly over the collar of his jacket, the allure of his beautifully formed mouth, those fascinating eyes of his . . .

Yesterday she would never, in a million years, have thought she'd not only agree to join Mr. Thane for luncheon, much less discover, to her astonishment, that she would have a pleasant time with him.

Yet here they were!

He'd apologized for his rude behavior on the journey here, saying that he hadn't slept well the night before, and of course she forgave him for that, because it was true that one never felt quite like oneself after a bad night. And he'd been asking so many thoughtful questions about her interests and her work—and listening with such flattering attentiveness.

These surprising developments more than made up for the fact that their journey out of Whittlesey had been cut short by a snowstorm just past the little market town of Oundle, where, additionally, the road had been blocked by a big fallen tree.

To own the truth, she was almost glad they hadn't been able to leave. Earlier today she'd been feeling rather blasé, but now everything seemed fresh and new, sparkling with possibility. Her feelings of disinterest and melancholy had melted away, and now, sure that she could confide in him one of her biggest goals, and one she'd been quietly cherishing for a long while, she took a deep breath and leaned forward. She said to him:

"I know it's ambitious, but when I have enough of these folk-tales, from all over the country, I'd like to publish them in a book."

"Why, that's marvelous. A book! I wish you every success."

She beamed. "Thank you very much."

"What gave you the idea of writing a book in the first place?"

"Oh, Aunt Seraphina's books have long been an inspiration, and also having read many seminal collections of folk-tales from abroad, it seemed to me that somebody ought to start collecting British ones as well."

He nodded. "How far along are you?"

"About halfway, I think. And Aunt Seraphina's publisher has agreed to read the manuscript when I've completed it."

"I'm sure they'll say yes."

Margaret smiled at him, flattered all over again by his encouraging words and his confident tone. "You can't know that."

"But I can." He smiled back. "I have special powers."

"Oh, you can see into the future?" She laughed. "That would be very impressive."

"I think *you're* very impressive. Writing a book is a remarkable accomplishment." Mr. Thane set aside his knife and fork, and patted his mouth with his napkin. "That was delicious. I'm almost as full as a *gulon*."

"You know that term?" said Margaret, delighted. Mr. Thane really *was* full of surprises!

"Yes, it's Scandinavian, isn't it?"

"That's right. Now I'm *truly* impressed."

"Don't be. I must have come across it in a book somewhere."

"Do you like to read then, Mr. Thane?"

"Very much."

Margaret looked at him across the table with a pleasure she didn't even try to conceal. He was handsome, he was intelligent, he was a lively conversationalist, he was kind and thoughtful, *and* he liked books! Could it be . . .

She caught her breath at the dazzling thought.

Could it be that after all these years, her poor bruised heart was healing, and that she had—through the wild and improbable coincidence of being stranded in Brampton and his being the first coach to pass her way—found her perfect man?

It was the stuff of romantic novels.

And yet it *had* happened.

Happiness seemed to fill her up from head to toe, and everywhere in between. She felt marvelous all over. And *alive*—exuberantly alive. She said, in her voice a joyful lilt: "What sort of books do you like, Mr. Thane?"

"Oh, just about everything, really. Have you by any chance read Miss Austen's *Persuasion* and John Keats' *Endymion*?"

"I haven't. Did you enjoy them?"

"Yes, a great deal."

"Tell me about them."

He did, in a concise and succinct and very interesting manner. Margaret listened attentively, but she was also noticing how pleasant it was to take in the cadence and nuances of his deep cultured voice as he spoke. Dreamily she watched his mouth, admiring its cleanly carved lines, the glimpses of his white straight teeth, and found herself wondering what it would be like to feel that enticing mouth upon her own.

And now she caught her breath all over again.

Why not?

She knew that he liked her. She could tell by the warm glow in his brown-green eyes, and the way he looked at her with such interest and appreciation. Between them seemed to crackle the sweet fiery energy of desire. She barely knew Mr. Thane, but perhaps down the road sometime, what harm could there be in a kiss? It had been so long . . .

Also, she wanted to plunge her fingers into his glossy hair, and trail her tongue along the warm skin of his throat, and smooth her bare hands along the hard planes of his chest, and more . . .

"Would you like that, Miss Allen?"

Margaret gave a start. "I beg your pardon?"

Mr. Thane smiled at her and she felt a hot flush spreading all over her face. Had she been staring at him in an embarrassingly obvious way? But he only said mildly:

"I was wondering if you'd like to go for a walk."

"Oh! Yes. Yes, I'd like that."

So they left the Cup and Saucer and strolled around the town, glancing into storefronts, each of them offering a donation to a nice couple raising money for the local convalescent home (Mr. Thane giving a *very* generous amount!), petting all the dogs they encountered, and chatting with a freckle-faced little boy in a jaunty red cap who had crouched down to stroke the butcher's tabby cat and whom Mr. Thane somehow already seemed to know, as he addressed him by his first name—Thomas. Then the two of them meandered into a confectionary shop and gallantly he bought her a box of marzipan, which of course she shared with him, and then they continued walking here and there, talking and laughing with an easy sort of naturalness, and altogether Margaret was in such a happy, giddy, tingling sort of daze that the next thing she knew they had come to a halt.

She blinked.

They were in front of the Apple Street Inn.

His inn.

The sun had just begun its long slow descent into dusk, and the world was bathed in soft, mellow light; shadows everywhere had begun to deepen. A cool invigorating breeze fluttered the hem of her gown and pelisse and toyed with the gleaming locks of his hair which splayed across the collar of his greatcoat. His dark brows were lifted inquiringly as he looked down into her face.

"Well?" he softly said.

"Well what?" she answered, just a little breathless.

"Would you like to come in?"

She glanced over to the door of his inn. "I don't think I should."

"You shouldn't, but do it anyway."

Margaret hesitated, her heart thumping hard. She *did* rather want to, she did want to kiss him—and be kissed, and caressed, and held close—but all at once it felt like she was being driven in a carriage that was going too fast. Too fast, and too reckless. Why rush things? They had the whole rest of the day ahead of them, and, hopefully, tomorrow a long journey toward Oxford during which they could continue getting to know each other, and . . . who knew what might happen after that?

She said, smiling, "Let's keep walking. There was that interesting gallery we passed—remember?—and I'd love to go back and go inside. You mentioned being fond of art, and you already know that I am, too. Shall we go do that?"

"Later," he suggested softly. "Why not come in with me now?"

"I don't think it's a good idea."

"On the contrary. It's the very best of ideas. Honestly, the finest idea anyone in the whole entire world has ever had. Let's go inside. I have a marvelous room—I want you to see it."

"I don't think I should, really."

"*I* think you should. I think *we* should."

The conversation was looping around again somehow and Margaret began to feel just a trifle frustrated. "Yes, well, but only consider, Mr. Thane—it's one thing for us to be seen together in public, but quite another for us to be private together."

"Who would know, or care? We'll be leaving Whittlesey tomorrow, never to return."

"I care," said Margaret, nettled. "I care about my reputation, even if I'm far from home."

"Yet you embraced me on a sidewalk once. Why would this be any different?" In his voice was a new note of impatience.

"I beg your pardon?"

"Nothing," he said hastily. "Never mind. I only meant that if we nipped inside, I'm sure that nobody would notice."

Margaret stared up at him. What on earth did he mean, she'd once embraced him on a sidewalk? *Had* she? She had to stop a moment to actually think about it, then dismissed it from her mind. She saw, now, that Mr. Thane's expression was earnest and mild again. But she'd clearly heard the impatience in his tone, as if . . .

As if he'd been playing a little game and she was being recalcitrant and all he wanted was his prize.

And *she* was the prize, to be smuggled into his inn and up the stairs and into his room.

Any lingering feelings of warmth and excitement she'd been feeling now vanished.

It was like dumping a bucket of cold water onto a kindled fire.

She shivered, goose-bumps rising all over her flesh despite the cozy warmth of her thick wool pelisse.

"My dear Miss Allen, you're chilled," he said, his voice soft, coaxing again. "Come inside, and let's warm you up by the fire."

"What I *am* is gullible," she retorted. "I should have known from the start that *yesterday's* Mr. Thane is the *real* Mr. Thane. Oh, how could I have been such a fool?" So much for her poor bruised heart healing, Margaret thought, angry and anguished all at once. "Goodbye."

He caught at her arm. "Wait. Don't go. You're right, we don't have to go inside. Let's keep walking. Please. I'd love to go back to the gallery."

She shook him off, disliking yet another change of tone she clearly heard: not impatient, not coaxing, but instead just a tiny bit urgent.

And that was too bad for *him*. He'd had his chance and had managed to muck up what had been a really lovely day.

"Thank for you the luncheon, sir," she said stiffly, hoping she was concealing how hurt and terrible she felt inside. "And pray erase from your mind all thoughts of taking my aunt and me along with you tomorrow. We'll find some other way of getting home."

"It could be a long while, though," he said hoarsely. "The snow could come in, you know. Heaps, piles, big mounds of it! You'd be trapped here. I'll—I'll ride up front with the coachman and I won't even talk to you. At all. You won't even know I'm there. Please don't go, Miss Allen. Please."

He sounded just like a frog, croaking.

Well, she was no princess, and she wasn't going to

kiss him. Nor was he a prince—he was a frog through and through. That was quite obvious.

"Goodbye," Margaret said again, even more stiffly, and turned on her heel and walked away as fast as she could.

Had she truly thought that maybe she'd found her perfect man in Philip Thane? Ha!

It was a joke, but not a particularly funny one.

Chapter 10

He and Margaret had been strolling about the town after a pleasant, uneventful luncheon at the Cup and Saucer. He'd been very, very careful this time around. No accidental slips of the tongue referring to their past history—of which, of course, she was unaware—and no gently steering them to the sidewalk in front of his inn. He'd abandoned his goal of having her in his bed by suppertime. *Anytime* today would be fine. Yesterday's disaster had shown him that he couldn't rush her; he had to be more subtle.

And so far so good.

They'd offered a donation to that friendly, cheerful, dowdily dressed couple raising money for the local convalescent home (and how glad he was to have borrowed money again this morning from the town dignitaries, so that he could hand over a fat wad of cash and see her eyes widen in admiration of his generosity), they petted all the dogs they encountered (which he honestly enjoyed very much), and they chatted with the irrepressible Thomas Abernathy (with whom he was careful to display no memory of their previous encounter on the day he'd sunk down onto the sidewalk with his boots in the gutter, stunned and horrified by what was happening to him).

He and Margaret also went into the confectionary shop again, where he'd purchased a box of marzipan for them to share, and now they were idling along another sidewalk, laughing and talking with an easy sort of naturalness that made him feel increasingly hopeful that today was going to be the day. She liked him. He could tell by the warm glow in her expressive blue eyes, and he could practically feel the sweet fiery energy of desire crackling between them. He was picturing Margaret, naked and rosy, in his eager arms at last, when suddenly he realized that she had paused, and was looking up toward the sky which had, without his noticing it, shifted from bright blue to softer shades of amber, dark blue, violet, and murky gray.

"Goodness, how late it is," she said in surprise. "It's almost dusk. I've had a wonderful afternoon, Mr. Thane, but I should be getting back to my aunt."

"Must you?" he said, carefully and mildly and regretfully. "She did say she'd be busy working on her galley-sheets, and that she'd be of no use to anyone else."

"Yes, but that was hours ago. How quickly the time has passed!"

"Too quickly," he replied, with perfect truth. "Are you sure you wouldn't like to go into that interesting gallery we passed? You mentioned being fond of art, and I am, too. Shall we go do that?"

"That does sound lovely, but I really do want to return to the Woodhull Inn."

Damn it, he thought, repressing an impulse to frown. Damn, damn, *damn*. Once she was back at her inn, the chances of getting her alone again would diminish—possibly even fade away to nothing. He'd been working so hard, and things had been going so well between them! What could he say or do to keep her with him? Surreptitiously he glanced around, and

his eye lit upon the window of the shop in front of
which they were standing.

It was the Whittlesey jewelry store.

Inspiration struck, lifting his hopes again.

Women were like crows, irresistibly attracted to
shiny glittery things, always so grateful for them, too.

And he still had plenty of money in his greatcoat
pocket.

"I'll of course escort you back, just as you like, Miss
Allen, but first come inside here, just for a moment."

"What? Why?" she said, looking surprised again
as gently he drew her toward the door.

"You'll see." He made sure to infuse his voice with
an easy, playful tone. Once inside, he led her toward
the main display case which was, naturally, still filled
with the same bracelets, aigrettes, brooches, rings,
necklaces (and even the same diamond and ruby one
which he had stolen), and so on. A clerk—the same
one from before, naturally—came over and said:

"May I be of assistance, sir? Madam?"

Philip turned to Margaret. "I'd love to give you
something, Miss Allen. A memento of our wonderful
time together."

"It's very kind of you, Mr. Thane, but it's not at all
necessary. Nor is it proper, you know."

"Surely we needn't dwell on the proprieties, not in
a little town like this."

"I don't agree. Besides, we hardly know each other,
and to accept a gift of jewelry from you would be in-
appropriate."

"What about a brooch? Something simple and
modest, like that one shaped like a butterfly. Do you
see it there? With the amethyst wings? I'm certain that
would be all right."

The clerk hastened to take the butterfly brooch

from the case, and held it out to Margaret. "See, madam, how it shines in the light."

But she only gave it a cursory glance. "Very pretty. You can put it away now, if you please." Then she looked up at him, Philip, and with a sinking heart he saw that her expression was cooler now, and even rather remote. "Thank you for the kind offer, Mr. Thane, but my answer is still no."

He stared down at her, a certain desperation setting in. What was *wrong* with her? He'd been thoughtful and respectful and generous and kind all day long, asking her a lot of questions about herself and listening with every appearance of interest, and taking her out to luncheon, and walking around and around this stupid dung-hill of a town until he wanted to bang his head against the nearest wall with boredom. He stepped a bit closer to her and whispered:

"If it's the proprieties you're worried about, why don't you just tell me what you like the best, and I'll buy it for you later? No one need ever know."

"*I'll* know." She moved away from him. "Why is it so important for you to buy me something, and why do you keep pressing me? I've told you how I feel about it."

"It's just that—it's just that it would mean a lot to me. I mean—we've had such a wonderful time together—I can't remember when I've had so much fun simply talking and walking around, and—and I really don't want our time together to end, and I thought a little gift would—would—well, make you want to stay with me. I mean—so that we could keep on having a wonderful time together."

Damn it, he was gibbering and stammering and croaking like a frog *and* he was sweating like a pig. But he kept going.

"I mean—I mean, haven't *you* ever had a day you wish would never end? I certainly am, today, with you. And I was hoping—hoping very much—that you felt the same way too—and we could—could have dinner together, perhaps—and you could tell me more about your book, and all those marvelously fascinating folk-tales—I honestly don't feel you've told me enough about them—time's going by so fast—"

And now he was babbling, too. He wanted to wipe away the sweat on his face, but wouldn't that look bad? Margaret was looking up at him in obvious perplexity and he could tell, out of the corner of his eye, that the clerk was, too.

Philip took another step toward Margaret. "Maybe—maybe we could go for another walk together. Wouldn't you like that? I would. You're a wonderful walker. Also, a wonderful talker. I mean—a wonderful conversationalist. I don't know when I've enjoyed talking with someone so much. Really, you're absolutely fascinating. And clever, too. And you're beautiful. So very beautiful. How about just another hour together? Would you like something to eat? I've got plenty of money. See?"

Hardly knowing what he was saying or doing, aside from the excruciating awareness that somehow everything was slipping away from him, *again,* Philip pulled from his greatcoat pocket all his borrowed money. Women liked money, didn't they? He waggled it at Margaret and said:

"We could go to the fanciest restaurant in town. I mean, it'll probably be as terrible as that ghastly hole in the wall where we had luncheon, but must needs when the devil drives, don't you think? You'll say yes, won't you? We'll eat, drink, and be merry. You and I. Together. The most marvelous couple in Whittlesey. What do you say, dearest Miss Allen?" He used the sleeve of his greatcoat to wipe the sweat from his fore-head and labored onward.

"Do say yes. We'll have the most marvelous time together. I promise. I *swear*. You can tell me all about your absolutely fascinating book. Are you *sure* you wouldn't like some jewelry? I'll buy you anything you want. And perhaps, after dinner, we could go to my inn—it's the nicest one in this godforsaken town. There are some prints in the common-room—they're not too bad. Honestly. Dogs and horses and old farm-houses, you know, pastoral scenes and so on. The occasional silo. And cows. Loads of cows. Wouldn't you like to see them? You said you liked art. And per-haps afterwards we could—we could—"

"Go up to your room together?" she said gently.

"Yes. Wouldn't you like that? I would. I think you would, too." He nodded several times. "A *lot*."

There was a silence.

Quietly the clerk put the butterfly brooch back into the display case. Philip wiped his face again with his coat sleeve. Margaret took a deep, deep breath, and all at once he noticed how white her face had gotten, and how expressionless. It almost looked like she was wearing a mask.

"I suppose," she said gently, even conversationally, "this whole day has been about getting me to your room and into your bed."

"No," he answered, but feebly. "Not at all. We've been getting to know each other. Hasn't it been fun? I've learned what a marvelous person you are."

"Marvelous? Actually, I'd say that I'm a pathetically gullible fool. And as for you, I've learned that the *real* Mr. Thane is the man I met yesterday. The *real* you is a cruel, conniving, deceitful, double-dealing, lecher-ous *ass*. I wish I'd never met you." Her voice was still calm, still even, but it rang with undercurrents of steel. "Thank you for luncheon, Mr. Thane. I enjoyed it, even if you didn't—I daresay you were laughing up your cosmopolitan sleeve at the idea of eating cutlets and green beans. Also, I do hope you've erased from your mind all thoughts of taking my aunt and me along with you tomorrow. We'll find some other way of getting home. I never, ever want to see you again. Goodbye."

She turned away, and this time Philip didn't even bother trying to tell her about snow possibly coming in or how he'd ride up front with the coachman. It was all over. *Again.* Helplessly he watched as Margaret left the jewelry store and vanished from sight.

Another silence ensued.

It was a heavy, awkward, embarrassing, humiliating, and altogether mortifying silence, in fact.

Then, after about a million years, came the sound of a throat being discreetly cleared.

It was the clerk, who stood behind the display case looking professionally wooden. As if he'd never been witness to a ghastly scene in which, he, Philip, had metaphorically speaking been crucified and left to be picked clean by crows, peck by peck by peck, until all that was left was his bones which would, in time, rot and crumble to dust. Ashes to ashes and all that. In a quiet voice the clerk said:

"I beg your pardon, sir, but the store is closing."

Splendid, Philip thought. Someone else who wanted to get away from him. He shoved the money back into his greatcoat pocket and without another word he went out of the store and onto the sidewalk.

Dusk had fully fallen, and the world had gone dark and shadowy and gloomy and vague somehow. Everything looked tenuous and uncertain; it was hard to tell what was real and what wasn't. The sidewalk was filled with people going to and fro, huddled close against the cold in their coats, pelisses, shawls, and hats, doing some last-minute shopping, making their way home to their families and loved ones, heading out to taverns or restaurants or the Plough Day banquet.

Then Philip spotted Matron hurrying along in his direction, of course still bundled up to her eyeteeth and looking cylindrical in her various shawls and wraps, and so he spun about and nipped around the corner and, with long strides, zigzagged his way back to his inn, looking nervously over his shoulder, as one might avoid an enemy ambush.

The last thing in the world he wanted was another charming conversation with Matron during which they could reminisce about his delightful habit of hiding in the laundry room where he would hug a sack of clothing and cry like a baby.

Ten minutes later he let himself into his room and into blessed safety, closed and locked the door behind him, and flopped onto his bed, where he lay staring up at the ceiling for a while and determinedly *not* thinking about his younger self hugging laundry and weeping but instead about Margaret.

He'd gotten *so* close today.

Tantalizingly close.

Trying to buy her jewelry had, in retrospect, been a mistake.

What *could* he buy her? Something she wouldn't repudiate, something a brainy woman like her would appreciate.

The marzipan had been a nice touch, and somewhat romantic, but nothing out of the ordinary.

Flowers were always nice, always acceptable, even to the most straitlaced, but it would be awkward for her to lug them around. What if tomorrow he had many dozens of roses sent to her room at the Woodhull Inn, surprising her when they (inevitably) got back from their futile attempt to leave Whittlesey? *That* would be a fine, big gesture, although if it turned out she had allergies it would be a disaster—just as it had been with that countess in Amsterdam who, while delighted to have received all those tulips from him, had also gotten all covered over in red blotches and sneezed so many times her wig had fallen off, which had rather spoiled the mood.

No flowers, then.

He thought and thought.

Then, at last, it came to him and he sat bolt upright, smiling a big, happy, confident smile.

Why hadn't it occurred to him earlier?

It was *perfect*.

Margaret could hardly believe what a lovely—what a *surprising*—day she was having with Mr. Thane. She stole a wondering glance up at him as they strolled along a sidewalk together. What a very nice profile he had!

In fact, everything about him was nice.

More than nice.

Splendid, even.

This day of astonishing discoveries had begun when she'd first spotted him early on at the Plough Day ceremony, walking with easy, athletic grace toward the platform—and toward herself. How different he had looked from the Mr. Thane of yesterday!

Gone was the cynical, sardonic, insinuating fellow from the carriage ride here; today he had been pleasant and fresh-faced. His speech had been inane, platitudinous, and rather forgettable, to be honest, but he himself was nothing less than a revelation. It turned out that he was thoughtful, kind, respectful, generous, intelligent, lively, and charming. *Such* a good conversationalist, and a good listener too!

It more than made up for the fact that their attempt to leave Whittlesey this morning had failed.

And wasn't it so sweet of Mr. Thane to have offered them all places in his barouche without anyone needing to ask him?

Too, it was equally sweet of him to insist they try again tomorrow when, with luck, the weather and the roads would cooperate.

Margaret felt very, very happy at the thought of spending all that time with Mr. Thane on the journey home to Oxford—talking, laughing, getting to know each other, just as they'd been doing over luncheon at the adorable little Cup and Saucer restaurant, and also as they walked all over Whittlesey together.

It occurred to her that she never wanted this magical day to end.

Suddenly she caught her breath.

Could it be . . .

Could it be that her poor bruised heart was starting to heal at last, thanks to the marvelous, engaging, and exceedingly attractive Philip Thane?

She hoped so.

Oh, she hoped so with every bit of her.

She felt like a book which had long been shut, but was now, tentatively, opening up to a new chapter. And maybe, just maybe, on its way to a happy ending.

"Penny for your thoughts."

Margaret gave a start and looked up again to see that Mr. Thane was smiling at her. "I beg your pardon," she said, a little breathless. "I was woolgathering. What did you say?"

"I asked if you'd like to go into this bookshop."

Margaret realized that they'd drifted to a stop without her even noticing it, right in front of a window filled with some of her very favorite things: books, glorious books, in all kinds of sizes and colors. Wasn't it such an amazing coincidence that she'd just been thinking about a book?

Sometimes the world could *truly* be magical.

"I'd love to, Mr. Thane."

Together they went inside, and Margaret gave an appreciative sniff.

"It even smells good in here, don't you think? If they ever made a perfume with a fragrance like new books, I'd buy it."

He smiled again. "It would be intoxicating."

"For some, not for everybody. Not everyone loves books like I do."

"Like myself as well. You know, someday soon, your book may be in here."

"Wouldn't that be nice."

"I have faith in you, Miss Allen."

She smiled up at him, happiness making her feel all light and floaty inside. "Thank you! If it happens, I'll be sure to give you a copy."

"*When* it happens. And signed by the author, I hope."

Herself, a real live author? That would be *amazing*—and a long-cherished dream come true. "One step at a time, Mr. Thane. First I've got to finish the manuscript."

"You will. You're here in Whittlesey, after all, which means you've gotten yourself one step closer."

She laughed. "Very true."

A clerk came over and asked if he might be of service, and Margaret inquired as to their new arrivals in botany. Her mother was an avid gardener and a book like that would make a perfect birthday gift. So she spent some time leafing through a couple of books and finally picked one she was sure Mama would like the best, and then her eye was caught by a new translation of Euripides' *Children of Heracles* that Papa would enjoy adding to his collection.

She purchased these two books, along with a handsome blank journal for Aunt Seraphina who was a faithful diarist, and showed them to Mr. Thane who admired them all. They left the bookshop and went outside again, where the first signs of dusk began to reveal themselves in the deepening shadows all around them, and, above, in the softening colors of the sky, at the moment a tranquil palette of dark blue, gray, and violet which would soon fade into the deep rich colors of night, a vast canvas for the twinkling stars which even now were faintly, faintly, beginning to emerge.

She gave a happy sigh. "How beautiful it is here."

"I agree."

Impulsively Margaret tucked her arm through his. "Oh, Mr. Thane, I'm so glad we met! And isn't it curious that we did by pure coincidence? Because *I* was stranded in Brampton and *you* were in the first coach to pass my way? Why, it's like a plot from a novel!"

"A very clever novel," he said, and laughed. "I like to think that if somehow you hadn't flagged me down, you still would have found your way here, and we'd have met regardless. Perhaps it was meant to be."

"Perhaps." Margaret looked up into Mr. Thane's face, wanting, more than anything in the world, to kiss him. To feel his mouth on her own, his arms around her and her fingers buried in his thick glossy hair; their bodies pressed together without an inch between them. How unfortunate to be standing on a busy public sidewalk, surrounded by people going to and fro, huddled close against the cold in their coats, pelisses, shawls, and hats, doing some last-minute shopping, making their way home to their families and loved ones, heading out to taverns or restaurants or the Plough Day banquet. All at once she was distracted from her delicious idea of kissing Mr. Thane and she exclaimed:

"Goodness, I almost forgot!"

"What is it?"

"I was intending to go to the banquet at the Publick House. In honor of Plough Day, you know."

"Don't let me keep you from your plans," he said, gallantly but also with a flattering tinge of regret in his voice.

"Well, why don't you come with me? If *you* don't have any other plans."

A look of pleased surprise came onto his handsome face. "Really?"

"Yes, I'd love it."

"I would too."

Happily Margaret squeezed his arm, noticing, as she did, that it was a very nice and muscular arm, and also thinking that she wouldn't mind one bit running her fingers along the bare skin of it, lingeringly and more than once while she was at it. "Let's go back to my inn so that we can tell my aunt, and I'll drop off these books as well."

"May I carry them for you?"

"Thank you very much." While she could carry them herself quite easily, there was something so sweet about his offer. It seemed chivalry wasn't dead after all in these fractious modern times! With a smile Margaret transferred her package to him, and together they walked in the gathering twilight to the Woodhull Inn.

Aunt Seraphina, who had warmed considerably toward Mr. Thane during their journey from and back to Whittlesey this morning, greeted them with affable cordiality, applauded the banquet plan, declined to accompany them, and declared her intention of enjoying a quiet, peaceful dinner in the private parlor and then reading a book by the fireside with her feet propped up on a stool and a glass of claret at her side.

So Margaret went off with Mr. Thane to the Publick House, satisfied that Aunt Seraphina was going to have a pleasant evening, and sure that she herself was going to have one also.

In the dining-room they spotted Mr. Lawrence sitting at a boisterous table of young people; he waved to them and they waved back, then found seats at a table not far away. On Margaret's right was a middle-aged man with an extraordinary set of eyebrows who heartily congratulated Mr. Thane on his speech this morning, and on Mr. Thane's left was an elderly lady in puce. They all chatted easily throughout the various courses and then dessert, and time passed as if on silver wings. Before Margaret even knew it the banquet was over, people were drifting away, and when after jovial farewells their respective neighbors left too, she and Mr. Thane continued talking, as if there was so much to say to each other that they couldn't even be bothered to get up and go somewhere else.

The room had emptied, and only a few of the serving staff remained, clearing tables and dimming lamps, and Margaret had finished telling Mr. Thane, at his request, about her large and (in her opinion) delightful family in Oxford. She was just about to ask him about his, when he pulled something from an interior pocket of his jacket—a small, flattish, rectangular package wrapped in paper and tied up with twine.

"A little something for you, Miss Allen."

A flutter of pleasure went through her. "Why, Mr. Thane, how kind!" She took it from his hand, another flutter sparking inside her when their fingers touched, and she smiled at him. "May I open it now?"

"There's no time like the present."

She pulled off the wrapping. "*The Collected Poems of Andrew Marvell*. And what a handsome binding, too. Did you get it at the bookshop while I was busy shopping for my family?"

He nodded, smiling back at her, and she went on, teasingly:

"How underhanded of you, sir. Thank you!"

"You're most welcome. Do you like poetry? I hoped you did."

"I do, but I must admit that thanks to my parents' enthusiasms I'm more at home with the ancient Greeks and Romans. Isn't Marvell from around the same time as John Milton—the seventeenth century? My brother Sebastian spent a whole year studying Milton's life and works, and would go around the house quoting verses."

"I'm not sure about Milton. I don't know much about him. But yes, Marvell was born around 1620 or so."

"Will you read something to me? My father always says that poetry is best appreciated when hearing it, rather than silently reading it to oneself."

He smiled again. "I quite agree."

Margaret passed him back the book, closing her eyes as he began to read "The Garden." She was hearing each word, each line, each stanza, but she was also relishing the sound of Mr. Thane's deep voice which seemed to bring the poem, with all its vivid imagery and graceful evocations of nature, alive in her mind.

"'How could such sweet and wholesome Hours . . . be reckon'd but with herbs and flow'rs?'"

These closing words seemed to hang in the air, and after savoring them for a few moments Margaret opened her eyes and smiled at Mr. Thane. "That was lovely! Mama would enjoy it so much. And you read with such feeling and sensitivity."

"Thank you. Another?"

"Oh, yes! Please."

He read "The Gallery," and after that Margaret, delighted to discover a new poet to admire, asked for yet another. Softly Mr. Thane began reading a poem called "To His Coy Mistress" and dreamily she closed her eyes again.

> "'Had we but World enough, and Time,
> This coyness Lady were no crime.
> We would sit down, and think which way
> To walk, and pass our long Loves Day.'"

He went on, and Margaret felt almost as if she were floating, all buoyant and weightless, on a warm, welcoming lake, basking in his voice and nearness and her happiness in this magical day.

> "'But at my back I always hear
> Time's winged chariot hurrying near . . .'"

His hand, warm and strong, found hers as it rested in her lap and with a jolt of pleasure Margaret intertwined her fingers among his own. She kept her eyes closed, thrilling to the sensation of this unexpected—but not at all unwelcome—contact between them, and after a few giddy moments reminded herself to keep listening as he went on:

"'Now therefore, while the youthful hew
Sits on thy skin like morning dew,
And while thy willing Soul transpires
At every pore with instant Fires,
Now let us sport us while we may;
And now, like am'rous birds of prey,
Rather at once our Time devour,
Than languish in his slow-chapt pow'r.
Let us roll all our Strength, and all
Our sweetness, up into one Ball:
And tear our Pleasures with rough strife,
Through the Iron gates of Life.
Thus, though we cannot make our Sun
Stand still, yet we will make him run.'"

He had leaned closer to her and his warm breath
stirred the tendrils of her hair near her ear. Margaret
shivered, but not with cold. With pleasure.

Hot pleasure, melting her all over and making her
limbs feel gooey and soft and warm and quite marvelous. It was a wonder she didn't slide, limp and melty,
from her chair and dissolve into a puddle on the floor.

"I say, you're still here!"

It was Mr. Lawrence, bounding into the room accompanied by the merry gaggle of his dining companions.

Margaret opened her eyes and straightened in her
seat, reluctantly pulling her hand free from Mr. Thane's;
and Mr. Lawrence, coming near, announced:

"They've closed the taproom, and now they want
all the guests to leave for the night. We're going to the
Whittlesey theatre just round the corner—it's the late
performance of *Macbeth*. It's supposed to be a *ripping*
play and I've always wanted to see it. Care to join us?"

Margaret looked to Mr. Thane, and for the merest
second thought she saw impatience flickering in his

brown-green eyes. But she must have been mistaken, for in the very next moment he was smiling at her, his dark brows raised inquiringly. "Miss Allen? I defer to you."

"Oh, let's," she softly said to him. "The night is still young, and I'm not ready to go back to my inn."

So they got up and went with Mr. Lawrence and his lively companions to see Shakespeare's *Macbeth* in the little theatre-house. The actors threw themselves with gusto into their roles and Margaret watched, rapt, as the hideous tragedy unfolded, all the way to its bloody, gloomy end—and all because of Macbeth's dreadful fixed ambition, wanting something that he shouldn't have.

Afterwards as they all crowded together in the tiny lobby Mr. Lawrence declared:

"It was terribly sad, but restorative somehow, isn't it?"

"Yes," chimed in one of his new friends, "but I could still use a drink. There's the Twopenny Tavern next door. Who's with me?"

Agreement from the others was swift and enthusiastic. Margaret saw that Mr. Thane was looking at her inquiringly again, and this time she shook her head and stepped close to him.

"This time I think I'll say no," she said in a low voice. "I'm rather tired, and ready to go back to my inn now. If that's all right with you?"

"Of course."

They parted ways outside the theatre, and then it was just the two of them again, strolling arm-in-arm along the quiet, dark sidewalks which were illuminated at regular intervals by the street-lamps, looking so cozy and friendly against the heavy curtain of night.

Margaret gave a happy sigh. "*What* a marvelous day. And what a shame that all good things must come to an end."

"Must they?" responded Mr. Thane quietly as they paced along.

She quoted from that lovely Andrew Marvell poem: "'Had we but World enough, and Time . . .' It's the human condition, I fear. 'But at my back I always hear Time's winged chariot hurrying near . . .' There's never enough, is there?"

Instead of answering, he was silent for some while, and curiously Margaret glanced up at his profile, just then framed in the soft light of a street-lamp. His expression was oddly stony.

"What's the matter?" she asked. "What's wrong?"

"Nothing." He came to a halt, and Margaret could just see, down the street from where they now stood, the Woodhull Inn, all lit up with lights in the downstairs rooms and which made it look so home-like and inviting.

"Actually," he said, "there *is* something. I really don't want to take you back to your inn."

"You don't?" She cocked her head, half curious still, half puzzled by the serious tone in his voice. "What is it that you want?"

"Listen," he said. "Please." And he quoted from the Marvell poem again:

"'*Now therefore, while the youthful hew*
Sits on thy skin like morning dew,
And while thy willing Soul transpires
At every pore with instant Fires,
Now let us sport us while we may;
And now, like am'rous birds of prey,
Rather at once our Time devour,

Than languish in his slow-chapt pow'r.
Let us roll all our Strength, and all
Our sweetness, up into one Ball:
And tear our Pleasures with rough strife,
Through the Iron gates of Life.
Thus, though we cannot make our Sun
Stand still, yet we will make him run.'"

"I *am* listening," Margaret said. "It's a lovely poem, truly. But I'm ready to be at my inn, Mr. Thane. I hate to say goodnight, but I'll see you in the morning, and we'll have all day tomorrow to be together. With luck the weather will be—"

"Here's the thing," he interrupted, sounding quite urgent. "I love you, Miss Allen. I love you with all my heart and soul, like I've never loved another woman. I want to sweep you off to my room at *my* inn so that I can show you just how much. And—and I want to marry you. I know my family—the Penhallows—and of course my step-grandparents the Duke and Duchess of Egremont—will welcome you with open arms. You'd practically be a Penhallow! *Please* say yes."

Margaret could feel her mouth dropping open in astonishment and she took a step back, releasing his arm. There was a lot to dissect in what he'd just said, but she chose the salient point first. "You *love* me?"

"Yes. Very much. Truly. Madly. Utterly."

"But that's impossible! We only met yesterday. I mean—I like you too, Mr. Thane. I like you a great deal. But *love*?"

"It happens. You know it does."

"In stories it does, but I'm not so sure about in real life. At any rate, let's not get bogged down debating such a thing. Please, Mr. Thane, only consider how— how *rash* you sound. This isn't—this isn't moderate."

Even as she said this, Margaret had a vague, fleeting memory—or was it from a dream?—of Mr. Thane saying placidly, *Moderation is overrated.*

She gave her head a shake, dispersing the strange little recollection. "Please let's just go on as we've begun," she said earnestly. "We had a bad beginning yesterday, but today has been wonderful, and I have a feeling tomorrow will be even more so."

"It won't. It will be worse."

She stared up at him. "But why? And how could you even know that?"

He didn't reply for a few long seconds, his eyes little more than dark, unfathomable sockets in his face. "Are you sure you won't come back to my inn with me? I'm aching with desire for you."

At these raw words, simply spoken, Margaret felt a flame leap within her. It was pure, hot, delicious lust; lighting her up inside like a thousand candles sprung to life. She felt no shame at her response, but neither did she intend to act upon it. Quietly she said:

"I'm sure I won't go. My answer is—it *must* be—no. It's too soon, Mr. Thane, and only time will let us discover if what we've been feeling today is real, and lasting. But that will only matter if you also want something like that, and not—not a secretive, hasty little tumble among the sheets." She put a gentle hand on his arm, and was shaken, and hurt, when he jerked it away as if her touch had scalded him.

"I keep trying to tell you, Margaret, I don't *have* time."

His voice was harsher now, and she was more baffled than ever. Not bothering to chide him for—or even remark upon—his abrupt use of her Christian name, she said, "Whatever do you mean? Why don't you have time?" Suddenly she caught her breath as a terrible possibility occurred to her. "Oh, Mr. Thane, you're not—surely you're not dying."

"Would you come to my room if I said yes?"

"Don't tease me. Pray don't. *Are* you—ill?"

"Unfortunately, I'm healthy as a horse, and will probably live forever." He gave a short, sharp, bitter laugh.

"So what do you mean about not having time?"

"Well, I'd tell you, Margaret, but you'd only forget."

"Try me. I have a fairly good memory."

"It still wouldn't help. But do you know what *would*?"

"I'd like to know. I'd truly like to help you if I could, Mr. Thane."

He laughed again, just as bitterly. "Good, kind, sweet, clever, beautiful Margaret. I know you mean well, but you never, ever help me. Here's your chance, though—right here and right now. Come back to my room with me, and let me make love to you. I assure you, I'd feel a whole lot better. And you would too."

Margaret stared at him, frozen, feeling as if this whole day had been nothing more than a carefully constructed house of cards.

Which were collapsing all around her.

Which *had* collapsed around her.

All her happiness, all her hopes—*gone*.

"Please," said Mr. Thane. "I love you, Margaret."

She stood as straight and as tall as she could. "Stop saying that. It's obvious that you're trying to seduce me. And if you're trying to seduce someone, you don't love that person. You don't even *like* that person. Mr. Thane, you're despicable." She took a deep breath, and said:

"'He that has light within his own clear breast may sit in the center, and enjoy bright day: But he that hides a dark soul and foul thoughts benighted walks under the midday sun; Himself his own dungeon.'"

"Uh . . . Shakespeare?"

"John Milton. And it should also be obvious by now, but do erase from your mind all thoughts of taking my aunt and me along with you tomorrow. We'll find some other way of getting home. Goodbye, Mr. Thane."

Margaret turned on her heel and walked back to her inn, both anguished and angry, and vowing to never, ever think of the horrible, awful, terrible, conniving, deceitful Philip Thane ever again.

Chapter 11

"**Y**ou *love* me?"

Margaret stared up at him, wide-eyed, her exquisite face illumined in the nimbus of a nearby street-lamp as they stood together on the sidewalk, with her inn far too close for comfort. He was taking no chances this time. He *wasn't* going to devolve again as he had yesterday. He'd rehearsed this particular, crucial speech in his mind, over and over and over again, all day long.

And so, thankful that the street was at present deserted, he sank with faintly theatrical fluidity onto one knee, then reached into a pocket of his greatcoat and pulled out a small box. Surely on *this* momentous occasion a bit of sparkle couldn't hurt, in addition to the book of Marvell poems he'd given her earlier. With a little flourish he opened the lid and held out the box to her. Nestled on a bed of white satin was an enormous square-cut ruby surrounded by a glittering frame of tiny, perfect diamonds. He still didn't much care for rubies, but it was the largest, flashiest ring the jewelry store had.

"Yes, I do love you, dearest, darling Margaret. Please marry me, and you'll make me the happiest man in the world." *Get her to say yes to the old ball-and-chain first,* he reminded himself. *Stick to the script. Then, when she's agreed, it's on to the Apple Street Inn.*

"But this is all so impossible!" she exclaimed. "We only met yesterday. I mean—I like you too, Mr. Thane. I like you a great deal. But marriage? And *love*?"

"I can't explain it. I just know that it's happened. Quickly, thoroughly, and utterly. Cupid's arrow, swift and true. I want to marry you, as soon as possible, and introduce you to my family. They'll love you just as much as I do, I'm sure of it."

"That's very kind of you to say, but—"

"I mean it. Once we're wed we'll be the most marvelous couple in London—the toast of the town. You'll be more or less an Egremont by marriage, you know, and practically a Penhallow, too. They're leaders of the *haut ton*—preeminent in Society—and have been for a long, long time. We'll go everywhere—be seen everywhere, at all the best and most exclusive parties."

"You say it as if I would care about such things."

"I only meant to—"

"Sway me? My own family may not be titled, or aristocratic, or have come over with the Conqueror, but they're wonderful and I couldn't be more proud of them or to be merely an Allen of Oxford."

Philip saw with inexpressible dismay that Margaret's eyes were blazing and that she'd gone as white as snow. Somehow, in some way, he'd touched a nerve. Usually people were instantly impressed when they heard about his family connections. Why, the loans he'd secured, the invitations he'd received, the country-house doors thrown open, the *bedroom* doors thrown open—all were innumerable. But with Margaret, instead of opening doors, they had only slammed shut.

Good Lord, was it all going bad *again*? For a brief moment he had an impulse to go to the nearest bridge and fling himself over it. *Get a grip, man,* he told himself urgently, even desperately. *Keep on talking about love, and whatever you do, don't say anything just yet about going back to the inn together.* Quickly he said, ignoring the fact that his knee, the one resting on the chilly sidewalk, had gone rather numb:

"What matters is that I love you, and that we belong together. Forever. You and I, dearest Margaret. What does family matter? What matters is *us,* and how we feel about each other. How much we enjoy each other. Wasn't today marvelous? Didn't we have such wonderful conversations? That's what each and every day could be like for us, over and over again."

Unfortunately, Margaret's eyes had *not* stopped blazing, nor had rosy color returned to her cheeks. Panic set in. No, no, no, no, *no.* He'd worked so hard all day long—*again*—being nice and charming and respectful and asking questions and looking so attentive and interested. It was *exhausting,* damn it! He opened his mouth to start talking again about love, sweet love, precious love, overpowering love, but, to his horror, the fatal words just came out, *again*:

"Won't you come back to my inn with me?"

There was a pause.

Then she said, her voice so frigid that he could practically feel his blood turning to ice:

"Get up. Get up and put that stupid ring away." From her reticule she wrenched out the Marvell book and thrust it at him. "'To My Coy Mistress,' eh? 'Had we but World enough, and Time . . .' Ha! What a charming hint, sir, and how incredibly foolish of me not to realize it earlier."

He stood up, feeling incredibly foolish himself. He

didn't want to take the book back, but he did, sheepishly, and slid it, and the ring-box, back into his greatcoat pocket, drooping with the most awful chagrin, hardly able to believe he'd somehow mucked things up *again*. What had happened to him and his time-honored powers of persuasion?

It might, he thought bitterly, have something to do with the word "time." No longer his friend, time had become not just his enemy, but his *nemesis*. Two more lines from "To My Coy Mistress" came back to him, like a dreadful tolling bell, clanging darkly in his brain: *But at my back I always hear . . . Time's winged chariot hurrying near . . .*

"I suppose I ought to thank you for the luncheon today," Margaret went on, sounding just as bitter as he felt. "And for the stroll around town, and the marzipan, and the book. But I'm not going to. It's obvious that you're trying to seduce me. And if you're trying to seduce someone, you don't love that person. You don't even *like* that person. Mr. Thane, you're despicable." For a few moments, she looked, suddenly, rather puzzled, as if recalling something that she couldn't quite put her finger on, and then she shook her head, took a deep breath, and said in that same icy, bitter voice:

"'He that has light within his own clear breast may sit in the center, and enjoy bright day: But he that hides a dark soul and foul thoughts benighted walks under the midday sun; Himself his own dungeon.'"

"John Milton," he said hoarsely, shocked at how much he sounded like a frog, croaking away.

"That's right. And it should be obvious by now, but do erase from your mind all thoughts of taking my aunt and me along with you tomorrow. We'll find some other way of getting home. Oh, and as it should also be obvious to you, Mr. Thane, I never, ever want to see you again. Goodbye."

Margaret turned on her heel and walked back to her inn, and he waited only long enough to see her safely inside before trudging back to his own inn, where it seemed to take forever for him to plod up the stairs and into his room, where he flopped onto his bed, rejected, dejected, and entirely, thoroughly, totally, achingly, miserably alone.

Warm and snug in her thick wool pelisse and cozy hat, Margaret looked around from her place near the festive bunting-bedecked platform with pleasure. It was a glorious morning, bright and cold and practically bursting with good cheer. Plough Day! Such a delightful scene lay all about: how much fun everyone was having, herself included. Wasn't she just so lucky to be here?

Yes, lucky indeed, as yesterday it had seemed there was a good chance she'd never get to Whittlesey in time. So why did she also have, tickling at the edges of her awareness, a bizarre feeling of foreboding?

Could it be because she'd had some unsettling dreams last night, most of them involving Mr. Thane? And wasn't Mr. Lawrence in one of them too, quoting lines from *Macbeth*? She seemed to remember him chanting, *Double, double toil and trouble, fire burn and caldron bubble. Time doth spin round and round, to each other you are bound. Double, double toil and trouble, fire burn and caldron bubble. Thwart it with your true love's kiss, thus the charm brings sweetest bliss.*

Which was even stranger, because that wasn't how the Song of the Witches in *Macbeth* really went.

Of course, in dreams things often got all curiously twisted around.

She sent a faintly uneasy glance to Mr. Lawrence next to her, but he was busy jotting down his impressions in his notebook. Suddenly she spotted a tall broad-shouldered figure coming toward the platform and, doing her best to ignore the ominous sensation tugging at her as if with icy fingers, she called out:

"Mr. Thane! Good morning!"

He came near and she noticed with surprise how slowly he was walking, and also that his expression was very different from what it had been when he'd dropped them off at the Woodhull Inn. Then he had been annoyingly suave and sardonic, and openly bitter about having to get up early for the Plough Day ceremony. This morning, however, he looked pale and haggard and exhausted, he hadn't shaved, and his eyes looked positively haunted. Was it *that* hard for him to get out of bed at the crack of dawn?

"Good morning," Margaret repeated, cautiously this time.

"Is it?"

"Are you all right, Mr. Thane?"

He didn't answer, only looked at her with such melancholy and longing—even with despair—that Margaret felt quite baffled. What had happened to change him so dramatically from yesterday to today? Was he ill? Had he been harmed in some way?

She repeated her question, but he still made no reply. She glanced again at Mr. Lawrence, who had lifted his head from his notebook and was staring at Mr. Thane with his gingery eyebrows raised high in puzzlement. Gently she said to Mr. Thane:

"It's just about time for your speech, I believe."

He gave the slightest of shrugs. Then, slowly, as if he was exhausted beyond words, he turned around and began trudging away.

"What was that all about, do you suppose?" asked Mr. Lawrence.

"I have no idea."

"These people from great families," he remarked. "Idiosyncratic, aren't they?"

"I daresay they are." Margaret was watching Mr. Thane's tall figure making its slow way among the crowd, and saw, also, a pair of pretty young women who bridled coyly at his approach, though he didn't seem to notice and simply trudged past them—to their obvious regret.

"I'm worried about him," Margaret said to Mr. Lawrence.

"Why? Because he walked right by two ladies who were dying to meet him?" Mr. Lawrence's voice was wistful. "How *does* he do it? Attract women to him like that?"

Margaret only shrugged, not being particularly interested in the subject, and Mr. Lawrence went on:

"I wonder where he's going. Do you think he's going back to his inn, and getting ready to leave town? I *was* hoping to ask if I—and you and your aunt, of course—could join him. There aren't any seats on the stage for several days."

"Yes, I inquired about that too. I'd prefer to leave also. But Mr. Thane doesn't look like he's in any shape to travel. Maybe he needs to go back to bed, or even see a doctor. Let's go talk to him."

"You're being awfully nice for a lady who was so disrespected yesterday," commented Mr. Lawrence. "Mr. Thane pretty much stared at you the whole way here. A bit caddish, if you ask me."

As someone who could never walk past a person in need, or a dog or a cat or a horse in trouble, without intervening, Margaret replied firmly:

"That was yesterday and today is different. Mr. Thane doesn't look at all well. Can you keep an eye on which way he's going? I'll be right back."

Quickly she went to the platform to inform the various town dignitaries clustering there that their guest of honor had unexpectedly been called away, after which she joined Mr. Lawrence again and together they hurried after Mr. Thane. She caught a glimpse of the fabled Straw Bear—a cylindrical figure all covered in sheaves of hay, from its head down to its ankles—waiting to burst upon the scene, and was sorry not to see more of the ceremony, but Mr. Thane's situation did seem urgent.

They caught up to him just outside a little restaurant called the Cup and Saucer.

"I say, Mr. Thane, what's the matter?" said Mr. Lawrence.

"Nothing."

"Oh? If that's the case, then, we were wondering if we might join you on your way out of town. If it doesn't inconvenience you, of course."

"I'm not going anywhere."

"The way you talked about Whittlesey yesterday on our way here," Mr. Lawrence said, surprised, "I would have thought you'd be champing at the bit to leave."

"Go on and take my barouche," responded Mr. Thane listlessly. "You're welcome to it."

Mr. Lawrence brightened. "Really, sir? That's very generous of you."

"On the contrary. It won't be any use. About half an hour from here, just when you've passed through a tiny village called Oundle, you'll drive right into a snowstorm. Also, your way will be blocked by a big fallen tree, and even if you *could* clear the road, Margaret would dissuade you from making the horses *or* the coachman travel under such conditions."

These words from Mr. Thane emerged with slow, desolate conviction, as if dragged from him, and Margaret exchanged a baffled look with Mr. Lawrence—partly because what Mr. Thane said made no sense, and partly because she seemed to have a vague but unnerving feeling that he was right. She gathered herself, however, and soothingly said to Mr. Thane:

"Let's not worry about traveling today. Would you consider seeing a doctor?"

"What for?"

"For—for whatever's ailing you."

"A doctor can't help me." He spoke with the same sluggish conviction, and Margaret was more worried than ever.

"Are you hungry, Mr. Thane? This restaurant looks nice. Why don't we go inside and get you something to eat?"

"I'm not hungry. But *you* go. Despite the unpromising look of the place, you'll enjoy the pastry platter. The muffins especially."

Margaret stared. How did he know that she loved pastries, and muffins in particular?

Well, many people did, so that could simply have been a casual sort of guess.

But that still didn't explain his oddly specific prediction about what would lie ahead for them in Oundle if they left Whittlesey.

And he looked so . . . haunted, quite like one would imagine a man who had seen a ghost.

Was it possible that there was something seriously

wrong with Mr. Thane? In other words, that he might be unbalanced? Or . . . *mad*? He hadn't seemed so yesterday—he had been annoying, but very much in control of himself. However, the Mr. Thane of today was so strikingly different.

"Let us take you to a doctor," she said. "There must be an infirmary somewhere here in town."

"There is, but I'm not going to let that quack look me over again."

"Again?"

"That's right. Again. He suggested I go see a practitioner in Peterborough or Cambridge, which seemed like a good idea at the time, but it didn't work out. I should have known."

"When exactly did you see this doctor?"

Mr. Thane shrugged, looking hopeless, and doggedly Margaret persisted:

"And what do you mean, it didn't work out?"

"Because there were the usual snowstorms and fallen trees on the way to Peterborough *and* Cambridge. Just like the one near Oundle."

"I say, sir, that seems highly unlikely," said Mr. Lawrence.

"It may seem unlikely, but that's what happened to me."

Oh dear, oh *dear,* Margaret thought anxiously. This was all deeply troubling. Mr. Thane had somehow found the time to seek out a local doctor yesterday evening *or* very, very early this morning? And if so, what complaint had he presented? What had the doctor told him that would require a consultation with other practitioners? Whom of course Mr. Thane couldn't have tried to go see between late yesterday and early today. Altogether it sounded serious.

"Let's go someplace where it's warm," she urged

him. "And perhaps there's another doctor in Whittlesey with whom you can speak."

"It doesn't matter if there is. It won't help. Nobody can help me."

"Oh, please don't give up hope," she said earnestly, still mystified but all at once feeling very sorry for him. Here was a man in the prime of his life, intelligent, handsome, well-spoken, vigorous, and graceful—and yet something was so wrong with him. (Beyond the fact that he seemed to be an incorrigible, sardonic, jaded rakehell, if yesterday's experience was anything to judge by.) She added:

"There's *always* hope. Truly."

"For you, maybe, but not for me." He nodded at them, once, as if it took a great deal of effort to do it, and then he began plodding away.

"Wait," Margaret said. "Where are you going?"

"I'm going back to my inn."

"We'll go with you."

"We will?" said Mr. Lawrence.

"Yes," answered Margaret firmly. She would tuck Mr. Thane into bed herself if she had to, and try to persuade him to drink a cup of tea or some nice hot soup. Anything to help him feel even just a tiny bit better.

"No, you won't," said Mr. Thane, stopping and slowly turning to face them. "You," he went on, addressing Mr. Lawrence, "you go on and try to chat up the ladies you were eyeballing at the ceremony. Though you won't have much luck, because you're gawky, awkward, maladroit, doltish, inane, and cloddish." Mr. Thane turned his mordant gaze to Margaret and went on:

"And *you* go back and have fun talking to all the rustics, provincials, hobnails, yokels, chawbacons, hicks, bumpkins, and loobies about the stupid Straw Bear. Oh, and also the hawbucks, joskins, and lump-kins. For your foolish, insignificant, trivial, pointless little book that will never be published. And do send my regards to your charming bluestocking aunt, who keeps reminding me just how valuable a thesaurus can be."

Sympathy for Mr. Thane vanished, and Margaret felt her mouth hardening into a thin bloodless line of anger and contempt. How *dare* he talk like this? Poor Mr. Lawrence looked as if he might burst into tears. And she couldn't bear the sarcasm in his voice when he mentioned Aunt Seraphina. "You're despicable," she said icily.

He looked down at her, his expression remote, his brown-green eyes lackluster. "You're repeating your-self. A bad habit for a writer, you know." He drew a long, deep breath and continued:

> "'*Tomorrow, and tomorrow, and tomorrow,*
> *Creeps in this petty pace from day to day,*
> *To the last syllable of recorded time;*
> *And all our yesterdays have lighted fools*
> *The way to dusty death. Out, out, brief candle!*
> *Life's but a walking shadow, a poor player,*
> *That struts and frets his hour upon the stage,*
> *And then is heard no more. It is a tale*
> *Told by an idiot, full of sound and fury,*
> *Signifying nothing.*'"

He turned away again, and this time Margaret made no attempt to stop him or to follow him, nor did Mr. Lawrence, who asked, after a minute or two when he had regained his composure:

"What was *that* from? It sounded like Shakespeare."

"It was. From *Macbeth*," she replied. *Macbeth* again! A horrid shiver danced up and down her spine, and not from the cold.

"That's funny—the theatre here in town is putting that on," remarked Mr. Lawrence. "I saw the marquee when we drove past it yesterday. Do you think Mr. Thane went and saw it last night? It's supposed to be a *ripping* play and I've always wanted to see it. At any rate, what does the quote mean?"

"Macbeth, the protagonist—or antagonist, actually— says it when all his ambitious plans start crashing down on him, and life comes to seem pointless and crushingly repetitive."

"Oh. Quite the odd thing for Mr. Thane to say, isn't it? And blast it, that 'tomorrow and tomorrow' bit sounds as if he really plans on staying here for a while," Mr. Lawrence said, disappointed. "Unless you think we *could* take his barouche?"

"I don't think we can take anything he says seriously," responded Margaret. She was fuming all over again. "That arrogant, insufferable man. I'm going back to the town square now. Do you want to come with me?"

"Yes, thanks. I'm going to try to get an interview with the mayor," he told her, and together they made their way back to the Plough Day celebration. It wasn't till Margaret's temper finally cooled that she suddenly wondered, with a frisson of uneasy surprise, how Mr. Thane knew about the book she was writing.

How very, very odd.

But what was even *more* odd was that somehow she wasn't nearly as surprised as she should have been.

Someone was knocking on a door.

Philip's eyes flew open. He stared with instant and

total comprehension at the familiar ceiling above
him, filled with so much dread and despair that he
might as well have been gazing up at the Sword of
Damocles, suspended overhead by the thinnest of
threads. In a low, ragged voice he muttered under
his breath:

"Wake up, sir."

A few moments later came the voice from outside
the room:

"Wake up, sir."

Philip braced himself, waiting.

Knock knock knock.

Then the voice again, and Philip mouthed the
words along with it:

"Mr. Thane, you asked to be awakened in time for
the ceremony. It's Plough Day, sir."

There was a pause.

Philip waited. Then here it came:

Knock knock knock.

It was his well-worn cue. "For the thousandth
time, I'm *awake*, damn your hide," he said loudly,
and waited. Then he mouthed the words as they were
spoken aloud outside the room:

"Very well, sir."

After that, there was silence once more.

Philip rolled onto his side and looked blearily
toward the window. If he got up to go glance outside,
he was going to see a clear, bright day, with a sky of
a soft cloudless blue. On the ground would be scattered splotches of gray slush. And he would see hordes
of people walking in the same direction—toward the
center of the town, all eager to partake of the Plough
Day fun.

Fun.

Ha!

It was a joke, but not a particularly funny one.

So if he got up and went to the window, just to confirm what he already knew he'd see, and after that if he were to get dressed and go downstairs, he'd have to face the horribly cheerful proprietor Mr. Lancross, and when that miserable ordeal was over, if he went outside and to the town square, he'd also have to deal with that couple asking for donations to the convalescent home *and* with Matron and her penchant for dredging up old terrible memories.

After he escaped their clutches, he would go toward the bunting-bedecked platform, like a bee inexorably drawn toward honey, and soon he would hear that feminine, pleasantly husky voice hailing him through the crowd:

Mr. Thane! Good morning!

And he would be forced to behold Margaret Allen, ravishing in her dark green pelisse and fashionable hat in the exact same shade of green and embellished with a charming spray of pink artificial roses that complemented her golden-brown hair quite beautifully.

Ravishing, fascinating, brainy, witty, kind, tenderhearted . . . and unattainable.

She would speak to him as one might politely address the merest acquaintance. And maybe she'd smile that glorious radiant smile of hers, which lit her up like a thousand suns, but it wasn't because she felt anything in particular for *him*.

Because for all she knew, she had only met him the day before.

And he was nothing more to her than some annoying, insignificant fellow who had happened to come along at just the right moment to offer her and her companions a ride, in a barouche which—had she but

known it for longer than a day—didn't even belong
to him.

Philip rolled onto his back again, staring sightlessly
up at the ceiling.

And she would be right.

He *was* nothing more than an annoying, insignificant fellow.

He owned no barouche, or a vehicle of any sort,
nor horses; neither did he have a home of his own, or
any kind of honorable profession.

What he *did* have were debts. So many of them, and
for so long. He didn't even know the total amount,
they were so numerous.

Into his mind, like a venomous ghost come to
haunt him, rose the quote from *Macbeth* which he
had hurled at Margaret.

> *Tomorrow, and tomorrow, and tomorrow,*
> *Creeps in this petty pace from day to day,*
> *To the last syllable of recorded time;*
> *And all our yesterdays have lighted fools*
> *The way to dusty death. Out, out, brief candle!*
> *Life's but a walking shadow, a poor player,*
> *That struts and frets his hour upon the stage,*
> *And then is heard no more. It is a tale*
> *Told by an idiot, full of sound and fury,*
> *Signifying nothing.*

How handy to have seen the play here in Whittlesey, in order to refresh his memory. He had been
made to study it while at Eton—with little success.
He hadn't done much studying there at all, in fact.

What a nightmare it had been: he a scrawny,
shocked, grieving lad, without a father but with a
new and illustrious family that, no matter how kind

and well-meaning, couldn't replace all that he had lost. And *he* merely the son of an obscure physician in some little-known seaside town to the north.

Some of the other boys had been less than kind, in the way that the powerful and the cruel will find the weak to hurt and rule over them. So he had, over time, as slowly he grew tall and strong, responded by reshaping himself with a hard impenetrable shell of breezy, uncaring braggadocio, suspiciously ignoring any friendly overtures, happily walking away from the place when he was ejected for a long history of pranks, threats, fights, and tawdry behavior involving some local ladies of the night *and* two of the dean's married daughters. If he had a tenner for every time he'd put frogs in other people's beds, he might actually have left Eton without debts.

An idiot, full of sound and fury, signifying nothing.

Yes: that was himself, and an all too accurate description.

A rake, a gambler, a wastrel.

No wonder old Henrietta Penhallow had looked at him with such skepticism and disdain.

He *was* a failure.

He had done nothing of real value in his life; had achieved nothing.

He was a nothing.

Why on earth had he thought he could entice the amazing, the wonderful, the utterly unique Margaret Allen into his bed?

How many times had they begun the day quite pleasantly, traveling from and back to Whittlesey, having luncheon together, walking around town, talking and joking and laughing and sharing a box of marzipan, but it always, somehow, ending so badly?

Over and over and over again.

He hadn't even managed to kiss her.

Feeling more and more desperate, he had reverted to his usual strategy of buying lavish gifts for a prospective lady-love. Flowers. Jewelry. Perfume. A whole *stack* of books. A giant box of marzipan so cumbersome that it obscured his view and he'd tripped, fallen, and spewed candy all over the sidewalk and into the gutter and street. (Naturally, somehow the irrepressible young Thomas Abernathy had appeared, grabbed up great handfuls of the stuff, and run off laughing merrily.)

Margaret had accepted nothing.

Still, he'd kept trying.

And trying.

And *trying*.

One day, with a kind of frenzied despair, he had even bought Margaret a *pony*. (He'd never forget the incredulous look she'd given him, after which she had taken the pony's reins and returned it to its owner.)

And every day ended the same way.

With Margaret storming away and whisking herself inside her inn.

"Despicable"—that was what she had called him, repeatedly, and that was what he was.

Philip groaned out loud and pulled the covers over his head, hoping against hope to be able to fall asleep again and so into unconsciousness.

He lay there for some time.

He tried counting sheep, but somehow the sheep kept turning into Straw Bears, who couldn't leap over the stile, but had to lumber up and over them, shedding bits of straw as they went.

Philip flopped from one side to the other, finally ending up in a messy, sweaty tangle of bedclothes.

At last he gave up and flung the covers off, letting them slither away from him onto the floor.

He needed a bath. And a shave.

Was he going to ring for hot water?

Unlikely.

He didn't even have the energy to get out of bed.

And without a fire, the room was miserably cold. God *damn* it, he hated winter.

He lay there shivering for a while, with goose-bumps running rampant along his arms and legs.

When at length his teeth started chattering, he leaned over the side of the bed and slowly dragged the bedclothes back up and over him, in a haphazard tumble which left one of his bare feet exposed to the cold.

It got colder, and colder, and colder.

After a while he listlessly brought his foot under the bedclothes.

Then he covered his head again, and closed his eyes, and drew a long shuddering breath. "Happy Plough Day," he muttered out loud and to no one. "Again."

As he did, a cry seemed to echo throughout his empty soul.

Why me?

There was a long, long silence.

Finally, there seemed to come a voice, distant, aloof, cool and amused. It almost sounded like Henri-etta Penhallow. Or God? Perhaps she *was* God. With what he was going through, anything was possible. The voice answered:

Why not you?

Philip groaned out loud again. He jammed the covers more tightly about his head, and waited for the voice to say something else.

Anything else.

A hint, a clue, a suggestion, or an order telling him what to do. He'd even be happy if a bolt of lightning seared through the roof and blasted him into cinders.

But there was only silence—the coldest, loneliest, most awful and implacable silence he had ever heard.

Chapter 12

The Plough Day ceremony was over. Margaret had had a marvelous time listening to the speeches and the music, seeing the fabled Straw Bear arrive to the acclaim of the crowd, and also talking to various townsfolk about this fascinating old agricultural tradition.

It *was* rather strange, though, that Mr. Thane hadn't shown up to deliver his speech.

Or was it?

Hadn't she been expecting it, really?

On the other hand, although yesterday on the ride here he had made his lack of enthusiasm clear, still he had given no indication that he was going to abandon ship.

Margaret found herself wondering if Mr. Thane was even in Whittlesey anymore. Maybe he'd gotten up early, at the first hint of dawn, had the horses hitched to his barouche, and was now somewhere on the road to . . . wherever it was that he had come from.

She was surprised to notice that she felt a pang of disappointment at the idea.

After which she felt very annoyed with herself.

Why should she care if she never saw Mr. Thane again?

He was—to quote Aunt Seraphina—brazen, brash, impertinent, impudent, brassy, shameless, lewd, lecherous, lubricous, satiric, dissolute, and dissipated.

Not a personality she could like, respect, or admire.

Still, he *was* dreadfully good-looking.

He had, she now recalled, the most delicious brown-green eyes, sparkling with intelligence and framed by gorgeous dark lashes. And he had equally gorgeous hair, brown with intriguing hints of chestnut, which curled just a little at the ends, in a way that one longed to caress and wind sensuously around one's finger. His mouth was very nice, too, beautifully molded and enticing, and he looked like just the sort of man who knew what to do with it. Oh, and also he had a long muscular body. She was sure he had lovely muscles in his arms and legs, and a hard flat stomach, and . . .

"I say, Miss Allen, what now?"

Margaret snapped out of her gauzy daydream. It was Mr. Lawrence's voice from right next to her. She blinked and gave him a mortified smile. Inside herself she was thinking mournfully: *What sort of shallow person fantasizes about a rake with an unappealing personality?* Didn't that make *her* brassy, shameless, lewd, and so on?

"I beg your pardon, Mr. Lawrence. My thoughts were . . . elsewhere. What did you say?"

"I was wondering about Mr. Thane. I was hoping to ask him if he was planning on leaving today, and if so, if we could join him. There's talk of a snowstorm coming in and there aren't any seats on the stage for several days."

Margaret nodded, glad to have her mind diverted to something less controversial and more practical. "Yes, I inquired about that too. I'd prefer to leave as well, if we can. Do you have any idea where Mr. Thane is?"

"No, but I'm guessing he overslept. Remember how he reacted yesterday when you told him the ceremony starts just after sunrise? He looks like a chap who doesn't ordinarily get out of bed before noon. One of those *haut ton* London types, I daresay. I mean— you saw his boots, and that greatcoat of his. All those capes." Mr. Lawrence spoke with wistful admiration.

Margaret said, "Shall we go to the Apple Street Inn and see if he's still there?"

"Yes, but later? I'm trying to get an interview with the mayor."

"That's all right. I'll go on ahead."

"Are you sure, Miss Allen?"

"Yes indeed. Good luck getting your interview." Margaret watched as Mr. Lawrence bounded toward the platform where the town dignitaries still clustered, then began walking toward Apple Street, soon coming in view of Mr. Thane's inn, a large, luxurious-looking hostelry with a wide front portico and a tall six-paneled door painted a cheerful red. She went inside, and in the foyer she glimpsed a spacious common-room, where a crowd of people was gathered about a big round table.

Curious, she went closer and saw that Mr. Thane was sitting at the table with his back to her. He was wearing—she squinted in surprise—what looked like a dashing black silk dressing-gown. His glossy brown hair was disordered and she could see, by tilting her head to peer beneath the table, that Mr. Thane had on elegant black velvet house-slippers, embroidered all over with green vines and leaves.

She could feel her brow wrinkling in astonishment.

Informality was one thing, showing up in an inn's public common-room dressed for the privacy of a bedchamber was another.

What was Mr. Thane thinking?

And what was *she* thinking—speaking of bed-chambers—to suddenly be imagining him taking off his dressing-gown, revealing that underneath he had . . . nothing on?

Just then, he said, in a voice of casual indifference:

"Four of hearts."

From the people gathered around him rose a murmur of amazement and appreciation, and Margaret saw that Mr. Thane sat opposite another man who had a deck of cards in his hands. This man also looked amazed; he turned the topmost card out for everyone to see.

It was the four of hearts.

Money was exchanged, with a lot of bank-notes placed atop the heaping pile in front of Mr. Thane.

"Do it again, sir," someone around the table urged, and the man sitting opposite Mr. Thane held up the deck of cards to him, showing only the back.

Without hesitation Mr. Thane said:

"Ace of spades."

The man flipped over the topmost card and displayed it to his left and right.

It was the ace of spades.

Another awed murmur arose, along with some scattered applause. More money was exchanged; more was added to Mr. Thane's pile. He reached for something, and Margaret saw that it was a bottle of expensive brandy. He brought it to his lips and drank deeply.

Goodness gracious, she thought. Drinking like a fish so early in the morning?

"Again," somebody else said, and seven times more he identified the cards before they were revealed for all to see. His money-pile grew taller.

"Are you a magician, sir?" asked one of the bystanders.

"Or are the two of you accomplices?" asked someone else, sounding skeptical.

The man opposite Mr. Thane declared, "Never seen the gentleman before in my life. Here. *You* hold the deck, and try for yourself."

So the other man did, with the same results.

Each and every time Mr. Thane without hesitation, in an indifferent monotone, announced the correct cards.

"How *do* you do it, sir?" another person asked him.

"I'm just lucky, I suppose." He took another long swallow of brandy.

"Can you do any other tricks?" somebody asked.

"I'll be walking on water after luncheon."

"No, really, what else can you do? Can you find my uncle Will's watch? We think he might've buried it in the garden before he passed."

"Well, if you offer me a treat, I'll sit up and bark like a dog."

Someone else said: "If you're so clever, my good fellow, tell me what I'm thinking right now."

Mr. Thane slowly swiveled his head. "You're thinking that you don't want your wife to know you're having an affair with her cousin who works in a chemist shop in Bath. Also, you worry that your undergarments have gotten shabby and you hope to replace them with something nicer before your next trip to Bath. And you're sorry you ate the fish stew last night, because it didn't agree with you."

There was a collective indrawn breath among the spectators, the man whom Mr. Thane had just addressed turned a brilliant crimson and hurried away, and some people applauded again. Unmoved, Mr. Thane only took another drink of brandy.

Margaret went closer, coming around the curve

of the table so that she could face him directly. And when she did, even though she had already been taken aback by his unconventional attire, still she could feel her jaw dropping in shock.

Gone was the suave, charming, devil-may-care rake from yesterday who had leaned against his barouche with casual grace, expecting to share its capacious interior with herself and herself alone.

In his place was a deathly pale, haggard, unshaven man with bloodshot, haunted eyes, his hair all tumbled and his black robe carelessly open to reveal (she couldn't help but notice) a hard-planed chest.

"Mr. Thane," she said, cautiously.

He looked up at her. "Hullo." His voice was cool and indifferent.

"You missed your speech."

"I didn't miss it at all. That's wordplay, in case you weren't aware."

She ignored the jibe. "But isn't that why you came to Whittlesey—to give a speech?"

"Oh, I've already given it. Loads of times." He gestured vaguely with the bottle, waggling it at the other people still around the table. "Do you know, *vous les gens stupides,* I'm now finding your presence *très ennuyant.* Can't you see this lovely lady is dying for an intimate *tête-à-tête* with me?"

They all moved away—with some people looking more offended by the insult than others—and with the toe of his slippered foot Mr. Thane casually pushed back a now-empty chair next to him.

Margaret sat down in it, aware, to her intense irritation, that she had to make a concerted effort to keep her eyes on his face and not on his bare chest. "What do you mean, you've already given your speech multiple times?"

"You wouldn't believe me if I told you." He held out the bottle, waggling it invitingly. "Drink?"

She shook her head. "No, thank you. So go ahead and tell me."

"I already have. And you never, ever believe me. So I stopped trying."

"You haven't told me. In case you aren't aware, you and I only met yesterday."

"So you say. But the truth is that you and I have a long, long history together."

Baffled, Margaret stared hard at him. He spoke in a reasonable tone, but the things he was saying were impossible. Doggedly she asked, "How did you know about that man's affair? And those other—ah—items?"

"Oh, he told me."

"When?"

Mr. Thane shrugged. "The other evening."

"*What* other evening? You've only been here since last night."

"I keep trying to explain it to you, but it's no use. You keep forgetting. In any event, he told me one evening when he'd had too much to drink."

"Where were you when he told you? What other city were you in?"

"We were here. In this common-room."

Impossible. She moved on, frustrated. "And what about that card trick of yours? How did you do it?"

"It's not a trick."

"Then how?"

"Let us say, it's the outcome of repeated observation."

Margaret leaned back in her chair, more baffled than ever. What he was saying made no sense at all. Was he playing her for a fool? Or was he diabolically clever? Or . . . worse . . . mad?

One thing *was* for sure: he didn't look at all well.

She abandoned the idea of asking if he was planning on leaving Whittlesey today, or anytime soon.

His appearance, his behavior, his overall attitude was very concerning.

So Margaret, who could never walk past a person in need, or a dog or a cat or a horse in trouble, without intervening, said gently:

"Mr. Thane, would you consider seeing a doctor?"

"I don't need your help."

"Perhaps you need a doctor's help."

"Nobody can help me." He drank some more brandy. "Why are you here, anyway? Did you miss me? Do you want to go upstairs and show me how much?"

She felt her sympathy waning. "No, I don't."

"Then go away."

"I'd like to help you."

"So come upstairs with me. My word, but you're dimwitted today."

She gritted her teeth. "I don't care to help you that way."

"Then you're of no use to me at all." Dismissively he waved the bottle at her. "Get out. Go commune with that stupid Straw Bear."

With careful deliberation Margaret ungritted her teeth and got up.

"Wait," he said.

"What is it?" she said frostily.

With his free hand he grabbed up a big fistful of bank-notes. "Do you want some money? I've got plenty."

"No, thank you. If you're looking to give your hard-earned cash away, the local convalescent home is soliciting donations not far from the town square."

"Why would I want to do that? I thought maybe

you'd like some flowers, or jewelry, or a damned pony."

"Good day, Mr. Thane," she said, even more frostily, and walked away, disliking both him and the fact that she was, it seemed, trapped here in Whittlesey for the time being. It was a very nice town, but she really, really wanted to get home.

It was odd, but somehow she wasn't the least bit surprised that her appeal to Mr. Thane had failed.

In fact, it felt surprisingly familiar.

Philip walked with long strides among the crowd toward the bunting-bedecked platform. The cheerful, lively sounds of the pipe and drum seemed to actually hurt his ears, and he couldn't bear to see the people around him having so much fun.

Why should they be having fun and not him?

Fools.

Damn them all, each and every one.

Soon he heard the familiar call in that feminine, pleasantly husky voice:

"Mr. Thane! Good morning!"

He loped to where Margaret stood, as ravishing and as unattainable as ever. Next to her, of course, stood Mr. Lawrence, scribbling away in his notebook as usual.

"Good morning," she repeated. "Happy Plough Day."

"Ha."

"I beg your pardon?"

"It's *never* a happy Plough Day."

Her smile dimmed. "Is something wrong?"

"Why would there be?"

"It's just that you—well, you look . . ."

"Incredibly handsome? I know."

Her lips thinned. "I was going to say that you look a trifle unwell."

"Quite the personal remark, isn't it, Margaret darling? I, for example, would never dream of saying that you look vacuous and stupid."

Philip watched with cynical amusement as her magnificent blue eyes flashed, and also he saw that Mr. Lawrence was staring at him openmouthed. "And you," he said to him, "look like a fish caught on a string. Try *that* expression on the ladies, old chap. I'm sure they'll run to you in slavering adoration."

"Why, you rude, despicable man," said Margaret icily. "How *dare* you."

He shrugged. "One should live dangerously, don't you think?"

No sooner had he said this than the merry sounds of the pipe and drum fell away, and the crowd fell silent too, turning as one toward the platform in joyful expectancy.

"I believe," Margaret said in the same cold voice, "that's your cue."

Philip sketched her a mocking little bow, then went up the steps of the platform, introducing himself to the various town dignitaries clustering there, one of whom gestured him toward the front.

He walked to the railing, swept his eyes over the crowd, and pulled a bottle of brandy from his great-coat pocket. He uncorked it and had a big drink. "This," he said in a clear, carrying voice, "is a joke. *You* are a joke—all of you. What normal human being gets excited about an event called Plough Day? Isn't that the stupidest thing you've ever heard of? And yet here you all are at the crack of dawn, freezing to death, milling about like the silly gudgeons you are, and waiting for some sapskull dressed up to look like a bear covered in straw. And you do this *every damned year*. Or should I say, every damned *day*. It's pathetic."

He paused, looking around at the sea of stunned, dismayed, angry faces, and waggled the brandy bottle at them, after which he had another long drink. "The truth hurts, doesn't it, *vous les gens stupides*?" With an exaggerated, theatrical flourish he gestured with the bottle toward the far edge of the crowd. "Oh, I see your precious Straw Bear has arrived. Well, I certainly hope you've enjoyed listening to my speech as much as I've enjoyed giving it. Have a nice day."

There was a brief, ghastly, amusing silence, and then the Straw Bear lumbered forward, the pipe and drum resumed, sounding hilariously tentative, and some people began to move and sway a bit, but also rather tentatively. Philip noticed that quite a few audience members had turned their backs to him. Also hilarious!

He strolled down the steps of the platform and to where Margaret and Mr. Lawrence stood. They, too, looked stunned and dismayed. Here again, yet more amusing hilarity. He said to Mr. Lawrence, whose mouth hung open even more widely than before:

"I do hope you wrote all that down for your tiny little newspaper, so that you can write a meaningless little story that nobody will read."

Then he looked at Margaret. In a sweet voice meant to jeeringly imitate her, he repeated her comment from the journey here:

"'The Straw Bear is meant to personify the winter season. Its appearance on Plough Day symbolically represents the banishment of winter, so that crops can grow again and the people will flourish.'" He grinned at her without humor. "Just so you know, my dearest, darling Margaret—oh, wait, you'll never be mine, will you? You've made that clear. Just so you know, winter isn't going anywhere. Ever. And neither are we. You were going to ask if you could invite yourself along for a ride in the Penhallow barouche, weren't you? Well, you can forget about it. Just as you always do—every single damned day."

Not waiting for a reply, he turned on his heel and strode away, still holding on to the half-empty bottle of brandy. Which he planned to finish in the very, very near future.

It was a bright, beautiful, sunny day—Plough Day!—and here she was, right in the middle of it all. Wasn't she just so fortunate, when yesterday it had seemed there was a good chance she'd never make it here in time? Warm and snug in her thick wool pelisse and cozy hat, Margaret looked around from her place near the festive bunting-bedecked platform with pleasure. What a delightful scene lay about: how much fun everyone was having!

And yet, almost like a mysterious dark patina dimming the bright sunshine, Margaret was also aware of an odd feeling of somehow *bracing* herself for something bad to happen.

But why would that be?

Everything had gone smoothly this morning.

She'd woken up with plenty of time to spare, gotten dressed, poked her head into the private parlor where Aunt Seraphina was already hard at work, met Mr. Lawrence in the common-room, and together they'd walked over to the town square without the least incident.

She sent an absentminded glance to Mr. Lawrence

next to her, he being busy jotting down his impressions in his notebook. Suddenly she spotted a tall broad-shouldered figure coming toward the platform, and, doing her best to shake off that odd mysterious feeling, she called out:

"Mr. Thane! Good morning!"

He came near and she saw at once that he was looking quite different than he had last night when he had dropped Aunt Seraphina, Mr. Lawrence, and herself off at their inn. Then he had been annoyingly suave and sardonic, and openly bitter about having to get up early for the Plough Day ceremony. Today there was a visible tension about him, almost like a nimbus of focused energy; his expression was hard and set.

"Good morning," Margaret repeated, cautiously.

"It's not yet, but it will be."

"I beg your pardon?"

"You'll see."

No sooner had he said this than the merry sounds of the pipe and drum fell away, and the crowd fell silent too, turning as one toward the platform in joyful expectancy.

Margaret said, puzzled and curious, to Mr. Thane:

"I believe that's your cue."

"Why, so it is." He turned away and went up the steps of the platform, introducing himself to the various town dignitaries clustering there, one of whom, Margaret saw, gestured him toward the front. Mr. Thane walked to the railing, swept his gaze over the crowd, and said in a hard, clear, carrying voice:

"Good people: we are gathered here today to celebrate farmers, farming, agriculture, growing seasons, winter, the end of winter—"

He paused and gave what sounded like an exceedingly bitter laugh.

"The end of winter. *Ha*. What a joke. Winter's not ending, ever, unless *I* do something about it. Unless *I* fix things. Today. Here and now. What you people need is a hero, and I'm it. Oh, and there's your precious Straw Bear."

He pointed toward the far edge of the crowd, which was, for the moment, silent and shocked. Then she saw the cylindrical figure all covered in sheaves of hay, from its head down to its ankles; people eagerly yielded before it. The figure lumbered forward, and everyone started to applaud, those closest to the Straw Bear reaching out to pat at his sheaves—a gesture which signified hope for an early spring. The pipe and drum resumed their merry, lilting beat and some people began to move and sway in happy little dances, both singly and together.

Margaret watched for a few moments, then looked uneasily back to the platform where Mr. Thane still stood.

He was staring at the Straw Bear.

She didn't like his expression.

It was strangely purposeful, still very hard, and even just a tiny bit desperate, and it was making her nervous.

He walked down the platform steps and swiftly she went to him, catching at his arm. "Where are you going?"

"Why should you care?"

"I'm—I'm worried about you."

"Don't be. I'm pretty sure I've figured it all out. How to turn the charm around. It all has to do with the Straw Bear, you see. It always has. I could kick myself for not realizing it sooner."

She stared up at him. Why was he talking about a charm, and why did that seem so familiar to her? *Stay focused, Margaret,* she sternly told herself, and demanded: "Realize *what* sooner? What on earth do you mean?"

"I already told you—you'll see. Did you forget already?" Mr. Thane shook off her hand and strode away. Puzzled and worried, Margaret continued staring at him.

"His speech wasn't at all what I was expecting."

It was Mr. Lawrence, who had come up to stand next to her. Without taking her eyes off Mr. Thane, feeling that she had been quite right to be bracing herself for something untoward to happen, Margaret replied:

"I'm not sure *what* I was expecting, but it wasn't that."

"These people from great families," he remarked. "Idiosyncratic, aren't they?"

"I daresay they are."

"If he's leaving Whittlesey today, do you think we could join him? There's talk of a snowstorm coming in and there aren't any seats on the stage for several days."

Margaret nodded. "Yes, I inquired about that too. But I have no idea as to Mr. Thane's plans. I'd prefer to leave also, if we can." Suddenly she gasped. "Oh, my *goodness*!"

"I say, what's he doing?" exclaimed Mr. Lawrence.

They both watched in astonishment as Mr. Thane grabbed at the Straw Bear and began hustling him away from the town square. It was evident that the people around him were too shocked to do anything, and also that Mr. Thane was very strong, able to easily overpower the Straw Bear who was flapping his arms in agitation, shedding bits of straw everywhere.

"My God," said Margaret, horrified. "He's shoved the Bear into someone's curricle. And now he's jumped up and taken the reins. Is he—is he *kidnapping* the Bear?"

"Now *here's* a story for my newspaper," declared Mr. Lawrence with enormous relish. "Let's go closer and see what happens."

They hurried toward the curricle, which Mr. Thane had deftly swung around and was now hurtling away with its unwilling passenger. A cry went up from many throats:

"Stop him! Stop him! Save the Straw Bear!"

And one lone aggrieved cry:

"He stole my curricle!"

It wasn't long before several other carriages were rolling off in hot pursuit. Behind them Margaret spotted a couple of constables, huffing and puffing and their faces red and enraged, trotting along as fast as they could—a laudable endeavor but, given the speed of the carriages preceding them, ultimately a rather futile one.

There was no way this was going to end well.

Just as she had, in fact, suspected all along.

"**I**sn't this fun?" said Philip casually to his companion, who was gripping the arm rail for dear life. "Would you like a turn with the reins?"

"No," said the Bear, in a panicky man's voice. "Wish you'd let me off. Don't like speeds."

"Faster is better, in this case, though in certain other, intimate situations it's quite the obverse. Don't you agree, my dear Bear?" Skillfully Philip managed to just barely miss a giant hole in the road, and the Bear gave a loud anxious moan. They were already on the outskirts of town.

"Where—where are you taking me?"

"Why, we're on the road to Oundle."

"Oundle? I don't want to go to Oundle."

"But we must. We've got to pass through it, you see, and beyond, and *you're* the key."

"Me? The key? I'm not even a Bear, you know. I'm just a man."

"You're the key to solving all my problems. You'll see." Now that they were barreling along at a spanking pace, the Bear's rate of straw-shedding had exponentially increased. No doubt they had left quite a trail behind them. That was unfortunate, but hopefully they had a large enough lead to give his plan sufficient time to be enacted.

Just enough to make it to, and through, Oundle.

And then he'd be *free*.

This morning, lying in his dumpy bed at the Apple Street Inn, he'd been thinking hard. Instead of wrestling with *why* he'd been trapped in Whittlesey, or *how,* he was trying to figure out a means by which to break the curse—the evil charm set upon him. In the absence of any suggestions or advice from that not very helpful Voice, it had occurred to him that perhaps the Straw Bear—the whole reason for him being in Whittlesey in the first place—was at the center of it all.

Maybe the Bear was his *lucky* charm.

And if so, having the Bear with him as he got to Oundle would somehow ensure that the road wouldn't be blocked by a big fallen tree; that there was no snowstorm getting in the way.

"Watch out!" shrieked the Bear, and Philip saw that a cow had wandered into their path. Just for fun, he drove straight toward it, veering to one side and bypassing it only at the absolute last moment. The Bear moaned again and said feebly:

"Think—think I'm going to be sick."

"Oh, for God's sake, Bear, don't," said Philip in a sharp voice.

"Can't help it," answered the Bear, apologetically, "I told you I don't like speeds," and without further ado he gave up his breakfast all over himself, and, as the curricle lurched over a rut, causing the Bear to jolt in his seat and twist about as hapless as a ragdoll, all over Philip, too.

Not even the best of whips could drive with sick in his eyes, and so, cursing furiously under his breath, Philip brought the curricle to a halt, snatching out his handkerchief to wipe his face. The Bear took advantage of his distraction to slither down from the curricle, go over to the nearest tree, vomit again, and when Philip approached him in a minute or two, he wrapped his arms around the tree trunk and refused to go anywhere—revealing, when Philip tried hard to tug him away, a surprising amount of both arm strength and unshakable determination.

Chapter 13

Margaret hardly knew whether to remain in the town square and wait for what she hoped would be the Straw Bear's rescue and return, or to go on about her business, but while she lingered among the angry, anxious crowd, it was all decided for her sooner rather than later when in twenty minutes or so, the stolen curricle rolled back, driven not by the Bear *or* Mr. Thane, but by one of the townspeople who had been among their pursuers; the other coaches followed in short order.

To the cheers of the crowd the Bear was tenderly helped down from another carriage, and borne away to a bench where he was surrounded by friends and admirers eager to be of assistance which, at the moment, seemed to be a need to be wiped down from head to toe.

The curricle's owner rushed to see to his horses, who were, thankfully, none the worse for wear.

One of the carriages didn't stop to disperse passengers, but instead kept going, and Margaret was just able to catch a glimpse of Mr. Thane sitting inside, along with two of the constables, no longer huffing and puffing but with faces that were, if possible, even more red and enraged.

"I say, isn't this *ripping*?" exclaimed Mr. Lawrence, coming up to stand next to her, all his journalistic instincts aquiver. "Everyone's saying it's the most memorable Plough Day since an alderman was so drunk that he toppled off the platform, tearing all the bunting as he went, rolled around in it, and rose to his feet looking so much like an Egyptian mummy that several people screamed and at least two women fainted."

For a moment Margaret found herself wanting to laugh, but repressed it and soberly said:

"Where are they taking Mr. Thane? Do you know?"

"Yes, they're taking him to the constabulary house. By Jove, *what* a story for my newspaper! What do you suppose Mr. Thane was thinking? I was hoping to get an interview with the mayor, but my editor would be ever so pleased if I could get Mr. Thane to talk. Would you excuse me, Miss Allen?"

"Yes, certainly," said Margaret. "Good luck."

Mr. Lawrence rushed off, and she remained in the town square just long enough to see that the Straw Bear was really and truly all right. Then she went back to her inn and into the private parlor, where she had a hearty breakfast and told Aunt Seraphina all about the events of the morning.

"My word!" exclaimed her aunt, her eyes as round as saucers. "I knew Mr. Thane for a rapscallion the moment I met him, but *this* is beyond the pale. Kidnapping the Straw Bear and stealing a curricle! It's outrageous." She gave a derisive sniff. "I daresay he's another one of those madcap young wastrels who think it's a great lark doing things like that—taking over the driving of the mail coach, or betting enormous sums on the movements of a fly. Or, closer to home, sneaking a cow into the dean's chancery. Do you remember *that* incident from a few years back? I thought your great-uncle Timothy would go off in an apoplexy."

"Yes, I do remember, Aunt, but Uncle Timothy was as much concerned for the cow as anything else. The poor thing had to be taken up three flights of stairs and then, once discovered, down them again. And only recall how quickly he identified the undergraduates who did it—his talk with them not only left them in tears of genuine remorse, you know, they both were so inspired by his truly Christian forgiveness that they ended up becoming clergymen. And, of course, he made them work tending cows for the whole summer half." Thoughtfully Margaret had another bite of her muffin and went on:

"The thing is, I don't believe it was a lark for Mr. Thane. He was so—so *odd* this morning, Aunt, before the kidnapping. He told me he had to 'turn the charm around,' and that it had to do with the Bear."

"Curiouser and curiouser! I hate to say it, my dear, but is it possible that Mr. Thane is—well—unbalanced?"

Margaret nodded. "It may be."

"Then we were more fortunate than we knew to travel here *safely* in his barouche yesterday," Aunt Seraphina said gravely. "And to think we were hoping to travel with him again! This unfortunate incident with the Straw Bear may well have been a strange stroke of luck for us."

"Strange indeed," said Margaret, and finished her muffin.

When her breakfast was over, she spent some time going over her Plough Day notes, went to inquire about any last-minute stage seats (alas, a futile endeavor), and decided to go for a long, invigorating walk about town. She had just enjoyed a chat with a freckle-faced little boy who had been petting the butcher's tabby cat when Mr. Lawrence came bounding along.

"I say, here you are!" he exclaimed. "I've been looking for you everywhere. Any chance you might be willing to come with me to the constabulary house? They won't let me in to see Mr. Thane, but *you've* got such a nice air about you, maybe they'll change their minds."

"Oi, mister!" piped up the little boy. "Can I come too? Never seen a *prisoner* before. Are they going to hang him, do you suppose?"

Startled, Mr. Lawrence glanced down at him. "I shouldn't think so, lad."

"Damn." He sounded very disappointed. "That *would* be jolly. Can I at least go into the constabulary house with you? Always wanted to do that."

"Best not," said Mr. Lawrence. "Sorry, laddie."

The little boy shrugged. "I'll go roast my chestnuts then." He started off, and Margaret called after him:

"Do be careful, won't you?"

The little boy only laughed and vanished round a corner, and after that she and Mr. Lawrence walked to the constabulary house, where they were indeed promptly admitted. Looking around the front room, Margaret thought that the little boy would like it here a great deal: it was suitably gray, dingy, dank, and altogether unpleasantly tomb-like.

A minute or two later they found Mr. Thane in a cold, drafty cell, sitting on a bare uncomfortable-looking bench, with one long booted leg crossed over the other and looking just as determined as he had been earlier this morning. There was a faint, unpleasant odor in the cell and instinctively Margaret wrinkled her nose in distaste.

"My apologies," said Mr. Thane at once. "The

Bear vomited on me, you see, and they've callously refused to let me have a bath. The amenities here are quite disappointing. In fact, they're nonexistent."

"What made you do it, sir?" Mr. Lawrence inquired.

"Better to ask what made the Bear vomit. This is a new and very expensive jacket."

"No, seriously, sir. Why did you kidnap him?"

"I *am* serious. My jacket is ruined."

Margaret's heart sank at this exchange. Either Mr. Thane was refusing to consider his situation with due gravity, which was bad, or he really was unbalanced, which was worse. Gently she said:

"You've been charged with theft, kidnap with intent of bodily harm, property damage, and disorderly conduct, and many people have given sworn testimony to the fact. I asked if you could be released on my recognizance—and I offered to pay the surety fee—but they said you're to be held here until tomorrow morning, when the magistrate will speak with you then and adjudicate your sentence. I should warn you, Mr. Thane, that the sentence may be harsh—a few years' incarceration, I'm afraid."

"Oh, I doubt that. I'll be a free man tomorrow."

"How can you know that?" asked Mr. Lawrence curiously. "The whole town is against you, sir, and the law is too. Everyone saw what you did."

"Luckily for me, people have short memories."

"Do they? The way people are talking, I expect they'll never forget *this* Plough Day."

"Trust me. They will."

Mr. Thane sounded so confident that Margaret actually found herself believing him. A little dazedly she put a hand to her forehead, as if she'd run into a lamp-post and rattled her brain so badly that *she* was getting unbalanced—especially when she now remembered all over again how she'd been dogged by a strange feeling of bracing herself before the Plough Day ceremony began, only to have the feeling justified when Mr. Thane acted so outrageously.

"What's the matter, Margaret?" said Mr. Thane.

She gave her head a shake, as if to clear it, and dropped her hand. "Nothing. Let's talk about you, though."

"My favorite subject."

Annoyance rose within her, and she was glad. She'd rather be annoyed at Mr. Thane than worried about the frailty of his mind. "I'm sure it is. Mr. Lawrence wants to interview you for his newspaper. Is that something you'd be willing to do?"

He shrugged. "Why not?"

Mr. Lawrence whipped out his notepad and pencil from his rucksack. "So why did you do it, sir? Steal the curricle and take the Straw Bear?"

"Because the Bear is my ticket out of here."

Margaret's heart sank all over again. He was back to *this*.

"How so?" asked Mr. Lawrence, looking baffled.

"I've been placed under an evil curse, you see, and it finally occurred to me that it's the Bear who's going to set me free. Today was my first go at escaping with him, but I think the problem was that I used someone else's carriage. Tomorrow I'm going to take the Penhallow barouche. It makes more sense, don't you think? I *came* in the Penhallow barouche, and I'm going to *leave* in the Penhallow barouche. So I'm fully expecting that the second time will be the charm."

Margaret had been listening to Mr. Thane with increasing dismay, but something about that last phrase caught her attention even more sharply. Didn't she have a memory of sitting somewhere with Mr. Thane—over a meal? In a restaurant?—and him saying:

Nothing ventured, nothing gained.

If at first you don't succeed, et cetera, she had answered. *Hopefully tomorrow, the second time will be the charm.*

I'll drink to that, Mr. Thane had said, and they had clinked their glasses in a convivial manner.

They'd been talking about . . .

Margaret thought hard. It was like trying to grasp at something through a vast, dense fog.

Something incredibly elusive.

What *had* they been discussing?

Then, at last, her mind lit on something.

They'd been talking about getting to Oundle in his barouche, but being forced to turn back due to a snowstorm, and . . . a big fallen tree blocking the way.

Margaret felt a keen sense of satisfaction at remembering, but it promptly dissipated when next she remembered that she'd never had this conversation with Mr. Thane in real life.

How bizarre.

It must, she now thought, have been a dream. It's the only possible explanation.

"This makes no sense at all."

Margaret gave a start. Then she realized that it was Mr. Lawrence speaking, and that it wasn't *her* he was addressing—thank goodness—but rather Mr. Thane, who seemed unperturbed by Mr. Lawrence's grave words and replied in a tone of the utmost reasonableness:

"On the contrary. It's the only possible explanation."

At this Margaret gave *another* start and stared hard at Mr. Thane. Why had he said that—"the only possible explanation"? Had he . . . had he *read her mind*?

Nonsense, she told herself. It's just a coincidence. She watched as Mr. Lawrence, looking puzzled, even frustrated, put away his pencil and notepad. He was giving up on the conversation, she saw. So was Mr. Thane, it seemed, for he said:

"Well, it was kind of you both to stop by. I'll see you tomorrow at the Plough Day festivities."

"*Today* is Plough Day," Mr. Lawrence reminded him gravely.

"And it will be again tomorrow."

Margaret said, just as grave as Mr. Lawrence, "Is there anything we can do for you before we go?"

"Yes, how about a kiss, darling Margaret? We've gotten close, but never close enough."

That's because you lied all day long, you awful toad, she nearly blurted out, then checked herself at the very last moment. Astonished, and more baffled than ever, she retreated a step. "Goodbye, Mr. Thane."

"Rather, let us say, *Je te reverrai aujourd'hui, demain.*"

They left him sitting on the bench, one leg crossed over the other, leaning casually against the wall, looking as if he was anticipating a full and purposeful day to come on the morrow instead of the fate which most likely was awaiting him: a visit from a magistrate, a substantial fine, and a sentence of significant incarceration.

"What did Mr. Thane say in French, Miss Allen?"

"He said, 'I'll see you again today, tomorrow.'"

"Really? Dash it, it's nonsensical. The whole thing is nonsensical! Poor fellow ought to be in Bedlam."

Margaret only nodded somberly. The way things were going, perhaps she'd be joining him there.

He was sitting in his cold, drafty cell, having disposed himself as best he could on a bare and very uncomfortable bench.

Margaret and Mr. Lawrence were standing outside his cell, looking gravely at him.

He barely noticed them. He was thinking about that weirdly prescient dream he'd had, long ago, on the morning of his second Plough Day. Slowly he had come to the horrifying realization that he was in a cage, entirely surrounded by cold metal bars. Just like he was now, basically. All this time, all those Plough Days, he'd been looping round and round, only to end up precisely where he'd started.

It was hopeless.

All his efforts were for nothing.

And by God, he was tired.

Not just tired—*exhausted*. In his body, his mind, and his soul. He was, he thought, nothing but an empty husk. Is that what ghosts felt like? He lifted an arm, checking to see if he'd started going transparent, or fading away. He saw that he was all still there, and hardly knew whether to be glad or sorry.

He heard, as if from a great distance, a feminine, pleasantly husky voice. It was Margaret's, of course. He roused himself from his dismal reverie, and realized that she was murmuring something to Mr. Lawrence.

"—honestly, I don't think asking Mr. Thane for an interview is a good idea. He seems so fatigued."

Mr. Lawrence looked disappointed, and she went on:

"Maybe you could go find the mayor. You said your editor would be pleased with an interview with *him*."

"Yes, that's true. Are you ready to go? I can escort you back to your inn, or wherever you like."

Philip bestirred himself to say, "Yes, go on, Margaret."

She hesitated, and a flicker of his old vanity stirred. He hated for her to see him like this—rumpled and bedraggled and defeated and *imprisoned*. So he said, summoning as much sharpness into his voice as he could:

"Go on and commune with that stupid Straw Bear, and leave me alone. I'm sick of you."

He watched, resigned, as her expression hardened.

"Very well, Mr. Thane. Goodbye."

"Goodbye." He closed his eyes, so he didn't have to watch her go.

Margaret and Mr. Lawrence had passed through the gray, dingy, dank, and altogether unpleasantly tomblike front room of the constabulary house, and now she stood looking at Mr. Thane in his cold, drafty cell, deeply shocked. Had he ever really leaned against the side of his barouche, all dashingly devil-may-care, looking so breezy and confident, as if he had the world at his feet? The man she saw now, sitting on a bare uncomfortable-looking bench and slumping against the wall, seemed incapable of rising to his feet without help.

To Mr. Lawrence, standing next to her, she murmured, "I know you went all that way to bring me back here with you, but honestly, I don't think asking Mr. Thane for an interview is a good idea. He seems so very, very tired."

Mr. Lawrence looked disappointed, and she went on:

"Why don't you go find the mayor? You said your editor would be pleased with an interview with *him*."

"Yes, that's true. Are you ready to go? I can escort you back to your inn, or wherever you like."

Mr. Thane suddenly spoke up. "Yes, go on, Margaret."

She hesitated, and he added in a sharp voice:

"Leave me alone, won't you? Go chat with the Straw Bear and take some more stupid notes. I'm sick to death of you."

For a moment Margaret was so angry and upset by this horrid, callous remark that she wanted to turn on her heel and storm out.

But something held her back.

She didn't know what it was, only that her hesitation somehow shifted into something else.

A determination to stay.

She felt like a tiny little ship sailing against strong headwinds that wanted to keep her at bay.

But she was a very *stubborn* ship.

So she said quietly to Mr. Lawrence, "You go. I'm staying."

His gingery eyebrows went up. "Really? He seems awfully surly."

"I'm sure. Good luck getting your interview."

"Thanks. I'm going to need it."

Mr. Lawrence went away, and Margaret remained where she was, looking sorrowfully at Mr. Thane. His eyes were closed now, and as a heavy silence fell in the wake of Mr. Lawrence's departure, she saw, to her shocked amazement, two tears, one on each cheek, rolling down his face.

"Oh, Mr. Thane," she said softly, her heart aching, "I'm *so* sorry."

She didn't know what exactly she was sorry about, but she *did* know that she was glad that she had stayed. As if somehow, in some way, she had failed him before. Or had they failed each other?

Someone was knocking on a door.

"Wake up, sir," said a voice from outside the room, "it's Plough Day."

Knock knock knock.

"Mr. Thane," said the voice, "you asked to be awakened in time for the ceremony. It's Plough Day, sir."

Slowly Philip opened his eyes.

There it was, the same old ceiling overhead.

And here he was, lying in the same old bed.

Again.

Again, and again, and again.

Knock knock knock.

"I'm awake," he whispered, barely able to get the words out.

"Very well, sir."

He lay there, stunned.

Just as stunned as he had been yesterday, and the day before that, and the day before . . .

He had indeed tried taking the Bear in the Penhallow barouche to Oundle. They'd gone flying along the road that time, fast and fleet, easily outdistancing their pursuers, and he'd stuffed the Bear *inside* the barouche while he himself drove, so that when the Bear lost his breakfast he could continue driving.

And just past Oundle, they'd encountered—to his unspeakable horror—a swirling snowstorm and a big fallen tree blocking the way.

So he'd been caught, rounded up, and thrown into jail again.

The next day he tried going to Peterborough.

They were met with a snowstorm and a big fallen tree. He'd been thrown into jail.

The day after that, he tried going with the Bear to Cambridge.

Snowstorm, fallen tree, jail.

The day after that, he'd tried going to Norwich, which was in the *opposite* direction from Somerset and Surmont Hall.

Snowstorm, fallen tree, jail.

After that, he'd tried for Ipswich, Colchester, Marham, Braintree, Stevenage, Kettering, Grantham, Sleaford, Coventry, Nuneaton, Bansbury, Leicester, and some other places whose names he couldn't even recall at the moment.

It didn't matter.

It was all the same.

Snowstorm. Fallen tree. Jail.

There was no way out.

Whether or not he was literally in jail at any given moment, he was definitely, totally, entirely, thoroughly, and absolutely trapped here.

Slowly Philip turned his head toward the window.

At this moment, beneath a sky of soft cloudless blue, people were heading toward the town square, passing scattered splotches of gray slush. The pipe and the drum could be heard, all merry and cheerful. Margaret was there, as ravishing as always and smelling like the sweet summer roses he'd never see again; Mr. Lawrence was standing next to her, scribbling in his notebook. The town dignitaries were in their places on the bunting-bedecked platform, waiting for him to show up and give his speech. And the Straw Bear—his stomach, Philip now knew all too well, comfortably full from his breakfast of kippers, sausage, eggs, and toast—was getting ready to make his appearance amidst enthusiastic fanfare.

Philip envisioned this scene over and over again, a living nightmare that he couldn't control and couldn't stop.

This had been his life.

This *was* his life now.

It was difficult to remember that there was a larger world out there.

A world in which he had flitted from one place

to another, from one woman to the next, dancing, drinking, gambling, copulating, and in general doing whatever he wanted, whenever he liked.

A world which was lost to him forever.

Oh, she was lucky, lucky! thought Margaret happily.

She was in Whittlesey on Plough Day, when yesterday it seemed she'd never get here and would be stuck in Brampton for who knew how long.

Warm and snug in her thick wool pelisse and cozy hat, she looked around from her place near the festive bunting-bedecked platform. What a delightful scene lay all about: how much fun everyone was having! She sent a smiling glance to Mr. Lawrence next to her, he being busy jotting down his impressions in his notebook.

And it was all due to Mr. Thane that she was here. Margaret felt another burst of gratitude for his happening to be in the right place at the right time. She'd thank him again, and as soon as possible.

Even as she thought this, a strange frisson of anxiety skittered up and down her spine. What if something bad happened today because of him? What if something bad happened *to* him?

It seemed all too likely, as if it were something that had happened before.

What a strange fancy, Margaret thought, mystified, and then she determinedly shook it off. Just then, she spotted a tall broad-shouldered figure coming toward the platform and she called out:

"Mr. Thane! Good morning!"

He came near and she saw that his expression was very different from what it had been when he'd dropped them off at the Woodhull Inn yesterday.

Then he had been annoyingly suave and sardonic, and openly bitter about having to get up early for the Plough Day ceremony. Today, however, she had a difficult time reading his expression: he didn't look satirical or even lively, but instead he seemed . . . flattened-out . . . and somehow *resigned*.

Maybe, despite yesterday's casual braggadocio, he was one of those people who dreaded speaking in public?

And so he had girded himself to give his speech, accepting his fate, but with reluctance?

Back home in Oxford she'd given talks on folk-lore, superstition, mythology, and so on, and at first she'd been nervous. For many people, herself included, it took time to get comfortable up on the podium.

"Good morning," she repeated, smiling reassuringly at him. "And thank you."

"For what?" His voice was flat.

"For bringing us here."

"You shouldn't be thanking me. You should be cursing me."

"I beg your pardon?"

"Nothing. It was nothing."

"Oh." Rather baffled, Margaret added, "I daresay it's almost time for the speeches to begin."

"Yes, I know."

"There's nothing to be nervous about. Everyone here is looking forward to hearing what you have to say."

Mr. Thane looked at her closely, his expression now one of faint surprise. "Do you think I'm worried about giving a speech?"

"Well—aren't you?"

"Good Lord, no. I'm quite the old hand at it."

No sooner had Mr. Thane uttered this than the

merry sounds of the pipe and drum fell away, and the crowd fell silent too, turning as one toward the platform in joyful expectancy.

"I believe that's your cue, Mr. Thane. Good luck! Not that you'll need it, of course."

"Oh, I've given up on luck," he said in that same flattened-out way, and went up the steps of the platform, introducing himself to the various town dignitaries clustering there, one of whom, she saw, gestured him toward the front. Mr. Thane walked to the railing, swept his eyes over the crowd, and delivered a brief, rather unmemorable speech about agriculture and the importance of annual traditions, which was received with a polite smattering of applause, and after that he announced the arrival of the Straw Bear with a cursory sweep of his arm.

Looking to the far edge of the crowd, Margaret saw people eagerly yielding to a cylindrical figure all covered in sheaves of hay, from its head down to its ankles. The figure lumbered forward, and everyone began vigorously applauding, those closest to the Straw Bear reaching out to pat the sheaves—a gesture which signified hope for an early spring. The pipe and drum resumed their merry, lilting beat and some people began to move and sway in happy little dances, both singly and together.

Margaret watched, fascinated, tapping one of her feet in time to the music.

After a while—perhaps ten minutes or so—at the edges of her awareness she felt herself wondering about something.

What was it?

She looked vaguely around her, like a person waking from a deep, dark sleep.

Like a person looking for something.

No—looking for *someone*.

Where was Mr. Thane?

It was as if she'd been expecting him to draw near while she was gazing at the Straw Bear, and to say something sardonic in that deep, cultured voice of his.

His *not* saying anything, not coming to her, felt like an odd absence.

Like a hole where there should have been *something*.

Earlier, she'd glanced away from the Bear for a moment and had seen Mr. Thane moving slowly among the crowd, passing right by two pretty young women who bridled coyly at his approach. Yesterday he'd seemed like just the sort of man who would find this an irresistible invitation—but today he hadn't even seemed to notice them, to their obvious disappointment.

What was wrong?

Margaret could have laughed at herself for worrying about a rake who missed an opportunity to make his next conquests, but now she couldn't help but feel that there really was something wrong with Mr. Thane.

Moreover, even though she couldn't explain it rationally, she somehow felt that she needed to be involved.

So Margaret, who could never walk past a person in need, or a dog or a cat or a horse in trouble, without intervening, gave one last appreciative look at the Straw Bear and followed in the direction she'd seen Mr. Thane going.

She left the town square and looked around. There was no sign of him. Had he gone back to his inn? She began walking toward Apple Street, but just as she came up to Plympton Street she caught sight of him.

To her astonishment, he was sitting on the edge of the sidewalk and his handsome, stylish, expensive boots were in the dirty gutter. His head was bowed; his eyes were open but he didn't seem to be gazing at anything in particular.

Margaret went to stand next to him. "Mr. Thane, are you all right?"

Slowly he turned his head to look up at her. "Never been better." His voice was flat.

"Would you—would you like to get up and go somewhere else?"

"No."

Early this morning, as she and Mr. Lawrence had walked together to the ceremony, she'd resolved to ask Mr. Thane about his departure plans, and if it would be at all possible for herself, Aunt Seraphina, and Mr. Lawrence to tag along to some convenient point where they might find other transportation.

But now it didn't seem important anymore. Impulsively she said, "May I join you?"

"Why would you want to do that?"

"To keep you company."

"Really?"

She nodded, surprised to hear the outright amazement in his voice. Was it because she'd been so cold to him yesterday? Strangely, she found herself thinking of how the frog in the old fairy tale might have reacted when the princess at last offered to kiss him. "Yes. I'd like that, Mr. Thane."

"Are you sure?"

"Yes, I am." She sat down at his side and tucked her skirts around her ankles. Then she looked hard at him.

Now that his face was, for some mysterious reason, wiped clean of the mockery from yesterday, that jaded, sardonic, concupiscent expression which seemed to be habitual—if half a day spent together in a carriage was anything to go by—Mr. Thane looked very different to her.

It was almost as if . . .

As if she could see him better now.

She was vividly aware of his masculine solidity, the long length of his body and its easy, graceful lines; the way his brown hair, with its interesting hint of chestnut, curled ever so slightly over the collar of his greatcoat, the allure of his beautifully formed mouth and the gleam of unmistakable intelligence in his brown-green eyes.

She had always found intelligence irresistible, and when allied with a great many appealing physical attributes, it all added up to something tempting.

Very, very, tempting.

But—which was the real Mr. Thane?

The cynical rakehell from yesterday, or this quieter, more soft-spoken man?

Or had the real Mr. Thane yet to reveal himself?

It was a puzzle, and she did enjoy solving puzzles.

Also, this air of resignation he had about him concerned her. As if he had somehow . . . given up. Gently she said:

"Mr. Thane, is something troubling you?"

He gave her a long, considering look tinged by surprise. "Do you really want to know?"

"Yes, I do."

"Now that you mention it, there *is*." But he didn't go on; instead he gave a deep sigh, one that seemed to come from a genuine place of darkness and even, perhaps, despair.

Sympathetically Margaret said, "Won't you tell me about it?"

"You wouldn't believe me if I did."

"Try me."

"It'll sound strange to you. Like something out of folk-lore, or mythology."

She smiled just a little. "Well, as you know, that's my speciality."

"I do know. Sometimes I've wondered if I'm a creature of your imagination."

"What do you mean?"

He turned to face her and quietly said:

"The thing of it is, I think I'm Sisyphus brought back to life."

Margaret stared. If he was joking, he was doing a very good job of concealing it. His tone was sincere, even earnest. "I beg your pardon?"

"I think I'm Sisyphus."

"The crafty, clever king of Ephyra in Greek mythology, who was punished for his misdeeds by being made to roll a giant boulder up a mountain—endlessly."

"Yes, that's right."

"But Mr. Thane, it's only a story."

"Stories come from somewhere, don't they? And sometimes they're based on real things."

"Yes, but . . . Sisyphus? Have you . . . have you been rolling boulders up a mountain?"

"No. It's a metaphor."

"For what?"

"Every single day, no matter what I say or do, I wake up in my bed at the Apple Street Inn, and it's Plough Day. *That's* the boulder I roll up the hill—endlessly."

"But Mr. Thane," said Margaret, befuddled, "that's impossible."

"It may be impossible, but it's true. There's no other explanation. I can only conclude, logically, that

I'm Sisyphus. And please don't suggest that I go see a doctor. I assure you, I'm not mad, or pulling a prank. I'm saying this based on things that have happened to me. That *are* happening to me."

A cold wind rattled past, sending a few dried winter leaves and other detritus scudding along the gutter at their feet, including a battered-looking crisp.

He went on:

"Wasn't it lucky for me I found a big fat volume on Greek mythology in the Whittlesey lending-library. It was all quite interesting, really, and it actually made me wish I'd paid more attention at school. Also it made me wish I'd been assigned a different figure from Greek mythology, with different attributes. I'd prefer to have *useful* powers, like being able to transform base metals into gold, or to fly, or to read people's minds. Although in your case, Margaret, I can—you're wondering if I *am* mad, even though I've already told you plainly that I'm not." He spoke without rancor.

"You must admit that what you're saying is . . . hard to believe."

"I'll readily admit it. But only consult your own expertise. Aren't there any stories or folk-tales about—what was the word again? I found a Greek dictionary in the lending-library as well. Yes: *metempsychosis*."

"The transmigration of souls, from one lifetime to the next. It's an old and persistent concept," said Margaret. "The Yoruba tribe in western Africa, for example, believe that people are continually reborn. They call their baby girls 'Mother Has Returned' and their baby boys 'Father Has Returned.'" She noticed how he seemed to wince, as if in pain, and quickly said:

"What is it? What's wrong?"

"A bad topic. Never mind. But now that we agree that soul transmigration is a time-honored concept, how can you be certain that I'm *not* Sisyphus? Or, at least, some kind of—of *revival*?"

"Because these are concepts! And stories!" exclaimed Margaret. "Not truths!"

"I can prove it."

"How?"

"Listen. Just listen."

Chapter 14

Philip looked at Margaret sitting next to him on the sidewalk. Her deep blue eyes were wide, and her face, which he had memorized in its every enchanting detail—the delicate arch of her tawny brown eyebrows, her broad high cheekbones, her long straight nose, her soft and generously curved mouth and the faint, charming smile-lines to either side—was rather pale.

"I'm listening," she said quietly.

"First of all, you should know that I've spent a great deal of time locked up in the constabulary house."

She took this in. "Which . . . which constabulary house? Where? And why?"

"The one right here in Whittlesey. And for all kinds of charges—for thefts of various sorts, public drunkenness, kidnapping the Straw Bear, and disorderly conduct."

"*Kidnapping* the Straw Bear?"

"Yes, I'm afraid so."

"But when, Mr. Thane? You only got here yesterday. And on the carriage ride here, you said it was your first time going to Whittlesey."

"Free your mind from the notion that yesterday was—well, yesterday. Try to accept the reality that a great deal of time has passed since the moment of our first meeting."

He saw the doubt and confusion in her eyes, and forged onward. "I've been thrown in jail many, many times. And you—in your infinite kindness and goodness—came to see me there. Sometimes you stayed for a few minutes, sometimes you left right away because I was rude to you—speaking of disorderly conduct. But quite a few times, though, you stayed for several hours to keep me company."

She was shaking her head. "That's—that's not possible."

"Yes, you did, and we've talked. Talked and talked and talked."

"About what?"

"For one thing, we had some very spirited debates about literature. I was shocked to discover that you prefer Walter Scott over Miss Austen. You acknowledged that you had only read *Emma* and didn't like it that much as you thought Emma Woodhouse to be an annoying character. So I told you all about *Mansfield Park* and *Persuasion*, and you agreed to give Miss Austen another chance."

"I . . . I do prefer Mr. Scott over Miss Austen. And you're right, *Emma* is the only book of hers I've read, and I didn't care for it." Margaret's eyes were wider than ever. "There's no way you could have known that. I don't think I mentioned it to Aunt Seraphina, or to my family at home, or—or to anyone."

"I know it because you told me one day in the constabulary house. By the way, once you argued so compellingly in Scott's favor that *I* agreed to give *him* another chance."

"You should," Margaret said, rather absently, then visibly marshaled herself to return to the more pressing topic. "So are there other things you believe you know about me, Mr. Thane?"

"Yes indeed," he answered, unable to keep a melancholy wistfulness out of his voice. "You come from a large and happy family in Oxford, many of whom are academics. Your father teaches classics at the University, and there are lots of professors and teachers among the Allen clan. Your mother is a respected translator of ancient Greek, her uncle Timothy is the Archbishop of Oxford, and your brothers are both vicars. Jasper, your oldest brother, stuttered as a child but doesn't anymore, and is, as you've said, one of the most eloquent people you know and his sermons are very well attended. Also, he knows an apparently limitless number of bad jokes. Sebastian, your other brother, once jumped off the roof on a dare and broke both his legs, and even though he sometimes limps a little, he still says he doesn't regret it."

"Yes," she whispered. "He says it was the best of larks."

"You went to a boarding school when you were eleven—at your own choice. It was in Cheltenham, with a well-deserved reputation for academic rigor, and you loved it, though the food was bad. You went home at sixteen, and moved into the room that Sebastian once had, because you like the view to the back, and also because it has a window-seat just right for reading. You speak French and German fluently, and also a smattering of Spanish, Gaelic, Dutch, and Swedish. You like pastry in general, and muffins in particular. You drink coffee for everyday, but tea when you're feeling ill, without any cream or sugar. You dislike licorice but love marzipan, and will go out of your way to not eat mushrooms if you can do it without being impolite."

"Yes," she said again. "I don't like their taste *or* texture."

He nodded. "I also know that you're extremely clever, but you're not one of those people who feel the need to boast about it. You feel lucky that you were raised in a family which supports your intellectual ambitions. You hate hurting the feelings of other people. Your great-aunt Patience, the family's long-lived curmudgeon, died four years ago and to your enormous surprise left you a modest bequest which renders you financially independent. You love animals, and you donate all throughout the year to help various charities and philanthropic endeavors in Oxford. At home your family has five dogs, two cats, a very loud parrot, and in the pasture at the back of your house there's an old horse and a miniature donkey you saved from a neglectful farmer in Iffley. You're kind, forthright, generous, tenderhearted, and you're the most beautiful woman I've ever met, both inside and out."

She was staring at him in wonderment. "You're flattering me, Mr. Thane."

"No. I'm simply telling you what I see, and feel, and know. You like going to balls and you love all the dances except the cotillion, which you find a trifle dull. You own over three hundred books, and one of your favorite things to do is to poke around bookshops—not necessarily to buy something, but just to be around books and see what's new and interesting. You're very sociable, but you're also happy in your own company. Though sometimes you *do* feel a little lonely. Once," he went on quietly, "you told me about James—or, I should say, the Viscount Mannering."

"I—I did?" faltered Margaret. "What did I tell you?"

"That he was a student at the University, and that you were head over heels in love with him. Things were going swimmingly between you, and he even hinted quite boldly about marriage. But then his parents found out and threatened to disinherit him for 'dallying,' as they put it, with a commoner, when he'd known for all his life that he was expected to marry a woman of rank. James had to choose, and he chose to align himself with his parents' wishes. Which pretty much broke your heart. And to make things worse, he didn't even have the courage to tell you in person—he sent you a letter, after he had left for the summer half. You've told me how much it hurt to be rejected as not being good enough, merely as a consequence of your social status. I'm so sorry."

Philip wanted, more than anything, to take her hand, and offer her some simple comfort. But he didn't dare. So he sat there and looked with sorrow at her beautiful, sad face. Her eyes gleamed with tears; then she swiped firmly at them and said:

"Yes, that's right. It was very painful, and it's left some scars, I'm afraid."

"Understandably. By the way, I also told you that three years ago I happened to meet Mannering and his wife at a Carlton House levée, and they got into a ferocious argument right in front of me. He told her he was sorry he married her, and she told him she was sorry he'd been born, and then he said he only married her because his parents made him, and she said she only married him because he's a viscount, and then they both stormed away in opposite directions. Which, you said, made you feel—in a guilty way—a tiny bit better."

The smallest of smiles briefly curved her lovely mouth. "It does. But—oh, Mr. Thane, this all so—well, so very confusing!"

"Understandably also. All I can do is tell you the truth. Every day, no matter what I do, or *don't* do, I wake up in my room at the Apple Street Inn. And every day it's Plough Day."

Philip saw the doubt and perplexity, still, in her eyes, and even though he accepted why she felt that way, it was like a tall, tall barrier looming between them, keeping them implacably separate. He on his side, she on hers. And he felt so much sorrow at the thought it was like a searing, scarring hurt in his heart. He almost put a hand on his chest, as if to try and hold back the pain, but instead kept himself very still.

Margaret murmured, "'There are more things in heaven and earth . . .'"

"'. . . than are dreamt of in your philosophy,'" he finished. "A clever fellow, that Hamlet."

"Oi there!" came a familiar voice, and Philip looked past Margaret to see young Thomas Abernathy approaching, as insouciant as ever. "What's wrong with you two?"

Margaret looked up at Thomas and smiled. "Hullo. Nothing's wrong."

"It's got to be. You're grownups sitting with your feet in the gutter." He leaned down to pluck up the dirty crisp and popped it into his mouth. "Aren't you being punished for something?"

"No, we're just sitting here having a chat."

Young Thomas looked skeptical. "You look barmy."

She smiled again. "I daresay we do. Would you like to join us, or are you on your way to school?"

"No school today, missus. It's Plough Day."

"Of course. That's nice for you."

"Yes, I've got these chestnuts I've been wanting to roast for ages." He pulled a couple from one of the pockets of his nankeen breeches to show them.

"They do look nice," said Margaret kindly. "You'll be careful roasting them, won't you?"

"*Oi* there!" It was the exasperated mother of their young friend, still stout and red-faced and wearing her distinctive purple hat. "Thomas Abernathy! You come right here!"

"Damn! It's my mum. Well, I'll see you later." He gave a jaunty smile and ran off, laughing, and about thirty seconds after that Mrs. Abernathy steamed by, arms pumping, and glared down at them both without breaking stride, within moments vanishing around the corner.

"I say, *there* you are!" It was, inevitably, Mr. Lawrence, pink-cheeked from the cold and with his rucksack hanging from his shoulder as he came rushing over. He stopped short and stared down at them, his gingery eyebrows high in his face. "Why are you sitting in the gutter?"

"To be clear," Philip responded mildly, "it's our *feet* that are in the gutter."

"So they are! You sound like my editor, correcting my writing mistakes. I do hope you don't mind my asking, sir, but are you planning to leave today? I was hoping I could tag along with you till Northampton—if it's on your way."

Margaret leaned closer to him and whispered: "Why don't we go? All of us? Wouldn't it help to get out of Whittlesey?"

He could smell her subtle, delicious fragrance, he could smell the summer roses, and another rush of pain and sorrow swamped him, for the past that was gone forever, and for the future he'd never have. He fought through it as best he could, and quietly answered:

"You're welcome to take the barouche, but with me

in it, I'm afraid I'll bring the curse along too. Just past Oundle, you see, we'd drive right into a snowstorm and the road would be blocked by a big fallen tree."

"How could you possibly know this?"

"The four of us did try to get out of here, but couldn't—that's how. Your aunt Seraphina with her usual wisdom insisted we turn around. She tatted all the way back here, Mr. Lawrence napped, and you read your book, glancing at me from time to time as if I was something nasty you'd found on the bottom of your shoe. Deservedly so, I might add."

She gave her head a little shake. "I don't understand this at all."

"Neither do I. Believe me, I've tried. But here's what I think—you *should* take the barouche and get out of town. You and your aunt and Mr. Lawrence. You know, of course, that there aren't any seats on the stage for days."

"Yes, I do know that, but—I'd hate to leave you here, Mr. Thane."

"Thank you, but there's that colloquium back home at which you're slated to speak—the one about fairy folk, the ballad of Tam Lin, and superstition. I know you're very excited about it, and I'd hate for you to miss it."

Her eyes widened yet again. "You know about that?"

"Yes, you told me all about it, and all the work you've done preparing for it, and also that your aunt's publisher is going to be there—the one who's agreed to read your manuscript when you've completed it."

"You know about that *also*?"

"Yes indeed. It sounds like a splendid book," Philip said, and this time he actually meant it. Actually *believed* it. Her passion for her subject, all her hard work, truly was impressive. He could see this now, no longer blinded by his casual and wholly selfish need to deceive and manipulate and thus to hustle her into his bed. Not that he didn't find her desirable anymore. He did. But it was all over now. He was done—he was *finished*. He gathered himself and went on, sincerely, "I wish you every success. Also, I think you should eat something before you go, because you've told me that you're worthless—*your* term—until you've had your breakfast and at least two cups of coffee."

"It's true," she whispered, looking at him wonderingly.

He got to his feet and held his hand out to her. "Then we have a plan."

Margaret put her hand in his and a shimmer of pleasure went through him. But he resisted the temptation to keep holding it, as only a cad would do, and released it as soon as she was on her feet again. She shook out her skirts and he said to Mr. Lawrence, who had been patiently waiting:

"You're all welcome to take the barouche."

He brightened at once. "I say, sir, that's awfully kind. Thanks ever so much. But aren't you coming too?"

"No." Philip could tell that Mr. Lawrence was bursting with questions but, a deep weariness coming upon him again, he merely said:

"Shall we go on? There's talk of a snowstorm coming in, so it might be a good idea for you to go sooner rather than later."

"You're right, sir," said Mr. Lawrence, "I heard that as well," and in his eagerness to get out of town he dropped the subject, much to Philip's relief, and the three of them made their way to the Woodhull Inn and into the private parlor, where they found the

elder Miss Allen enjoying a substantial breakfast.
The plan was explained to her and she too brightened, and with a noticeable thaw in her demeanor
toward Philip, she even invited him to join them at
table. This invitation he refused, however, and went
off to the stables to see the barouche made ready for
the journey ahead.

Feeling dazed, mystified, befuddled, and confused,
Margaret stood in the courtyard of their inn watching as Mr. Thane handed Aunt Seraphina into the
big black barouche while Mr. Lawrence assisted the
coachman in securing the baggage behind.

"Thank you, Mr. Thane," said Aunt Seraphina
graciously, and then he turned and held out his hand
to *her*.

She took it with her own gloved one, feeling again,
as she had earlier today when he'd helped her up from
the sidewalk, a shimmer of pleasure at this contact
between them. But she also looked up into his handsome face with grave misgivings. "Are you *sure* you
don't want to come with us?" she said, very quietly.

"I'm sure."

"Will you promise me something, then?"

"What is it?"

"Promise me you won't do anything—rash, or foolish today. Like kidnapping the Straw Bear. Or worse."

He gave a crooked smile. "Old habits die hard."

Margaret gripped his hand rather tightly. "Just for
today. Please, Mr. Thane. *Promise*."

Bit by bit, his smile faded. "I promise."

"Good. And remember the story of the cow and
the fly."

"I don't know that one."

"It's an old folk-tale out of Africa. A cow faces dire consequences for breaking her promise to a fly."

"Are you comparing me to a cow, Margaret?"

"Only metaphorically. Besides, that would make me a fly."

"I can't picture it somehow."

"Nor you as a cow." She smiled a little. "At any rate, it's quite the cautionary tale."

"Maybe you'll tell it to me sometime."

"Maybe I will."

"Do come along, Margaret, my dear," called Aunt Seraphina from within the barouche. "It's getting chilly in here."

"Well—goodbye," Margaret said to Mr. Thane, "and thank you again. It's wonderful of you to have helped us like this. I'll never forget it." She stepped into the barouche and reluctantly let go of his hand. Moments later they were rolling away, and she kept her eyes fixed on him until he had vanished from sight.

Philip kept his eyes on the barouche until it had vanished from sight.

"*Au revoir,*" he murmured out loud.

A phrase which usually meant goodbye.

Literally, however, it meant *to the reseeing.*

Would he see Margaret again?

Or would they actually manage to get out of Whittlesey?

For her sake, he hoped so.

Then he gave a deep, shuddering sigh, noticing how shockingly, *achingly*, empty the courtyard seemed all at once.

What to do now?

What to do with this long, empty day ahead?

Dark impulses tugged at him, seductively offering the promise of distraction, diversion, even if only for a while. *Steal some jewelry, go get drunk, break something, have a tumble with the shepherdesses . . .*

He could almost *feel* his spirit drifting . . . leaning . . . yielding . . . like a storm-damaged tree on a riverbank, giving way to the pull of the water's inexorable flow . . .

Promise me.

It was Margaret's voice he heard again in his mind. Sweetly husky, pleading, firm.

Promise me you won't do anything rash or foolish today.

And he had answered, as if the words were dragged from him:

I promise.

But he had never been very good at keeping promises.

Will you try harder at your schoolwork?

Yes, he had said to his mother and to his step-grandparents and to his teachers.

He hadn't.

Will you stop the ill-natured jests and the pranks, the teasing and the fights?

I will, he had replied, but he hadn't.

Later, women had said to him:

Last night was lovely. Will I see you again?

Of course, he had responded, but quite often they hadn't.

People would say, handing him a cheque or some bank-notes:

Here you are. You'll pay me back, won't you?

Certainly, he had said. But he never did.

Promise me, Margaret said.

And so Philip stood there in the courtyard, as still

as a statue, feeling the impulses within him pull, push, pull, push.

It was like a silent, invisible war raging.

Both sides were very strong.

And he was so very, very tired.

Which side would win?

You're right on time.

He gave a little shake of his head, trying to remember who said that, and when, and where.

You're right on time . . .

After a few puzzled moments it came to him.

Mrs. Roger, the so-called Riverton oracle, had said this to him last week—last year? Last century?—after he'd arrived from Bristol. She'd marched over to him on the high street, just as if she had been waiting for him to show up.

It hadn't occurred to him, then, to say:

Right on time for what?

She'd had her husband, who happened to be standing nearby with his gig—which had seemed like a convenient stroke of luck at the time—ferry him over to Surmont Hall, where old Henrietta Penhallow had eyed him with cool shrewdness, was patently unconvinced by his breezy claim to have changed his ways, and said in a crisp, sardonic manner:

Old habits die hard. . . . Handsome is as handsome does.

And she had sent him on this fool's errand, with the assurance of payment in order to keep him out of debtors' prison.

So who was the fool now?

He was. That was quite obvious.

He thought of a tree, stuck on a muddy bank, listing dangerously close to a swift-running river.

It would be so easy to let gravity take its course.

To simply let go, to lean, to fall . . .

And to be swept away.

You're right on time.

Handsome is as handsome does.

Promise me.

Promise me you won't do anything rash or foolish today.

Promise me . . .

I promise.

Philip drew a deep breath, and was surprised at how good it felt to have the cold, invigorating air going in and out of his lungs.

The proverbial breath of fresh air.

And just like that, he made up his mind.

Just for today, he'd keep this one small, simple promise.

He wasn't going to think about the past. Or the future.

Just for today, he would keep his word.

And now, what would he do? Where would he go?

Someplace that might, perhaps, bring him a tiny bit of happiness, no matter how ephemeral?

He thought about it.

And then he walked to the Whittlesey bookshop, where he poked around for a while, browsing among the shelves, and made a purchase. No poetry this time, but something he liked even better: novels. Two of them, in fact.

One of them he looked at with fresh curiosity. He was willing to give it another try and, he hoped, lose himself among its pages.

"We're here," Margaret said, and Aunt Seraphina looked up from her tatting and out the barouche's window, answering just a trifle gloomily:

"So we are, my dear." She nudged Mr. Lawrence, who sat next to her with his gingery head lolling against the squabs, with her tatting-shuttle. "We've arrived back in Whittlesey."

Mr. Lawrence woke up from his nap with a glottal snort and glanced out the window. "At least the snow didn't follow us here. That was lucky, wasn't it?"

"Yes," Margaret agreed, a bit absently. Her mind stretched back to what they'd encountered just past Oundle. It was just as Mr. Thane had predicted.

How uncanny.

Also, strange and unnerving.

But—not that she'd want to admit it out loud—hadn't she also been expecting it in some tiny way?

And wasn't she actually rather glad that Philip had been right?

She still didn't think he was some kind of reborn Sisyphus, of course, and there was no *rational* way to explain his apparent situation, but here they were in Whittlesey again and she would, she hoped, get to see him again.

At the thought of this Margaret felt a pulse within her, like a sunbeam breaking through a cloud.

Like happiness.

A few minutes later the barouche pulled into the courtyard of the Woodhull Inn.

And she saw Philip Thane, sitting on a bench, one long booted leg crossed over the other and his dark head tipped forward. He was reading a book.

Another pulse rippled through her, this time more like the excited tingle that had shot through her when they'd first clapped eyes on each other.

This time it felt like happiness *and* . . . something else.

Something warm, even hot.

Something quite pleasurable.

What was better than seeing an interesting, intelligent, attractive man deeply absorbed in a book?

He looked up and it happened again—that *pulse*.

Their eyes met.

He smiled at her.

Not the bold, piratical, devil-may-care smile from the other day, but nonetheless—a smile, one that reached his eyes, and that lovely, hot pulse rippled through her once more.

Margaret smiled back.

He got up from the bench and when the barouche came to a stop, he walked over to pull down the steps himself, open the door, and, in a nice courtly gesture, he handed out Aunt Seraphina first.

"Thank you, Mr. Thane," her aunt said. "Here we are again, bad pennies, I daresay, who keep turning up."

"Not at all, ma'am. As long as you're safe." He held out his hand to Margaret; she took it gladly, and stepped out of the barouche; then she released his hand with some reluctance.

Mr. Lawrence climbed out behind her. "We drove right into that snowstorm everyone's been talking about," he told Mr. Thane. "And a big fallen tree was blocking our way too."

He nodded. "It sounds as if you had no choice but to turn around."

"Yes, we all agreed on that. It would have been rotten for the coachman *and* the horses, even supposing we could have somehow cleared the road. Well, it seems we're stuck here for now. Maybe I'll see if I can find the mayor for an interview after all. But first, shall I go get our rooms back, ladies?"

"I asked the proprietor to hold them for you," said Mr. Thane. "On the off-chance you'd be returning."

"How thoughtful of you, Mr. Thane," Aunt Seraphina said, bestowing upon him an approving smile. "Thank you."

"It was my pleasure, ma'am."

A bustle commenced in the courtyard as their baggage was unloaded by the coachman and two of the inn's staff, and Margaret looked up wonderingly into Mr. Thane's handsome face. She saw that he was looking at her, too, in his dark eyes a somber, wistful melancholy that made her heart rather ache.

"Aren't you coming inside, my dear?" said Aunt Seraphina, and Margaret gave a start.

"It *is* cold out," Mr. Thane said. "Don't let me keep you."

She smiled, just a little. "Not *that* cold. Would you like to go for a walk together?" She saw how into his eyes came just the tiniest bit of light, like a candle trying to flicker back into life, and her own heart lifted. Quietly he said:

"Would *you* like that?"

"Yes."

"Then—yes, I'd like that very much."

So Margaret said, "Aunt, Mr. Thane and I are going for a walk. If that's all right? What are you going to do?"

"Why, I'll have some luncheon, and then I'm going to work on my book, very likely taking up every inch of the private parlor with my things and having a marvelous time and being of absolutely no use to anyone else." Aunt Seraphina looked at both Mr. Thane and her, and Margaret could practically hear the gears in her aunt's brain whirling with new speculation. Then she gave a puckish smile and added:

"Mr. Lawrence, would you care to join me for a bite to eat? My treat, of course."

"I say, that *would* be jolly. Thanks ever so much, ma'am."

The two of them vanished inside the inn and, her concerns allayed, Margaret turned again to Mr. Thane.

"Welcome back," he said, still quietly.

"Thank you. Were you surprised to see us?"

"I'm not sure that anything could surprise me anymore. But I'm sorry you couldn't get away. I'm afraid my curse went along with you."

"Do you know," Margaret said, "I'm really not all that sorry that we had to come back." She watched as just a tiny bit more light came into his eyes, and felt her heart lift a bit more, too. "What were you reading?"

"Rereading, actually—*Waverley*."

She laughed. "You said you'd give Walter Scott another try! How is it going so far?"

"I'm a third of the way through but it's still hard sledding, I must admit." Mr. Thane went over to the bench and picked up the two books stacked there; one of them he gave to her. "This is for you."

She took it and looked at the title. "*Mansfield Park*. Oh, it's the book you mentioned earlier, isn't it? Thank you! What is it about?"

"Fanny Price, an impoverished little girl from Portsmouth, is sent away to live with wealthy relations in Northamptonshire."

"I'm already intrigued. What an interesting plot."

"I think so too." He paused, an arrested expression coming onto his face, and added slowly: "Perhaps because it's like my own life-story in a way."

"Really? How so?"

"My father died when I was nine, and not long after that my mother married the Marquis of Ellington, who had come to Embleton—my hometown—to visit a health-clinic. He had weak lungs, you see, and the sea air was thought to be beneficial as part of his treatment. He and my mother met at the clinic—it had been my father's, who was a physician, and my grandfather, also a physician, still ran it at the time."

How slowly—how *cautiously*—Mr. Thane was speaking, Margaret thought. It summoned to mind a person treading on a frozen lake, wary of thin ice cracking at any moment. She stayed very still, watching him. Waiting with unwavering patience. And finally he went on:

"Once, I told you that all doctors are quacks. In my heart of hearts I don't mean it. Both Father and Grandpapa were excellent physicians. It was bitterness that made me blurt it out. Not even Grandpapa could save Father—nor could anybody, I daresay—but still I blamed him. Father had gone to treat an indigent family suffering from typhus, caught it himself, and didn't survive. For years I blamed Grandpapa, I blamed the poor family, and I even blamed Father. It was . . . a kind of poison."

Margaret put a gentle hand on his arm. "Oh, Philip, I'm so very, very sorry."

He sighed. "Thank you. Shall I go on?"

"Please do."

"After the Marquis arrived, things happened fast. My mother married him six months later, and we went to live at Hathaway Park, the Egremont country seat in Northamptonshire. It was, to say the least, a big change. Like little Fanny Price, I too felt like the proverbial fish out of water."

"I can understand that. Did you—did you blame your mother also?"

"No. My mother Almira is like a well-meaning

butterfly, blown here and there by the wind. Even as a child I could see this about her. She'd loved my father, but she loved the Marquis too. She was very happy to marry him."

"And you? Were you happy?"

He hesitated. Finally: "No. People were kind, but still I felt sad, mostly, and—overwhelmed and inadequate, and—missing my father."

Margaret slid her hand down his arm and intertwined her fingers with his own. "I'm so sorry, Philip," she said again.

And quietly he said, again, "Thank you. I can't remember ever telling anyone this. Admitting that I was unhappy. I always thought it would make me sound—weak. Frail."

"Not to me it doesn't."

A small, crooked smile curved his mouth. "Because, as I already told you this morning, you're kind and generous, and altogether marvelous."

Margaret gave him a little smile in return, filled with a tenderness that both shocked her and made her feel happy. So happy. "That's very kind of *you* to say."

"It's all true. At any rate, I think that's one reason why I like *Mansfield Park* so much—because I see myself in it. And it's beautifully written, too."

"High praise indeed. What happens to young Fanny Price?"

"There are plenty of travails she must face, of course, as does any proper heroine. Do you want to know the ending, or would it spoil it for you?"

"Perhaps just a hint."

"In the end Fanny gets what she deserves—recognition for her true worth, and marrying her one true love."

"Just my sort of book." Margaret smiled up at him again. "It's a lovely gift, Philip, thank you."

"You'll only have it for today, I'm afraid."

"Why? Oh—because tomorrow . . ." Margaret trailed off. She knew he believed that tomorrow would be Plough Day all over again, and that she wouldn't remember anything from today. It would be like a slate wiped clean. No little interlude at the Plough Day ceremony early in the morning. No long, astonishing, revelatory conversation sitting next to each other on the sidewalk. No bittersweet farewell in the courtyard of the Woodhull Inn, as she and Aunt Seraphina and Mr. Lawrence tried to leave town. And no leap of the heart when she saw Philip again, sitting on the bench with his dark head bent over a book as he waited for them—for *her*.

And her heart gave another happy, excited leap within her breast.

She thought about everything Philip had said today. About all the things he—oh so curiously—knew about her.

Could it be possible . . . that it was all *true*? That he really was living the same day over and over again?

Maybe because she'd been chewing on this idea all day long, it somehow didn't seem as odd as it should have.

Philip said, "You're woolgathering, Margaret."

"I was just thinking about something from Greek mythology. About how their concept of time isn't linear—that is, that one day follows after another, in a long sort of line, like a ruler, that can never be repeated. Instead the stories, thought to evoke the agricultural cycle of repeating seasons, describe a *circular* concept which is very different from our own contemporary one."

"Well, to paraphrase you, just because an ancient belief differs from our own doesn't mean it's worthy of scorn."

She smiled. "From our conversation in your barouche,

when we were traveling here from Brampton. Oh, Philip, that *does* seem so long ago! Now listen—we need an extension to our plan."

He was silent for a few moments, and then gravely he said, "Shall we go see if there's any sudden availability on the stage? So that you can evade the curse and leave town?"

"That's not what I meant. I think our plan should be that we spend the day together."

Philip looked surprised. And then some of the gravity left his expression. "Would you like that?"

"Yes, I would." She released his hand, but only to slide *hers* around his arm, noticing, as she did, that it was a very nice and muscular arm, and also thinking that she wouldn't mind one bit running her fingers along the bare skin of it, lingeringly and more than once while she was at it.

"Where shall we go, Margaret?"

"Wherever you like. Lead the way."

Chapter 15

So they walked around Whittlesey together. It had warmed up since the dawn's crisp chill, and in midday the sun was bright and strong. Everything seemed to sparkle a little in the light.

Philip showed Margaret the capacious lending-library, the confectionary shop (where he bought her a box of marzipan which generously she shared with him), the theatre where *Macbeth* was being performed, a quirky and crowded store selling antiquaries, the tiny civic museum, an art gallery, the bookshop where he'd made his purchases earlier on, the Publick House in which the Plough Day banquet was to be held in the evening, and the tall imposing building which, he told her, was said to have once been visited by the controversial Roundhead Oliver Cromwell though, he added, sentiment among the townsfolk ran about fifty-fifty as to its veracity.

And now they came to the town square, which had quieted down since the morning's revelries. The festive bunting-bedecked platform was gone, but there were plenty of people strolling about, lending the scene a cheerful, lively quality. They sat together on a bench, and Philip looked wonderingly at Margaret.

How strange to be so satisfied with something as simple as walking and talking.

To be so satisfied with merely being with another person.

Of course, it helped that that person was Margaret. She was smiling as she watched some boys playing a noisy game of catch. And then, as if aware of his gaze upon her, she turned to look at him and his heart seemed to rise up in his throat at her beauty and the keen intelligence which plainly shone through her face, her eyes, her expression, even the tender lines of her mouth. Teasingly she said:

"You're woolgathering, Philip."

"I beg your pardon. Would you mind telling me the story of the cow and the fly?"

"Oh yes, gladly! It's a story which belongs to the people of Akwa Akpa, in western Africa. It's about a cow who's presiding over a great feast, and who, in her arrogance, neglects to ensure that all her guests, even the lowly fly, are served. The fly asks, the cow promises, but as course after course goes by, the fly gets nothing and must go to bed hungry. So the fly complains to the mighty queen Adiaha Umo, who decrees that as punishment the fly will henceforth be allowed to feast on the liquid of the cow's eyes."

"Most certainly a cautionary tale," said Philip, and couldn't stop the wave of melancholy and regret that broke over him as he thought again of all the promises *he* had never kept.

But . . .

But *today* he had kept a promise.

After Margaret had left this morning, he hadn't gone off and done something stupid.

That was *something*, wasn't it?

He couldn't change the past.

But he could, at least, make the most of today.

He let the great wave of regretful sadness crash and begin to slowly ebb away.

"Philip."

He blinked, and saw her face again. "Yes, Margaret?"

"Speaking of feasts, I'm hungry for luncheon. There's a sweet-looking restaurant just across the street—shall we go there? Are you hungry, too?"

"Very," he answered, surprised to have rediscovered his appetite.

Together they went to the Cup and Saucer where, *un*surprisingly, the only table available was the same cozy one in the corner. Margaret ordered the pork cutlets and green beans, and so did he, and this time he found, having set aside his snobbish derision from before, that they were quite tasty. They talked about the places to which they had traveled, voiced their mutual dislike of the Prince Regent's governing philosophies (if they could even be called that), deplored the rapacious purchase by the British Museum of the so-called Elgin Marbles, agreed as to the lamentable effect the Gothic trend in literature was having on fashion, and Margaret shared some of her brother Jasper's bad jokes which actually had Philip laughing.

It felt like such a long time since he'd laughed. *Really* laughed, with genuine amusement.

After that they walked to the edge of town, where the Straw Bear cooperative was hosting a demonstration on how to dredge effective drainage ditches, and Philip mentioned to one of the organizers that he had come to Whittlesey at the behest of his relation Mrs. Henrietta Penhallow, whose bailiff had brought the cooperative to her attention.

And so the organizer hallooed to one of his col-

leagues, who came over, introduced himself as Dan
Collins, the brother of the bailiff, and wrung both
Philip's hand and Margaret's before sweeping them
away to his nearby house where they met his pleasant wife and his several children. Then they all went
outside and toured the Collinses' extensive gardens
which included dozens of fruit trees, several raised
beds for vegetables, a bustling poultry-yard, and a
very pretty arbor.

Margaret inquired as to how they managed to keep
insects at bay, an ever-present concern of her mother
in managing *her* garden, and the conversation turned
to an animated exchange of remedies, techniques, and
strategies, successful or not. Philip leaned against the
fence-rail, content to listen, and to watch Margaret as
she talked, gestured, smiled and laughed. He *ought* to
have been bored to death—but he wasn't.

How very strange.

But also how very wonderful.

They left an hour later, with expressions of great
cordiality on all sides and Margaret carrying a little
basket with some tea-cakes Mrs. Collins had baked
and insisted on giving to them. By mutual agreement
they walked to the art gallery and this time went
inside where they had a merry time pointing out their
favorite artworks and affably debating the value of art
across the ages.

"I do wish I could paint or draw," Margaret remarked, as they paused before a large and handsome
landscape. "I admire visual artists so much."

"What, no daintily executed watercolors gracing
your walls at home? Isn't that a crucial accomplishment for all gently reared young ladies?"

She laughed. "They tried hard to teach me at school,
but without much success, I'm afraid. All my houses

are lopsided, my flowers are execrable, my horses look like potatoes on sticks, and I *cannot* render hands or feet in any way that looks even remotely human. What about you? Have you some of the artist in you?"

He thought about it. He wasn't usually one to ever look to the past. But she'd reminded him of something. "I was a great doodler in my youth, much to the exasperation of my teachers. Not that I'd call that art, of course. But I liked doing it."

"Ah ha! You've given me an idea. Come along." Margaret drew him out of the gallery and to a shop a few blocks over. "Thanks to our stroll all over Whittlesey," she said, "I remembered this place." It was a general mercantile, and she gestured to something in the window-front, placed between a tray of hair ribbons and a couple of iron cooking-pots. "I'll be right back." She whisked herself inside and soon returned with a sketchpad and a clutch of colored pencils, already sharpened. "You gave me a gift, Philip, and now I can give *you* something."

"You didn't have to do this," he protested.

"I didn't *have* to, but I *wanted* to. Do you like them?" She looked up at him a little anxiously, and he couldn't help but smile at her.

"Very much. Thank you."

She smiled back. "You're very welcome. Will you draw something for me?"

"It's been ages since I have."

"I'm not a harsh critic—I promise. But only if it's something you want to do."

"For your sake, I'll try."

"Splendid. Shall we go sit?" There was a small park down the street, and together they went to it and sat on a bench. Margaret took a tea-cake from the basket and offered it to him; he shook his head and so she began to nibble at it. "Oh, it's delicious! Now, I won't bother you at all while you draw, Philip. I'm going to start reading *Mansfield Park,* if you'll kindly withdraw it from your coat pocket."

He did, and Margaret opened it at once. In turn he opened up the sketchpad and gazed at the blank page.

There was something both terrible and wonderful about it.

Was it an intimidating nothingness—or an inviting field of pure possibility?

He looked around.

Across the street was a shoemaker's, a coffee-house, a butcher shop, and a milliner's. Two women were dawdling in front of the milliner's, eyeing its enticing window display of bonnets and caps, and the butcher's prosperous-looking tabby cat came mincing along, its tail waving lazily behind it. In the park where they sat, a little girl rolled a hoop under the benignant gaze of an older woman—grandmother? Governess?—and a small gray bird came to rest on a nearby tree branch, its bright eyes surveying the scene and then seeming to focus on the tea-cake Margaret held in one hand as she read. All at once it darted down to her feet, plucked up a crumb, and flew away with an air of palpable triumph. Absorbed in her book, Margaret didn't even notice, and Philip looked for a long, long time at her profile.

With her lowered eyelids, long straight nose, and tenderly curved mouth, she resembled a Renaissance Madonna, he thought with a kind of awed admiration. Even the softening light of a late-afternoon sun added to this impression, for it seemed to cast upon her a gentle, glowing, golden patina.

Beautiful.

And slowly he picked up a pencil.

Margaret drifted up from her stay at Mansfield Park, with its tangled web of personalities, the conflicts and desires and the hopes and fears, the great house and the parsonage, the gardens and the shrubberies, the disastrous theatre and *Lovers' Vows,* and returned with a little jolt to the bench in Whittlesey which she shared with Philip Thane.

He was looking at her, looking at her with a glow in his dark eyes, and without thinking about it at all she smiled at him, feeling as if her heart shone without reserve, without fear, in her own eyes as she looked back at him. Softly she said:

"How's the drawing coming along?"

He held out the sketchbook.

Margaret smiled at him again and looked through the first couple of pages.

Charmingly rendered images, in a loose, evocative style, of a tabby cat, a row of shops, two women looking at bonnets, a bright-eyed bird on a branch, an elderly woman with a young girl who was rolling a hoop. He had captured the sense of motion with marvelous precision, and the cat in particular looked so smug and cheerful, she could practically hear it purring. And—

She caught her breath.

Herself, in profile, her head bent over her book. The lines sure and confident; unfussy, deliberate. A soft effect of the light, almost like a nimbus around her. Margaret looked up and at Philip. "Is this really me?" she asked wonderingly. "Is this how you see me?"

"Yes."

"It's lovely. So lovely."

"*You* are, Margaret."

"I—I don't know what to say. Except—thank you."

He smiled a little. "Believe me when I say that it's my pleasure. What do you think of the other drawings?"

"I love them! You have a real gift."

"I don't know about that, but I enjoyed myself. Speaking of which, you looked as if you were enjoying *Mansfield Park*."

"Oh, I was—I *am*! I find poor Fanny Price a much more sympathetic heroine than Emma Woodhouse."

He nodded. "And yet, in a way, despite all her advantages Emma's to be pitied, I think, for her disastrous conceit. She's so oblivious for much of the story."

"A trenchant observation! I may have to try *Emma* again." Margaret took another tea-cake from the basket next to her on the bench and held it out to him. He shook his head and she began to nibble thoughtfully on the cake. "I'm sorry you didn't like *Waverley*. It was good of you to try again."

"It was worth a try. Whenever we read a book again, it's a different experience, don't you think? The book hasn't changed, but we have."

"Oh, that's true! I remember reading *The History of Sir Charles Grandison* when I was a girl and adoring it—I was *quite* in love with Sir Charles who seemed so dashing to me!—but when I tried to pick it up a few years ago I'm afraid I found it horribly overblown. Have you read it, by any chance?"

As the afternoon light began to fade into soft, dark violet and deep gray, they talked more about books, and Margaret was amazed by him all over again. On the carriage ride here she could tell he was clever, he was very well-spoken; but she would have assumed he'd been too busy chasing women to have ever picked up a book. How wrong she would have been, too! His breadth of knowledge was impressive. And oh, how easy it was to talk with him. Never in a million years would she have dreamed she'd be having a day like this with Philip Thane.

Yesterday seemed like ancient history.

The hours were going by so quickly.

Philip could have laughed at himself for feeling like Cinderella at the ball, but there it was. Like her, he *was* enjoying himself beyond anything he'd ever known, and even though he wasn't going to be dressed in rags after the stroke of midnight and see his carriage turned back into a pumpkin, it was still a fact that for both Cinderella and himself, time wasn't on their side. Where was *his* fairy godmother? he wondered, half seriously. Surely it couldn't have been that mysterious Voice saying—in response to his anguished cry of *Why me?—Why not you?*

As darkness fell softly all around them, his spirits sank. In a quiet voice he said, "Shall I take you back to your aunt now?"

Margaret looked surprised—and a little mischievous. "Goodness, it's dusk, isn't it? I didn't even see it coming on. I *would* like to drop off this basket, and change for dinner. I have a beautiful new gown I'm dying to wear. It's periwinkle, and it has the prettiest spangles in the world. But must we end our time together, Philip? For one thing, I haven't yet shared with you my unshakable opinion that *Hamlet* is better than *King Lear,* and I'm still hoping to convince you that paintings can far better express emotions than sculptures. I'm not sure I'll rest till I've won you over to my side. Also, you'll probably be astounded by my apparently infinite capacity for food, but I *am* getting hungry again. Shall we go to the Plough Day banquet? Would you like that?"

He couldn't say anything for a moment, as he was flooded by that same sense of almost dizzy amazement he'd had this morning when Margaret had come to talk to him after the ceremony and said, *May I join you?*

Join him . . . as if he wasn't just some awful, obnoxious, dissolute, trifling sort of fellow, but someone who was actually worthy of her time.

Was it even possible . . . ?

It was dark outside, but within him he felt somehow illuminated.

With humility.

With happiness.

He smiled at Margaret. "Yes. I'd like that a great deal."

An hour or so later they were sitting in their usual spots at the banquet. Mr. Caterpillar Face—whose name, it turned out, was John Samuelson—sat to Margaret's right, of course, and Puce Lady—Mrs. Selina Richmond—was naturally on Philip's left, and together they chatted easily throughout the various courses and then dessert. The room began to empty and people started drifting away, as did Mrs. Richmond and Mr. Samuelson, who parted from them with an amiability that didn't even have any outraged puffing or snorting, and this time the feathers in Mrs. Richmond's turban waved serenely as she went away. Only a few of the staff remained, dimming lamps, clearing tables and setting them again for the morrow with fresh linens, plates, and silverware.

Margaret had a sip of her coffee. "Thankfully, *this* is much better than the wine. Could you pass me the cream? Thank you. Philip, would you mind telling me what happened to you after your mother married the Marquis and you moved to Hathaway Park?"

"Very little happened."

"I don't believe you."

He shrugged. "Alas, it's merely a 'tale told by an idiot, full of sound and fury, signifying nothing.'"

"You're not Macbeth, murdering people out of ruthless ambition!"

"No, I haven't murdered anyone, but that's a fairly low bar, don't you think?"

"Please tell me, won't you, if you can? I want so much to know you better."

"You're going to forget all about it." His spirits were sinking again, as if into quicksand, and he could hear the undisguised melancholy in his voice.

"That may be, but we're here—right here and right now. Couldn't that, perhaps, be enough? Just for this moment?"

He was silent for a while, toying with the stem of his half-full wineglass. At last he lifted his eyes to hers again and said, quietly, gravely:

"I'm afraid, Margaret, that if I *do* tell you you'll despise me."

"Try me."

"Don't say I didn't warn you." And, feeling rather like a man on his way to the gallows, slowly he went on:

"With the best will in the world, they sent me to Eton. I didn't want to go and I begged my mother to let me stay on at Hathaway Park, but she was thrilled at the opportunity she believed this offered to me. Me—the son of an obscure physician in some equally obscure seaside town, going to *Eton*. It was a dream come true for her. And my step-grandparents were willing to pay for it. But when I got there, some of the other boys were—let us say—unkind about my background. As the idiotic James was toward you."

Margaret nodded soberly. "It's all so stupid, and so wrong! I'm sorry, Philip."

He gave another shrug and told her how, as he grew taller and stronger, he purposefully developed a hard shell of breezy braggadocio, and how he had happily walked away from the place when he'd been ejected for his long history of pranks, threats, fights, and tawdry behavior involving some local ladies of the night along with two of the dean's married daughters. "Despise me *now*, Margaret?"

"No, I don't. What happened after that?"

"After a few years of moping around Hathaway Park in disgrace—reading mostly, the house has a stupendous library—I went to London and launched myself into the *ton*, shamelessly coasting along on the Egremont prestige and that of my Penhallow connections. How they open doors in Polite Society! I was invited everywhere. So I'd be in London for the Season, then go to various people's estates for the rest of the year. Europe when I could, when the war ended. My step-grandparents cut off my allowance when I was twenty-three, as they were well and truly tired of paying for my expenses *and* my debts. So I kept gambling mostly, to keep myself afloat, and also I indulged in a great deal of . . ." He paused. "I'm searching for a good euphemism."

"Do you mean wenching?" Margaret said calmly.

"Yes, that's right. I deservedly earned my reputation as a libertine. In fact, I was quite proud of my international renown."

"Did you . . ." she began, then trailed off.

"Did I what?"

"I was wondering if you *enjoyed* yourself all those years."

He was silent again for a while. At length he answered, "I thought I did."

"And now?"

"Now I don't know anymore. I'm nearly thirty years old. What have I accomplished? Nothing. *Nothing.* Last year, in Vienna, I was shot in the chest by a jealous husband and almost died. I barely managed to get back to England and to an operation which saved my life—which my step-grandparents paid for, of course. Perhaps it was a waste of their time and money." Suddenly he laughed. Bitterly. "My God, only listen to this rubbish. An outburst of maudlin self-pity. I *am* an ass. Forgive me."

"There's nothing to forgive," Margaret said, reaching out to cover his hand, which lay against the base of his wineglass, with her own. "No matter what's happened in your past, it's all behind you. There's always—" She stopped.

"Tomorrow?" he said, very quietly.

Margaret leaned forward. "Yes. Philip, isn't time the most precious commodity any of us have? And somehow, for some mysterious reason, you now have more of it than anybody else. Maybe you've been given some kind of—well, some kind of opportunity. Some kind of *gift*."

He looked at her rather fixedly. "An optimistic perspective. Do you believe we live in the best of all possible worlds?"

"You're thinking of the German philosopher Leibniz and his argument for hopefulness?"

"Yes."

"I don't know his theories very well, but doesn't he take the position that the darkness of the world provides an important contrast to goodness—that the darkness offers us a chance to find our way into the goodness we seek? Into light, happiness, connection, peace, joy?"

"Yes, a position for which he's been savaged by his fellow philosophers for over a hundred years."

"I say, you're still here!" It was Mr. Lawrence, of course, bounding into the empty dining-room accompanied by the merry gaggle of his new friends. Margaret discreetly drew her hand away as Mr. Lawrence announced:

"They've closed the taproom, and now they want all the guests to leave for the night. We're going to the Whittlesey theatre just round the corner—it's the late performance of *Macbeth*. It's supposed to be a *ripping* play and I've always wanted to see it. Care to join us?"

Philip looked to Margaret. It was up to her. Previously she had said yes. She'd *always* said yes. How many times? But tonight, she said to him softly:

"Would you mind if we didn't?"

He let out the breath he hadn't known he was holding. "No, I wouldn't mind," he answered just as softly, and so they politely thanked Mr. Lawrence for his kind invitation, and he and his friends bounded away again.

When the big banquet room was quiet and they had it to themselves once more, Philip turned back to Margaret, and saw that she was abruptly deep in abstraction, tracing on the tablecloth some kind of pattern with her forefinger.

He found himself wishing he had the sketchpad with him again, so that he could try and capture the expression on her lovely face. Pensive, dreamy, yet bright somehow too.

After a while he said, "You're woolgathering, Margaret."

She looked up at him and her hand stilled. "Oh! I do beg your pardon."

"What were you thinking about?"

"About Sisyphus. About that boulder he must roll up the mountain, over and over again. What if, every time he gets to the top of the mountain, he takes a bit of it with him when he trudges down to the bottom again? A clump of earth, a weed, a stone. Each and every time. Eventually, the mountain would get smaller and smaller, and finally disappear, and then there'd be no mountain for Sisyphus to climb anymore. Maybe then he'd be free."

He took this in. "Margaret," he said, "one of the things I like most about you is that you make me think."

She smiled. "Is that a compliment?"

"Do you know, it really is."

"I'm pleased to hear it. Oh, Philip, I'm so glad I've met you!"

"Are you? I'm not sure I've ever heard anyone say that before, especially having spent time with me."

"Well, I mean it."

At this he could almost feel his heart actually expanding within him, crowding out melancholy, making room for sudden happiness. But even as he looked at her in the cozy dimness of the room, admiring both her intellect and her beauty, he could also feel the hard rush of lust—the blind, driving, selfish kind—reasserting itself.

And old habits threatened to stir.

Coax her into going to your room at the inn.

Persuade her . . .

You can wrap her around your little finger, if only you try . . .

Tonight's the night, it has to be the night . . .

Time's running out . . .

He lifted his shoulders, as if shrugging something off, and got up from his chair. "Did you know that I've come here a lot?"

"Have you? For the banquet, you mean?"

"Yes, for that, but often I've returned after everyone else has left. There's a door in the back which is easily jimmied open."

"And what do you do when you're here?" she said calmly.

"I'll show you." He went to the table next to them, grasped the edge of the tablecloth in both hands, took a moment to focus, then yanked hard.

There was a tremendous crash as everything tumbled into a scattered heap on the floor.

"Damn," said Philip mildly, and explained to Margaret: "I've always wanted to do this trick, but in my previous life it would have been difficult to practice." He gestured at the mess. "For obvious reasons. Now, of course, I can destroy the entire room and it'll be all nice and tidy again in the morning, with no one the wiser."

He went to the next table and yanked at the tablecloth, with the same result. He tried another one. And another one. "Damn."

Margaret said, interested, "I wonder if it might help to keep your hands lower than the table height? And instead of pulling the cloth toward you, if you pulled it downward?"

"I'll give it a try." He went on to the next table and did as she had suggested. Everything on the tablecloth toppled to the floor again, but he simply continued to the next table and yanked on its cloth. Everything toppled off again.

"If at first you don't succeed, et cetera," he said to Margaret, who nodded, then looked rather puzzled. "What is it?" he asked.

"Oh, nothing, really. It's just that I seem to remember saying that to you sometime."

"Given our very long acquaintance, it's entirely possible." He went on to the next tablecloth and yanked at it again. Everything tumbled off. Methodically he went around the room. Once he got close to success, but not quite. And when finally he returned to where Margaret sat, watching him with a kind of thoughtful curiosity, he said:

"I'll get the hang of it eventually, I daresay. It's only a matter of time—and I've got plenty of that, after all."

She nodded, but he could tell that something was on her mind. He said again:

"What is it?"

"It's not important."

"Try me," he said, echoing her own words from a little while ago.

"It's just that—oh, it's none of my business how you spend your time. I'm not in your shoes, after all. Please do forget I said anything." She stood up and shook out her skirts. "Are you tired of me prosing on, or would you like to come to my inn and sit by the fire for a while?"

"Really?"

"Yes."

"I'd like that very much." Philip took another look around the banquet room in all its extravagant disarray, and tried not to think ahead to the hundreds—thousands—millions of times he'd be yanking tablecloths off a table, over and over and over again.

Chapter 16

Aunt Seraphina had gone upstairs to bed by the time Margaret and Philip arrived at the Woodhull Inn, and so they had the private parlor to themselves. Margaret didn't mind one bit, especially when she and Philip sat cozily together on a small sofa they'd pushed closer to the fireplace. They talked for a while about nothing in particular—as if, by tacit consent, avoiding the heavier topics of time and tragedy—and they each had a glass of claret.

She was tired from the long day, but also warm and toasty after their walk from the Publick House in the chilly dark of night. And she was, all over again, vividly aware of Philip's delicious masculine solidity right next to her, the long length of his body and its easy, graceful lines. As she gazed into the flames of the fire, leaping and dancing and sending out such pleasant warmth, she couldn't help but wonder, privately, what tomorrow would bring. How could she forget what a wonderful, magical, amazing day she'd had with Philip?

It's time to take your own advice, Margaret, she told herself. Earlier she had said to him, *We're here—right here and right now. Couldn't that, perhaps, be enough? Just for this moment?*

And this moment was more than enough.

In fact, it felt like all she had ever wanted or needed.

And if that wasn't magic, what was?

"Penny for your thoughts, Margaret."

She looked up at him and smiled. "I was thinking how happy I am."

"Are you? I'm glad."

"Are . . . are you too?"

He didn't answer right away; he seemed to be thinking hard about it, on his face an expression of dawning wonderment. Finally he said, "Yes, I am," and she heard the sincerity in his voice, as clear as a bell.

"Then I'm glad too." Margaret took a deep breath, thinking of this particular moment and this particular man, and bravely she added, "Do you know what I'd like to do right now?"

"Tell me."

"Well, I—I'd like for us to kiss. I've been wanting to for ages. If—if *you'd* like that also?"

He stared at her, transfixed, which gave her another chance to admire the fascinating green flecks within the brown depths of his eyes. Then he swallowed, and slowly replied:

"'Like' doesn't quite do justice to how I feel about it."

"That's good," she said, with both relief and dreamy joy, reaching out for him, and the next thing she knew, he had caught her up in his arms and brought his mouth, hard and hungry and delightfully urgent, upon hers. Her lips parted without hesitation and she kissed him right back.

It took just a few seconds for Margaret to realize that not only was Philip an excellent conversationalist, he was also an excellent *kisser*.

She hoped he felt that way about her too, and guessed that he did when some time later he lifted his head, smiling in a flatteringly dazed way and breathing rather noticeably and looking at her with his eyes all filled with light. He said with unmistakable sincerity:

"My God, but you're marvelous."

"Thank you." Margaret, in her turn, was quite breathless. "And ditto." She lifted her hand to play with a lock of dark hair that had tumbled onto his forehead. It was glossy and silky and she loved the sensuous feel of it between her fingers. "Did you know that your hair has a gleam of chestnut in it?"

"Is that good?"

"Very."

"Then I'm happy to hear it. May I kiss you again?"

"I wish you would, and the sooner the better."

"Your wish is my command." Hungrily he brought his mouth to hers again and kissed her deeply, at the same time bringing forward one of his hands where it had been holding her tight so that he could cup her breast in his palm.

"That's nice," Margaret murmured dreamily against his mouth, arching her back, and Philip slid his thumb over the rich swell of flesh to where her nipple was. "Oh, *very* nice." Clearly he wasn't just an excellent kisser; he knew what to do with his hands, too. Just as she had suspected all this time. And how wonderful to have such glorious confirmation: he was ardent and generous and so sensitive and adept that her own swift response was a fiery hot thrill running through her from her head to her toes, and everywhere in between.

She slid her hands up into his hair, gripping him hard, and kissed him, feeling all the ravenous urgency he clearly did, too.

Time passed.

A minute, an hour, a lifetime?

It was only the need to take a long full breath that forced her to finally break the kiss. She inhaled, exhaled, smiled at him, radiant. "Very, *very* nice."

Philip smiled back. Then, as light and gentle as snowflakes falling, he kissed her lips, her jaw, her cheeks, the tip of her nose.

"You're so beautiful, Margaret, and wonderful beyond words. Thank you."

"For what?"

"For . . . everything."

Margaret leaned back a little, studying him—and taking a moment to study herself as well. They were at a crossroads, she knew. Should they keep going, kissing, caressing, exploring, and more? All the way to the ultimate intimacy? It would not be difficult to slip away together, upstairs to her room, where they could lock the door and be private. She wanted him; he wanted her. That part, at least, was uncomplicated.

And if—*if*—it really was true that tomorrow was going to be Plough Day again, there wouldn't be any risk of a baby being made, or possible regret for an interlude of wild, sweet recklessness.

And some wild, sweet recklessness, *right now*, would be *wonderful*.

On the other hand . . . she wouldn't remember it.

Philip would, however.

Only he could lay claim to the memory of what they'd shared together.

It was one thing for him to tell her about the many conversations they had had; it was something quite different to have made love.

Margaret envisioned herself at some future date

listening as Philip described what they'd done and felt her spirit cringe at the thought. No matter how tactful and respectful he might be, it would still be . . . awful. Because it would all be a blank to her.

And so she drew away a bit more. "I'm sorry," she said, meaning it. "But I think we should stop for now."

She continued studying his face and saw the disappointment in his expression, and the regret too. But it passed away and he nodded. He even smiled a little. "I understand."

"Thank you for that," she said, and lightly kissed him.

"Do you want me to go, Margaret?"

"No. Will you stay?"

"You'd like that?"

"Very much."

"Then I'll stay—with pleasure."

"Oh, I'm glad! Will you read to me? At home we like to read aloud to each other in the evenings and it's one of my favorite things to do."

"*Mansfield Park*?"

"Yes, please. I wouldn't inflict *Waverley* on you again."

So he went to his greatcoat where he'd flung it over a chair, pulled the slim volume from one of the pockets, and returned to his place on the sofa next to her. "Where shall I begin?"

"I was up to page ninety-four."

He opened up *Mansfield Park* and began reading it in his deep, cultured voice. How beautifully he did it, too, she thought, without hurry, without haste, lending a lovely inflection to each and every word, bringing the story to vivid life. She snuggled closer to him, sure she had never in her life felt so warm and cozy and comfortable. Philip was so solid and so strong. A man to lean upon. To rely upon. To trust. She slipped her hand around his arm, bringing them yet closer together, and let her head come to rest on his broad muscled shoulder as she listened.

The scenes flitted across her mind's eye.

The ill-fated theatricals . . .

Poor Fanny's courageous efforts to resist them, and her pain in watching her beloved Edmund falling under the sway of the sophisticated, glittering Mary Crawford . . .

That awful Aunt Norris, so busy and obsequious and nasty . . .

Mr. Bertram's unexpected return to the family estate . . .

Maria's marriage to the doltish Mr. Rushworth . . .

The scenes converged, blended, fell away, and then, exhausted by her very long day, snug and secure against Philip, Margaret drifted into the pleasant haze of a deep and peaceful sleep.

Philip opened his eyes and above him saw, in the murky dimness before dawn, the familiar ceiling of his room at the Apple Tree Inn.

Here he was again.

Of course.

He sighed a little, and turned onto his side, glancing at the curtained window where, he could see, dawn had yet to break.

His mind was alive with memories from yesterday.

His absolute and utter despair in the morning, feeling nothing but emptiness inside him. He'd been sure that he was defeated, vanquished, undone. *Finished*.

His astonishment when Margaret had found him;

when she'd sat down on the sidewalk with him. Talked with him, *listened* to him.

Later, the look of unfeigned gladness on Margaret's face when the barouche rolled back into the courtyard of her inn and she'd seen him sitting on the bench waiting for her. His wonderment at *her* being glad to see *him*.

Their golden afternoon together, strolling here and there, doing this and that, talking, laughing, getting to know each other, minute by minute, hour by hour.

The banquet at the Publick House. How easy, how pleasant it had been. Looking back, he found that he actually liked their table-mates Mrs. Richmond and Mr. Samuelson. Perhaps there *was* something to be said for not going around insulting people all the time.

After the banquet, Margaret had revisited the subject of Sisyphus and his intolerable burden:

About that boulder he must roll up the mountain, over and over again . . . What if, every time he gets to the top of the mountain, he takes a bit of it with him when he trudges down to the bottom again? A clump of earth, a weed, a stone. Each and every time. Eventually, the mountain would get smaller and smaller, and finally disappear, and then there'd be no mountain for Sisyphus to climb anymore. Maybe then he'd be free.

And when he, Philip, had looped around the room yanking the tablecloths off the tables, he had seen how she'd been watching him with a kind of thoughtful curiosity.

"What is it?" he had said.

"It's not important."

"Try me."

"It's just that—oh, it's none of my business how

you spend your time. I'm not in your shoes, after all. Please do forget I said anything."

She'd gotten up and lightly changed the subject.

Now, as he lay here in bed, he pondered what exactly she'd meant.

It's none of my business how you spend your time.

He set this aside for a moment and remembered how it felt to finally, finally, hold Margaret in his arms, how it felt to kiss her and be kissed by her.

Pure magic.

There was no other way to describe it.

And *she* had asked him to kiss her!

He hadn't needed to jockey her into it, to cajole or to coax or to hint or to suggest or even lie through his teeth. He had simply . . . been there with her.

She wanted to *kiss* him.

It had been as wonderful as he had dreamed. Not only was Margaret clever and beautiful and charming and kind and fascinating *and* an excellent conversationalist, she was also an excellent kisser; and her hands had a kind of delicious power in them. She set his flesh, his bones, his very spirit on fire.

He had wanted more, of course.

More kissing, more caressing, more exploring . . . all leading up to the ultimate intimacy for which he had waited for so long.

But when she had gently brought things to a halt, he had *listened*. He had respected her choice. He had honored her choice. And been rewarded with a smile of such piercing sweetness that he seemed to feel it directly in the region of his heart.

He lifted a hand to his chest. He had a dense, gnarled scar there, from the old bullet-wound. Was it his imagination, or had the scar healed somewhat since the last time he'd touched it?

That seemed rather magical, too.

He thought again to last night, to how he had been disappointed, regretful, but had only said to her, *I understand*.

Never would the old Philip Thane have simply let go of his own desires.

The old Philip would have at once started in on the coaxing, the hinting, the cajoling, caring only about his own wants and needs.

Instead—strangely enough—it was *Margaret* he had wanted to please.

It was Margaret's happiness that mattered more than his own.

And even more strangely, it had taken no effort on his part to see this, to feel this, to act accordingly. It had come to him as naturally as breathing.

He lay there in his bed, shocked to his very core.

Was this how life could actually be?

He relived in his mind how it felt to have Margaret leaning so confidingly, so trustingly, against him as he'd read *Mansfield Park* to her. How it felt to breathe in her familiar scent of summer roses. How . . . *happy* he had been.

When she'd fallen asleep, slowly he had closed the book and looked at her as she lay utterly relaxed with her head on his shoulder, tawny-brown lashes feathering her cheeks, her lips slightly parted. Within him had bloomed a mix of emotions unlike anything he'd ever experienced.

He had been awed by her beauty.

Dazzled by her soul.

Humbled by just being with her.

And he was flooded with something else, something powerful, cleansing, curing, sweet, glorious . . . and unfamiliar.

It had taken him a while to figure out what it was, for it was like a tapestry comprised of many colors, many different threads. He could identify among them liking, respect, admiration. Desire: intense, carnal, and fiery. Companionability. Hopefulness. An urgent need to be of service, a drive to bring her happiness, to see her smile, to keep her safe. All woven together into the most gorgeous creation in all existence.

And then he had finally realized.

It was *love,* in point of fact.

He lay there stunned and shocked and amazed.

He, Philip Thane, rapscallion extraordinaire, who had left a trail of broken hearts all across England and Europe, dancing lightly and indifferently from woman to woman, his own heart as cold as ice, had fallen in love with the magnificent, the wonderful Margaret Allen.

He loved her.

He soaked in this revelation for a while, humbled and awed, as he brought to life in his mind her beautiful face.

And he thought of one of his favorite passages in *Mansfield Park.*

You have qualities which I had not before supposed to exist in such a degree in any human creature. You have some touches of the angel in you.

Philip turned on his back again, awash with a feeling of gratitude more profound than any he had ever before felt in his whole entire life.

He loved Margaret Allen.

Someone knocked on the door.

"Wake up, sir," said a voice from outside the room, "it's Plough Day."

Knock knock knock.

"Mr. Thane," said the voice, "you asked to be awakened in time for the ceremony. It's Plough Day, sir."

Knock knock knock.

"I'm awake, thank you," he said mildly.

"Very well, sir."

But Philip didn't get out of bed just yet.

He was thinking, again, about something Margaret had said.

It's none of my business how you spend your time.

Whether or not that was true, she'd raised a good point.

How *was* he going to spend his time today?

She had been dreaming.

Lazily, luxuriously, Margaret turned from her back onto her side, tucking the covers more warmly about her neck and shoulders. It wasn't quite sunrise yet, so she had a few more minutes in which to enjoy her cozy bed and recall her very interesting dreams.

How vivid they had been, how *real* they had seemed.

And strangely enough, they all seemed to have Philip Thane in them.

Even more strangely, they featured a different Philip from the one she had met yesterday on the ride here from Brampton.

In her dreams he wasn't an aggravating, insinuating, jaded libertine, but instead he had become . . .

In point of fact, he was literally the man of her dreams.

He was interesting and clever and thoughtful . . .

Well-read and a wonderful conversationalist, with a lively sense of humor, too . . .

Also he was all strong and muscled and exceedingly

attractive, with the most fascinating brown-green eyes which sparkled with lively intelligence . . .

They had walked around what seemed to be Whittlesey. They'd gone out to look at—of all things!—drainage ditches, and someone's garden . . . sat in a park and watched the world go by . . . went to a big dinner-party, where her neighbor dressed in eye-catching puce and wore a great befeathered turban . . . Philip had yanked tablecloths off tables, over and over, sending dishes and silverware crashing to the floor . . . and they'd ended up in the private parlor here at the Woodhull Inn, where they sat before the fire, and kissed each other, quite passionately and delightfully . . .

Even now she felt warm and tingly just remembering it.

He was the *best* kisser, and his hands were, well, magical.

How she had wanted him!

How she had liked and enjoyed him!

How she had . . . *loved* him.

Margaret gave a long, deep sigh and turned onto her back again.

It was curious just how much the dream felt like a genuine memory, and not just the creation of her busy, wistful nighttime brain.

She had wanted Philip Thane to be something he wasn't in real life.

If he even showed up this morning to give his speech, he'd be just as sardonic and lecherous and off-putting and annoying as he was yesterday.

Damn.

Double damn.

Triple damn.

But there was no point wallowing here in bed

feeling all melancholy and lonely and yearning for something that couldn't be.

It was Plough Day, after all, and she was very curious to see the fabled Straw Bear and add to her notes.

So Margaret pushed aside the covers, got out of bed, and began to get dressed, trying hard to shake a lingering feeling of sadness and loss.

Philip turned onto the sidewalk fronting a variety of stores and shops and came across the rickety table, covered with a neatly ironed cloth, behind which sat the middle-aged couple, the woman and the man, looking cheerful and friendly.

The woman picked up a basket and held it out to him. "A donation for the convalescent home, sir? For our brave war veterans."

For the very first time, Philip paused.

He thought about Margaret, and her generous spirit.

Then he reached into his greatcoat pocket and put into the basket all the bank-notes he had in the world. Not because Margaret was around and he wanted, deviously, to impress her by giving away the dignitaries' money—but because she did things like that all the time. She never *could* walk past a person in need, or a dog or a cat or a horse in trouble, without intervening. Why not try it for her sake, simply and quietly?

"Thank you, sir," said the woman warmly. "It's *most* kind of you to help."

"You're welcome, ma'am," Philip said, "it's my pleasure."

And it really *was* a pleasure.

He suddenly felt as if he was ten feet tall and walking on air.

But just as suddenly he realized that if he didn't make a detour right away, he'd run into Matron again. O God: he didn't want to be dragged back into the past, he didn't think he could endure it. So he loped across the street, where he came upon a little girl selling posies made from snowdrops, their graceful drooping blossoms tipped with cheerful yellow, and tied together with a bit of green ribbon. She told him they grew to the back of her house and she was hoping to earn enough money for a doll, one she'd been admiring in the window of the toy-shop for ages. It occurred to Philip that he'd never noticed how, even in deepest winter, flowers could still grow and bloom.

He bought a posy from the girl, and gave her a generous tip, too.

Her smile of thanks seemed to brighten the day even more, and as Philip made his way into the town square, under his breath he whistled along with the merry, lilting sounds of the pipe and drum.

Warm and snug in her thick wool pelisse and cozy hat, Margaret looked around from her place near the bunting-bedecked platform with a pleasure tempered by that lingering feeling of wistful sadness and also by a rising curiosity.

When would she see Philip Thane again?

What would happen then?

Impatiently she scanned the crowd. Where *was* he? And why on earth—having met him only yesterday— did she care so much? Now *that* was odd. Suddenly she spotted a tall broad-shouldered figure coming toward the platform and, all at once feeling very relieved, she called out:

"Good morning!"

He came near and she saw at once that he was looking quite different—*remarkably* different—than he had last night when he had dropped Aunt Seraphina, Mr. Lawrence, and herself off at their inn. Then he had been annoyingly suave and sardonic, and openly bitter about having to get up early for the Plough Day ceremony.

Today he was looking surprisingly pleasant, even . . . happy. Which made him look so handsome, and so much like the man in her dreams last night, that Margaret, astonished, her curiosity piqued even more, found that she was actually glad to see him. And to her further surprise she saw that he was carrying a pretty little bouquet of white and yellow flowers.

"Good morning," she said again, smiling at him. "Happy Plough Day."

He smiled back at her. "Happy Plough Day. Will you excuse me for a moment?" He went up the steps of the platform and chatted for a minute or two with the dignitaries clustering there. Then he came back and said to Mr. Lawrence who stood next to her:

"Good morning. I mentioned to the mayor that you're a journalist from Watford, and asked if he'd be willing to let you interview him for the *Bugle*. He said by all means, and to come see him after the ceremony."

"By Jove, that's splendid, sir, thank you very much! How did you guess I was hoping for that? My editor will be ever so pleased with me."

"I just assumed you would," Philip Thane said, and Margaret gave him a long, wondering, curious, approving look.

This was all quite uncanny.

He was so kind and thoughtful. *Just* like the man of her dreams. And oh, how attracted she was to him. She found herself hungering to kiss that smiling and very, very tempting mouth. Hungering to kiss him, and do more than just kiss. Had she . . . had she somehow dreamed this new Philip Thane into existence?

All at once a wisp of memory—from a dream?—floated across her mind.

Double, double toil and trouble, fire burn and caldron bubble. Time doth spin round and round, to each other you are bound. Double, double toil and trouble, fire burn and caldron bubble. Thwart it with your true love's kiss, thus the charm brings sweetest bliss.

"Margaret."

She gave a start. "Yes, Philip?"

"Do you like snowdrops? They don't quite match the roses in your bonnet, but I hoped you might like them anyway."

He held out the sweet little posy and Margaret took it at once and tucked it into the vee of her pelisse, just below her throat. "Thank you so much," she said, pleased, even delighted. "I love it. Sometimes the simplest gifts are the best, don't you think?"

He smiled at her, with such tenderness in his dark eyes that she felt a responsive flicker within her leap into life.

"Yes," he said. "I've been learning that."

Philip sat at a table in the Whittlesey lending-library, a couple of great thick books open before him. One was a volume of German philosophy, over which he had been poring, day after day; the others were translational and pronunciation dictionaries. Lately he had been studying the eighteenth-century philosopher Immanuel Kant, and just now he was working on translating something, painstakingly, word by word:

Regeln für das Glück: etwas zu tun, jemanden zu lieben, etwas zu hoffen.

Rules for . . . happiness . . .

The translation emerged bit by bit, almost like a flower unfurling.

. . . something to do . . .

. . . someone to . . .

. . . like?

No, that wasn't it. He rifled through the translational dictionary.

Ah! He had it now.

Love.

. . . someone to love . . .

. . . something to . . .

. . . hope for.

And there it was:

Rules for happiness: something to do, someone to love, something to hope for.

Philip read this over and over again, feeling rather like an arid desert receiving the sweet and precious benediction of rain, and then he looked up and around him, smiling. This lending-library—a square, old-fashioned building, dark-paneled but with plenty of windows to admit the light—had become, over time, almost a kind of home to him; he spent so many hours here. How *many* hours exactly? Thousands? Tens of thousands? More than that?

He had no way of specifying other than a vague realization, which surfaced now and again, that it was a lot. Some time ago he'd stopped trying to count the hours or keep track of the days. He had begun to let them flow past him—no, to *submerse* himself in them, like slipping into a river he'd once wished he could dam up, and he had surrendered to its greatness and its inevitability. The sum of all his days was no longer a burden.

It was Margaret who had once said to him: *Isn't time the most precious commodity any of us have? And somehow, for some mysterious reason, you now have more of it than anybody else. Maybe you've been given some kind of—well, some kind of opportunity. Some kind of gift.*

Maybe, just maybe, Margaret was right.

And so here in this library, time and time again, he had roamed among the shelves, trailing his fingers along the leather spines, pausing to read the titles one after the other, until he pretty much knew all the books housed in here.

The table at which he sat was in the sciences section, so there were books on philosophy, natural history, pure science, anatomy, medicine, mathematics, and so on. Opposite him were the sections in literature, art, music, languages, history, and geography. Every day—like Sisyphus, perhaps, taking a little something from atop the mountain to bring back down with him—he borrowed a book to take back to his inn, having, of course, to each day keep borrowing the same book until he finished it.

So far he had read or reread works by William Blake, Frances Burney, Robert Burns, William Cowper, Germaine de Staël, Daniel Defoe, Maria Edgeworth, Henry Fielding, Oliver Goldsmith, Mary Hays, Eliza Haywood, Samuel Johnson, Ann Radcliffe, Mary Shelley, Charlotte Turner Smith, Tobias Smollett,

Jonathan Swift, Johann Wolfgang von Goethe, and Horace Walpole.

He reread all of Miss Austen's books, too, and ignored without remorse everything by Walter Scott.

At present he was on a double jag: philosophy and German.

It was slow going, but immensely satisfying. At school he couldn't have cared less about philosophy, or about reading books in their original language, and so now he felt as if he'd been given a second chance at his education.

Altogether it was no hardship to spend these hours in the library, reading, studying, thinking.

Bong . . . bong . . . bong . . .

Somewhere in the distance, church bells were chiming.

Eleven bells. An hour before noon.

Which meant that any moment now, over at the Woodhull Inn, the Penhallow barouche would, in all likelihood, be pulling into the courtyard with Margaret, her aunt, and Mr. Lawrence inside. They had wanted to leave town and he offered them the barouche, without saying anything about the snowstorm and the big fallen tree they'd encounter just past Oundle.

Sometimes he met them there in the courtyard, and they all had luncheon together.

Quite often he and Margaret would go for a stroll, during which he said nothing about his peculiar situation. Neither did he reveal that he knew her so intimately—the kind of person she was, her likes and dislikes, her habits and routines, the names of her parents and brothers and cousins and aunts and uncles and also all the family pets, her history, where she had gone to school, the subjects in which she excelled, the tale of her sad romance with the idiot James, even the fact that she was a marvelous kisser who lit him up with ecstatic joy. Nor did he let her know that he was head over heels in love with her.

Instead, he did his best to simply enjoy his time with her, moment by moment.

Every day gave him the chance to see Margaret.

And that was something worth getting out of bed for.

Sometimes he asked Mr. Lawrence if he'd like a second pair of eyes on the article he was writing up for the Watford *Bugle,* and so the two of them would go to a tavern where, over a glass of crisp ale, they would discuss the finer points of journalistic prose and grammar. They'd play some darts, too, just for fun.

Sometimes he'd wander into the toy-shop that was next to the jewelry store he had robbed long ago. There he'd met the Kings, the affable couple who owned it. It turned out, in a remarkable coincidence, that years ago Mr. and Mrs. King had been part of a traveling troupe of actors which had come to Embleton when Philip was a small boy.

Amazingly, they had met his father, who had helped Mrs. King when she'd been stricken by a severe bout of influenza. The Kings had had little money to spare, but Father had insisted on caring for her in his clinic, rather than in their less than hygienic inn, and refused to accept any payment.

Moreover, when Mrs. King finally was well again, he also insisted that he be allowed to pay for their expenses in catching up with their troupe which had had to move on the previous fortnight.

The Kings couldn't say enough nice things about the late Dr. Thane and Philip found himself basking vicariously in their praise; as if their grateful recollections truly helped keep Father's memory alive within him.

Once, returning from the Plough Day ceremony, Philip struck up a conversation with Mr. Lancross, the proprietor of his inn, whose normally smiling countenance drooped into lines of deep anxiety when, Philip having admired the handsomeness of the place, he blurted out that there was a large hole in the roof he couldn't afford to repair, and neither could he fix it himself—not being, he said, as young and spry as he used to be.

At first Philip thought about borrowing money from the Whittlesey dignitaries as he'd done before, and giving the money to Mr. Lancross, but soon dismissed the notion. He offered to fix the hole, but only if Mr. Lancross would teach him how to do it, step by step.

Do you mean it, sir? Mr. Lancross would exclaim, brightening.

Yes, I do, Philip would answer, and could almost see the heavy, fearful burden lifting from the older man's shoulders.

So day after day, Mr. Lancross would instruct Philip in the art and science of roof repair.

In his old life, Philip would have scoffed at the idea of doing manual labor. He, a scion (even if disgraced) of the Egremont and Penhallow families, crawling around a roof?

Unthinkable!

But that was his old life. In his new one, he had said yes.

It was miserable, dangerous work. At first Philip was clumsy, embarrassingly clumsy, with the tools. Once he nearly severed his thumb and had to be rushed, bleeding profusely, to the infirmary. He dropped a hammer

on his foot and broke four of his toes. Several times he
fell off the ladder. He got chilblains. He choked on the
dust. A rat bit him. Twice he slipped off the roof and
knocked himself silly.

And, of course, every day the hole was back to its
original size.

Over time, however, Philip became more skillful.
And quicker. And more confident. It wasn't that he
grew to *like* the dirt, the dust, the danger. But he
remembered Mr. Lancross' anxious face, his nervous
twisting hands, and doggedly he kept at it.

And then, at last, there was the afternoon, when
the violet light of sunset was deepening in the sky, that
he finished repairing the hole *on the same day*. He
and Mr. Lancross drank a whole bottle of champagne
together, got enjoyably tipsy, and ended up regaling
the common-room with such crowd-pleasing songs as
"The Joys of the Country," "Egad We Had a Glorious
Feast," "With Love My Heart Is Beating," "Robin
Adair," and "Look'ee Dear Ma'am," with everyone
joining in on the choruses at the top of their lungs.

Now *that* was a good day.

Not all of them were, though.

Some days he was consumed by grief, or burning
anger, or bitterness, or morose lassitude, or a self-pity
so raw that he wept, or even by a terrible gnawing
envy of people who could wake up each morning to a
new and different day.

There were days when he was rude or openly lascivious or sardonic to Margaret, and he hated himself
as he watched her lovely face harden and close off to
him. Or he might be unkind to young Mr. Lawrence,
or insult somebody—*anybody*—at random. Or he
might behave in other ways that reminded him of the
bad old days.

He would try harder, the next day, to make up for his lapses.

He wasn't perfect, but he was trying to be better.

Trying to become a man Margaret could like, respect, and possibly . . . possibly even love.

Chapter 17

Margaret sat with Philip on a wide swing they'd discovered now that the festive bunting-bedecked platform had been removed sometime earlier today. They were swinging back and forth, her arm linked companionably through his. The golden light of afternoon had just begun to fade into the softer, darker colors of dusk, and the town square was beginning to empty out. Even the boys who'd been playing a riotous game of catch had gone.

"This has been *such* a nice day," she said, warmly, truthfully, to Philip. "I'm not the least bit sorry we had to come back to Whittlesey."

"Nor am I." He smiled at her with such tenderness that for a few moments she felt as if the earth had shifted beneath her feet. On the ride out of town today she had been flooded with such intense regret at leaving Philip that she had been shocked. It had felt, somehow, as if she was leaving a part of herself behind, and she had vowed to never do it again.

Again?

That made no sense, nor, too, did the intensity of her feelings.

She barely knew Philip, and yesterday he had been

so annoying and obnoxious on the journey here from Brampton.

Yet, curiously, yesterday seemed so very, very far away.

And today was sparkling with bright promise. She was happy, *happy*.

Because of Philip Thane.

A Plough Day miracle, Margaret thought, half seriously, then reverted back to the subject they had just been discussing. "I'm very impressed that you're teaching yourself German."

"Thank you. I'm trying to make up for lost time, you see. I wasn't the best of students while at school. It's lucky for me that *you're* fluent, Margaret. Would you mind explaining to me how plurals work in German?"

"Not at all. It's a trifle more complex than in English, in which we simply add an 's' to the end of a word. In German you usually—but not always—add an 'e.' For example, *der Hund*—'dog'—becomes *die Hunde*. But with *der Vater,* say—'father'—the plural is *die Väter,* with an umlaut over the 'a.'" She went on to explain other exceptions, and then Philip carefully said, after repeating them after her:

"*Vielen Dank, ich bin Ihnen sehr dankbar, fräulein.*"

Thank you very much, I'm very grateful to you, miss.

She smiled. "*Gern geschehen. Du bist ein ausgezeichneter Schüler.*"

You're very welcome. You're an excellent student.

He smiled back. "I'm trying."

It was Plough Day, bright and early, and on his way to the town square Philip had paused to put all his bank-notes into the basket of the woman asking for donations for the convalescent home, received her thanks and acknowledged them as warmly as she had tendered them, and was just about to make his usual detour across the street to avoid Matron, whom he could see, at the far end of the sidewalk, coming his way, as always bundled up in her shawls and wraps.

But today, for some reason, he didn't.

He stepped back, half-turned away, and waited. For what, he didn't know, but there he stood anyway.

Matron came to the table. "Oh, good morning, Mrs. Jenkins! Mr. Jenkins, good morning! Have you collected many donations today? I hope you don't mind my coming round, but Jacob's been wondering, and so have I." Her voice was soft and full of what sounded like poorly concealed worry, contrasting so profoundly with her beaming smile and cheerful manner from before, that Philip stood stock-still, listening as hard as he could.

At the same time, he let his mind go back to the past.

He let himself summon up memories of himself at Eton, his misery and wretchedness, and this time he remembered how unfailingly kind Matron had been to him. That horrible day she'd found him crying in the laundry, desperately missing his father and hugging a sack of clothes as if it were Father himself he was clutching, she had patted his shoulder and sat by him, with the utmost patience despite all the many duties calling her, until he'd managed to pull himself together.

After that she'd slipped him tiny treats, too, a caramel or a bit of licorice, and took special care of him when he'd catch a cold or was shivering in bed with an ague. And always she was careful to not overtly distinguish him among the other boys as needing some extra attention, as that would have, naturally, singled him out for additional scorn and bullying.

Jacob Parcell, Philip now recalled, was her son and only child, a rifleman in Sir John Moore's Fifty-second Foot regiment. How proud Matron had been of him! She carried a rough little likeness of him, folded into a locket which she always wore around her neck. Once, while on leave, he'd come to visit his mother at Eton, and Philip had met him. He'd been only a young boy, and had looked up with awe at Matron's great strapping son who had, like his mother, shown him nothing but affable kindness during the three or four conversations they shared.

So why was Jacob wondering about donations to the convalescent home?

"Oh, there's never enough, is there, dear Mrs. Parcell?"

It was the woman—Mrs. Jenkins—sitting at the table who spoke, bringing Philip back to the here and now. Mrs. Jenkins added, gesturing at *him*:

"But this gentleman just gave a very generous donation."

Philip turned back to the table and watched as Matron's face lit up.

"Why, goodness me, if it isn't Philip Thane!"

He went to her, and held out his hand; she took it in her own and clasped it tightly, exclaiming in wonderment:

"Just fancy meeting you here, after all these years, Master Philip! Why, it's quite the Plough Day miracle!"

"Hullo, Matron," he answered, smiling at her. "It's good to see you too. And do call me just 'Philip,' won't you? And I'll call you 'Mrs. Parcell,' if I may.

It *is* quite the coincidence seeing you again. I don't remember your being from Whittlesey."

Some of the light left her expression then, and the worry returned. "Oh no, I'm from Bray, Master Philip—I mean, *Philip*. You see, there was a specialist here—ten years ago—I brought Jacob to see him. Perhaps you remember Jacob? My son?"

"Of course I do. What sort of specialist did Jacob need?"

"A doctor specializing in treating gangrenous wounds—he was also the director at the home for war veterans here in Whittlesey. My Jacob had been hurt in Ireland, and right bad."

"I'm very sorry to hear that. Is he all right now?"

"Oh, well, he's had some amputations, Master—I mean, Philip—but he's done well for himself, really. He's alive, when there were months—years—when I—well, I despaired for him, to own the truth, and because of the Black Dog—the melancholy, you know—which ate at him, too. He said he felt so *trapped* by his injuries—by his circumstances. He came round in time, though, and he's the director himself now, and managing it all so nicely! But there never *does* seem to be enough money, no matter how hard we all try. And the home is full to bursting, which makes it even harder. Oh! And here I am, wasting your time telling you of my silly troubles. I'm sure you have many more important things to do than listen to an old woman like me. What brings *you* to Whittlesey?"

"I'm here to give a speech at the ceremony. But after, may I go see Jacob? Could you join me for that?"

"You're giving a speech? Why, Philip, how impressive!"

"Not so much, ma'am. What your Jacob has done—that's truly impressive."

Mrs. Parcell looked pleased. "That's very kind of you to say. Shall I wait for you here, and we'll go on to the home after?"

"It's cold out, however. Would you like to wait for me over at the Cup and Saucer, just across from the square? You'd be warm in there, and maybe you could have a nice cup of tea." Philip saw the fleeting look of embarrassment on Mrs. Parcell's face and he pulled from his greatcoat pocket a couple of coins which surreptitiously he pressed into her hand. "Will this help?" he softly asked her.

She beamed up at him. "You're a thoughtful lad! Thank you!"

He held out his arm and escorted her to the Cup and Saucer and saw her established at a cozy table by the window, which was where he found her again after his speech was over. Together they went to the convalescent home, a ten minutes' walk from the square, and he saw it was a low, long building, very much in need of new paint; to the front was a scrubby, dilapidated sort of garden with a few lonely-looking benches placed here and there.

Inside it wasn't much better, but he could see at once that people had been trying to make it as cheerful as possible. It was impeccably clean, for one thing; the aged furniture was placed so as to invite gathering and conversation; the plants set here and there were thriving; and on the walls were all kinds of paintings and drawings, many with simple frames or none at all, and Mrs. Parcell explained that they'd been made by the residents over the years. She led him to a group of men around a table, two of whom were playing chess.

A very tall, broad, bearded man, who stood rather than sat, looked up as they approached and Philip recognized him right away, though it was a shock to see Jacob Parcell leaning on crutches; one of his legs had been amputated below the knee and the cuff of his trousers was rolled up neatly beneath the joint and pinned securely. Jacob smiled and limped forward to meet them, and Philip was sure that he'd lost his other foot. But he managed to walk nonetheless, however arduously.

"Hullo, Mum," he cheerfully said, then held out an enormous hand to Philip. "How d'you do, sir?"

Philip warmly shook Jacob's hand. "Hullo. You don't remember me, I daresay, but I remember *you*. I'm Philip Thane. You came to visit Mrs. Parcell while I was a student at Eton."

Jacob's smile widened. "Indeed I do! Bright as a button you were, sir. We had some splendid chats, and you asked some awfully clever questions for a young shaver like yourself. Wondered if you might go into the military someday."

"No, I never did. Mrs. Parcell was telling me that you're the director of the home, sir, and that you're doing a marvelous job at it too."

Jacob glanced affectionately at his mother. "Well, I do try, Mr. Thane—we all do—but it's hard sledding sometimes making do, I'll admit. Still, I love the job, and I still get up excited every day to try and make the best of things. Would you like a tour of the place?"

"Very much."

And so Jacob Parcell showed him around the home. It wasn't easy meeting the injured former soldiers, especially those who were the worst off; their difficulties tore at the heart. But Philip was impressed by what was being accomplished despite the home's straitened circumstances.

He left an hour later, having parted from Jacob and his mother with great cordiality, and as he walked thoughtfully back toward the Apple Street Inn— where he planned to have another crack at the roof, if only to lighten Mr. Lancross' load for the day—he mused with admiration upon Jacob's resilience and extraordinary strength of character. No air of the Black Dog, melancholy, hung about him, no hint of self-pity—just a cheerful determination to get on with his life as best he could.

It made Philip wonder at his own bouts of feeling sorry for himself. The wise Shakespeare had said, *Comparisons are odious,* and there was little value in comparing one's burdens to those of others; but it wasn't hard to conclude that, all things considered, he, Philip, had been singularly blessed.

His thoughts went back to the convalescent home.

The resident physician, a Dr. Saltonstall, had joined them about halfway through the tour, and mentioned some of the recent advances in wound care and rehabilitation which he had been implementing there; the talk had turned to a clinical discussion of infection treatments, diseases of the blood, effective splinting techniques, tissue repair, and so on.

He had listened with interest, thinking, inevitably, of his own father and grandfather. He could remember, even now, the animated discussions between the two of them—though of course he, as a little boy, could understand almost nothing. The impression that chiefly remained after all these years was their passion and excitement for their work.

In the sciences section of the Whittlesey library, Philip suddenly recalled, there were three or four shelves of books about anatomy and medicine. He hadn't looked into any of them, as he had been busy pursuing his interests in literature, languages, and philosophy.

Maybe he would—

He broke off his train of thought. He had heard someone, a child, exclaiming, *"Damn!"* and after that, a loud yelp, as if of pain, and into Philip's nostrils came the strong smell of smoke. Just as quickly he realized that he knew that voice, and he began running toward the sound of it.

The Plough Day ceremony was over, and Margaret had had a very interesting and enjoyable time. How delightful to see the fabled Straw Bear! And hadn't it been just so kind of Philip to help Mr. Lawrence get an interview with the mayor for his newspaper?

What a different Philip from yesterday, too. Margaret could hardly believe how pleasant—how civil—how agreeable—how incredibly *attractive* he was today. In fact, she had actually been sorry when he hadn't lingered after the ceremony, saying that he'd run into an old friend from his schoolboy days who was waiting for him at the Cup and Saucer restaurant. Margaret had gazed rather wistfully at his tall, broad-shouldered figure as he made his way among the crowd.

Naturally she couldn't have invited herself along, but she *could* have asked to meet up with him later.

Maybe she'd do that tomorrow.

Tomorrow—?

Why on earth was she expecting another chance to ask him after the Plough Day ceremony?

Tomorrow wouldn't be Plough Day again.

How odd that she would have thought that.

Slowly, pensively, Margaret went back to her inn

and into the private parlor, where she enjoyed a hearty breakfast with Aunt Seraphina, after which she got out her notes, poring over them and making additions while her aunt continued reviewing the long printer's galley-sheets of her forthcoming book.

It was very cozy and convivial.

But something was tugging at Margaret—quietly, subtly, insistently. She didn't know what it was precisely, but it refused to go away and she found she couldn't concentrate anymore. At last she got up. "Aunt, I'm going out for a while."

Aunt Seraphina muttered, "Drat! Yet *another* printer's error. Dear me, how difficult it is—spotting mistakes in one's own work. I do beg your pardon, my dear. What did you say?"

Margaret smiled lovingly at her aunt. "I said I'm going out for a while."

"Very well, my dear," replied Aunt Seraphina absently. "Enjoy yourself." And, pen clutched firmly in one hand, she went back to scrutinizing the galley-sheets.

So Margaret put on her pelisse, hat, and gloves again and went out into the bright sunlight of midday. She started walking briskly. It was impossible to explain, but it was almost as if her *feet* knew where to take her, as if she was being tugged along by an invisible string.

She turned a corner onto Plympton Street and was astounded—shocked—to see Philip rapidly coming toward her, in his arms a young freckle-faced boy who was crying hysterically, clutching one of his arms to his chest. As they came closer she could smell a horrible charred smell and realized that the boy had burnt his arm very badly.

"Good God," she gasped, hurrying to them. "What's happened? What can I do?"

"We're going to the infirmary, just up the street," Philip said, not checking his stride, and Margaret spun about and kept pace with him by taking three steps to one of his own. Philip went on, "Poor little chap was roasting chestnuts and let the fire burn too high. Can you find his mother, a Mrs. Abernathy? She may be walking about looking for Thomas. Stout lady wearing an enormous purple hat."

"Of course," Margaret answered, and hurried with him to the infirmary, just long enough to hold the door open for them. "Oh, good luck!" Then, standing alone on the sidewalk, she looked left and right. Which way to go?

Her heart was pounding hard in her chest with distress, and she took a few deep breaths to calm herself. Then, a bit desperately, she cocked her head, as if listening.

It came to her after a few moments.

Go to the right.

Without bothering to question the instinct guiding her, Margaret began walking quickly to the right of the infirmary. At the corner of Plympton Street she paused.

Cross the street and go left on Maple Avenue.

She did that, walked two blocks, then turned right onto Chestnut Street.

There she saw a woman steaming toward her, red-faced, heavyset, and wearing a big, purple, old-fashioned hat. Margaret went swiftly to her. "Mrs. Abernathy?"

She was indeed the mother of young Thomas, and the moment Margaret told her what had happened to her son all her hostile belligerence melted away and what remained was only horrified concern. Together they hurried to the infirmary, where the doctor was busy bandaging the burnt arm of poor Thomas, who had been given a dose of laudanum to help with the pain but was still in agony; Philip sat next to him on the table where he lay, holding his uninjured hand.

Thomas burst into tears again at the sight of his mother, and *she* wept too. Philip at once yielded his seat to her, and when—after an excruciating half hour till Thomas' suffering abated, followed by an hour of careful observation—the doctor was ready to send Thomas home, Philip carried him there as gently as a baby, Mrs. Abernathy and Margaret trailing just behind them.

After Thomas was settled in his bed, as comfortably as possible, Mrs. Abernathy turned to Philip and thanked him over and over again.

"I was so angry with him," she said, weeping once more and swiping at her eyes. "He didn't come home for luncheon. That's all I cared about. *Luncheon!*"

"You couldn't have known, ma'am," said Philip, and Margaret thought she heard him murmur, as if to himself, "But *I* could have." He went on to Mrs. Abernathy in a reassuring voice, "Thomas will be all right. I promise you."

"But—but the doctor said my poor Tom'll be scarred for life, and in so much pain for such a long time!"

"Tomorrow will be better," Philip said, with such confidence that Mrs. Abernathy stopped crying and looked at him with new hope. And Margaret looked at him too, filled with amazement and awe. How had she misjudged him so badly before? Why, he was *wonderful.*

Someone was knocking on the door.

"Wake up, sir," said a voice from outside the room, "it's Plough Day."

Knock knock knock.

"Mr. Thane," said the voice, "you asked to be awakened in time for the ceremony. It's Plough Day, sir."

Knock knock knock.

"I'm awake, thank you," he said mildly.

"Very well, sir."

But Philip didn't get out of bed just yet.

He was thinking back to that terrible day when he had hit rock-bottom.

It had begun as this day did, as all his days did: with someone knocking on his door and letting him know that it was Plough Day.

But on this particular morning it had sent him plummeting into the deepest, darkest pit of despair, hopelessness, and agonized self-loathing.

Life had seemed utterly worthless. Without meaning or value. A devastated cry had echoed throughout his empty soul: *Why me?*

How long ago that was.

So much had changed.

This morning, Philip thought again:

Why me?

And this morning, he went on to ponder:

Why have I been lucky enough to be given this gift?
This chance to make things just a tiny bit better?
What can I bring down from the mountain today?

He didn't know all the answers, but simply asking the questions filled him with so much peacefulness that he practically floated on air, all the way to the town square.

Warm and snug in her thick wool pelisse and cozy hat, Margaret looked from her place near the festive bunting-bedecked platform as Philip Thane lightly climbed the steps and introduced himself to the various town dignitaries clustering there, one of whom gestured him toward the front. Philip walked to the railing, swept his eyes over the crowd, and said in a calm, pleasant, carrying voice:

"There was a time, once, when I would have told you how much I hated winter. I would have railed against the cold, the snow, a frozen world cloaked in what seemed to me nothing but a barrenness and a desolation as still, as unchanging, as ice itself. I might have quoted to you the old medieval poem by Neidhart von Reuntal:

"'*Summer, we are missing your good weather.
This cold winter gives us sorrow and longing.
My beautiful beloved does not give me solace.
What shall I do during these long, heavy times,
as the meadow and the flowers have withered?
The birds in the wood are defeated by you
and have to stop singing.*'"

Philip paused, and smiled, then looked directly at Margaret, and she smiled right back, all at once feeling so happy and joyful that she half wondered if she was dreaming.

"But now," he went on, "I stand here today to tell you that my thoughts have changed. My feelings have changed. *I've* changed. I've learned that we can't stop the seasons from coming, one after the other, in life's eternal circle. We can't wish the seasons away, or long for them to be anything other than they are. Nature presents herself to us with absolute honesty: '*To every thing there is a season, and a time to every purpose under the heaven.*'

"And so I've learned that winter isn't a burden or a

curse. While the earth is quietly sleeping, it offers to us its own unique gifts, and we do ourselves an injustice to try and refuse them.

"When winter comes, we can accept it. We can decide what each of us can contribute, to life and to each other, when it comes.

"I couldn't be happier to be here, now, with you—with all of you—to welcome winter, and wait, with patience and with hope, for the beautiful spring to come."

Philip smiled again, seeming to encompass everyone in his smile, and the crowd burst into loud applause that lasted for a long time.

Margaret gazed wonderingly at him, as with a modest nod or two he acknowledged the applause, then graciously he introduced the Straw Bear, gesturing toward him with a sweep of his arm. Looking to the far edge of the crowd, she saw people eagerly yielding to a cylindrical figure all covered in sheaves of hay, from its head down to its ankles. The figure lumbered forward, and everyone began applauding again, those closest to the Straw Bear reaching out to pat at the sheaves—a gesture which signified hope for an early spring. The pipe and drum resumed their merry, lilting beat and some people began to move and sway in happy little dances, both singly and together.

Margaret looked back to the platform and saw how all the dignitaries, one after the other, enthusiastically wrung Philip's hand, every one of them looking so pleased and cheerful. She could understand their reaction. What a magnificent and inspiring speech he had given!

And . . . how handsome he was, how clever and attractive, how personable!

Just being near him made her happy.

Margaret caught her breath in sudden amazement.
Was it possible . . .

Was it possible that just like *that,* she'd fallen in
love with Philip Thane?

It was strange, but what was even stranger was that
it didn't feel like love at first sight. Rather, it felt like a
love that was tested and *true.*

Filling her up with radiant joy.

When he walked down the platform steps and
came to her, with that light and graceful tread of his,
she said, a little breathless:

"Your speech was *wonderful,* Philip."

He smiled with such tenderness that she was surprised all over again, for it felt entirely natural. Familiar.
As if Philip smiled like that at her every day.

"Thank you," he said. "That means the world
to me."

Next to Margaret, Mr. Lawrence, who had been
scribbling away in his notebook, writing down the
speech as quickly as he could, raised his head and said:

"It *was* wonderful, sir. I hope my editor prints it on
the front page of the *Bugle.*"

Philip smiled at Mr. Lawrence. "I'm glad you enjoyed it. Thank you. By the way, I mentioned to the
mayor, Mr. Garvey, that you're a journalist from Watford, and asked if he'd be willing to let you interview
him for your newspaper. He said by all means, and to
go on over to the platform as soon as you're ready."

"By Jove, that's splendid, sir, thank you very much!
How did you guess I was hoping for that? My editor
will be ever so pleased with me."

"I merely assumed you would. Also, he mentioned
that his daughter Elizabeth, who's just about your
age, is interested in journalism, and wondered if you'd
be willing to talk with her about it."

"To be sure I would!" agreed Mr. Lawrence, and as he bounded away toward Mr. Garvey, Margaret gave Philip an approving look, filled with so much happy radiance that she wondered that she wasn't literally glowing like the sun, sending out rays of light everywhere. Wasn't that just like Philip? Always so thoughtful, kind, and generous.

He said, nodding toward the Straw Bear:

"Magnificent, isn't he?"

"Yes, he is. And it's entirely because of you that I got to see him at all! If you hadn't happened to come along at just the right time, I never would."

He smiled at her again. "And *you* were in the right place, so let's call it a joint effort."

She laughed. "An early Plough Day miracle."

"Yes indeed. I used to scoff at the idea of miracles, but now I'm not so sure anymore. Well, I wish I could stay and linger here, Margaret, but I've got a lot of things to do."

"Things to do? What sort of things?"

"This and that. I hope I'll see you again later on today."

He turned away and Margaret quickly said:

"Wait."

Philip paused and turned back. "Yes?"

"May I come with you?"

She saw light springing into his eyes and he smiled once more. "Of course. Only—I may be rather busy. If you don't mind that?"

"Not at all." And then, almost without her realizing it, the words just came out:

"As long as we're together."

They were, she knew right away, the *perfect* words to say.

Chapter 18

First they went to a nearby restaurant, the cozy-looking Cup and Saucer, where they found a table by the window.

"Do we have time to eat?" asked Margaret. "You said we'd be busy."

He smiled at her. "You need your breakfast. And some coffee. Besides, I intended to stop here anyway."

The pot-girl came to take their orders. Margaret asked for a pastry platter and—Philip being absolutely right—a coffee, and he did the same, adding:

"By the way, is the owner a person who doesn't mind a little friendly suggestion?"

"He's my father, sir, and the nicest man in the world," answered the pot-girl.

"In that case, you may want to mention that the buffet in the kitchen where you keep your dishes has started to rot a bit around its base, and that you'd all be safer if it were buttressed. A couple of sturdy chocks would make all the difference."

"Oh, that's good to know! I'll tell him, sir, right away." The pot-girl hurried off, returning in a few minutes with their coffees and a platter heaped tower-ingly high with delicious-looking pastries. "Dad was ever so grateful for your mentioning that, sir! He went and looked, and you were spot-on! Thank you *very* much."

"You're most welcome," said Philip.

They ate heartily but swiftly, mindful of the passing time, and when they were done Philip took Margaret to a toy-shop not far away, housed between a tobacconist's and a jewelry store, where he purchased a sweet-looking doll with cloth limbs and a smiling china face.

"For a young friend of mine," he explained to Margaret, and so they went back toward the town square where he gave it to a little girl named Lydia, who was selling posies of cheerful white and yellow snowdrops which grew to the back of her house.

She exclaimed in ecstatic surprise and delight, declaring she'd use the money she was earning to buy fabric, so that she could make all manner of gowns and caps and shawls for her new charge whom she had already dubbed Miss Lucinda Carissa Minerva Jilly Simmons, which they all agreed was a marvelous and perfect moniker, especially as she shared the same pleasing surname as Lydia. Margaret gave Lydia her fine cambric handkerchief to help with Lucinda's forthcoming wardrobe, into which she tucked a half-sovereign, and in return received the biggest, prettiest posy from Lydia's little bucket.

Warmly Margaret thanked her, tucking the posy into the vee of her pelisse, just below her throat, and said it was the nicest bouquet she'd ever received—a compliment which had Lydia beaming more than ever.

Then Philip and Margaret went to a bookshop where they were just in time to prevent an overconfident clerk from dropping an enormous pile of books he was ferrying in from the back and which, Margaret saw, would have likely injured a frail-looking elderly man browsing amongst the new arrivals. The clerk, horrified, apologized to the old man, who merely said, pleasantly, that all was well that ends well, and went back to his peaceful browsing.

Once outside again, they continued on their way, stopping at a butcher's shop where—while Margaret petted a friendly tabby cat which curled around her ankles, purring—Philip bought some large cuts of cheap meat which he asked the butcher to chop up and wrap in two separate pieces of paper.

They went into the alley behind the shop and walked until they came to a tumbledown collection of old wood boxes, a discarded rug, a broken-down chair, and other such things that were no longer of interest to their former owners. Huddled timidly beneath a curl of the rug was a big yellow dog with great pointy ears and sad brown eyes. Philip opened up one of the packages and, moving slowly, he crouched down on his heels and set the meat in front of the dog, who inched its way out, gobbled it all up, then retreated into its makeshift burrow.

"See you next time," Philip promised the dog, and after that they walked for a few minutes toward a similar-looking pile of rubbish.

"I hear meowing," said Margaret, quickening her steps, and shortly they came to the pile and saw, almost invisible to the casual eye, a white-furred mother cat snugged up against an old dumpy mattress over which a heap of ragged canvas had been tossed, creating a kind of protective canopy. The mother cat was nursing two tiny black-and-white kittens, but looked up, wary, at their approach.

"Oh, how adorable!" Margaret exclaimed quietly to Philip, and he nodded, then opened up the other package he was carrying and, with similar slowness and care, set the meat in front of the cat.

"She'll eat it when she's ready," he said.

They didn't wait, but instead walked for a few minutes and went into an art gallery, where their arrival forestalled, at the very last moment, a young woman from reaching up to hang a large, heavy painting on a wall.

"Pardon us," said Philip, "but would you mind if we took a look at the wire on the back?"

"If you like," said the young woman, surprised, but Philip's tone was so courteous that she at once rested the painting on a nearby counter so that the wire could be examined.

"There, do you see?" he said. "It needs to be fastened more securely. If I may?"

The young woman nodded and Philip made the adjustments, then helped her hang the painting onto the wall so that it lay perfectly straight. It was a handsome landscape, rendering an immense and thriving field of wheat just at the moment of harvest, in rich shades of gold and yellow which evoked all the fullness of summer and a farmer's labors—and hopes—realized.

"It's splendid," said Margaret warmly, and the young woman smiled and confided that it was her very first painting to be shown in a gallery. How lucky for her that a pair of kind strangers had come along at just the right moment! She hated to think what might have happened if her beloved painting had crashed to the floor.

"Well, it didn't," said Philip, "and I daresay it's going to be much admired."

After that they walked into an area of town with several vacant lots, all scrubby and neglected. There, standing over a pit filled with wood and brush, was a little boy, perhaps eight years old, slender and fine-boned and with a generously freckled face, dressed neatly in nankeen breeches and a dark blue woolen coat. On his head was a red wool cap set at a jaunty angle.

"Oi there," said Philip in a casual voice, and the little boy swung around.

"What is it?" he answered, bristling.

"I was hoping to have a roasted chestnut or two. If you don't mind sharing?"

"Did my mum send you to look for me?"

"No."

"Oh." Then the boy squinted suspiciously. "How did you know I've got some chestnuts?"

"For one thing, your pockets are bulging like anything."

This explanation seemed to satisfy their young friend, and as Philip and Margaret drew near, Philip glanced with that same casualness into the pit. "Going to roast them in there?"

"Yes, isn't it jolly? I thought I'd have a bonfire too."

"It's definitely jolly, but I tend to think that if you really want those chestnuts, you may want to leave off the bonfire for another time."

The boy looked mulish. "Yes, but look at all the branches and wood I dragged over! Took me a long time."

"It's just that a bonfire might be a trifle dangerous, and overdoing it."

"I'm not afraid," boasted the boy.

"I can see that. But I'd hate for you to be burned, you know. It would hurt like the devil, and you'd have scars and you wouldn't be able to play the violin for ages."

Shocked, the boy demanded, "How did you know I play the violin?"

Philip shrugged. "I get around. And I know how much you love it."

"Yes, I do. I'm going to play in London someday, in front of loads of people! But that's a long way off and I *did* want a bonfire."

Margaret said, "I'd love to see how you roast chestnuts. Somehow mine always come out underdone."

"That's just it, missus, you can't hurry it along," said the boy.

"Will you show me? But I'm rather afraid of a big fire, you see. Once my brother Sebastian started a fire to the back of our house—he wanted to roast chestnuts, too!—and almost burned down our chicken coop. And the poor chickens were so frightened they didn't lay eggs for a whole month."

"Well, that's bad," the boy said. "Was Sebastian in trouble?"

"Oh, no, he felt so sorry for what he'd done! He spent hours and hours hanging round the coop apologizing to the chickens. I wish you could have seen how *haughty* they were to him, as if they knew what he'd done and blamed him. It took a great deal of corn before they finally forgave him. My mother said she'd never seen a child so filthy in her whole entire life."

The little boy laughed, and Philip said, "Why don't we pull out some of the wood and branches? Then you can show my friend Margaret here how to properly roast chestnuts."

"All right then," agreed the boy, and together the three of them did as Philip suggested and soon a small fire was burning merrily. The chestnuts were carefully set among the embers and they poked at them from time to time with some long sticks. The boy—whose name was Thomas Abernathy—chatted away, and told them all about his violin lessons, his favorite foods, the books he liked to read, his cousin Sam in Weymouth whom he got to visit every year in the spring, the tobacconist shop his widowed mother owned, the horrible toothache he'd had last year, and also about his troubles in school. He didn't mind the academic part too much, he said, but there was another boy, Edmund Carter, who bullied him all the time.

"I wish I had a horse, a great big tall one," said Thomas wistfully. "As high as a house. That way Edmund couldn't get at me. Oi! The chestnuts are popping! They're ready."

With their sticks they poked out the chestnuts, all browned and fragrant, and let them cool a bit before eating them.

"Oh, these are *delicious*," said Margaret. "Honestly, the best I've ever had."

Thomas grinned proudly. "You should tell Sebastian to try it my way."

"I will."

"Do you know, Thomas," said Philip, peeling open another chestnut, "I was bullied most awfully at school when I was your age."

"*You*, mister? But you're so big and strong."

"I wasn't back then. And it took me a long time to figure out how to deal with them."

"Mum says I ought to ignore Edmund. I try, but it never works."

"That was my experience too."

"So what did *you* do?"

"I was lucky enough to meet a kind, clever chap named Jacob Parcell—a soldier and a rifleman, you see, so he knew all about fighting—who told me that there were two things I had to do to keep the bullies from bothering me anymore."

"What were they?" asked Thomas eagerly.

"First he said that I had to stand up to them. Show them I wasn't frightened, even if I *was*. But to pretend if I needed to, at first."

"How did you do that?"

"I stood very tall, as tall as I could, and I kept my chin up. And I puffed out my chest and I pretended that I was Heracles."

"I know who that is!" Thomas exclaimed. "One of those old Greek heroes, and he was terribly strong."

"Yes, that's right. So I pretended that I was just as strong as he was."

"Did that scare the bullies away?"

"Well, there *was* that other thing Jacob taught me."

"What was it?" Transfixed, Thomas held an unpeeled chestnut in his hand, forgotten, and stared up at Philip.

"He showed me how to use a fearsome left hook."

"Like a *boxer,* mister?"

"That's right. I practiced and practiced till I got it right—I daresay just like you practice with your violin till you've got the piece down perfectly."

Thomas nodded. "Can you show *me* how to do it?"

"Yes. But you must promise to only strike out if you need to—that you won't just lash out. I want you to give Edmund a chance to back away first."

"I promise," said Thomas eagerly, and gave his chestnut to Margaret. He held up balled fists, looking very determined. "I'm ready."

So Philip spent an hour showing Thomas how to administer a powerful and effective left hook. "Adjust your foot placement a little . . . you'll have better balance and mobility if you put your feet in toe-heel alignment . . . The hook begins from the ground, really, and how you're holding yourself . . . Yes, that's better . . . Now bend your knees while at the same time you drop your head forward, then rotate your body to the right as you throw the hook . . . Very good! . . . Keep your fist tight when it hits your opponent . . . Remember to stop your punch when you connect, just as I showed you, or you'll over-rotate. Try it again."

Philip watched closely, nodded, and continued:

"You're nearly there, Thomas. When you finish your hook, you want your head, fist, body, *and* feet to be facing to the right . . . Once more . . . Good! Now try the 'weak and strong' technique I showed you earlier . . . Remember? You throw a soft jab, just to make your opponent shift his weight defensively, then come on with a strong one, to throw him off. Well done!"

He smiled down at Thomas. "If you decide not to become a professional violin player, lad, you could take up boxing instead."

Thomas grinned and lowered his hands, then picked up his stick to poke out another chestnut from the fire. After a minute or two he started peeling it but stopped abruptly. "I was supposed to go home for luncheon. Wonder if my mum's worried about me? She's not bad, really—just a bit of a fuss-bucket."

"Mothers are like that, aren't they?" said Margaret sympathetically. "But it's because she loves you, you know."

Thomas nodded, all at once looking thoughtful.

"Shall we walk you home?" suggested Philip.

"*Would* you? She won't be cross if I showed up with you."

"Let's put out the fire first."

They doused what was left of it by kicking dirt over it, an activity into which Thomas entered with great enthusiasm. They began walking back toward the more populated part of town, pausing to make a quick detour onto a side-road where they came across a horse and cart stuck in a muddy, rutted sort of wallow.

The cart's owner stood looking ruefully at the wheels so deeply entrapped in mud, but brightened when he saw that help was on the way. Margaret went to the horse's head, to coax it forward while the owner, Philip, and young Thomas pushed hard at the back of the cart.

In a trice the cart was free, and the owner thanked them all very heartily, fishing into his pocket to offer Thomas a snippet of licorice he had stowed there. Thomas accepted the licorice with equal heartiness, and then the three of them continued walking. In ten minutes or so they arrived in a pleasant neighborhood of small, neatly tended houses with gardens to the front and mature trees everywhere.

Mrs. Abernathy was inclined at first to be surly and belligerent, especially when she saw Thomas' muddy brogues, but rapidly mellowed under the influence of Philip's courtesy and Margaret's kindness, even, after a few minutes' conversation, going so far as to invite them to stay for luncheon. This they tactfully declined, but before they left Thomas begged them to listen to the piece of music he was currently working on—it was Mozart's Sonata Number 20 in C major—and of course they stayed to hear it, and when Thomas was done they both complimented him warmly *and* sincerely, and so left the little house with mother and son beaming, inviting them back anytime, and waving with real enthusiasm.

Outside, Margaret turned to Philip, eyes sparkling. "Well? Now what?"

He gestured in the direction of Apple Street. "And now I'm going to fix a hole in a roof."

As they walked along he told her about Mr. Lancross' anxiety about being unable to either repair it himself *or* pay for it, and how, earlier this morning, he'd promised Mr. Lancross he would come back and have a crack at it.

Half an hour later Philip was on the roof, with Margaret, in the attic below, handing him up various tools and pieces of tar-paper. He had warned her about the possibility of an unwelcome encounter with a rat, but fearlessly she had pooh-poohed it and promised to keep an eye out.

With her capable help—and without any cantankerous rodents showing up—the repair went more quickly than any of Philip's previous efforts and so it was only a little past four when they were done. He clambered down safely to the ground again, returned the ladder, tools, and extra supplies to the inn's cellar, and met her again in the common-room, dirty and sweat-stained but otherwise none the worse for wear. He apologized for his grimy state, and she only smiled, plucked a napkin from a nearby table, and wiped from his forehead a patch of dirt.

"You look splendid, dear Philip. You *are* splendid."

Mr. Lancross came hurrying over, to fervently thank them both, and offered them tea which they were glad to accept, being both thirsty and hungry again after such a full and busy day. As they enjoyed their tea, amiably they debated as to whether *Hamlet* was better than *King Lear,* Margaret being unshakably firm on plumping for *Hamlet,* and also they tried to determine whether paintings could better express emotions than sculptures, with Margaret advocating for the former and Philip, for the sheer joy of light-hearted argumentation, taking up the side of the sculptures.

When she finished her second sandwich and third cup of tea, Margaret twinkled at him from across the table. "Now that I'm fortified, I'm ready for our next adventure."

He smiled back at her. "Would you like to go to the Plough Day banquet? I've invited two old friends of mine to join me there as well."

"Oh, I'd love to! I have a new gown I'm dying to wear. It's periwinkle, and—" Margaret broke off, and then, after a pause, slowly she went on:

"It's periwinkle, and it has the prettiest spangles in the world. But . . . you've seen me in it already, haven't you, Philip?"

Something hung in the air between them, like a grace note between the end of a song and the beginning of a new one. Tentative, sweet, then deepening and lingering in the ear, the mind, the heart.

Then the moment passed, easily and naturally, as would a second-hand on a clock pause before resuming its rhythm, counting out the minutes and the hours and the days, over and over again, and Philip smiled and nodded and softly said:

"Yes. I can't wait to see you in it—again. But first I'm going to have a bath and make myself presentable for you."

"I'll do the same." She laughed. "As I'm quite sure I have cobwebs in my hair and that I reek of roasted chestnuts."

"You look beautiful," he said quietly. "As you always do. Always."

"Thank you *very* much. I'm glad you find me so."

Impulsively Margaret reached out to lay her hand on his. "Oh, Philip, I'm having the most marvelous day! Thank you for that, too."

"It's my pleasure. I am also."

"We make a good team, don't you think?" she said, twinkling at him all over again.

"I couldn't agree more," he said, turning over his hand to clasp hers within it.

They smiled at each other again, and sat there for a while holding hands, doing nothing and doing everything, till Mr. Lancross came over again, asking if they'd care for some more tea or additional sandwiches, and reluctantly they let go, Margaret to whisk herself off to her inn and Philip to go upstairs to his room.

They met again at the Publick House an hour later, when darkness had fully fallen and overhead, the immense canvas of the sky was filled with glittering stars, and together they went into the banquet room. Softly he said to her:

"I didn't think you could look more beautiful, Margaret, but somehow you do. The periwinkle brings out the blue of your eyes. You look like a queen."

"Thank you! And you look quite regal yourself. You carry yourself with such strength and grace."

"You're very kind."

Tonight they went to a different table, Philip having been asked this morning by the mayor, Mr. Garvey, to join him and some other of the town dignitaries. He'd agreed, and requested that two or three extra seats also be left open; and no sooner had he and Margaret sat down than Jacob Parcell and his mother Mrs. Parcell came into the banquet room. Philip jumped up to go to them and usher them over, and soon they were all sitting together. Philip made the necessary introductions, and conversation flowed from there.

By the time dessert was served, Margaret's new acquaintance with Mrs. Parcell had ripened into a warm friendship and Philip's respect and admiration for Jacob deepened yet further. Mr. Garvey had revisited what had been only a cursory knowledge of Jacob's endeavors at the convalescent home and now he promised, along with the other dignitaries, to seek out new sources of funding. His daughter Miss Elizabeth Garvey, accompanied by Mr. Lawrence, joined them from the table where they'd been sitting with a merry gaggle of young people, and in a matter of minutes Mr. Lawrence was asking if he and Miss Garvey might stop by the home tomorrow to interview Jacob, and then together write up an article he was sure his editor would run, and maybe on the front page, too.

Jacob graciously assented, and Mr. Lawrence and Miss Garvey shared an excited look.

Many people—including Mrs. Selina Richmond in stately puce and Mr. John Samuelson, he of the splendid eyebrows—stopped by their table to congratulate Philip on his magnificent speech, accolades which he acknowledged with modesty and with pleasure.

The wine was still awful, but nobody cared.

Fortunately, the coffee was still good.

Everyone lingered for a long while after dessert had been eaten and enjoyed, and eventually, after many cordial goodnights had been exchanged, people started drifting away and the room began to empty. Only a few of the staff remained, dimming lamps, clearing tables and setting them again with fresh linens, plates, and silverware.

Margaret and Philip stayed at their table, talking and laughing about nothing in particular. Finally, when it was nearly time for the Publick House to close, they stood up and began to leave the banquet room. Then Philip paused.

"Just one moment, Margaret."

"What is it?"

"There's something I must try."

She watched as he went to a table which had been freshly set for tomorrow. He grasped the edge of the tablecloth, keeping his hands lower than the table height, took a deep breath, and yanked the cloth downward in a smooth, swift, decisive motion.

A moment later he stood holding the tablecloth.

On the table remained all the plates, silverware, glasses, the crystal centerpiece filled with flowers, and napkins, just as they had been before.

Philip grinned, Margaret applauded, and he gave a low bow, playfully flourishing the cloth. "Thank you. I've been following the suggestion you once gave me, and practicing."

"It's obviously paid off."

They laughed, and she helped him move everything off the table; they replaced the tablecloth and put it all back. Then they made their way to the foyer, got their wraps, and went outside, into the full dark of chilly night. Margaret slid her arm through his, gave a happy little sigh, and said:

"How beautiful it is here."

"I agree. May I walk you to your inn, Margaret?"

"Yes, please. I'd like that."

They strolled along the quiet, dark sidewalks which were illuminated at regular intervals by the street-lamps, looking so cozy and friendly against the heavy curtain of night. When the Woodhull Inn came into view, all lit up with lights in the downstairs rooms which made it look so home-like and inviting, Margaret came to a halt. She turned, released his arm, and looked up into his face.

"Philip, something's been tugging at me all day.

I hope I don't sound—well, odd—but there's something curious—something *magical* happening, isn't there? As if somehow—I can't explain it exactly, but as if—as if someone's sprinkled fairy-dust over Whittlesey. If that makes any sense at all?"

He nodded. "It does make sense, to me at least. I don't understand it, and I gave up trying to quite a while back. But what truly matters, as far as I'm concerned, is that I've had the most wonderful day with you today, Margaret. And no matter what tomorrow brings, nothing can take that away." He reached down to gently take hold of both her hands, which willingly she gave to him. He went on:

"There's something that's been tugging at me, too. Something I've been wanting to say to you. Is that all right?"

"Yes. You can tell me anything. *Everything.*"

He smiled. "Thank you. It's this. It's . . . you, Margaret. I wanted to tell you—I *want* to tell you—that I adore you. That I love you. That you're everything I've ever wanted or needed. Although I'm sorry to say that for a long, long time I was too much of an ass to know it. But I know it now, and I'll know it forever. You're my light, my love, my guiding star, and I'll always be grateful that you came into my life. *That's* the magic for me. And I believe that come what may, we can do anything—*be* anything, when—as you put it earlier—as long as we're together."

To Philip's relief, to his immense and infinite joy, Margaret smiled back. "And all because of a broken shaft outside of Brampton, and me flagging down your barouche to brazenly beg for a ride."

"Thank God you did." Philip looked wonderingly down into her lovely face. She was still here with him. *She was still here.* She hadn't stormed away, justifiably furious after he'd said or done something rash, stupid, ill-advised, reckless, shifty, rude, cretinous, feather-brained, careless, self-serving, conceited, arrogant, insincere, cavalier, presumptuous, and any other words that might possibly be found in her aunt Seraphina's thesauruses under the general heading of "chucklehead."

All that, he thought, was yesterday.

And today . . .

Today was the best day he'd ever had in his whole entire life.

"Margaret," he said, very quietly, "do you think—do you think you could come to care for me too?"

She pulled her hands from his, but only to put them on his shoulders, her deep blue eyes alight, and went up on her toes, and the next thing he knew, she was kissing him.

And then he was kissing her back.

It felt like a first kiss *and* like a kiss that they had shared many times before.

Utterly, completely, entirely magical.

His body was on fire and his heart so full of love for Margaret that he was sure, absolutely sure, that he was the luckiest man in the world.

He could face anything now.

He could endure a hundred—a thousand—a million more Plough Days.

Because he had at last become a good man.

An honest man.

A caring man.

Rules for happiness: something to do, someone to love, something to hope for.

Philip brought Margaret yet closer, deepening their kiss.

Mouth to mouth, body to body, soul to soul.

He couldn't have said for how long they stood there like that, held tightly in each other's arms, only that time itself seemed to have stopped—as if a benignant universe was softly, kindly, whispering:

Let the rest of the world rush on without you, just for a little while.

Enjoy this precious gift.

Because against all odds, you've found your perfect woman.

Here's your moment, Philip Thane.

You've earned it.

Take it, grab on to it, own it and cherish it.

Together you and Margaret exist beyond time and place.

Love has taken you, enveloped you, transformed you.

You've become the man you were always meant to be.

And here at last is your true love's kiss, bringing you both the sweetest bliss.

Bliss indeed, unlike anything he'd ever known before.

And when finally, finally, Margaret ended their kiss, to lean back a little, eyes glowing, cheeks rosy, her tender mouth curved up in the sweetest of smiles, Philip could not regret being gently delivered back into the here and now.

Because here and now was a wonderful place to be.

She said softly:

"Did that answer your question, Philip?"

So dazzled was he that it took him a few seconds to recall it.

Margaret, do you think—do you think you could come to care for me too?

He swallowed, hard. "I think," he slowly said, "I think that was a 'yes'?"

And Margaret went up on her toes to kiss him again. "Yes, yes, a thousand times yes." She gave a glad laugh. "Oh, Philip, dearest, darling Philip, I never dreamed I could be so happy."

"I too," he said, and tightened his arms around her. "Margaret, you look like an angel."

She laughed again, softly. "I'm no angel. Just a mere woman, whose nose is doubtless turning red in the cold."

He leaned down to kiss the tip of that charming nose. "Let's get you inside again, and warm."

Together they walked to the Woodhull Inn, where they stopped on the front portico. Tenderly he said:

"Goodnight, Margaret, my love. I'll see you to-morrow."

"Yes, you will, my darling," she said firmly, went up on her toes, kissed him again, smiled, and went inside—leaving him alone, but not lonely.

Chapter 19

Something woke him up.

Philip lay in bed, unmoving and his eyes still closed, patiently waiting for the usual knock on his door.

Then the voice from outside the room:

Wake up, sir, it's Plough Day.

But . . . there was nothing.

Only silence.

Now *that* was odd.

He opened his eyes and looked to the window, expecting to see around its curtained edges just the faintest, murkiest intimations of dawn.

But what he saw was . . . soft ribbons of light shimmering in the gap between the curtain and the window, and the dark fabric of the curtain itself paled against the day's illumination.

His heart gave a giant leap.

This was something altogether different.

Different.

Had he . . . overslept?

Had the owner of that voice, with the unseen hand that knocked on his door, overslept as well? Or forgotten to show up?

How strange.

Philip slid aside the covers, got out of bed, and then—moving with the caution of a man navigating a narrow tightrope over a high precipice—he went to the window and took hold of the curtain, his heart now hammering hard in his chest.

When he looked outside, was he going to see the same view yet again? The clear, bright blue sky? On the ground the familiar, scattered splotches of gray slush? A few late stragglers all walking toward the center of town, eager to partake of the Plough Day fun?

If so, he'd get dressed and join them. He'd get to see his beloved Margaret again, he'd walk up the platform steps to give his speech once more, and then he'd use his time today to keep bringing down from the mountain whatever he could.

Again.

He took a moment to look within him for his new strength, his new resolve.

It was still there, like a tree with deep sturdy roots, stalwart against whatever winds might blow its way.

And so Philip pulled aside the curtain and looked out the window.

And he stared.

Outside, the world was blanketed in white.

Last night, the snowstorm had come at last.

Gone were the splotches of slush; instead, there was a thick, heavy covering of the stuff—that glorious white wonderful stuff—everywhere, and the sky overhead was a beautiful pearly gray. On the sidewalks were only five or six people . . . walking in *different directions*.

He stared all over again.

Was it really possible . . . ?

Had Plough Day come . . . and gone . . . and today . . .

And today was a *new day*?

He turned away from the window, as if to give the world a chance to rearrange itself back into the usual formation: the bright blue sky, the big yellow sun, the splotches of gray slush.

He waited for a minute or two, schooling his heart to resume its usual rhythm.

Then, calm again, he turned back to look out the window.

And his heart gave *another* leap, an exuberantly joyful one this time, a butterfly bursting into flight, a frog jumping high in a pond, a whale leaping out of the sea.

Because the thick covering of snow was still there. The sky was a beautiful pearly gray. And those half dozen people were going in different directions.

A *post* Plough Day miracle?

Philip's brain whirled wildly.

He stood there, dazed. *Amazed*. Hardly daring to breathe.

But one thing was clear: he had to see Margaret.

He had to see her as soon as possible.

Quickly he scrambled into his clothes and loped down the stairs and into the common-room. Mr. Lancross came sailing over, wreathed in smiles.

"Good morning, Mr. Thane! Did you see that it snowed last night? Weren't we lucky it didn't snow the night before? Would've interfered right bad with the Plough Day festivities. And if it wasn't for you and Miss Allen, working so hard as you did yesterday, the attic would be a terrible mess right now."

Cautiously, aware that he sounded rather stupefied, Philip said: "The roof is *still* fixed?"

"Why, to be sure it is! I went up and checked on the attic first thing. Thank you again, Mr. Thane. Thanks to you both."

"You're welcome, Mr. Lancross. Very welcome indeed."

"It's good people like you and Miss Allen who make the world go round—that's what *I* think. Well! It's a lovely morning, isn't it? The young 'uns'll be sledding and building snowmen all over town, I reckon. Will you be wanting your breakfast before you go out?"

"Later, perhaps—if you'll excuse me?"

"To be sure. We've got some fresh-made muffins which are especially good."

"Excellent," said Philip, then went swiftly to the front door, flung it open, went outside to the portico—and paused. And stared yet again. For there, coming toward him, was none other than Margaret herself, ravishing as always in her dark green pelisse and . . .

Not her usual fashionable hat in the exact same shade of green and embellished with a spray of pink roses.

Today she had on her head a charming woolen confection in the prettiest shades of pale orange and pearly gray, topped with a dashing white feather which curled jauntily to one side, altogether setting off her lovely face to marvelous advantage.

He caught his breath and went to her, eagerly, joyfully, and saw that she was smiling at him and that those deep blue eyes of hers were sparkling like sapphires. She held out her hands and he took them, just as they had done last night. And she said, with a happy lilt in her voice:

"Good morning."

"Never have truer words been spoken."

"Because it's not Plough Day anymore, is it?"

"No." He gave a laugh, merry and free. "It's not Plough Day, Margaret, dearest Margaret, and you're here with me."

"Of course I am. I had to see you right away."

"That's how I felt too. I was coming to find you." He smiled down at her. "By the way, that's a gorgeous hat you're wearing."

"Thank you! I felt like wearing something different this morning. Isn't it lucky I brought two of them with me from home?"

"Very." Suddenly Philip added, almost as if doubting what he had just heard: "Wait—you said it's not Plough Day *anymore*."

She nodded. "Yes, it's the strangest thing. Last night I had dream after dream, Philip, and—it may sound odd, but I dreamed that you and I lived Plough Day over and over again. And that we were trapped here in Whittlesey, even though we kept trying to escape in your barouche. We *always* drove right into a snowstorm, and the road was blocked by a big fallen tree. Do you know those dreams where it's all so vivid and real-seeming? That's what they were.

"And—well, I'm sorry to say it, but in the beginning I didn't like you at all. As the dreams went on, though, things changed—you changed—*I* changed! And it wasn't long before I fell head over heels in love with you. Then they were the best and happiest dreams in the world."

Margaret paused, smiling, then her expression became thoughtful, and a trifle puzzled. She went on:

"And then it got even odder. After having dreams like this seemingly all night long, I was still asleep in my bed at the Woodhull Inn, and then someone was knocking on my door. 'Wake up, Miss Allen,' the voice said, 'it's not Plough Day anymore.' I was quite befuddled, as I had no idea why somebody would come along to do that. So I simply called out, 'I'm awake, thank you.' And whoever it was just went away. I lay there awhile, wondering if those were dreams I'd had, or—or *memories*.

"Somehow it seemed *so* important that it was the day *after* Plough Day. And then I remembered yesterday, and what an amazing day we had together, and I couldn't wait another minute to see you again. So I scrambled into my clothes, left a note for Aunt Seraphina in our private parlor, and stopped to ask the proprietor if anyone among the staff had come to knock on my door. He had no idea what I was talking about. So I left, and walked over here as quickly as I could. Oh, Philip, what does it all mean?"

"It's a long story, my darling. How about some breakfast, and I'll tell you everything?"

"I'd like that. I'm ravenous, and as you know I do need some coffee as soon as possible. But first . . ."

Margaret went up on her tiptoes and kissed him soundly, there on the front portico for all the world to see, and of course he kissed her right back, and even though a half dozen people saw them, they only smiled to see a young couple so happy together.

After that Philip and Margaret went into the Apple Street Inn, where Mr. Lancross brought them a lavish breakfast—including some delicious muffins which had a tasty, buttery crumble of chopped nuts and sugar on the tops, and some really excellent coffee, served piping hot—and Philip related to her the mysterious tale of the Plough Day that repeated itself over and over again. And when he had indeed told her everything from beginning to end, he added, rather hesitantly:

"I know I sound quite mad, Margaret, and deserving of being carted off to Bedlam. But it's the truth."

"I believe you, Philip," she answered at once.

"You do? It's all so fantastical, don't you think?"

"It is, but I trust my instincts. I trust *you*. And

in addition to everything you experienced, how can we explain that mysterious voice at *my* door, on the very same day it was silent at yours? Too, only consider—so many fables and folk-tales, for example, are fantastical. What if, within them, reside kernels of truth, softened and obscured by the passage of time, but based on genuine mystical events? Didn't you once say that stories come from somewhere, and sometimes they're based on real things?"

"I *did* say that to you, long ago."

"Yes, I thought so. And perhaps there's more to life than we realize. Maybe there's more inside us than we can know." She smiled, reaching out to cover his hand with her own, just as she had yesterday here in the common-room, although, reassuringly, when they had been sitting at a different table. "Maybe—just maybe—we've all got inside of us a little magic, all our own."

He nodded, and clasped her hand in his. "Margaret," he said, "I love you. I love you with all my heart and soul. Everything that I have, everything that I am, belongs to you. And I'm hoping you'll agree to marry me, so that I can spend the rest of my life doing anything and everything I can to bring you happiness, each and every day, now and forever."

Margaret smiled again. "Well," she softly said, "yesterday was a very good start, and today is even better. Which means we've already begun, don't you think? I love you, too, Philip Thane—always. And my answer is yes."

His heart seemed to overflow with happiness. With joy. With optimism for a future so glorious, so magnificent, that it filled him with deep, humble, infinite gratitude. He was lucky, *lucky*. Then he said, a bit ruefully:

"Not a very romantic setting for a proposal, is it? I'm sorry about that."

"What's romantic is what's inside us—and how we feel about each other," replied Margaret firmly. "I'll never regret that we made up our minds here, Philip. Besides, the muffins are *tremendous*."

He laughed. "That matters, too."

After that, Margaret had another muffin, and he did too, and they talked and talked, glowing with their shared happiness. Histories were shared, hopes and aspirations discussed, plans made. Mr. Lancross came over with another pot of coffee, thanked them again for their help yesterday, and made mention of the fact that due to the big snowstorm, travel out of town might be difficult for a few days—which he hoped they wouldn't mind too much?

Neither of them did.

As they waited for the roads to clear, those four disparate souls who had, seemingly, ended up by chance traveling into Whittlesey together kept themselves busy.

Aunt Seraphina, commandeering the private parlor, peacefully continued working on her forthcoming book. Having apologized with real sincerity for his unfortunate behavior on the journey there, Philip volunteered to help read the long galley-sheets and proved himself to be so eagle-eyed in spotting printer's errors that Aunt Seraphina—surprised and pleased at how her first, unfavorable impression of him had dissipated—declared she was going to include his name, with fulsome thanks, in the acknowledgements section.

Margaret had *her* book to work on and notes to go

over, along with deepening her friendship with Mrs. Parcell and, of course, enjoying every minute spent in Philip's company.

As for Philip, he spent a lot of time over at the convalescent home, learning from Jacob Parcell and Dr. Saltonstall, and helping there in whatever ways he could—talking with the patients and listening to their stories, changing bandages, bringing meals, sweeping floors, washing dishes. He also got a couple of sketchbooks for himself, and had a marvelous time reacquainting himself with his early love of drawing. His favorite piece, during this time, was a pen-and-ink portrait of Jacob which his mother begged to keep; and so Philip had it framed and when he gave it to Mrs. Parcell she wept happy tears, then hugged him for a long, long time.

Additionally, he and Margaret went multiple times a day to feed the stray dog and the mother-cat and her kittens, and to make themselves familiar to them. The dog they named Victor, for his bravery in surviving his rough life; the mother cat Snowdrop, for her white fur, and the black-and-white babies Charles and Cassandra, for no other reason than it somehow seemed to suit them.

Mr. Lawrence, meanwhile, working alongside Miss Garvey, wrote up an interview with Jacob Parcell accompanied by an article about the convalescent home that was so comprehensive, so eloquent and powerful, that it would end up being published by the Watford *Bugle* as well as by several of the national periodicals, a feat which not only would bring donations to the home pouring in, it would add such luster to Mr. Lawrence's budding reputation that he would soon be promoted to Assistant Editor at the tender age of twenty-three and find himself the recipient of a gratifying boost in pay which, he would rejoice, make it feasible for him to offer hand, heart, and hearth to Miss Garvey, who in turn would be gratifyingly prompt in accepting, and with whom, in time, he would come to be the partner in one of Britain's most celebrated journalistic duos.

Early on the morning when it was at last deemed propitious to travel again, Margaret, Philip, and Aunt Seraphina gathered in the private parlor of the Wood-hull Inn for breakfast, Mr. Lawrence having gone off to bid a long and sentimental farewell to Miss Garvey. When they had finished eating, Margaret reached for Philip's hand and said:

"Aunt, Mr. Thane—Philip—and I have some news."

"Do tell." Aunt Seraphina's eyes were twinkling.

"We're engaged. I know it must seem quite sudden, but we love each other, and I'm absolutely, entirely, and *completely* certain about it. And so very, very happy!"

Her aunt laughed. "Goodness gracious, my dear, it's been obvious since Plough Day that the two of you get on like a house on fire. So while I'm not surprised, I *am* delighted. And I wish you both the happiest of lives together, though I don't think you need any wishes to make that happen. I can see it on both of your faces." She beamed across the table at them. "Welcome to the family, Mr. Thane."

"Thank you, ma'am, I'm most fortunate to be joining it. And won't you please call me 'Philip'?"

"I certainly will. And now, I want to hear all about your plans."

So Philip told Aunt Seraphina that, to his immense shame, his debts were many, and that he had intended to clear them all before marrying Margaret; but here Margaret intervened, saying that she stood firm on her decision not to wait, and that while her income wouldn't permit them to live in grand style, they could nonetheless be perfectly comfortable.

"I admit I'd prefer to marry you sooner rather than later," he told her. "Tomorrow if we could. Or even better, today. But you'll be marrying a pauper, you know. Actually, worse than a pauper."

"I'll take you just as you are, dear heart."

"Now that," said Aunt Seraphina, "bodes well for present *and* future happiness. I always say that unconditional love is the *best* sort of love. Are you going to take up a profession then, Philip?"

"Yes, ma'am. I've been thinking about it a great deal, and I've decided to follow in my late father's footsteps and become a physician."

"A worthy vocation," she commented approvingly. "How are you going to go about it?"

"I've read a fair number of books to get me started, studying on my own, but what I'm going to need now, of course, is formal education and an apprenticeship."

"As it happens, my cousin Horace is the Regius Professor of Medicine at the University of Oxford, and I'd be glad to introduce you to him. Perhaps he can help."

"That would be splendid, ma'am. I'm much obliged to you for that."

"Think nothing of it, my dear boy," said Aunt Seraphina graciously. "We must all help each other along in life, don't you think? Well! Who knew that our little jaunt to Whittlesey would have such a momentous outcome?"

They all three smiled at each other, and Margaret felt so happy that she could have floated up to the sky like a balloon. But she didn't. Because she never wanted to leave Philip's side.

Within the hour, their original party of four boarded the Penhallow barouche once again, accompanied, this time, by Victor the dog, who was less thin *and* less shy, and who lay at their feet on a warm thick blanket; and also by Snowdrop, Cassandra, and Charles, who shared a flannel-lined basket which Margaret held on her lap. Even with the lid closed, they could hear Snowdrop purring, as she did quite a bit these days.

They passed through Oundle without the slightest incident, dropped Mr. Lawrence off in Northampton, where he would proceed in short order to Watford, then continued to Oxford where Philip stayed for a few days with the Allen family in their capacious home, receiving from them such a friendly, delighted welcome that by the time his visit concluded he was declared to already be an honorary Allen. (As were Snowdrop, Cassandra, Charles, and Victor, who fit right in also and who, like Philip, were prime favorites in particular with the noisy parrot.)

Margaret had been disappointed, but philosophical, about missing the colloquium at which she had been slated to speak. As it turned out, so many of the other speakers as well as attendees had been delayed due to various weather conditions, the colloquium was rescheduled to early spring and she could look forward with fresh pleasure to giving her talk. In the meantime, she was going to continue working on her folklore book as well as on a new idea for another book she had had.

Philip met with Aunt Seraphina's formidable cousin

Horace Allen who, after a long, searching conversation, offered him—to his great surprise and delight—admission to the University's medical school and an internship in his own medical practice, along with a small stipend which would help defray Philip's educational expenses and give him a little something extra to contribute to the shared expenses of the cozy household he looked forward to establishing with Margaret in the very near future.

So though it was a wrench to part, Philip was nonetheless able to kiss Margaret goodbye with a buoyant heart and a promise to soon return to Oxford.

He arrived at Surmont Hall on a bright, chilly afternoon and was ushered into the same drawing-room, all elegant and warm, in which he had had his memorable conversation with Henrietta Penhallow on a day which had occurred three weeks prior *and* a lifetime ago.

"Good afternoon, Philip," Henrietta greeted him, sitting indomitably upright as ever, and with considerably more cordiality than she had displayed back then. "Won't you sit down?"

"Thank you, ma'am." Philip was secretly rather glad to see that she was wearing a different gown today, this one being made of soft violet wool and ornamented with an old-fashioned fichu, instead of the dove-gray one from before. The gray gown had been exquisite, but he appreciated the difference in her attire more than he would ever say out loud.

"May I offer you some refreshments?"

"Yes, thank you, Aunt Henrietta." He recalled with an inner flicker of pleased amusement that on his previous visit she had made no such offer. A sure sign that he was moving up in the world! "You'll join me, I hope?"

"A cup of tea and a scone would not go amiss." Henrietta rose from the escritoire at which she had been sitting, went to the bell-pull and tugged on it, then continued to a handsome old rococo chair opposite his and sank with majestic unflappability down into it. Her eyes were sharp as they regarded him, but without that sardonic, cutting quality from before which had given him the distinct impression of being (metaphysically speaking) flayed alive.

"Thank you for your letter from a fortnight ago, informing me of the snowstorm which prevented your prompt return to Surmont Hall. It was courteous of you to keep me informed."

"But of course."

"And, more importantly, may I tender my felicitations upon the announcement of your betrothal? I know several of the older members of the Allen family—in particular Timothy Allen, the Archbishop, and his son Horace, with whom you'll be working and studying—and I also know that the family in general is greatly esteemed and admired throughout the Oxford community."

"That's my understanding as well."

"Based upon the glowing description in your letter, your Miss Allen sounds a delightful young lady."

He smiled. "She is, Aunt Henrietta. Clever and kind and charming and beautiful, and I'm the luckiest man in the world to be marrying her. And whenever the opportunity presents itself, it will be my honor and privilege to introduce you both to each other."

"I'll look forward to that." Henrietta smiled back at him. "In the meantime, I wish you *very* happy, and I'm certain that all your Egremont family will join me in wishing you well also. On another note, I was pleased to read the transcripts of the speech you gave at the Plough Day ceremony. May I say, Philip, that I was both surprised and impressed. You represented the family in a way which makes me very proud."

Philip wasn't the least bit surprised himself that somehow Henrietta knew about his speech. "Thank you, ma'am. It came from the heart, and I'm very thankful to you for entrusting me with the responsibility to give it."

"Despite your obvious antipathy when last we met."

"That was then, Aunt Henrietta, and this is now."

She nodded. "It's fascinating how our expectations can sometimes be confounded, is it not? For example, when Gabriel was betrothed to Livia, I indulged in the darkest, most pessimistic predictions as to their future happiness. And how wrong I was. Too, I expected to hear nothing but shocking reports as to your conduct in Whittlesey."

"My time there was—shall we say—a transformative experience."

"It has not escaped my notice. You seem greatly changed, my dear Philip. Not in appearance, but in essence."

"I believe I *have* changed."

"Indeed. Further confounding my gloomy expectations from our earlier encounter. I am gratified to see it. Incidentally, you may be interested to hear that the day after you left for Whittlesey, Sir Gregory Stoke underwent a sudden recovery which he described as nothing short of miraculous. Most curious."

Philip was silent for a few moments, reflecting. If not for Sir Gregory's sudden attack of gout, he wouldn't have been sent to Whittlesey in his place; if not for the broken axle that had left Margaret stranded in Brampton, he might never have met her . . .

He suddenly found himself thinking again of the old lady, Mrs. Roger, who had marched up to him that day he had arrived in Riverton, intent on cajoling Henrietta Penhallow out of as much money as possible.

Mrs. Roger had firmly said:

You're right on time.

As if . . . she had somehow been expecting him.

And then she'd hustled him over to where her husband happened to be standing with his gig, and told him to drive to Surmont Hall.

In his hurry to get his hands on Henrietta's money, he hadn't paid much attention to these strange details, and merely thought it was all very convenient for *him*.

Because back then his focus had only been on himself.

That was all he ever cared about.

God, what a poor, limited life he had been living all those years.

Into his mind now came an image of Margaret.

Beautiful, wonderful Margaret, her deep blue eyes alive with intelligence and warmth and sweetness.

Margaret, who had inspired him to change.

He really *was* the most fortunate man in the world to have joined his life with hers.

As for all these various, odd details, they were impossible to logically reconcile.

Nor could he understand the mechanism of living the same day over and over again.

He could, of course, spend a great deal of time chewing over this knotty and perplexing question; instead, he chose to simply acknowledge that it had happened, and that the experience had at last brought him out of darkness and into the welcome light.

Philip roused himself from his reverie and looked again at Henrietta, smiling. "As Hamlet says, 'There's a divinity that shapes our ends, rough-hew them how we will.'"

"Very true," said Henrietta, nodding wisely, and then came a tap on the door, which opened to reveal a couple of servants bearing silver trays. As they two enjoyed their tea, Philip told her about his determination to repay each and every loan, his and Margaret's wedding plans, and how he was going to travel home to Hathaway Park when he left Surmont Hall, to see his mother and step-grandparents and half-brother Owen and share his news with them in person; after which he was going back to Oxford to begin his studies.

Henrietta listened, approved of it all, then got up again and went to her escritoire where she picked up her pen to write him out a cheque. "You've truly earned this, my dear Philip."

"Thank you, ma'am, but no. I've enough to get me to Northamptonshire and then to Oxford."

"Are you quite sure?"

"I am."

She looked at him with a kind, shrewd smile. "It's not often in your former life, I daresay, that you turned down an offer of money."

He returned her smile. "No indeed. But I'm learning how to say 'I have enough,' and mean it. Although, Aunt Henrietta, if you *are* inclined to issue a cheque, there's someone I know who truly doesn't have enough. For a cause I believe you may be interested in supporting."

He told her about Jacob Parcell and his work at the convalescent home for injured veterans of the war, and how he himself had spent a lot of time there and could attest to how very great was the need for help. To Philip's immense satisfaction Henrietta promised to send along a substantial donation right away, and in thinking about Jacob's joy in receiving that donation, and how much good it was going to do, Philip felt that he could hardly thank Henrietta enough for all the good *she* was doing.

Dinner that evening was a pleasant affair, during which he was glad to see his cousin Gabriel's chilly reserve—which, Philip admitted to himself, he fully deserved—thaw into something approaching amiability, and to make the acquaintance of his pretty, lively wife Livia.

Philip left for Northamptonshire the next day, refusing Henrietta's generous offer to borrow a Penhallow carriage and horses again, but he did accept a ride into Riverton where he could catch the stage. Half an hour later, as the stage rolled along the high street, his gaze fell upon a stout form all bundled up in a heavy cloak and enveloping hat marching along the sidewalk.

It was Mrs. Roger.

Her eyes came to him and she nodded, affably, and he had the distinct impression that she was silently conveying a message.

Well done.

Upon his arrival at Hathaway Park, he was received with the usual careful, uneasy caution. He could almost hear his family anxiously wondering what uncomfortable revelations he would drop upon them, what requests for money he would make, what careless insults he would hurl. It was therefore with considerable pleasure that he was able to disabuse them of their entirely justifiable concerns. A nice change it was, too, to see no furrowed brows or alarmed expressions, and to hear no despairing reproofs, and he looked forward to experiencing none of them ever again.

While he was there, he made a special effort to get to know the younger half-brother whom he barely knew, Owen FitzClarence, the Marquis of Ellington—at age twenty a tall, thin, and rather shy young man. His half-sister Helen wasn't there, having last year married a Frenchman and gone off to France with him, and taking all her horses, too.

A week later, Philip left his family with their glad promises to attend his wedding still resonating in his ears, and after two days of uneventful travel he arrived in Oxford, where he was received by Margaret with a comprehensive hug and kiss that lit up his soul all over again.

They were married three months after that, in a ceremony presided over by Margaret's great-uncle Timothy, whose warm, sonorous voice filled the church with solemn beauty. The pews were crowded with relations and friends from the two families who, in defiance of the accepted custom and by tacit consent, freely intermingled on both sides of the aisle. It gave Philip a quiet, particular pleasure to see Henrietta Penhallow at her most gracious and congenial, and also that the shy Owen had with him a cousin of sorts, young Francis Penhallow, like him a student at the University and with whom he seemed to converse with ease.

The newly married couple took no honeymoon journey—as Philip had already begun both his studies and his internship—and so, after the festive wedding-breakfast hosted by Margaret's parents had finally wound down by mid-afternoon, they two walked hand-in-hand in the mild spring sunshine to their very own cottage which was just around the corner from the big Allen house.

They opened the low white gate and as they strolled past the promising little garden to left and right of the meandering walkway, Margaret, radiant in lilac silk, said with a happy sigh:

"Oh, was there ever such a lovely home?"

"Never," answered Philip firmly, pausing on the portico to open the front door and then catching her up into his arms to carry her over the threshold. When they were inside with the door closed behind them he didn't let her go, and tenderly said:

"What would you like to do now? What can I do for you, my darling?"

Her blue eyes were sparkling as she replied without hesitation, "Let's go upstairs."

And so he carried her up to their cozy bedchamber, which Margaret, her mother, her aunt Seraphina, and several Allen cousins had, over the past several weeks, fashioned into the most delightful little bower with soft linen bed-coverings embroidered in a repeating pattern of fleur-de-lis, long matching curtains, and coverings for the pair of comfortable old armchairs—formerly occupying a place of honor in Margaret's bedroom—now set so invitingly before the fireplace.

There was a tall bookcase, too, already filled to overflowing with books, a pretty carpet of soft wool, and several framed artworks on the walls, including some by Philip himself. On a small table by a sun-filled window stood an antique crystal vase which had once belonged to Margaret's great-aunt Patience. In it was a riot of gorgeous pink and white roses which filled the bedroom with the nicest, sweetest scent in all the world.

Philip lowered Margaret onto the bed, as lightly as a feather, and stood smiling down at her.

"Well, Mrs. Thane?"

"I like the sound of that." Her eyes like stars, she held out her arms to him. "Do come here, Mr. Thane."

He did, bringing himself alongside her and holding her tight. "Have I mentioned to you lately how much I love you?"

"Yes, but I don't mind if you tell me again."

"I love you, Margaret." He kissed the tip of her nose. "I love you today, and tomorrow, and forever."

"I like the sound of that also! And I love *you*, dearest, darling Philip. Now and always."

He kissed her on her smiling mouth, and it wasn't long before they decided that their clothes really weren't necessary at the moment and, moreover, were quite awfully in the way. They rose to their feet and helped each other disrobe, then stood, naked, for a few moments in open admiration, he of her and she of him.

"You," he softly said, "are so very, very beautiful."

She caught at his hand, smiling. "I'm so glad you think so! Oh, Philip, we've been waiting so long for this moment, haven't we? How *good* we've been! I'm amazed at our extraordinary patience, aren't you? But now let's make up for lost time." And she drew him back into bed, where they did, in fact, make up for lost time at length and very satisfactorily indeed.

In no time at all Margaret and Philip settled happily into their charming little cottage, which of course was graced by the presence of Victor the dog and the three cats, who all rapidly mellowed into serene domesticity marred only by a spirited competition for places on the drawing-room sofa which was warmed by morning sunshine and also offered a prime view of the street and its passersby.

Margaret continued working on her folk-lore book, traveling every few months to various places throughout England with the intrepid Aunt Seraphina for company, and two years after her marriage completed her manuscript which was soon accepted for publication, just as Philip had predicted. It received many positive reviews and its sales surpassed the publisher's modest expectations—thanks in large part, Margaret stoutly maintained, to the marvelous pen-and-ink illustrations Philip managed to execute despite his busy schedule.

This flattering claim Philip acknowledged with pleasure, but said that it was all due to Margaret's passionate interest in her subject, careful research, and graceful writing, and that he would always be honored at having been able to play a very small role in the book's success. Also, he said, he'd leap at the chance to illustrate her next book if she wished. It was a radical reenvisioning of *One Thousand and One Nights,* in which the selfish, controlling king was peacefully overthrown and the brilliant storyteller Scheherazade installed as a just and kind ruler, thereby creating much more pleasant and less anxious lives for all concerned, with the possible exception of the sulky former king who had gotten what he richly deserved, and who wandered moodily about town, kicking at pebbles with shoes that used to be grand, and was generally ignored.

Philip's medical studies and internship with his uncle-in-law Horace, meanwhile, progressed swimmingly, and it wasn't long before he discovered within him a real aptitude for surgery, also developing as a result of his time at the convalescent home in Whittlesey a strong side interest in the field of wound care and treatment. The repayment of his debts was a process that took a long while, keeping Margaret and himself on a strict budget which neither minded, as they had in each other, their family and friends, their pets, and their professions all that they wanted and needed. Money would come to them in time: they were never wealthy, but they were always comfortable, and there was enough, in due course, to support the happy, healthy children who were born to them and who filled their little house with yet more joy and the most delicious and delightful chaos.

As the years passed, never once did Philip—with eyes, body, mind, or heart—stray from his Margaret, for he'd become that rare, remarkable thing: a rake redeemed, and well and thoroughly, too.

Nor did he ever repeat his curious dance with time, which had so fortuitously given him the opportunity to halt in his tracks, to reflect, and to grow—an interval in his life he always remembered with the deepest gratitude, for he had lost nothing that mattered and in return had gained everything that did.

There is but one solution to
the intricate riddle of life;
to improve ourselves,
and contribute to the happiness of others.

—*Mary Shelley*

To understand and be understood,
those are among life's greatest gifts,
and every interaction is an opportunity
to exchange them.

—*Maria Popova*

. . . the question can no longer be
"What can I expect from life?"
but can now only be
"What does life expect of me?"
What task in life is waiting for me?

—*Victor Frankl*

A note from Lisa Berne

Whittlesey, England, is a real place, and the Straw Bear festival is a real event there, though I've adapted both the town and the tradition to suit my authorial fancy. Similarly, Plough Monday is an ancient British agricultural holiday which makes its appearance in this book as Plough Day.

In the story, when Margaret is pondering the myth of Sisyphus and proposes to Philip the notion of taking a bit of the mountain down with him, over and over again until there's no longer a mountain to climb, I'm borrowing the idea expressed in Manfred Kopfer's *The Philosophy of Recursive Thinking,* which offers an innovative solution to Sisyphus' arduous punishment by the gods for his misdeeds.

It also speaks to the power of incremental progress— that is, the process of achieving goals through small steps that, in time, add up to something big. It's a power that Philip slowly and painstakingly learns to harness, much to his eventual betterment and which, at last, makes him a worthy hero for my heroine . . . and gives them both the happily-ever-after which I so much enjoyed creating for them.

I hope you did, too.

For your further reading enjoyment: some questions to ponder about *The Redemption of Philip Thane*

- Do you think Philip Thane deserves to be trapped in the same day over and over again? In other words, has he brought it upon himself by his prior actions and behavior?

- In the end, why do you think he's freed from what initially feels like a curse?

- As the story progresses, Margaret seems to continually sense some aspects of the ever-repeating day, although no one else around her does. Why do you suppose that is?

- Do you believe that mystical events can, and do, happen in real life?

- What would *you* do if you had to repeatedly live the same day? Is there a particular day in your life you would choose? Are there things you'd do again? Or differently? What new things might you try?

- In Chapter 15, Philip says, "Whenever we read a book again, it's a different experience, don't you think? The book hasn't changed, but we have." Margaret then describes a book she read as a girl and loved, but which falls rather flat for her as an adult. Have you had this experience yourself as a reader?

  Conversely, have you ever had the opposite experience? That is, rereading a book you didn't much care for and finding that now you're enjoying it?

- Also in Chapter 15, Margaret mentions the philosopher Gottfried Wilheim Leibniz: "I don't know his theories very well, but doesn't he take the position that the darkness of the world provides an important contrast to goodness—that the darkness offers us a chance to find our way into the goodness we seek? Into light, happiness, connection, peace, joy?"

  Similarly, young Francie Nolan, the heroine of *A Tree Grows in Brooklyn,* reflects on her tumultuous schooldays: "There had to be the dark and muddy waters so that the sun could have something to background its flashing glory."

Does this philosophy—which asserts that light (or goodness) shines all the more brightly in the presence of darkness, that in fact they have a kind of symbiotic relationship to each other—have any resonance for you?

- In the author's note, Lisa Berne touches on the power of incremental progress in achieving large goals that may, at first, seem overwhelming or even impossible—in Philip's case, the drive to change into the best man he can be. It's a strategy that people in all walks of life employ.

Author and teacher Anne Lamott, for example, urges writers to tackle the challenge of the blank page by taking it "bird by bird"—that is, word by word, a process that will, in time, lead to a completed manuscript. The prolific Stephen King jokes, with perfect truth: "When asked, 'How do you write?' I invariably answer, 'One word at a time.'"

In her efforts to encourage children to make positive food choices, First Lady Michelle Obama said to officials in charge of school nutrition: "I'm not asking any of you to make drastic changes to every single one of your recipes or to totally change the way you do business. But what I am asking is that you consider reformulating your menu in pragmatic and incremental ways to create healthier versions of the foods that we all love."

What are the big goals that have challenged you in your own life? How have you met them—or not? Does the idea of incremental progress, breaking down large tasks into their smaller components, work for you?

- Speaking of change, Philip undergoes a great deal of it throughout the story, transforming himself from a selfish, idle rake to a man of true worth. Margaret does, too—by opening her heart again to love. Do you believe that people can, in real life, change? And change significantly? Or do you think it's something that happens only in fiction?

- If you had to guess, how many Plough Days do you think Philip experiences?

**Keep reading for a sneak peek at the next
book in Lisa Berne's irresistible
Penhallow Dynasty series . . .**

. . . coming soon from Avon Books!

It seems to me that love is everywhere. . . .
If you look for it, I've got a sneaky feeling you'll find
that love actually is all around.

—from *Love Actually*, 2003

Chapter 1

Whitehaven, England
November 1827

Francis Penhallow sat alone in the ancient stone church over which his grandfather, the late Mr. Mantel, had presided as vicar for many years. From outside, mild autumnal sunlight made its presence known through the stained-glass windows to left and right, suffusing the lectern, the marble font, the mellow old oak pews, the unlit candles with a delicate multicolored glow—and had he but known it, illuminating Francis' golden hair with a soft glimmer almost like fire.

Even if he *had* known, he wouldn't have cared.

He was long accustomed to frequently being compared, like all his three brothers, to a Greek god from classical antiquity, and other such fervent descriptions. They were each of them tall, muscular, broad-shouldered men, with eyes of a vivid blue and hair the color of ripe wheat: attributes which, he had long felt, while pleasant ones, he had done nothing to earn and were merely accidents of birth.

Besides, there were far more interesting and important things to think about.

Just now, for example, he was musing with great happiness over the fact that—at age twenty-eight having worked hard at his studies for nearly fifteen years—he was on the verge of ordination and taking orders at last. This beloved church in his hometown was his for the asking, he'd been assured by the Archdeacon of West Cumberland, who had added warmly:

How pleased your grandfather—God rest his soul—would have been.

Francis hoped, and believed, this was so.

He thought of the big, cozy parsonage house nearby on George Street. A convivial and welcoming place he had visited nearly every day as a child to be tutored by Grandpapa. But for two years now it had been empty. A sad reality. And yet, along with grief, and acceptance, there was the promise of a new beginning, too. Francis liked to think that the parsonage house was, well, waiting for him to come back. He pictured one room in particular: the study, with its great tall windows overlooking the garden and its rows and rows of shelves, filled shelf by shelf with familiar well-thumbed books.

The light inside the church brightened, as if clouds had been drifting across the sun and just a moment ago passed it by. It almost seemed as if the candles had been lit, or an invisible lantern brought in.

All at once Francis suddenly found himself remembering an incident from several years ago. He and his sort-of cousin Owen FitzClarence had gone to London to support their respective sisters' *débuts*. It had been a generally uninteresting experience, but of course he had shown up for his sister Gwendolyn's sake. One evening there had been a little family birthday celebration for Owen's sister, Helen, and Francis had wanted out of simple politeness to purchase her a gift of some kind, especially as he was a guest in the townhouse belonging to Owen and Helen's grandparents the Duke and Duchess of Egremont.

He had puzzled over what to get Helen. He'd known her for years, but not well at all. An inarticulate, rough-and-tumble, horse-mad sort of girl who hung about pinching people, at least she had in her youth and when *he* had been around. Finally, stumped, and recalling the old maxim about getting someone else a gift that one would like to receive, he'd presented her with a copy of Wilberforce's magnificent treatise, *A Practical View of the Prevailing Religious System of Professed Christians in the Higher and Middle Classes in This Country, Contrasted with Real Christianity.*

It was a handsomely crafted, leather-bound first edition *and* it had an index, which he—completely subsumed by his studies and his passionate intellectual pursuits, living quite entirely inside his own head—had thought a nice touch.

Instead of seeming pleased as he had naively expected, Helen had only looked quite blank, and turned the book over and over again in her hands as if she had never before seen such a thing in her life and was afraid it might explode.

Owen had guffawed and exclaimed, *Lord, Francis, you're a corker!*

At the time Francis didn't know what Owen had meant by that. But now he smiled, stretching out his long legs underneath the pew in front of him.

He did understand.

It had taken him rather a long time, however—most of his twenties, in fact, in which to slowly emerge from the insular life of the obsessively dedicated scholar and find his way into a far more complex, even messy world in which people lived, loved, laughed, lied, struggled, fought, triumphed, lost, learned, and found *their* own ways as best they could. Just as he was doing.

Not, however, that he'd abandoned his intellectual interests.

By way of example, there was a deeply flawed article on determinism, Democritus, the early Hellenistic movement, logical necessity, and natural phenomena in this month's *Eclectic Review,* and he wanted to finish the draft of his letter to the editor denouncing it.

He closed his eyes, the better to picture his draft, written in his neat, precise handwriting. In his mind Francis drifted pleasurably among the sentences he'd already written, the arguments he was marshaling, and the perfectly devastating summation which needed only a bit of polishing to hone it as sharp as a knife's edge.

After a while, the words in his draft seemed to fade away, nor could he summon them again to his mind's eye, no matter how hard he tried.

Before him, rather, was a blank page.

Frustrating, yet also, undeniably, filled with possibility. And then frustration gave way, as if inexorably, to the possibility, filling his mind with a deep and tranquil silence. Within this vast peaceful silence, Francis felt himself to be very small—a mere speck—yet he was also part of something so much bigger than himself. He was both insignificant *and* interconnected, a leaf in the wind, a ship on the ocean, a tiny star floating in an infinite galaxy . . .

With his eyes closed and his focus elsewhere, Francis didn't realize that inside the church, it had gotten yet brighter. It was sunnier now than even on a mid-summer's afternoon, and strong white light, like warm spreading honey, was purling about, filling up all the empty spaces. The lectern, the font, the pews seemed almost to glow in the brilliant incandescence, the colors of the stained-glass windows were supersaturated and vividly intense, and the glimmer of Francis' hair had lit into a nimbus of shining gold.

As he drifted, as he floated, into the great deep silence of his being came a vague awareness which slowly, slowly, gathered and formed—in precisely the same way, in fact, in which the stars themselves were born—until finally the awareness sharpened into a thought which bolted across his mind like a lightning strike.

Was there someone in the church with him?

Because it rather felt like it somehow.

Francis' head jerked up and his eyes shot open. He looked all around, but there wasn't anyone else. No, it was quiet and serene in here, with the same mild autumnal sunlight streaming in through the windows, just as it had before he'd closed his eyes. That curious sensation—of a kind of *presence*—was gone.

And yet something remained.

It was as if . . .

As if he was being called to do something.

The odd thing was, he knew exactly what it was, too: he needed to go see Owen in Northamptonshire, and right away.

As to *why* he had this feeling of very specific urgency, Francis had no idea.

Maybe it was because he'd just been thinking about Owen . . . ? Had he slept after that, had he dreamed a fanciful dream of floating about like some kind of celestial speck?

He sat up a little straighter in his pew. He didn't *think* he'd fallen asleep; he felt alert, energized.

He hadn't heard from Owen in months, but that was understandable as Owen had assumed a lot of new responsibilities. Two years ago his grandfather the Duke of Egremont had passed away, and as Owen had also lost his father quite some time ago, it resulted in Owen ascending to the dukedom. No doubt he'd been awfully busy, doing whatever it was dukes did. Running things, one supposed, like the prime minister of a small country.

He and Owen weren't cousins exactly, but they *were* related somehow through old and tangled lines of Egremont–Penhallow connection. Besides, they had, along with Francis' twin brother Percy, been the best of friends ever since meeting each other at Eton at age fourteen.

So if Owen did happen to need help, he, Francis, would certainly do his best to provide it, whatever form that might take.

If, on the other hand, it turned out to be a wild-goose chase, and he traveled all the way to Hathaway Park merely because of a strange fancy—well, that would be all right too.

Briskly Francis stood up, and with a last affectionate glance around he left the church.

One week later . . .
Hathaway Park, Northamptonshire

With an unobtrusive deftness born of long practice Elinor de Vries guided her employer Lady Almira past a console table on which stood a large, expensive, extremely fragile vase filled with fragrant hothouse blooms. Such a vase practically called out for Lady Almira to bump her elbow against it or for her shawl to somehow get entangled in it or to otherwise cause the vase to go crashing onto the floor.

"Well!" exclaimed her ladyship, blithely oblivious to her near-brush with calamity as they proceeded along a hallway toward the big drawing-room where the Egremont family received visitors. "To think that it's *already* time to plan for our annual Christmas theatricals! How can it be *November*? It seems like just yesterday it was summer. Dear me! How time *does* fly."

"It certainly does, ma'am," agreed Elinor, checking her stride only briefly to pick up the reticule which had slipped from Lady Almira's wrist. She passed it without comment to her ladyship who gratefully said:

"Oh, *thank* you, my dear! I can't think how the silly thing fell off. I *did* tighten the string quite ruthlessly to keep it secure, and—oh, I must have frayed it. Look there! Do you see how it's coming apart?"

"Just a little, ma'am. I'll repair it later."

"Would you? How *very* kind. Thank you, Elinor dear. I *would* try to sew it myself, you know, but I always end up poking myself dreadfully with the needle, and I can never seem to find my scissors. Too, the pins scatter *everywhere*! Abigail always *says* she'll take on my little sewing jobs—I don't know how it is, but she never seems to get around to it. Goodness me," marveled Lady Almira, for perhaps the thousandth time, "imagine being named Abigail and *becoming* an abigail! The most curious thing, don't you think, Elinor dear?"

Elinor was spared the necessity of issuing some kind of appropriate reply—while also thinking that

there was something so childishly sweet about Lady
Almira's insistence on calling Abigail by her first
name, rather than her surname as was more typical;
and additionally thinking that not only was Abigail
not a particularly good abigail, there was something
about her personality which Elinor found faintly
repellent—when abruptly there came a sound of feet
pounding along a nearby hallway, perpendicular to
their own, and a high girlish voice shouting:

"*Je ne vais pas!* I *won't*! You cannot make me! *Moi*,
I am going *riding*!"

Both Elinor and Lady Almira flattened themselves
along the wall, just in time to avoid a collision with a
small sturdy figure in a scarlet riding-gown which had
rounded the corner and came pelting along the corridor in a defiant flurry of skirts, boots, dark red curls,
a fluttering white sash, and an adult's riding-crop held
out in front of her like a flaming sword.

"*Do* slow down, Eugénie dear," called Lady Almira
to her granddaughter, but without any real expecta-
tion of being attended to, and was duly ignored by the
fleeing child who shot into another side-corridor and
vanished.

More footsteps followed, heavier ones and at a
slower pace. Moments later Miss Danton, Eugénie's
governess, burst into the hallway, looking distraught.
"Do forgive me!" she exclaimed, breathless and apol-
ogetic, her damask cheeks an agitated crimson, as
she hurried past them in her own flurry of skirts and
plunged into the side-corridor.

"*Poor* Miss Danton," said Lady Almira feelingly,
"and poor Eugénie, too, to have lost her father, and
being made to leave the only home she'd ever known
and come here, all the way from France. Not that I'm
not *glad* to have her, and to have dear Helen too, of

course, home again. Dear me! It's still *so* surprising that Helen married a Frenchman in the first place—she doesn't speak French, for one thing, and for another she never showed the *slightest* sign of liking Monsieur de Montmorency during her Season. But there! Love is so *mysterious*, don't you think, Elinor dear?"

Elinor nodded, in full agreement with Lady Almira. Love *was* mysterious, and at Hathaway Park it also seemed to be in short supply. But she wouldn't—couldn't—let herself care too much. That led to messy emotional entanglements and she had learned over the years to remain detached and thus keep things tidy and clear-cut. Life was easier that way. She said to her ladyship:

"Shall we go on, ma'am?"

They both stepped away from the wall but paused again when they heard another set of footsteps.

Soon Helen de Montmorency, the widowed daughter to Lady Almira and the mother of little Eugénie, came barreling around the corner. She too wore a riding-habit, although hers was a deep, rich blue which contrasted sharply with her bright red curls and hard emerald-green eyes and even the plentiful freckles dotting her round face. "Which way did they go, Mama?" she demanded of Lady Almira.

Her mother gestured vaguely, which made her shawl drift off one of her shoulders and a fringed corner to dangle on the floor. "Oh, Helen dear, I'm *sure* Miss Danton has things well in hand."

"That great fat thing?" said Madame de Montmorency, her voice taut with contempt. "The only thing *she* has in hand is her latest meal."

In a perfect world, thought Elinor, as with the lightest of touches she restored Lady Almira's shawl to its proper placement upon her shoulder, one would feel free to audibly deplore the need some people felt to cruelly denigrate other people's appearance, or to wish out loud that certain people would just shut up, or even to administer a swift kick in the arse to deserving recipients, but when one was a lady's companion, one was nothing more and nothing less than hired help and one also recognized that discretion was the better part of valor if one desired to remain employed and therefore fed, clothed, and housed—a reality which led one to conclude that the world, alas, was a far from perfect place, and also that eating was better than starving.

It was a further reality that yet another reprimand from the hot-tempered Madame de Montmorency could possibly reduce Miss Danton to floods of anguished tears and even trigger one of her debilitating nosebleeds. That would be bad for Miss Danton and also bad for her, Elinor, as there was a chance that she'd then be asked to look after Eugénie until Miss Danton recovered. A scenario to be avoided at all costs. So Elinor said, in a neutral tone:

"You're coming to the meeting about the theatricals, aren't you, Madame?"

"What do I care about a stupid play?" retorted Madame de Montmorency, and Elinor saw with satisfaction that she had drawn Madame's fire, for she turned away from the direction in which her child and the governess had gone in order to gaze scornfully at Elinor.

"Oh, but Helen, it's an Egremont *tradition*," her mother protested in distress. "You know it is. For all your life we've hosted the Christmas theatricals here at the Park. And of course for *countless* years before that."

Madame shrugged. "So what?"

"Surely, Madame, everyone will be turning to you and your brother the Duke for leadership," said Elinor, perjuring herself shamelessly for Miss Danton's sake and therefore her own. "And inspiration."

"Ha! As if Owen will have anything useful to say."

"Oh, Helen *dear*," said Lady Almira, even more distressed, but Elinor saw that her suggestion had indeed struck a chord within Madame de Montmorency, for she said in her sharp, blunt way:

"I suppose if I don't go, Owen will panic and let that bossy Sir Richard take over. It's absolutely pathetic. Come along, then."

She turned on her boot-heel and meekly Lady Almira followed along in her wake, with Elinor trailing behind to pick up the amethyst brooch that detached itself from Lady Almira's bodice and plunked onto the floor. She had arrived here at Hathaway Park this past January, and so had not had the dubious pleasure of either observing the planning stages of the theatricals or witnessing last year's performance, although she *had* heard a great deal about it.

George Hawkridge, the owner of an estate adjoining Hathaway Park and in addition the author of several unpublished novels for which he had high hopes—apparently all romantic tales of sensitive, talented, good-looking men in their late twenties unexpectedly finding their soulmate—had written a play called *Love Among the Holidays* and managed through relentless pleading to persuade the new young Duke to approve it.

According to the gossip with which Elinor had to both her disinterest and boredom been regaled by people above *and* belowstairs, the play featured an enormous cast, multiple costume changes, several rotating panels for the set, and an orchestra of seven, altogether creating not just a lot of expense but also very high expectations for the '26 theatricals which were more or less dashed when the play turned out to be a soggy, four-hour-long retread of *Romeo and Juliet*, only with a Christmas theme and with the role of the Friar replaced by an actor dressed up as Jolly Saint Nick.

Too, the hero and heroine didn't die and instead triumphantly lived and closed the play by hugging and kissing each other on top of a tomb, a dramatic, even shocking display which scandalized quite a few members of the audience but which eight-year-old Eugénie de Montmorency had found entrancing and tried to reenact with the nine-year-old son of one of the grooms, resulting in her immediate disgrace and three days spent forcibly sulking in her bedchamber with only Miss Danton for company—a punishment which gave the household a welcome interval of peace but which also culminated with Eugénie believing herself to be head over heels in love with young Luke Gorlie, the groom's son, and Miss Danton taking to her bed with a nosebleed that lasted nearly a week.

Just before they went into the drawing-room Elinor gave Lady Almira the amethyst brooch.

"Oh, thank you, my dear! I can't *imagine* how I came to lose it. Oh! *Ow!* The dratted thing's pricked me—no, no, it's only a *little* blood—where *is* my handkerchief? I was *sure* I had one in my reticule! Oh, thank you, Elinor dear! How kind of you to lend me yours! I'll just wrap it round my finger, and—why, you've pinned the brooch so nicely. I do believe I had it on upside-down before. I wonder why Abigail hadn't noticed it. But perhaps she was busy with other things."

Elinor tactfully said nothing about the real possibility that Abigail *had* noticed but chose to do nothing about it, and so they passed into the drawing-room where she shepherded Lady Almira around chair-legs simply crying out for someone to stub their toe on them or to trip over them and go sprawling, and also she took a quick look around.

Sir Richard Bellington, the local magistrate and the man of whom Madame de Montmorency had spoken with great dislike, sat upright in the nicest armchair, exuding his usual air of imperturbable self-assurance. His wife Lady Bellington, cousin to Lady Almira, wasn't here, but her twenty-five-year-old son Charles was, staring about like a mooncalf as he seemed to do a lot these days.

Alphonse de Montmorency, the younger brother of Madame's late husband, had of course planted himself next to the room's only woman under the age of sixty to whom he *wasn't* related by marriage, the quiet and demure Miss Davidson, while her equally quiet and demure friend Mr. Miller sat nearby; next to him was Mr. Forte, the longtime director of the theatricals who had never once in Elinor's acquaintance with him *not* looked harassed.

Just now he was casting uneasy glances at Nicholas Lambert, the flamboyant middle-aged actor who had once performed in two plays in London and since returned to his hometown in nearby Uppingham where he never ceased reminiscing about his glory days and also publicly plotting his artistic comeback. Mr. Lambert was saying to George Hawkridge, the local scribe, in his distinctive, carrying drawl:

"Can't go wrong with Shakespeare in his original form, my dear boy. Why go to all that trouble to re-invent the wheel when the wheel is perfectly good in the first place?"

Mr. Hawkridge looked both offended and hurt. "You didn't object to playing Romeo in my play last year."

"Well, of course." Mr. Lambert chuckled. "It was the lead. What other role would I take? I, who have played Lord Townly in *The Provok'd Husband* and Mr. Hardcastle in *She Stoops to Conquer*. In Town, you know—performances for which I was greatly acclaimed. *Your* play was a painful compromise, naturally, but I like to believe I helped elevate it above the commonplace."

At this, looking very woebegone, Mr. Hawkridge drooped to one side, so much so that Elinor made sure to guide Lady Almira past his listing form, and then they took their places on a sofa set near the enormous hearth in which a fire merrily crackled, sending out pleasant warmth on this chilly day, and which also provided a panoramic view of the massive drawing-room, from the wide double doors leading to the hall-way and Great Hall, all the way to the distant far end where additional groupings of chairs, sofas, and tables were to be found and were at present unused aside from the handsome, mercurial Siamese cat which had belonged to the late Duke and who now lay stretched out on a divan eyeing everyone and everything with open contempt.

"Acting," said Mr. Scott the vicar to no one in particular, "is a dubious profession. As is the writing of plays. Writing in general is suspect. Aside from morality tracts, of course, of which there can never be too many." He pulled from his jacket pocket a handful of pamphlets and plucked from among them one emblazoned with the words RESTRAIN YOURSELF! printed in tall black letters and extended it toward Madame de Montmorency who was occupying the seat next to his. "I wrote these myself," he said with poorly concealed pride.

Madame looked at the pamphlet with her hard green eyes, then at Mr. Scott, and curled her lip. "As this is a meeting about plays and acting, I'm not even sure why you're here."

Mr. Scott somehow managed to look prim, virtuous, righteous, smug, offended, and superior all at once. "I heard about the meeting, ma'am, and knew it was my duty to attend, no matter how spiritually onerous." He got up and went over to where the Duke of Egremont sat, in a chair rather far removed from everyone else's, looking tense and pale. He was a tall, wiry young man in his late twenties, having like his sister Madame de Montmorency bright red hair and a generously freckled face, though in form he was attenuated and she was rounded.

"Your Grace," said Mr. Scott, and with a little flourish held out the pamphlet.

The Duke took it, looked at the title, sighed, muttered his thanks, and opened it up. Mr. Scott hovered there for a bit, clearly hoping that the Duke would lift his head and the gush of flowery compliments would then ensue, but when that didn't happen—the Duke only stared fixedly at the pamphlet in a way which made it unclear whether or not he was actually reading—he finally gave up, retreating to his chair where he opened up another one of his pamphlets (LUST IS THE SIN OF SINS) and seemed to lose himself in it right away.

Elinor watched in secret amusement. In a way, the meeting for the planning of the theatricals was itself as good as a play. As the only servant in the room, she was by definition an outsider; no contributions were expected from her, and so in this passive role she could simply sit back and enjoy the proceedings.

Really, as jobs went, this one wasn't bad.

Lady Almira was a sweet old lady and the kindest of souls, and Elinor's duties were far from onerous. She had plenty of time to go for the daily walks which were so important to her, and to systematically plunder the library here which was magnificent although somewhat antiquated. Of course, young Alphonse de Montmorency was a nuisance, but his aims were helpfully obvious and one could generally avoid him.

Some of her previous posts had been far less congenial.

She had been paid less and worked more, often tasked with providing the services of not just a companion but also those of a lady's maid, governess, general maidservant, seamstress, and even a cook. Too, the men in her employers' lives could not always be trusted to keep their hands to themselves. All this helped to explain why she'd had nearly a dozen positions to date. She had moved on, in search of the proverbial greener pastures, without a backward glance, though by now she was convinced that no such pasture existed.

Having moved about so much, at age twenty-nine Elinor sometimes felt as if she had lived multiple lifetimes—although, she now thought, it might be more accurate to say that she had lived but two lives: the before and the after.

In her life from before, she had been the daughter and only child of Sir Geoffrey de Vries of Falmouth. Their circumstances were comfortable, and there had even been talk of a Season for Elinor, but when both her parents perished in a curricle accident when she was just seventeen, she had learned to her infinite dismay that Sir Geoffrey's debts were many and his assets few. Thus had the "after" part of her life begun, in shock and in tragedy. Rather than throw herself upon the grudging mercy of a handful of distant cousins with daughters of their own to dispose of, she had taught for a few years in a Falmouth girls' school and after that served as a companion, drifting to Bath to Sheffield and Norwich and from there to Weymouth and then, most recently, to Hathaway Park.

Glancing idly around the drawing-room, Elinor wondered how long her post would last, and if her next one would be better or worse.

"Well," said Sir Richard in his pleasant, self-assured way, "I believe we're all here. Shall we begin?"

Madame de Montmorency glared at him. "Owen's going to chair the meeting."

All eyes turned toward the Duke, who looked up from the pamphlet with a palpable start, set it aside, and muttered:

"It's fine with me if Sir Richard wants to."

"*You* do it, Owen," snapped Madame de Montmorency. "*You're* the Duke—or have you forgotten, you big looby?"

"Oh, Helen *dear*," said Lady Almira, distressed.

"*Hamlet*," put in Mr. Lambert the actor. "Let's do *Hamlet* this year. Everyone loves it."

Mr. Hawkridge sat up straight. "But—but everyone *dies*! That's no way to celebrate the holidays!"

"Maybe you could do another rewrite, like you did with *Romeo and Juliet*," said Madame, malice in her tone.

Mr. Hawkridge started to droop again, but rallied sufficiently to say: "Now that you mention it, I—"

"I was *joking*. Four hours of *Romeo-ho-ho-ho and Juliet* was enough."

"If we're considering Shakespeare," said Sir Richard, "what about *Twelfth Night*? It's a comedy, after all, and surely more cheerful than *Hamlet*."

"It was meant to be performed on Twelfth Night," said Miss Davidson. "But the play has nothing to do with the holiday itself." As Miss Davidson never said much in company, several people looked at her in surprise.

"*A dire vrai*, I would give my soul for twelve nights with *you*, Mademoiselle Davidson," Alphonse breathed, his dark eyes all limpid and full of yearning. There was a brief, awkward silence in the wake of this remark and Miss Davidson did not reply, only, instead, looked down at her demurely folded hands.

"I vote for *Hamlet* over *Twelfth Night*," Madame de Montmorency said, more, Elinor thought, to establish her authority over Sir Richard than anything else. Her brother the Duke, sitting at the edge of the circle, looked between them with painful anxiety.

There was a loud crashing noise and an even louder screech from the nearby Great Hall, and before anybody could even rise from their seat to investigate, Eugénie came charging into the room, still with her riding-crop held out before her like the sword she no doubt wished it was, followed by two footmen, a panting Miss Danton, and, finally, the butler Wattle, who arrived at a more measured pace and said to the Duke in a voice of terrible icy formality:

"I trust you will forgive my Intrusion, Your Grace, but it is my Duty, I fear, to inform you that the Young Person who preceded me, and is now at present beneath one of the Sofas, has toppled the suit of armor belonging to the Sixth Duke."

Elinor eyed the rigidly upright, professionally wooden, superbly dignified Wattle with admiration. Not only was he both competent and unflappable, he also managed to articulate certain of his words with uppercase letters. She was very fond of hearing him speak.

"*Eugénie!*" hissed her mother Madame, her face a bright brilliant red. "Get out from under there *at once!*"

"*Non! Je ne vais pas!*" Eugénie hissed back, waggling her riding-crop defiantly.

"*Miss Danton!*" Madame hissed at the governess, who stood wringing her hands in agony.

The Siamese cat, Brutus, yawned, gave a lazy stretch, and leaped lightly from the divan, leaving behind a visible bolus of fur, after which he minced over to the vicar Mr. Scott and sniffed at one of his shoes. Offended, Mr. Scott drew his foot away and scowled at Brutus, who looked right back at him with such calm insolence that Elinor had to bite back a laugh.

"Hullo," came a new voice, deep and mild and rather charming, and everyone in the room—with the possible exception of Brutus the mercurial cat who did what he wanted at all times no matter the inconvenience to others—turned to look at the source of that voice, which proved to be a very tall, very handsome man with eyes the color of cornflowers and hair a bright gleaming gold, and clad in a plain serviceable greatcoat and dusty dark boots which somehow looked extremely dashing on him. He went on, with a note of apology, which was also rather charming, in his voice:

"There was nobody about, so I came in."

The Duke leaped to his feet with instant gladness. "I say, *Francis!*"

"Dear *Francis!*" exclaimed Lady Almira, with a great wide smile of surprise and delight.

"*Qui est* Francis?" asked little Eugénie from her hidey-hole.

"Francis," murmured the demure Miss Davidson and her friend the equally demure Mr. Miller in a single low breath, gazing with rapt attention at the newcomer from head to toe and everywhere in between.

"*Francis!*" echoed Madame de Montmorency, her face abruptly going a ghostly white as she slumped back against her chair, her eyelids fluttering closed.

There was a sudden loud silence in the room as it dawned upon everyone gathered there that the robust, hardy, seemingly indomitable Madame—who could spend a whole day amongst her horses riding them and training them and grooming them and ordering grooms about and riding some more and then return to the house at dusk with the same energy and vigor she had exhibited ten hours earlier—had, for some strange and startling and mysterious reason, actually fainted upon the surprise arrival of the handsome stranger, thereby unwittingly confirming Elinor's earlier prediction that this planning meeting for the Christmas theatricals really *would* be as good as a play.

*Next month, don't miss these exciting
new love stories only from
Avon Books*

Highland Wolf by Lynsay Sands

In all her daydreams about her wedding day, Lady
Claray MacFarlane never once imagined being dragged
to the altar by her greedy uncle and forced to marry a
man she didn't know. But that's what would have
happened had a handsome Highland warrior with
black-as-sin hair called Wolf not snatched her up at the
last minute and ridden off with her in his arms . . .

His Lessons on Love by Cathy Maxwell

The Earl of Marsden—better known as Mars—has lived
his life by his own rules . . . until he is presented with a
very big problem in a very tiny package: his baby
daughter cast off by his ex-mistress. Mars doesn't know
the first thing about babies. Panicking, he turns to
Clarissa Taylor, village spinster, matron-in-training,
and Mars's greatest critic. Still, who better to tend a
motherless child than a woman who was abandoned as
a babe herself?

RELB 12 21

NEW YORK TIMES BESTSELLING AUTHOR
ELOISA JAMES

The Wildes of Lindow Castle

Wilde in Love
978-0-06-238947-3

Too Wilde to Wed
978-0-06-269246-7

Born to Be Wilde
978-0-06-269247-4

Say No to the Duke
978-0-06-287782-6

Say Yes to the Duke
978-0-06-287806-9

Wilde Child
978-0-06-287807-6

EJ6 1021